About

Lowe is a RIT ... or. Whether her ... back Australia or i ... tow.. s with big hearts and warm and likeable chara... th.. make you fall in love. Sign up for her newsletter ...ttp://bit.ly/1FmSvHN All social media links are at ...alowe.com

...anna Neil had her future planned. She enjoyed her ...rk as an infant teacher and didn't envisage any ...anges to her way of life. But then she discovered ...ll.. & Boon. She was surprised to find how absorbing ...interesting they were and read them on a regular ... The more she read, the more she had the ...whelming desire to write one. Encouraged by her ...ly, she persevered until her first book was ...ted, and after several books were published, she ...ded to write full time.

... completing a degree in journalism, then working ...vertising and mothering her kids, **Robin Gianna** ...what she calls her awakening. She decided she ...ed to write the romance novels she'd loved since ...eens, and now enjoys pushing her characters toward ...own happily-ever-afters. When she's not writing, ...in's life is filled with a happily messy kitchen, a ...dy garden, a wonderful husband, three great kids, ...rooling bulldog and one grouchy Siamese cat.

A&E Docs

A&E Docs: Emergency Medicine

FIONA LOWE

JOANNA NEIL

ROBIN GIANNA

MILLS & BOON

First Published in Great Britain 2021
By Mills & Boon, an imprint of HarperCollins*Publishers* Ltd
1 London Bridge Street, London, SE1 9GF

www.harpercollins.co.uk

HarperCollins*Publishers*
1st Floor, Watermarque Building,
Ringsend Road, Dublin 4, Ireland

A&E DOCS: EMERGENCY MEDICINE
© 2021 Harlequin Books S.A.

Career Girl in the Country © 2011 Fiona Lowe
A Doctor to Remember © 2014 Joanna Neil
Flirting with Dr Off-Limits © 2014 Robin Gianakopoulos

ISBN: 978-0-263-29941-0

MIX
Paper from
responsible sources
FSC™ C007454

CAREER GIRL IN THE COUNTRY

FIONA LOWE

To Sandra, with many thanks for keeping us
neat and tidy!

CHAPTER ONE

FEMALE SURGEON TAKES BAMPTON AWARD

Ms Stanfield's meteoric rise in the male-dominated field of surgery was recognised last week. *Journal's* 'on the ground' photographer snapped Ms Stanfield wearing last season's black suit (right), and we're left wondering if rather than taking the 'Old Boys' Club' by storm she's actually joined it. Rumour has it she's in negotiations with two prestigious hospitals for Chief of Surgery.

POPPY STANFIELD'S 6:00 a.m. sip of Saturday coffee turned bitter in her mouth as she read the five-line article on the back page of the Perth newspaper. She didn't give a damn about the bitchy comment on her cinch-waisted black suit but how the hell had the gossip columnist found out about the job interviews? One job interview especially—the one she'd very carefully and deliberately kept quiet because it was hard enough being female in this business, let alone having the temerity to want a top job. A top job she was determined to get one way or another, which was why she'd applied for the post of

Chief of Surgery at Southgate as well as Perth City, the hospital she currently worked for.

And now 'one way' was her only remaining option.

Her disappointed gaze caught sight of the envelope with the Southgate crest that had arrived yesterday containing a letter with the words 'unsuccessful candidate'. She hadn't read past them because there'd been no point. Poppy Stanfield didn't lose, she just regrouped and planned a new strategy. It would have been a huge coup to land the Southgate job ahead of the Perth City one, but the interview panel had been hostile from the moment she'd walked in.

The Bampton win had ruffled more than a few feathers in surgical ranks, and the media attention had been unexpected. The memory of the ditzy and pen-less journalist, with hair flying, who'd arrived late to interview her, sent a sliver of irritation down her spine. Poppy reread the article and the bald, incriminating words. Hell, why hadn't she spent more time with the journalist instead of rushing through the interview?

The faint echo of mocking laughter sounded deep down inside her. *You spend all your time at work and when have you ever really spent time with anyone?*

Steven.

Her phone chirped loudly, making her jump. Given it was 6:00 a.m., the call was most likely the hospital needing her for an urgent consult and absolutely nothing to do with this tiny article buried in the centre of the paper. Yes, an emergency consult would be the best scenario. The worst scenario would be— *Stop right there.* She refused to contemplate the worst scenario, but still she checked the screen before answering it.

She groaned into her hand. The name of the hospital's

executive medical officer and her current boss blinked at her in inky and unforgiving black. *Damage control.* Tilting her head back and bringing her chin up, she answered the call with a firm, crisp greeting. 'Hello, William.'

'Poppy.' The professor spoke her name as if it pained his tongue to roll over the combination of letters. 'I've just seen the paper.'

Show no weakness. 'You must be pleased.' She ignored the vividly clear picture of him in her mind—tight face and stern mouth—the way he always looked when he believed a staff member had let him down. She infused her voice with enthusiasm. 'It was an excellent article about your groundbreaking in utero surgery.'

'It was, and surprisingly accurate, but that's not the article I'm referring to.'

No way was she admitting to anything so she let the deliberate silence ride, biting her lip not to say a word.

William continued. 'In your thank-you speech at the Bampton awards you said you were committed to Perth City.'

She pushed the Southgate envelope under the paper and out of sight. 'Absolutely. City's given me every opportunity.' The words of her speech flowed out smoothly, in stark contrast to the reality, which had involved her fighting to get into the surgery programme, working harder and longer hours than her male counterparts and ignoring the advice that surgery took beautiful young women and turned them into ugly old ones. She'd stopped thinking of herself as a woman long ago and with it had gone the dream of marriage and a family of her own. 'Should the board see fit, it would be an honour to serve as the Chief of Surgery.'

'An honour?'

His tone bristled with sarcasm, which Poppy ignored. 'Yes, indeed, and as I outlined in my interview with the board, I can start immediately and provide a seamless transition period before Gareth leaves for Brisbane.'

'The board's still deliberating on the best person for the position.' His voice dripped with disapproval. 'But I'm reassured by your commitment to the hospital, and by knowing how much of an honour you consider it to be working for the WA Healthcare Network.'

She let go of a breath she hadn't realised she'd been holding. 'Excellent.'

'So it stands to reason that you were the *first* person we thought of when Bundallagong Hospital requested a visiting surgeon.'

'Excuse me?' Of all the possible things she might have anticipated him saying, that wasn't one of them.

'Bundallagong Hospital.' William repeated the name slowly, a hint of humour skating along the cool steel of his voice, as if he was party to a private joke.

Her brain stalled, trying to think why the name of the town was vaguely familiar, and with a start she frantically flicked the pages of the paper open until she found the weather map. Her gasp of surprise was too quick for her mouth to stifle. 'But that's fifteen hundred kilometres away!'

'Or nine hundred and thirty-two miles, which is why they need a visiting surgeon for three months.'

Years of well-honed control started to unravel. 'William, this is ridiculous. Sending me out into the boonies is only going to make the day-to-day running at City even tighter than it is.'

'We've allowed for that.'

Her stomach clenched at his terse tone. 'We've been chasing staff for over a year and what? Now you've just pulled a surgeon out of a hat?'

'One of the east coast applicants will fill your position while you're away.'

The staccato delivery of his words shot down the line like gunfire and she rocked back as if she'd been hit. The board was deliberately sending her away so they could observe her opposition in action without her being around to counteract any fallout. Incandescent fury flowed through her. 'And let me guess, that surgeon would be male.'

A sharp intake of breath sounded down the line. 'Poppy, you know I can't disclose information like that. Besides, as you've always pointed out, gender is irrelevant and it's all about expertise.'

He'd used her words against her to suit his own ends.

'Let's just be totally honest, shall we, William? You're seriously ticked off that I applied to Southgate and now you're punishing me for doing what any other surgeon in my position would have done.'

'Now you're being irrational, which isn't like you at all. Go to Bundallagong, Poppy, do your job and let the board do theirs. My secretary will be in touch about flight details but start packing because you're leaving tomorrow.'

The phone line suddenly buzzed and she realised he'd hung up on her. Blind anger tore through her and she shredded the newspaper, venting unprintable expletives at the journalist, William, the hospital and the system in general. Who the hell was this interloper from the east coast? She had contacts and she'd find out because learning about the enemy was a vital part of the strategy of winning.

But as the final strips of paper floated to the floor, her anger faded almost as fast as it had come and unchar- acteristic tears of frustration and devastation pricked her eyes. Suddenly she was whipped back in time to when she had been a gangly ten-year-old girl valiantly trying to hold back tears after a drubbing in the first set of a tennis final, one of the few matches her father had actually turned up to watch.

He'd crossed his arms and stared down at her, his expression filled with derision. *'Don't be such a girl. Do you think boys cry? They don't. They just go out there and win.'*

Shaking her head as if that would get rid of the memory, she stomped into her bedroom and hauled a suitcase out of the wardrobe. If Bundallagong Hospital needed a surgeon then, by God, they were getting one, and the staff there wouldn't know what had hit them. She'd clear the waiting list, reorganise the department, overhaul the budget, meet every target and make William and the board sit up and take notice. Nobody put Poppy Stanfield in a corner.

Dr Matt Albright was on an island beach. The balmy tropical breeze skimmed over his sun-warmed skin and a book lay face-down on his naked chest, resting in the same position it had been for the last half-hour.

'Daddy, watch me!'

He waved to his daughter as she played in the shal- low and virtually waveless water, then he rolled onto his side towards his wife, who lay next to him, reading.

At that precise moment he knew his life was perfect in every way.

She glanced up and smiled in her quiet and unassuming way.

He grinned. 'You do realise I've loved you from the moment you hit me with play dough at kinder.'

Her tinkling laughter circled him and he leaned in to kiss her, knowing her mouth as intimately as his own. He reached out to curve his hand around her shoulder, trying to pull her closer, but his fingers closed in on themselves, digging into his palm. He tried again, this time cupping her cheeks, but they vanished the moment he tried to touch them.

'Daddy!'

He turned towards his daughter's voice and saw her evaporating, along with the water that tore all the sand from the beach. Panic bubbled hot and hard in his veins and he sat up fast, hearing the sound of his voice screaming 'No!'

His eyes flew open into darkness, his heart thundering against his ribs and sweat pouring down his face. His hands gripped something so hard they ached and he realised his fingers were digging deep into the edge of the mattress. He wasn't on a beach.

He was in a bed.

Slowly his eyes focused and he recognised the silhouette of his wardrobe, and he heard the thumping and scratching of the goanna that had at some point in the last few months, without any protest from him, moved into the roof.

Bundallagong. He was in Bundallagong.

He fell back onto the pillow and stared blindly up at the ceiling. His heart rate slowed and the tightness in his chest eased and for one brief and blessed moment he felt nothing at all. Then the ever-present emptiness, which the dream had momentarily absorbed, rushed back in. It expanded wide and long, filling every crevice, every cell and tainting every single breath.

Sleep was over. He swung his legs out of bed, walked into the lounge room, stared out into the night, and waited for the dawn.

'And how long have you had this pain, Sam?' Poppy pulled the modesty sheet back over the young man's abdomen.

He shrugged. 'Dunno. I think I saw Dr Albright about a month ago but then it just went away.'

'And is today's pain worse than a month ago?'

'A lot.'

'The nurse tells me you've been vomiting?'

'Yeah, sorry about that.'

Poppy tried not to smile. Dressed in tough mining workwear, and looking like not even a bullet could take him down, Sam's politeness and air of bewilderment reminded her of a young boy rather than a strapping and fit man of twenty.

'I'll be back in a bit, Sam.' Poppy pulled the screen curtains shut behind her as she stepped out into the compact emergency department, running the symptoms through her head—fever, high white blood cell count, rebound tenderness and an ultrasound that showed nothing unusual, although that in itself wasn't unusual. The process of diagnosis soothed her like the action of a soothing balm and she relaxed into the feeling.

The shock of landing two hours ago on the Mars-scape that was Bundallagong still had her reeling. The green of the river-hugging suburbs of Perth had not prepared her for the barrenness of the Pilbara. When she'd exited the plane, her feet had stuck mutinously to the roll-away airport stairs as her gaze had taken in the flat, red dust plains that stretched to the horizon in three directions. Then the ferocious dripping heat had hit her like an impenetrable wall and it had been like walking into a raging furnace with an aftershock of wet, cloying steam. The irony wasn't lost on her—William had sent her to hell.

The only way to reduce her 'sentence' was to start work so she'd asked the taxi driver to take her directly to the hospital. The fact it was a Sunday afternoon mattered little because the sooner she started her rotation, the sooner she could finish. She'd planned to spend a couple of hours studying medical histories and drawing up her first week's surgical list but as she'd arrived, so had Sam. The nurse on duty had happily accepted her offer of help with a smile, saying, 'Thanks heaps. It'll give the on-call doctor a break.'

Now Poppy walked briskly to the nurses' station and dropped the history in front of Jen Smithers, whose badge read 'Nursing Administrator'. 'Sam's got appendicitis so if you can arrange everything, I'll meet him in Theatre in an hour.'

The nurse, who Poppy guessed was of a similar age to her, looked up, a startled expression on her face. 'So it's an emergency case?'

'Not strictly, but he'll be better off without his appendix and there's no time like the present.'

'Ah.' Jen spun a pen through her fingers, as if considering her thoughts.

Poppy rarely took no for an answer and the 'Ah'

sounded ominous. She made a snap decision: she needed the nursing staff on her side but she also needed to show she was the one in charge of the team. 'Jen, I call a spade a spade and I don't play games. I'll be straight with you and you need to be straight with me. I want to operate on Sam this afternoon and I expect you to do your job so I can do mine.'

Jen nodded, her demeanour friendly yet professional. 'Fair enough. I can get nursing staff in to staff Theatre and Recovery, but that isn't going to be enough. It's the anaesthetic registrar's weekend off and he's not due back from Bali until this evening's flight.'

Gobsmacked, Poppy stared at her, not knowing whether to be more stunned that a person could fly direct to Bali from the middle of nowhere or the fact that it left the town without an anaesthetist. 'Surely there's someone else?'

'Well, yes, technically there is, but...'

A tight band of tension burned behind Poppy's eyes. Hell, she really *had* come to Mars. She didn't have time for staff politics, especially if they got in the way of her doing her job and proving to William that she deserved the chief of surgery position back in Perth. 'Just ring the doctor and get him or her here, and leave the rest to me.'

Jen gave a wry smile. 'If you're sure, I can do that.'

'Of course, I'm sure.' Poppy headed back to her patient, shaking her head. It seemed a very odd thing to say but, then again, she was a long way from Perth. She busied herself inserting an IV into Sam's arm, administered Maxolon for his nausea and pethidine for the pain.

'This will have you feeling better soon.'

'Thanks, Doc.'

'No problem.'

She clicked her pen and started scrawling a drug order onto the chart when she heard voices coming from the direction of the nurses' station. She couldn't make out Jen's words but could hear her soft and conciliatory tone, followed quickly by a very terse, deep voice asking, 'Why didn't you call me first?'

'Because Ms Stanfield was here and I thought I could save you—'

As Poppy hung the chart on the end of the trolley, Jen's voice was cut off by the male voice. The anger was unmistakable and his words hit painfully hard. 'Save me? I don't need you or anyone else in this town making decisions for me, do you understand? I'm the on-call doctor today and that means I get called.'

Sam's head swung towards the raised voices, his expression full of interest.

Staff politics. She'd asked Jen to call in this guy so she needed to be the one to deal with him. 'Back in a minute, Sam.' Poppy grabbed the cubicle curtains and deliberately pulled them open with a jerk, making the hangers swish against the metal with a rushing ping to remind Jen and the unknown doctor that there was a patient in the department. She marched briskly to the desk.

'Oh, Ms Stanfield.' Jen glanced around the man standing with his back to Poppy. Her organised demeanour had slipped slightly but instead of looking angry or crushed at being spoken to as if she was a child, her expression was one of resignation tinged with sadness and regret. 'Poppy Stanfield, meet Dr. Matt Albright, Head of ED.'

The tall, broad-shouldered man turned slowly, his sun-streaked chestnut hair moving with him. It was longer than the average male doctor's and the style was either deliberately messy-chic or overdue for a cut. A few strands fell forward, masking his left cheek, but his right side was fully exposed, and olive skin hollowed slightly under a fine but high cheekbone before stretching over a perfectly chiselled nose. A dark five-o'clock shadow circled tightly compressed lips, leaving Poppy in no doubt of his masculinity.

With a jolting shock she realised he wasn't handsome—he was disconcertingly beautiful in a way that put everyone else into shadow. In ancient times he would have been sculpted in marble and raised onto a pedestal as the epitome of beauty. Poppy found herself staring as if she was in a gallery admiring a painting where the artist had created impossibly stunning good looks that didn't belong on battle-scarred earth.

He was heart-stoppingly gorgeous and she'd bet anything women fell at his feet. Once she would have too but thankfully, due to years of practice, she was now immune and not even a quiver of attraction moved inside her.

Nothing ever does any more.

Shut up. Work excites me. She extended her hand towards him. 'Matt.'

His hand gripped hers with a firm, brisk shake, and a faint tingling rush started, intensifying as it shot along her arm. *Immune, are you?*

Compressed nerve from a too-firm grip, that's all.

'Poppy.' He raised his espresso-brown eyes to meet her gaze. She expected to see at least a flicker of interest in a new colleague, almost certainly a calculating professional sizing-up, and, at worst, a derisive flare at the fact she was a surgeon and a woman. None of it worried her because she knew exactly how to handle the men she worked with—she'd had years of experience.

But what she saw was so unexpected that it sucked the air from her lungs, almost pulling her with it. A short, sharp flame flickered in his eyes for a split second, illuminating hunger, but as it faded almost as fast as it had flared, she caught deep and dark swirling shadows before clouds rolled in briskly, masking all emotion.

She swayed on her heels as his hunger called up a blast of her own heat but as she glimpsed the misery in his eyes, she shivered and a jet of arctic cold scudded through her. Fire and ice collided; lust and pain coiling together before spiralling down to touch a place that had been firmly closed off and abandoned since—

She abruptly pulled her hand out of his, breaking his touch and moving her gaze to his left shoulder. *There you go, simple solution: no eye contact.* She didn't want to care about what hid behind that flawless face and now that his heat wasn't flowing through her, she marshalled her wayward thoughts and valiantly recomposed herself. This was no time to be discomfited. She needed to be in control and in charge, her future depended on it.

'As Jen will have explained, I need you to anaesthetise Sam Dennison.'

Long, lean fingers on his right hand crossed his wide and casually clad chest, flicking at the sleeve band of his white T-shirt. 'This is my department and I need to examine *my* patient before any decisions are made.' He turned and walked towards the cubicle.

Poppy matched his stride. 'And as Bundallagong's

resident surgeon for the next ninety days or less, it's my considered opinion that—'

'You've had time to examine Sam and now you need to extend that courtesy to me.'

He didn't alter his pace and before she could reply, Matt Albright stepped through the curtains and closed them in her face.

CHAPTER TWO

MATT could hear the new surgeon pacing, her black heels clicking an impatient rhythm against the linoleum floor. Well, she could just wait. He wasn't a stickler for protocol but Jen had overstepped the mark by not calling him in to examine Sam first. God, he was sick of the town walking on eggshells around him and trying to protect him when all he wanted was normality. *Yeah, and what exactly is that these days?*

'You OK, Doc?' The young miner lay propped up against a bank of pillows, his eyes slightly glazed from the opiate pain relief.

Hell, if a spaced-out patient noticed he was shaking with frustration then things were really spinning out.

Matt, how can you always be so calm? Lisa's slightly accusing voice sounded faintly in his head. But that conversation had taken place in another lifetime, before everything he'd held dear had been brutally stolen from him. He hadn't known calm in over a year.

'I'm fine.' *Pull the other one.* 'But you're not. That appendix rumbling again?'

'Yeah, although whatever that other doctor gave me is good stuff.' Sam grinned happily.

Matt smiled as he examined him. 'Have you got any family up here?'

Sam shook his head. 'Nah, came for the job and the money.'

'I'll arrange for a phone so you can talk to your mum because there's a very high chance you'll be parting with your appendix. We'll fast you from midnight and observe you overnight.'

'OK.'

'Any questions?'

'Nah, you explained it all last time and then it got better.' Sam's eyes fluttered closed as the drugs really kicked in, tempering any concern over the surgery that he might have.

Matt decided he'd explain it all again to him later. He pulled the curtains open and the new surgeon immediately ceased pacing, but she held her wide shoulders square and tight. It struck him that there was nothing soft about this woman except for her name.

And her mouth.

Guilt kicked him hard. His initial top-to-toe glance of her had stalled unexpectedly on her mouth and a flash of lust-filled heat had sparked momentarily, shocking him deeply. There'd only ever been *one* woman for him, and until ten minutes ago no one else had ever registered on his radar, let alone elicited such a response. But there'd been something about Poppy Stanfield's plump mouth that had held him mesmerised. Lips that peaked in an inviting bow were the colour of crushed strawberries and hinted at tasting like an explosion of seductive sweetness. He'd almost licked his own in response.

It was a totally ridiculous and over-the-top reaction given the contrast between the softness of the lips and the precise and no-nonsense words they formed. Everything else about Poppy Stanfield was sharp angles and harsh lines. Her long black hair was pulled straight back exposing a high and intelligent forehead. Black hair, black brows, black suit, black shoes; the monotone was only broken by her lush mouth and the most unexpectedly vivid blue eyes.

Eyes that were fixed on him, full of questions and backlit with steely determination.

He deliberately sat on the desk and put a foot up on a chair, the position screaming casual in stark contrast to her starchy demeanour. For some crazy reason he had to concentrate really hard to get her name correct because, apart from being the colour of her lips, Poppy didn't suit her at all.

Her fingers tugged sharply at the bottom of her suit jacket, which was ludicrously formal attire for Bundallagong, and she seemed to rise slightly on her toes so she wasn't much shorter than him. 'Dr Albright.'

'You're in the bush now, Poppy.'

Her gaze drifted to the red dust on his boots before moving up to his face. 'Oh, I'm *very* well aware of that.'

Her tone oozed urban superiority and for the first time in months something other than anger and despair penetrated his permanent sadness—the buzz of impending verbal sparring. No one had faced up to him or even questioned him since Lisa. Hell, half the time his friends and colleagues had trouble meeting his gaze and, like Jen, their well-meaning attempts to help only stifled him. But he had a citified stranger in front of him who knew nothing about him and he realised with unexpected relish that he was looking forward to this upcoming tussle.

He met Poppy's baby-blue eyes with a deadpan expression. 'Excellent. Oh, and by the way, we use first names here even when we're ticked off.'

Her eyes flashed but her mouth pursed as if she was working hard not to smile. It was the first sign that a sense of humour might lurk under all the superficial blackness.

'Thank you for that tip, *Matt*. So you agree with my diagnosis that Sam has appendicitis?'

'I do.' He tilted his head ever so slightly in acquiescence. He didn't have any problem with her diagnosis, just her modus operandi. 'The pain he was presented with last month has intensified.'

Poppy schooled her face not to show the sweet victory that spun inside her. 'So we're in agreement. He's been fasting due to his nausea so Jen can prep him for Theatre and—'

'I said I agreed with your diagnosis.' He raised one brow. 'That doesn't translate into agreeing with your treatment plan.'

The coolness of his tone didn't come close to soothing the hot and prickly frustration that bristled inside her, and she silently cursed William for sending her to the middle of nowhere where men ruled and women had no choice but to follow. 'So you're going to sit on it until his appendix bursts and we're faced with dealing with peritonitis?'

Emotionless molasses-coloured eyes bored into her. 'Not at all. He requires surgery and he'll have it—tomorrow.'

So this is a power play: my turf versus your turf. 'But

he could deteriorate overnight and we'd have to come in anyway. Tomorrow is an unknown quantity, whereas right now it's quiet, we're both here, so why wait?'

'Technically you don't even start work until 8:00 a.m. tomorrow.'

'That's semantics.'

He lowered his gaze and stared at her bright red suitcase stowed by the desk and then he moved the stare to her. 'Is it? It's Sunday and I would have thought seeing as you've only just arrived, you'd want to get settled in the house, hit the supermarket and fill your fridge.'

Something about his unflinching gaze made her feel like he saw not just the persona she showed the world but way beyond it and down deep into the depths she hadn't allowed anyone to enter since Steven.

But he really didn't want to—
I am so not doing this now!

She shut the voice up, hating that her hand had crept to the pendant that sat just below her throat. She forced her arm back by her side and her voice came out stiff and authoritative. 'You don't have to concern yourself with my domestic arrangements.'

'Very true.' He radiated a controlled aura that was an odd mix of dark and light, although the dark dominated. 'But I do concern myself with my staff's. They have lives outside work, Poppy.' His expression intimated that he thought perhaps she didn't. 'This is not an emergency and therefore we are *not* interrupting their family time, their fishing and sailing time, and, for some, their afternoon naps.'

'Afternoon naps?' Her voice rose in disbelief as her brain tried unsuccessfully to wrap itself around such a foreign concept. 'You're joking.'

Matt gave a snort that sounded like a rusty laugh as his face creased stiffly into lines that bracketed his mouth and for a moment his lips broke their tight line. A streak of something close to warmth followed, giving life and character to his face, which up until this point had been almost a caricature of unmarred features.

Her gut lurched as a flicker of delicious shimmers moved through her and she wished he'd stop. Perfection she could resist. Deep life lines around those dark and empty eyes, not so much.

His expression neutralised as the shadows returned. 'Life is slower here and, as you'll discover, the humidity at this time of year really saps your energy.'

She thought of the chief of surgery job back in Perth and went back into battle. She knew this game and she didn't plan to give an inch. 'Nothing saps my energy. I'm here to work, not to relax.' She reached for her briefcase and pulled out a folder. 'In regard to staff, I have a surgical budget and my own staffing ratios, and it's my call when to operate, not yours.'

'It is, and come tomorrow, your first official day, when David, the anaesthetic registrar, is back on duty, you can order him about to your heart's content. Today, as the ED doctor and the back-up anaesthetist, it's my call. We're not operating on Sam just so you can rush in, set a precedent and get some runs on the board.'

'This has *nothing* to do with me and everything to do with patient care.' She protested too quickly as his words hit far too close to home. Sam's case technically wasn't an emergency but it wasn't strictly elective surgery either. She hated that he'd guessed at her need to operate so she could stake her claim as the incumbent surgeon, competent and in charge.

He slid to his feet, the movement as graceful as a gazelle's but with the calculation of a panther. Everything about him screamed, *I don't believe you.*

'Should Sam's condition change, I'll call you straight away. Meanwhile, go stock your fridge and turn on the air-conditioning so you can sleep tonight.'

Her body vibrated with rage. 'Don't patronise me.'

Genuine surprise raced across his face and he gave a sigh filled with fatigue. 'I'm not. I'm actually trying to help. Your life here will be a lot easier if you don't get the staff off-side before you've officially started.'

She wanted to stay furious with him, she wanted to cast him in the role of obstructive male, but his gaze wasn't combative and amid the darkness that hovered around him, she detected a sliver of goodwill. It totally confused her.

'I see. Well, we may not agree about Sam but I take on board what you're saying.' She made herself say, 'Thank you.'

'No problem.' His fingers pushed through his straight hair, the strands sliding over them like water on rocks.

With a shock she caught the glint of gold on his ring finger. How had she missed that? But it didn't matter how or why—what was important was now she knew. Married men didn't interest her.

It's been a long time since an unmarried one interested you.

Get off my case!

She had a gut feeling that she and Matt Albright would probably spend the next ninety days disagreeing but now it would be without fear of those strange and unwanted shimmers. Working with Matt would be uncomplicated and all about the job, and that was what she did best.

She pulled out a business card and held it towards him.

'This is my mobile number should Sam deteriorate, and meanwhile I'll let you get back to your Sunday afternoon and your family.'

The goodwill vanished from his eyes as his lean body ceased all movement, and an eerie stillness hovered around him.

So much for her attempt at being polite. She couldn't work him out.

The card hung between them for a moment and then he slowly raised his arm and plucked it from her fingers. 'Right. See you around.'

'I guess you will.' What else was there to say?

'Wait!' Jen hurried over as two bloodied men supported and half dragged another man into the department.

'What happened?' Matt hauled his way back from the black despair Poppy's innocent comment had plunged him into, hating that it had, and was glad to be able to focus on the patient.

'Patient involved in a brawl, suspected head injury and possible fractures.'

He grabbed a gown and stifled a groan. In years gone by, drunken brawls had been exclusively Saturday night's domain but the mining boom had brought more people into the town and some of them had more money than sense. This patient could have anything from a broken toe to a subdural haematoma, with a million possibilities in between.

He threw Poppy a gown. 'I think you just got a

reprieve from filling your fridge but just so we're clear, this is my emergency and you're assisting.'

'Oh, absolutely.' But deep sapphire blue shards scudded across her enormous baby-blue eyes, making a mockery of her supposed compliance. 'It's your emergency right up to the point when you realise he needs surgery and you're totally out of your depth.'

No one had been that blunt with him in a long time. A noise rumbled up from deep down inside him and for a moment he didn't recognise the sound. With a shock of surprise he realised that for the first time in months he'd just laughed.

Matt moved into action, work being one of the few things in his life he didn't question. He called out to the two men, 'Help me get him onto this trolley.'

They half hauled and half dropped the injured man onto the mattress and as soon as the sides had been pulled up, Matt asked, 'Do either of you have any injuries or is that your mate's blood?'

'We're OK.'

Matt wasn't convinced. 'Sit over there and wait. As soon as we've checked out your mate, someone will examine you both. No one is to leave until you've been examined, do you understand?'

Both men looked sheepish. 'Yeah, Doc.'

He pushed the trolley into the resus room. 'What's his pulse ox?'

Poppy slid the peg-like device onto the end of the patient's finger. 'Eight-five.' She unravelled green plastic tubing and turned on the oxygen. 'Mr…?'

'Daryl Jameson.' Jen supplied the information.

'Mr Jameson. I'm Poppy Stanfield, this is Jen Smithers, and on your left is Dr Matt Albright. You're in good hands. We're just going to give you some oxygen and help you to sit up.'

Matt tried not to show his surprise that Poppy had failed to mention her qualifications and that unlike many surgeons she was actually quite personable with an awake patient. 'Daryl, how's the breathing, mate?'

'Hurts.'

'Where does it hurt?' Poppy adjusted the elastic to hold the nasal prongs in place.

'It's me chest and arm that's killing me.'

'Do you know what day it is?' Matt flicked on his penlight.

'Sunday. I remember everything up to the moment the idiot hit me.'

Matt flashed the light into his patient's eyes. 'Pupils equal and reacting.'

Jen tried to ease Daryl's shirt off but resorted to scissors when Daryl couldn't move his arm without flinching. The soft material separated, revealing purple bruising all over the thin man's chest. The nurse gasped.

Matt looked up from the IV he was inserting, hating that he knew exactly what would have caused such trauma. 'Steel-capped boots. Welcome to the seedier side of Bundallagong, Poppy.'

She attached electrodes to Daryl's chest, and at the same time Matt knew she was examining the rise and fall of his chest given the complaint about pain on breathing. 'Sinus tachycardia. Jen, organise for a chest and arm X-ray.'

'On it.' The nurse started to manoeuvre the portable X-ray machine into position.

While Poppy wrapped a blood-pressure cuff around their patient's uninjured arm to enable automatic readings, Matt swung his stethoscope into his ears and listened to Daryl's breathing. He could hear creps and he palpated a paradoxical movement of the chest wall. 'Flail chest. I'll insert prophylactic chest tubes.'

A frown furrowed her smooth, white brow. 'Good idea but it's the damage under the fractured ribs that worries me.'

Matt nodded. 'We're in agreement, then.'

'There's a first time for everything.'

The words sounded precise and clipped, but her plump, berry-red lips twitched. Like the siren's call, he felt his gaze tugged towards them again and wondered what they'd feel like to kiss.

The blood-pressure machine beeped loudly, ripping into his traitorous thoughts and grounding him instantly. He pulled his shame-ridden gaze away, reminding himself that he loved Lisa and he had a patient who needed his total concentration. 'Pressure's dropping.'

'He's bleeding somewhere.' Poppy's hands went direct to Daryl's abdomen, her alabaster fingers, with their neatly trimmed nails devoid of polish, palpating expertly. 'Any pain here?'

Daryl barely managed a negative movement of his head.

'No guarding. It's not his abdomen.' Poppy's frown deepened, making a sharp V between her expressive black brows. 'His O2 sats aren't improving. What about a haemothorax?'

'If he does have that, it's not massive because there's no mediastinal shift or tracheal deviation.'

But the blood-pressure machine kept beeping out its worrying sound as Daryl's heart rate soared and his conscious state started to fade. Matt stared at the green lines racing across the screen. PQRST waves scrawled the heartbeat but he thought he saw something unusual. He hit the printout button and studied the paper strips, detecting a change in the ST segment. Combining it with Poppy's musings, he had a sudden idea. 'Check his jugular vein.'

Matt shoved his stethoscope back in his ears and listened carefully to Daryl's heart beat. Instead of a loud and clear lub-dub, the sound was muffled.

'Cardiac tamponade.'

They spoke in unison, their thoughts and words meshing together for the very first time. 'He's bleeding into the pericardial sac.'

Poppy ran the ultrasound doppler over his chest, locating the heart. 'There you go.' She pointed to the dark shadow around the heart that squeezed the vital muscle.

Matt snapped on gloves and primed a syringe, knowing exactly what he had to do. Under ultrasound guidance, he withdrew the fluid from around the heart. 'Hopefully that will stabilise him until you work your magic.'

Her teeth scraped quickly over her bottom lip; the slightest of hesitations. 'A pericardial sac repair without the back-up of bypass isn't quite what I'd expected.'

He understood her concerns and he had some of his own. 'The anaesthetic will stretch me too.'

'It's going to be touch and go.'

'I know.' He met her direct and steady gaze, one devoid of any grandstanding or combative qualities, and wondered not for the first time about the many facets of Ms Poppy Stanfield.

CHAPTER THREE

IT HAD been a hell of a piece of theatre. Matt couldn't help but be impressed by Poppy's expertise. Except for requests for unanticipated instruments, she'd been virtually silent throughout, but it hadn't been an icy silence that had put the staff on tenterhooks; the case had done that on its own. Given the complexity of the surgery, she'd done the repair in a remarkably short space of time, giving Daryl the best chance of survival. It had been a lesson to Matt that she knew her stuff and did it well. Although many visiting surgeons had her air of authority, not all of them had the skills to match.

It had been one of the most challenging anaesthetics he'd ever given due to the patient being haemodynamically unstable, and maintaining his pressure had been a constant battle. Thankfully, Daryl had survived the emergency surgery and was now ventilated and on his way to Perth.

Once the flying doctor's plane had taken off and the night shift had arrived, Matt no longer had a reason to stay at the hospital. As he took the long way home it occurred to him that even Poppy had left the hospital before him, finally taking with her those bright red cases that matched her lips.

Again, shame washed through him. He hated it that he kept thinking about her bee-stung lips. He didn't want to because they belonged to a woman who was so different in *every* way from his wife that it didn't warrant thinking about. When he thought of Lisa the words 'fair, soft and gentle' came to mind. Poppy Stanfield wouldn't understand the description.

He pulled into his carport and as he reluctantly walked towards the dark and empty house, memories of past homecomings assailed him.

'Tough case, honey?'

'Yeah.'

'Well, you're home now.' Lisa leaned in to kiss him. 'Annie's already in bed and our room is deliciously cool.'

His key hit the lock and the door swung open, releasing trapped and cloying heat, which carried silence with it in stark contrast to the past. God, he hated coming back to this house now.

Yeah, well, you hated not living in it.

He dropped his keys in a dish he'd brought home from the Pacific and which now sat permanently on the hall table, and thought about the months he'd stayed away from Bundallagong. Being back hurt as much as being away.

He turned the air-conditioner onto high, poured himself iced water and briefly contemplated going to bed. Picking up the remote, he turned on the television, rationalising that if he was going to stare at the ceiling he'd be better off staring at a screen. He flicked through the channels, unable to settle on watching anything that involved a story and eventually stared mindlessly at motor racing, the noise of the vehicles slowly lulling him into a soporific stupor.

He was back on the beach again, with dry heat warming his skin and coconut palms swaying in the breeze, a peaceful idyll that promised so much. Set back from the sand line was a grass hut, its roof thatched with dried sugarcane leaves, and he strode towards it quickly, anticipation humming through his veins. His family was waiting for him. He stepped up onto the lanai but instead of cane chairs there was a stretcher. Bewildered, he stepped over it and walked into the fale, expecting to see the daybed, but instead he was in an operating theatre that looked like a set from *MASH*, with patients lined up row upon row, some with sheets pulled over their heads. Voices shouted but he didn't recognise the words, and he turned back, wanting to run, but the lanai had vanished, leaving splintered timber as the only evidence of its existence.

Deafening noise roared and his arms came up to protect his head and then his eyes were suddenly open and the television was blaring out so loudly the walls vibrated. He must have rolled on the remote, taking the volume to full blast, and he quickly pumped it back to a bearable level, but the ringing in his ears took a moment to fade. He shook his head, trying to get rid of the buzzing, and thought perhaps bed was a better option than the couch—not that he wanted to sleep because the dreams would terrorise him.

As he swung his feet to the floor, a woman's scream curdled his blood. He quickly shoved his feet into his shoes, grabbed a torch and ran outside.

He heard a wire door slam and he moved his torch round to the house on his left, the house owned by the hospital. With a start he saw a tall, barefoot woman dressed in a long T-shirt standing on the steps, her arms wrapped tightly around her.

He jogged over as the outside lamp cast her in a pool of yellow light. 'Poppy? What the hell happened? Are you all right?'

She shuddered, her height seeming slightly diminished. She swallowed and it was if she had to force her throat to work. 'Mice.'

He knew his expression would be incredulous. The woman who'd stormed into his department with an approach similar to a man marking his territory had been reduced to a trembling mess by a mouse. For months he hadn't been able to laugh and now he had to try hard not to. '*You're* scared of a mouse or two?'

Her head flew up and a flash of the 'take no prisoners' woman he'd met nine hours ago surfaced. 'Not generally, no. But I opened the wardrobe to hang up my clothes and *mice* streamed out, scurrying over my feet, into my case and...' She took a steadying breath. 'I defy anyone, male or female, not to let out a yell of surprise when confronted by fifty of them.'

His mouth curved upwards, surprising muscles stiff from lack of use. 'That has to be an exaggeration of about forty-eight. Are they in the kitchen too?'

'I don't know!' Her voice snapped. 'I didn't stop to enquire if they'd taken over in there as well.'

Don't get involved. But he couldn't resist a dig. 'I did suggest you settle in to the house earlier in the day.'

Her chin shot up and she gave him a withering look. 'I am *not* exaggerating, and if that is the extent of your useful advice then I suggest you shut up now and leave.'

She crossed her arms and he suddenly noticed she had breasts. Small but round and… He hauled his gaze away. 'It's been a few months since anyone's lived here, although I would have thought someone would've checked out the house before you arrived. Who did you talk to in Administration?'

She stepped back inside, her gaze darting left and right and her long legs moving gingerly. 'No one.'

He followed. 'No one?' Usually Julie was very efficient.

'Me coming up here was—' She stopped abruptly for a moment. 'I rushed up here because the town was desperate. The fax telling you I was coming probably only arrived a few hours before me.'

They'd been desperate for weeks so her hasty arrival without the usual planning didn't make a lot of sense and he was about to ask her about it when a mouse raced out from under the couch.

Poppy leapt into the air, her long T-shirt rising up to expose creamy white thighs.

Matt tried not to look and instead marched like a foot soldier on patrol, punching open the kitchen door. Every surface was covered in mouse scats.

He heard Poppy's shocked gasp from the doorway but by the time he'd turned, her face was the usual mask of control, although she had a slight tremble about her.

'Just fabulous. This really is the icing on the cake of a stellar few days, and yet the poets wax lyrical about the bush.'

A startling fragility hovered around her eyes despite her sarcasm and he had an unexpected moment of feeling sorry for her. He shrugged it away. 'Living with a few creepy-crawlies is all part of the Bundallagong allure.'

'Not from where I'm standing it isn't. I think we have definition conflict on the word "few".'

Again he found himself wanting to smile yet at the same time a feeling of extreme restlessness dragged at him. He flung open cupboards and found mice squeaking and scurrying everywhere amidst bags of pasta, cereal, oats and biscuits, all of which had been chewed and their contents scattered. He slammed the doors shut. 'OK, you were right. It's a plague and with this many mice it probably means you don't have a python.'

Her eyes widened like the ongoing expanse of Outback sky and her hands flew to her hips. 'No snake? And *that's* supposed to make me feel better? Hell, and they give surgeons a bad rap about their bedside manner.'

This time the urge to smile won. 'Actually, a python would have meant fewer mice. I haven't seen an infestation like this in years. Your predecessor must have left food and I guess the cleaners figured it was nonperishable and left it for the next occupant. Thing is, time marched on and the mice moved in. Julie can get the exterminator to come in the morning.'

'The morning.' The words came out as a choked wail loaded with realisation. Another mouse shot past her and she stiffened for a second before hastily retreating to the lounge room.

Matt crossed the kitchen and leaned against the architrave, watching her. She had her back to him and was standing on tiptoe, reducing her contact with the floor to the bare minimum. One hand tugged at the base of the T-shirt in an attempt to make it longer, and the other pressed her mobile phone to her ear as she spoke briskly.

'Yes, I need the number for motels in Bundallagong. I don't have a pen so can you put me through direct?'

He thought about the suit she'd worn when they'd met and how it had been followed by surgical scrubs. Both garments had given her a unisex look, but the baggy shirt she wore now hid little. Poppy Stanfield might sound like a general but she had the seductive curves of a woman.

Heat hit him, making him hard, followed immediately by a torrent of gut-wrenching guilt. He loved Lisa. No woman could match her but for some reason his body had disconnected from his brain and was busy having a lust-fest. He hated it and every part of him wanted to get the hell out of the house and away from Poppy Stanfield and that damn T-shirt. But he couldn't leave, not until he knew she was settled in a motel. So he moved instead, putting distance between them by crossing the room and tugging his gaze away from the sweet curve of her behind that swelled out the T so beautifully that his palm itched.

He stared at the blank walls and then at the couch with a ferocious intensity he'd never before given to decor. He noticed a significant-size hole in the material covering the couch and realised the inside was probably full of rodents too. It would take days before baits and traps took effect, making the house liveable again.

He started making plans in his head to keep his mind off those long, shapely legs. As soon as he knew which motel she'd got a room at, he'd set the GPS in the hospital vehicle for her so she wouldn't get lost at this late hour. There'd be no point driving her because she'd need the car to get to and from the hospital.

Yeah, that, and you don't want to be in a car alone with her.

Poppy's voice suddenly went silent and the next moment, with a frustrated yell, she hurled her phone with a great deal of feeling onto the soft cushions of the couch. It was her first display of 'surgical temper'.

The outburst—so very different from Lisa's quiet approach—made him feel less guilty about getting hard, and yet it was so full of energy and life that it swirled around him, both pulling him in and pushing him away. After months of not feeling anything this maelstrom of emotions confused and scared him, and when he spoke, the words shot out harsh and loud. 'No instruments to throw?'

She didn't even raise a killing look. 'I have *never* thrown anything in Theatre, although I did train with a master thrower and once had to dodge a chair.' She plonked herself down hard on the couch, threw her head back and closed her eyes. 'This is a nightmare.'

Grey shadows hovered under her eyes and she looked exhausted.

'Actually, it's probably not a good idea to sit on that.' He pointed to the gnawed hole.

He'd expected her to fly off the couch but she merely shuddered and stayed put. Eventually she opened one eye and stared accusingly at him. 'You could have told me that the Australian billfish competition is on!'

Was it? Had that many months passed? 'Sorry, I didn't realise it was that time of year.' Once he'd had his finger on the pulse of his hometown and been part of the committee for one of the biggest events on the calendar, but not any more. Now days just rolled together into one long and empty period of time.

She frowned at him as if she didn't quite believe him. 'Every motel between here and a hundred k up and down the coast is fully booked out with anglers hoping to catch a two-hundred-and-twenty-kilo marlin. God, I hate this dust-impregnated town.' She picked up her phone and stared at it as if willing it to ring with news of a bed.

A mouse scuttled between his feet.

She can't stay here.

She's not staying with me.

Why not? You don't care about much any more so why care if she stays a few nights?

She sighed. 'I don't suppose you know if my office at the hospital has a couch?'

Her tone was unexpectedly flat, as if all the fight had gone out of her, and a tiny crack appeared in the blackness of his soul. His mouth started to work before his brain had fully thought it through. 'You can stay at my place until this joint is clean and mouse-free.'

Her smooth brow creased in uncertainty. 'That's kind of you but don't you think you should discuss it with your wife first?'

Your wife. He felt the darkness sucking at his heart and soul, threatening to drown him over again the way it had so many times in the last year and a half. His heart thumped faster, pumping pain with every beat, but he somehow managed to growl out, 'No need. Come on, grab your stuff. It's late.'

He turned and strode out of the house, not waiting for her, not offering to carry her case, and not looking back because if he did he might just change his mind. Not even Poppy deserved that.

* * *

Poppy lugged her unopened and mouse-free case the short distance to what she assumed was Matt's house—lights on, front door open—and wondered what on earth this man's deal was. He lurched from sarcastic to ironic, friendly to downright rude and a thousand emotions in between. Why offer her a bed if he clearly wasn't happy about her staying? She assumed he'd gone on ahead to let his wife know they had an unexpected guest. She thought of her gorgeous apartment in south Perth with a view of the river and silently cursed William and the hospital board.

She stepped into the empty foyer of a house considerably larger than her hospital residence, and unlike the minimalist furnishing of rental accommodation she could see the hand of a woman in the decor. Silence hovered and given it was close to midnight she didn't want to call out and wake anyone. For all she knew, there could be children asleep.

A closed door on her left was probably a bedroom so she left her case by the front door and padded down the well-lit hall, which opened into a formal lounge-dining area. Despite its stylish couches and polished wood table, it had an air of 'display only', lacking the personal touches like ornaments or photos that created living spaces. She kept walking and passed through a doorway into another huge space, which wasn't well-lit but she made out a kitchen and assumed beyond was a family room and bedrooms.

She spoke softly. 'Matt?'

He appeared through a door off the kitchen, his arms full of bed linen and his face set in unforgiving lines. 'Your room's this way.'

She expected him to turn towards the yet unexplored part of the house but instead he headed back from where she'd come from and entered the bedroom at the front of the house. A stripped white-wood queen-size bed dominated the room, which had a feature wall wallpapered in alternating cool blue and white stripes. Matching white-wood bedside tables held reading lamps with gold stands and white shades, although Poppy noticed the plugs had been pulled from the sockets. No books or boxes of tissues adorned any surfaces but gauzy curtains hung softly in front of a white blind, which was pulled down. The room should have said, 'restful haven for adults' but instead it looked abandoned.

Matt threw out the bottom sheet and Poppy moved to grab her side. She was almost certain this room had been designed to be the master bedroom. 'Are you sure this is OK?'

Matt deftly made a hospital corner with the top sheet and didn't meet her gaze. 'The en suite and walk-in wardrobe is through there.' He waved towards a doorway. 'The hot water's solar and it's really hot but it takes a minute or so to come through. Catch the water in the bucket unless you like to wake up to a cold shower.' He shoved a pillow so hard into the pillowcase it bunched up and he had to thump the feathers back into place before throwing it on the bed.

He strode to the door, his hand gripping the handle and his gaze fixed firmly on the cornice where two walls met. 'We leave at 7:30 a.m. and you'll find something for breakfast in the kitchen. Good night.'

The door closed firmly behind him, the click loudly stating, 'this is your space so stay here.' Poppy fell back onto the bed, her relief at being out of the infested house short-lived, and she wondered if she'd have been safer sharing with the mice.

Perhaps it had been sheer exhaustion but, despite Poppy's misgivings, she'd slept soundly. Now, as she dressed, she could feel the temperature climbing despite the early hour and her suit, which she donned automatically, felt hot. Still, if she had her way she'd be in scrubs soon enough. She opened her door, expecting to hear a household in full Monday morning action mode—radio or television news blaring, the drone of a kettle as it neared boiling and the ping of the toaster—but although she could hear the harsh squawk of cockatoos outside, she couldn't hear anything much inside. She made her way to the kitchen, which was empty, but with morning light streaming in she saw that, unlike the front part of the house, which held an unlived-in air, the kitchen showed more than the occasional sign of occupation.

Newspapers were piled so high on one end of the long granite bench that they'd started to slide onto the floor. Used cups and glasses sat abandoned close to, but not in, the dishwasher. A supermarket bag filled with tins took up more space rather than being stored in the adjacent pantry and every other surface was covered in clutter from half-opened mail to nails and paperclips.

A casual eating area off to the left had a table and chairs but instead of the polished jarrah having placemats it held a laptop and was covered in screeds of paper. She glanced into the family room and saw a similar chaotic mess that jarred with the decor, which had obviously been undertaken with care and a great eye for detail. Poppy wasn't a domestic queen by any stretch of the imagination but even she managed better than this. She was amazed the Albrights didn't have mice!

She filled the kettle and while she waited for it to boil for her heart-starter morning cup of coffee, she emptied the dishwasher, guessing where items went, and then reloaded it with the dirty cups and glasses. She located the coffee and then opened the fridge. Milk, a loaf of bread, three apples and a tub of yoghurt hardly made a dent in the cavernous space that was big enough to store food for a family of six.

'Morning.'

His voice startled her but at the same time it reminded her of a Cabernet Merlot from Margaret River: deep, complex and with a hint of tannin. She turned around and stifled a gasp as her body betrayed her with a shot of delicious, tingling lust.

He stood on the other side of the bench, his hair still slightly damp and rumpled from the shower, the ends brushing the collar of his open-necked shirt. His long fingers tackled the last few buttons and his tanned and toned chest fast disappeared under the placket. His wedding ring glinted in the sunshine through the window and when he raised his gaze, the Kelly green in his shirt lightened his dark eyes but the shadows remained, and fatigue hung over him like a threatening cloud.

What are you doing? Get yourself under control; he's married, off limits, and even if he wasn't he's too damn moody and you've sworn off men for all time.

The moody man spoke. 'Did you sleep?'

His question sounded almost accusatory. 'I did, thank you.' *But you don't look like you did.*

He seemed to be staring at her suit and she thought she detected relief in his eyes, which made no sense whatsoever so she was probably totally wrong. She had no clue why she was letting Matt Albright unnerve her. If anyone unnerved her it was usually other women. Men she understood because she worked in a man's world but the whole women and friendship thing she'd always found challenging and unfathomable, and that dated back to primary school.

You're conveniently forgetting Steven, are you?

He didn't unnerve me, he just broke my heart.

And now you avoid men.

I work with men all the time!

That's not what I mean and you know it.

To distract herself she picked up a cloth and started to wipe down the bench. 'No one else up yet?'

'You don't have to do that.' He swooped, his fingers brushing her skin as he tugged the cloth out of her hand.

Trails of desire shot through her. This was crazy on so many levels and she had to act. 'Look, Matt, I'm sorry I had to prevail on your family for a bed, although you were the one who offered. Obviously me being here is a problem and I'd like to apologise to your wife for the inconvenience.'

He lowered the dishcloth onto the sink, the action slow and deliberate. When he raised his head she experienced a chill.

'My wife isn't here.'

And you're an incredibly gorgeous guy that women viscerally react to even when they're sensible and know they shouldn't. 'And she's not OK with me being here. I get it.'

He grimaced. 'No, you don't get it at all, Poppy.' The ping of the kettle sounded bright and cheery, in sharp contrast to the strain in his voice and the emptiness in his eyes. 'She died.'

His grief rocked through her, sending out waves of shocked surprise, and her fingers immediately crept to the pendant at her neck. *Death*. She hadn't expected that. Suddenly everything fell into place: the vacant master bedroom; the messy kitchen; Jenny's lack of anger towards him yesterday; and his aura of immense sadness. 'I'm sorry. I shouldn't be here. I'll find somewhere else today.'

He scooped ground coffee beans into the plunger and dashed the hot water over them. 'It makes no difference to me if you stay or not.'

And she realised he spoke the truth. His perfectly handsome face that could have graced the cover of any magazine was a façade. Underneath it, pain burned inside him, making caring for anything difficult.

You should leave. 'When does the billfish thing finish?'

He consulted a wall calendar that was two months out of date, and turned the pages. 'Next Sunday. Everything will be booked solid until then.'

Hope sank in her gut like a lead weight. 'That's probably how long it will take them to get the house under control.'

'Could be.'

'So you're saying it's a waste of time even trying to find somewhere else?'

He shrugged as his hand closed around the coffee-pot. 'It's your call.' Lifting two clean mugs from the cupboard, he poured the coffee and held up the milk carton.

She shook her head at the milk and reached over,

lifting the black ambrosia to her nose, and breathed in deeply. The aroma sparked up her synapses, firing her brain into action. Was it such a bad thing if she had to stay here? She'd be working long hours so she'd hardly be in the house and when she was, she had her own room and bathroom so they'd hardly have to see each other. She had no doubt in her mind that Matt Albright was still very much struggling with the death of his wife so her occasional errant feelings, which she was certain she could squash, wouldn't be reciprocated at all, leaving everything as it should be: colleagues only.

'I came to operate, not to spend time trying to find a room, so, thanks, I'll stay.'

His blank expression and lack of response reinforced her decision and she brought the mug to her mouth, closed her eyes and drank in the brew. With a sigh of bliss she licked her lips and savoured every drop. She finally opened her eyes to find Matt's *chocolat-noir* gaze fixed intensely on her mouth and a spark of something broke through their blackness.

A shot of heat way beyond the definition of delicious tingling, and fully loaded with longing, rocked through her so hard and fast her knees sagged.

Get out now. 'I better get to the hospital and meet my staff.'

He gave a curt nod as the shadows scudded back in place. 'Don't give 'em hell.'

She bristled. 'I'll give them what they need.'

'I imagine you will.' His tone held resignation but his mouth curved slightly and the hint of dimple hovered in the darkness of his stubble, foreshadowing how heart-stoppingly magnificent he'd look wearing a full smile.

Poppy fled.

CHAPTER FOUR

POPPY flicked the switch on her Dictaphone to Off, having finished her last surgical report for the day. Her first couple of official workdays had arranged themselves into a routine of rounds, surgery, reports, phone calls to her spies in Perth to get an update on her opposition, and then arriving back at the house very late and falling exhausted into bed. Work consumed her, as it always did, only this time she appreciated that it left no space in her brain; no space to think about the way her body had gone into sensual overload when Matt Albright had looked at her through his heavy-lidded eyes.

She rubbed her forehead and wondered what on earth was wrong with her. Sure, he extended the handsome scale by about ten numbers but he was grumpy and short with everyone except patients, and obviously still grieving for his dead wife. Just like her, he wasn't fit for a relationship and she surely didn't even want one so there was absolutely *no* reason for her to be even thinking about him.

So why did thoughts of him sneak under her guard at random moments in the day? It made no sense and many times she'd needed to shake herself back into full-focus work mode because she had far more important things to think about, like the chief of surgery position in Perth.

'Ready, Poppy?'

The words broke into her thoughts and she glanced up, expecting to be asked for an emergency consult. Instead, Jen stood in the doorway dressed in casual clothes. 'Um, ready for what, exactly?'

Jen grinned. 'All work makes Poppy a dull girl.'

She straightened a pile of folders on her desk. 'All work is what I'm here to do.'

'Sure, but day is done and there's drinks at the pub.'

'Thanks but I'll pass.' Making small talk wasn't something that came easily to her; in fact, she was shockingly bad at it.

The nurse shook her head. 'Not an option, Poppy. It's a Bundallagong tradition that the nurses buy new medical staff a drink.'

She must have looked horrified because Jen hurriedly continued on with, 'Think of it as a girls' night out and a way of getting all the goss on the place.'

Her horror intensified. Poppy had no clue what a girls' night out entailed, having never been on one. *Getting the goss.* The words pierced her horror and she realised with a buzz of clarity that this might just be the solution to her problem of random thoughts about Matt interrupting her concentration. It was a normal human reaction to have natural curiosity when you heard unexpected news; healthy even, and Matt's statement about his wife being dead had been totally unexpected. She was pretty certain Matt wouldn't tell her any details and although she was known for her brusque, straight-shooting style, asking someone 'When and why did your wife die?' wasn't something even she would do. But if she found out the story from Jen then knowing would end the curiosity and banish all her unsettling feelings.

Decision made, she stood up, slung her handbag over her shoulder and joined Jen in the corridor. 'So how far away is the pub?'

'Next door.'

'There's a pub next to the hospital?' She couldn't hide her incredulity. 'Why haven't I seen it?'

'Its position is historical. Mining towns back in the day were pretty rough and I guess putting the two together was a short walk for the drunks. Today things are more PC so there's limited signage advertising the pub. It's mostly used by the hospital and college staff, so a fun crowd but not too rowdy.'

They stepped outside into the dusk and the ever-present heat enveloped them. Streaks of vermillion slashed the sky as the sun sank low against the horizon and the bright white light of the first star pierced the rising darkness. 'This sunset belongs on a postcard.'

'Yeah, it does from this direction, but turn one-eighty degrees and the port's infrastructure gets in the way. Mining dominates everything but I guess without it the town wouldn't exist.'

The sunset unexpectedly mellowed Poppy. 'Does the pub have a garden? Now you've planted the idea of a drink, a glass of champagne while watching this sunset might go down very well.'

Jen roared laughing. 'You can have any drink you like as long as it's beer or rum and Coke. Welcome to the north-west.'

The pub was busy and Jen made a bee-line for a table with a banquette seat on one side that had a reserved sign on it. The waitress appeared with a tray of glasses, a jug of beer and bowls of peanuts. Poppy, not normally a beer-drinker, accepted a glass of the icy-cold amber fluid. As it trickled down her throat she was surprised at how good it tasted, and put it down to the heat.

Jen raised her glass. 'Welcome.'

'Thanks. It's been an interesting start.' And the perfect segue into the information she wanted. 'I'm sorry if I got you into trouble with Matt on Sunday.'

'No worries. Matt has good days and bad, and they're hard to pick so we just roll with them.' Jen fiddled with a thick cardboard coaster already damp from condensation. 'It's been an awful eighteen months. It's hard to know what to do or say when someone goes through something like that, you know?'

Something like what? Cancer? Car accident? 'How did—?'

'Hi, sorry I'm late!' Sarah Fielding, Poppy's theatre nurse, slid into the bench seat, all sparkling green eyes, wild red hair and a handbag the size of the Outback. She looked very different from the competent woman who'd made the morning's theatre session run so smoothly. 'Justin got home earlier than I thought and as the kids were already in bed we took advantage of it.' She winked and raised a glass. 'To fast sex.'

Jen laughed and clinked glasses with Sarah and threw Poppy a conspiratorial grin. 'To long-distance phone sex. David's out in the Kimberley for another month.'

The hairs on Poppy's arms stood up. God, this was why she never went out in a group. Joking about sex with women she barely knew wasn't something she was comfortable doing.

Let's face it, you're not comfortable doing sex, full stop.

Shut up.

But she wasn't fast enough and the memory of Steven's voice echoed through her. *Sexually, a fridge is warmer.*

She realised with a jolt that the two women were staring at her, expecting a response to the toast. She gripped the edge of the table to keep her hand from touching her pendant. 'Actually, I'm not planning on having sex here.'

Jen's eyes blazed with interest. 'So it's phone sex for you, too. Have you left a gorgeous man behind in Perth, pining for you?'

'Uh, no.' He left me.

Jen's brows rose in surprise. 'So you're unattached?'

Poppy sipped her beer against a tight throat, wishing she could mutter a magic word and conveniently vanish. She didn't do this sort of chitchat well, and she was even worse when the focus was on her. 'I am, and I came here to work. Given the amount there is to do, I won't have time for sex.'

'You can't go three months without sex!' Sarah's expression combined abject horror with good-natured scheming and she glanced around the bar as if she was looking for someone.

'Oh, I can *easily* go three months.' Poppy drained her glass.

But it was as if Sarah hadn't heard her and she turned back, her face fill of dismay. 'Damien isn't here tonight but, Poppy, you have to meet him. He's the new flying doctor pilot. He's totally gorgeous, unattached and he'd be the perfect diversion for you.'

She was having trouble trying to align this sex-obsessed woman with the one who'd been so professional this morning, and it took a lot of effort to keep the biting tone out of her voice. 'I don't need diverting.'

'We all need diverting. Life in this town is tough.' Sarah gave a sincere and friendly smile with no agenda, while she refilled Poppy's glass.

Poppy stuck to her mantra. 'I came here to do a job, pure and simple.'

'But why not have some fun at the same time?' Sarah tucked her curls behind her ear. 'Damien would be the perfect reward for being stuck out here, although you will have a bit of healthy competition from every other single woman in town and probably the occasional married one as well. Any single, professional man who arrives is immediately considered as a ticket out of here, or a way of making the town work for you.'

Poppy smiled stiffly. 'Well, I don't need a ticket out because I've got a huge job back in Perth.'

Not necessarily. She tried to close her mind to the undermining thought and at the same time wrestle back some control in the conversation. She spun the spotlight back on Sarah and raised her brows. 'So, did marrying Justin make this town work for you?'

Sarah laughed; a big, congenial chuckle. 'Touché, Poppy. OK, I get it—you don't want to be matched up. But to answer your question, Justin and I met in Canberra during his intern year. He came out here as a med student, fell in love with the Outback and wanted to come back. As I loved him, I said I'd come out for a couple of years and see if I could love it too.'

Love *and* career support. The answer slugged Poppy, totally demolishing her preconceived ideas and stabbing her with a combination of jealousy and remorse. Sarah had what she'd never been able to achieve. 'And?'

Sarah shrugged. 'It's a man's town and there needs to be more of a focus on the women. I'm on the neighbourhood house committee and we're setting up groups based on interests that we hope will spin off into support, mentoring and friendship groups.' Her face suddenly lit up. 'Hey, what else are you good at besides surgery?'

She tried to focus on the unexpected question. 'What do you mean?'

'Hobbies, interests, things like that.'

Her mind was a blank space because for years all she'd done was haul herself up the surgical ladder with long and punishing hours, leaving no time for anything other than sleep. Often there'd been scant time for that. 'The last few years have all been about work.'

'What's on your "to-do" list? What do you crave to do when you have the time?' Jen leaned forward, her eyes filled with unexpected sympathy.

Poppy bristled at the look. Why on earth would a nurse be feeling sorry for her? But her usually quick and logical mind struggled to think of an answer to the question. Desperate to banish Jen's air of pity, she dug deep but nothing surfaced. 'I've always wanted to...' God, what had she always wanted to do?

Win.

Win Dad's love. Steven's love.

She grasped at straws, needing to give them something, needing to show them she was a successful woman in control of her life *and* with interests. Interests she didn't have. For some reason, she thought of how she enjoyed singing in the shower and belting out a tune. Shower singing was something she did most mornings and it reminded her of how she'd sung in the choir at school and at uni. Singing would do as an answer. 'I'd go back to music and rejoin a choir.'

Sarah squealed and clapped her hands together. 'You sing? That's fantastic.' She high-fived Jen.

Another prickle of apprehension washed through Poppy, this time stronger than the last. 'Have I missed something?'

Sarah beamed. 'I've wanted to start a women's choir because it's so much more than just singing and so many women here would benefit. Jen plays piano and now you've arrived with choral experience so we have a musical director. It's just perfect!'

'Musical director?' She heard her voice rise and she shook her head hard. 'I don't have time for something like that.'

Sarah's eyes narrowed and her carefree aura vanished, replaced with a very professional and determined one. 'Poppy, you're a successful woman in a field dominated by men and that makes you a mentor. We have women here who are isolated, living in tough conditions, dealing with their partners' shiftwork and dislocated from their families because they've followed their partners out here for work. It can all add up to depression and low self-esteem.' The passion in her voice carried clearly out above the noise of the room. She leaned forward. 'I know you're busy but seeing as you're so adamant about not having sex while you're here…' she winked '…that frees up time for some community service. Think of it as improving women's health, and as a doctor you can hardly walk away from that.'

Checkmate.

Poppy wanted to plead too much work and no time

but she knew both these women were intimate with her workload and would juggle rosters to create the time for her if she didn't find it herself. Sarah, with her air of good fun and no cares, had her over a barrel with her well-developed sense of social justice.

Poppy sighed. 'We start small, right?'

Sarah gave a long, slow smile. 'We'll start with whoever's interested.'

Poppy reluctantly raised her glass. 'To the Bundallagong's women's choir.'

'To the choir and friendship.' Jen titled her glass towards Poppy's and gave her a wide, open smile.

'To fun, friendship and service.' Sarah joined the toast.

A flurry of movement caught Poppy's eye and she turned towards the door. A tall man had entered and was crossing the room towards the bar, where he pulled up a stool and sat down next to another man. The chatter of the room dropped for a moment as all the women turned and followed his movements.

She instantly recognised Matt as the guy already sitting, his wild hair gleaming like a dark and rumpled halo in complete contrast to the golden fire of the man next to him. Side by side the two men looked like light and dark, storm and sunshine. Her gaze should have been tempted by the freshness, youth and sheer vitality of the unknown man but instead it was stalled on Matt. Stalled on the way his hair curled around his ears, stalled on his toned shoulders that filled out his shirt, giving it a precise and square fit; stalled on him full-stop.

'The blond delight is Damien and you have the right to change your mind about sex but not the choir.' Sarah leaned back with a conspiratorial smile on her lips. 'Rumour has it he can take a woman flying in more ways than one.'

Matt had been quietly getting drunk when Damien had arrived. He hoped that after one drink, the pilot would be taken away by one, two or more of the many women who'd been waiting so patiently for his arrival. That would mean he could resume his relationship with the barman, and wipe himself out for the night.

It had been a very long time since he'd got drunk, but during the first few weeks after returning to Bundallagong, alone, it had been a regular event. It had been the only surefire way to stop the dreams that broke his sleep and took him back to the heart of his grief, never allowing him any time to breathe without it. But the morning he'd woken up on the back steps after sleeping rough because he hadn't been able to work out how to put the key in the lock had been the day he'd stopped drinking hard. That, and the fact he knew it was a very fine line between himself and the alcoholics he treated in Emergency.

He'd been sober for weeks. He'd even started running again at dawn now he was able to get out of bed without a thundering headache, but Poppy Stanfield's arrival had changed everything. The only way he was going home tonight was completely buzzed so he could fall into the black oblivion of deep and uninterrupted sleep.

He threw back a shot. God, he hated himself. He despised the way he couldn't get Poppy out of his mind when he should be honouring Lisa's memory. He couldn't believe that on Monday night he'd left the hospital on time and cooked a meal in anticipation of

Poppy's arrival home. All day she'd jumped in and out of his thoughts and he'd found himself looking forward to sitting down at a table with her, hearing about her day and sharing his own with a living person rather than the silent walls of the house.

But he'd eaten alone. By 10:00 p.m. he'd thrown out the food and gone to bed—to bed but not to sleep. His silent monologue had veered between cursing life in general that he no longer had Lisa and Annie, and cursing himself that he'd been so pathetic as to think he could try and have a normal evening, although he had no clue what normal was any more. He'd heard her car pull in at midnight and when he'd finally fallen asleep, his dreams had been filled with a woman who had looked like Lisa but whenever he'd got close, he could only see vibrant blue eyes. Poppy's eyes.

He spoke to the barman. 'I'll have another Scotch and...' He turned to the pilot. 'What can I buy you, Damien?'

'Soda water, thanks, I'm on call. Your night off?'

'Yep.'

'Hey, Doc, third drink in an hour—time for your keys.' Lewis, the barman, held out a container with a couple of sets of car keys at the bottom.

'I walked, Lew.' He had a standing arrangement with the barman so he avoided doing anything really stupid. A couple of times soon after Lisa's death, when being alive had almost been too much to bear, he'd got way too close to stupid.

'Good to hear it.' Lewis slid the two drinks across the counter.

Damien sipped his and surveyed the room. 'So how's that guy I flew down to Perth the other night getting on?'

'Not bad. You'll probably be transporting him back here in a couple of weeks.'

Damien raised his hand in a wave and Matt glanced around to see who'd caught his attention. With a shot of surprise he recognised Sarah Fielding. Why on earth was Sarah beckoning Damien?

She and Lisa had been firm friends from the moment the Fieldings had arrived in town and as a result the two young families had socialised together a lot. Since coming back to Bundallagong, he'd only seen Justin at hospital functions and at the GP in-service he conducted every few months. He hadn't been able to face a social gathering with Sarah and the kids.

He stared at her and then made out Jen's profile behind her, before realising there was a third person at the table.

Surprise rolled through him. Poppy sat on a chair, looking awkward and completely out of place.

Sarah arrived at the bar, her gaze cautious, and she seemed to breathe in before she spoke. 'Justin was sorry you didn't make golf the other day, Matt. He's on for next Wednesday and looking for a partner, so call him?'

He didn't want to play golf. 'Sure.'

She nodded, her expression worried, and then she turned and gave Damien a flirty smile. Sliding her arm through the pilot's, she urged, 'Come and meet our new surgeon. She has the most amazing eyes you've ever seen and is in town for three months with no one to play with.'

Damien looked over Sarah's head towards the table of women. 'Ebony and ivory?'

Matt didn't like the way the pilot was scoping out Poppy and his voice came out on a growl. 'That's her, but be warned: just like a praying mantis, she'll play with you and then she'll eat you.'

But instead of being put off, the pilot grinned. 'I love a challenge.' He slid off the bar stool and strode towards the table.

The thought of Damien hitting on Poppy had Matt up and off the stool. *What are you doing? She'll probably tear strips off glamour boy and even if she doesn't, what do you care?*

But he picked his drink up anyway and let his feet carry him to the table. He arrived just as Damien was suggesting to Poppy that the only way to really appreciate the Pilbara was from the air.

Poppy's fine black brows rose in a look Matt was starting to recognise as pure sarcasm. 'If flying means not missing out on every single millimetre of the thousands of kilometres of endless, flat gibber plain and red dust, yes, I suspect you're right. Fortunately I flew in on a clear day so I don't feel the need repeat it any time soon.'

Damien looked slightly taken aback that his usual invitation had failed and Matt hid a smile before sitting down next to Poppy. Her fresh floral scent hinted at the newness of spring and it spun around him, urging every cell in his body to lean in close and breathe deeply. 'Actually, the only way to appreciate the unconventional beauty of this area is by four-wheel drive and getting a hands-on perspective.'

'Unconventional is right.' Poppy's fingers closed around the base of the pendant at her neck.

Jen's quizzical expression moved between Poppy and Matt. 'Matt's right. You should make sure you visit Walker's Gorge while you're here.'

'It's a fair distance from here, though. I could fly you in,' Damien countered. 'Just let me know when you have a free day.'

Poppy's hand fell back to her lap and she gave a short laugh. 'That's very kind but given that my surgical list is endless, and Sarah's already shanghaied me into starting a women's choir, I think my time in Bundallagong is pretty much full.'

A choir. Matt did a double-take, not able to imagine her in a musical role, but was that just another piece of the puzzle that was Poppy? His eyes met hers and he watched the vivid blue of her irises almost disappear into rapidly dilating inky discs. A flash of undisguised attraction burned bright for a heartbeat and then faded, but not before a wave of her heat crashed into him. Like a chain reaction, every part of him vibrated with hungry need.

She pulled her gaze away and rose to her feet, her movements jerky. 'Thanks, everyone, for the welcome drinks. It was really kind but it's time to call it a night.'

Damien moved towards her. *No way, mate.* For the second time, Matt found himself shooting to his feet and he spoke without thinking. 'I'll come with you.'

Her fingers tugged at the fine, silver pendant and her expression mixed hesitation with determination. 'Really, there's no need.'

But he wasn't letting her leave alone or giving

glamour boy an opening so he shrugged casually. 'I need the ride.' Instinctively, he slid his hand into the small of her back and guided her around the group, through the crowd and out into the night, ignoring the stunned looks of his colleagues.

The heat from Matt's hand flooded Poppy, streaming through her veins like hot vapour and culminating in a tingling pond of undeniable lust. Her breath came too fast and the muscles in her legs threatened to melt as the sensations spun through her with their intoxicating promise of pleasure.

Pull yourself together. It's just the touch of a well-mannered man. Steven had exemplary manners and remember what happened? The thought grounded her momentarily. Gathering her tattered self-control, she passed through the doorway into the starlit night and stepped away from his touch.

She hadn't been surprised that Matt had been drinking alone at the bar, given the way he held himself aloof from people and coupled with the townsfolk not seeming to know how to treat him, but the fact he'd joined them at the table had caught her off guard. His offer to leave with her had totally floored her. From the moment he'd sat down next to her she'd struggled to keep up with the conversation as every part of her had been absorbed by his closeness.

Now his gaze stayed fixed on her, and she shivered. *Find your strength, defuse the tension.* 'Where's your car?'

'At home.' He had no trouble matching her stride. Unlike her stiff and jerky gait, his was fluid. 'I walked because I'd planned to drink more than the legal driving limit.'

He didn't look drunk and she wouldn't call him relaxed but something about him was different. Less guarded perhaps? 'And have you?'

'Probably.' He leaned casually against the car, waiting, with his toned arms crossed over his T-shirt-clad chest and the light from the streetlamp spilling over him. It gave him the quintessential look of a bad boy.

Her mouth dried and her well of strength drained away. Flustered, she dropped her gaze and fumbled in her handbag, searching for her car keys. She breathed out in relief when her fingers closed over metal and she quickly activated the lock release button and swung up into the vehicle. She just had to get through a short drive. How hard could that be?

He sat down next to her, filling the cabin with his fresh scent of laundry soap and everything male. She let it fill her nostrils, pour into her lungs, and suddenly her hands trembled.

Intelligent brown eyes zeroed in. 'You OK to drive? We could always walk.'

'I'm fine.' *Liar.* She wasn't drunk but she was a long way from fine. With Matt so close her brain had closed down under the assault of her body's wayward pleasure-seeking mission and she couldn't think straight. She hit the on button of the radio with the palm of her hand, filling the cabin with music, and then she planted her foot. She tried valiantly to focus on the music but even that was against her with a raunchy song about make-up sex. Her hand wanted to leave the steering wheel, reach out and press her palm against the stubble on his cheek. She turned left at the first intersection and right at the second, and then drove straight.

'Uh, Poppy?'

'What?' It came out far too snappy as her body mocked her every good intention to stay aloof by sending rafts of hot and cold streaking though her.

He tilted his head, a lock of hair falling forward. 'I'm not so drunk that I don't notice where we are. You're going the wrong direction and the house is back that way.'

She squinted through the windshield. Oh, God, he was right. With her mind complete mush, she'd taken the wrong turning at the first intersection and now she had no clue where she was. 'It all looks the same at night.'

'Sure, it pretty much does except for the bright lights of the port, which gives you a whopping big navigational tool.' His voiced teased as he turned towards her, his face clear in the moonlight. His mouth was curved up into a broad smile, a smile that banished the usual hovering sadness as it raced to his eyes, creasing the edges and making them dazzle with fun and wicked intent.

She almost drove off the road.

She'd wondered what he'd look like when he truly smiled and now she knew—completely devastating. Hauling her gaze back to the road and loathing herself on so many levels for her total lack of control over her body, she tried desperately not to sneak another look at his sexy grin. Usually when she was proved wrong she got defensive, but there was something about the unexpected softness that had momentarily surrounded him that made her laugh. 'I'll concede you have a point.' She slowed in preparation to do a U-turn.

'Keep going. We're pretty close to Estuary Road and you get a great view of the town from there. It looks pretty at night.'

She changed gears. 'What, no red dust?'

'The key to Bundallagong is to focus on the ocean. The turtles and the whales will amaze you.' He stretched out his arm. 'Turn here.'

The headlights beamed onto a break in the trees and she slowly navigated the vehicle down a narrow track. 'Are you sure this is a road?'

He leaned back in his seat. 'You're such a city girl. Live a little.'

'I live plenty.' *You love deluding yourself, don't you?*

The track opened up into a wide parking area with a boat ramp and she parked. Matt jumped out of the car and quickly walked round the front of the vehicle, reaching her door before she'd finished unlatching her seat belt. Surprise piggybacked on every other rampaging emotion.

He opened her door. 'Come on, you need to see this.'

She followed him across the stony area until they stood on the curve of the bay. Across the moonlit water, the massive port with its heavy equipment that looked like a scar on the landscape during the day sparkled white, yellow, blue and orange. 'I concede it has its own charm.'

He laughed—a rich, deep sound that made her think of the bass notes of a clarinet. 'Careful, Poppy, you're in danger of gushing.'

He stood so close to her she could feel his heat, hear his breathing and smell his spicy scent—all of it swirling around her, taunting her to reach out and grab it for herself. 'It's nothing like I expected.'

His head leaned in, his eyes smoky and intense. 'Nothing ever is.'

'No.' She barely got the word out as his breath

caressed her face and her heart bruised itself against her ribs. She spoke almost as much to ground herself as to reply. 'I belong in Perth.'

'Who really belongs anywhere?' His warm hand slid along her jaw, and then long, strong fingers tilted her head. His dark hair fell forward, stroking her cheek, before his lips brushed hers—soft, hot, partially testing but mostly firm and sure.

He tasted of malt, tropical heat and arousal. He was kissing her and, God help her, she wanted it like her body needed air. Her hand wrapped around the back of his head and she pulled him into her, feeling the hard muscles of his thighs pressing against her and his heart thundering against her own. He murmured a groan and his tongue flicked at her closed lips, seeking entry, and she opened them to him, needing to have him inside her, wanting him to explore, lick, taste and take. Wanting him to treat her like a woman.

Every part of her burned as Matt's expert mouth dismantled any lingering doubts that kissing him was a bad idea. She kissed him back. She kissed away the past, banishing Steven's cold, hard voice and releasing the barrier on her femininity, letting it flood her and then flood Matt.

He gasped, his hands tangling in her hair and then gripping her head to gain access to her throat. He trailed spine-tingling kisses along her jaw before dropping his head lower, tracing the hollow of her neck with his tongue. She sagged against him as she heard a mewling sound in the back of her throat.

She hauled his mouth back to her own, needing that intimate contact and tasting salt and her own heady desire. Nothing mattered except losing herself in the heat of that hot, throbbing place, and she turned herself over to its power, allowing her mind to spin out on bliss and her body to burn.

She was boneless, wet with need, weak with longing yet strong with the power of her body and she gloried in it. His hand covered her breast, the thin material of her blouse and bra feeling like a concrete slab between them. She wanted to feel the heat of his palm against her skin, let the weight of her breast fill his hand, and she ached for the graze of his thumb on her tightening nipple. She popped her shirt open and guided his hand. 'Touch me.'

His body stiffened against hers, rigid from head to toe, and suddenly his hands were on her shoulders, pushing. He ripped his mouth from hers, stepping back, breaking the kiss, breaking all contact.

'This is a mistake.' His words shredded the night air—harsh, ragged and uncompromising.

You're a machine, Poppy, not a woman. The memory of Steven's voice taunted and the fire in her body chilled to ice. Her legs shook, followed by the rest of her, and she desperately wanted to evaporate like water against parched ground. Instead, she lifted her chin, locked down every emotion and pulled her blouse shut tight. 'That's what they all say.'

She strode to the car, slamming the door against his voice, and gunned the vehicle out of the car park, not caring how the hell he got home.

CHAPTER FIVE

'EXACTLY *where* is Victor Chu's fluid balance chart?'
Matt's head pounded and the backs of his eyes ached.

Jen frowned but her mouth moved into an anxious smile. 'It's clipped to his chart board.'

'If it was there, I wouldn't be asking.' He spun the chart board so it skidded across the desk. 'His pulmonary oedema is worsening and he's now on a strict fluid intake, which I'd write on the chart, if I could find it.'

She pulled the sheaf of charts out of the folder and started going through them one by one. 'You don't look very well. Do you need some of my winning combination of complex B and C vitamin drink?'

'I'm *not* hungover.'

She smiled overly brightly as if she didn't believe him and produced the elusive, pink, fluid balance chart.

'I'm not.' He sighed and tried to swallow his defensive tone. 'I had a terrible night and no sleep.' He wrote his orders on the chart and added a new drug regime in an attempt to dry Victor's lungs and maximise the effectiveness of the weak beats of an old and tired heart. 'I just need coffee.'

'There's a fresh pot in the lounge.'

He nodded his thanks and backed away from her

sympathetic glance. He didn't deserve it. Not this time when his lack of sleep had nothing to do with grief and everything to do with Poppy. God, why on earth had he kissed her?

But he knew why. He'd had plenty of time to think about it as he'd walked the three kilometres home. He poured himself a large mug of the aromatic brew and closed his eyes, instantly seeing Poppy's plump, lush lips. He forced his lids open but it didn't help—he could still see the after-image of their shape and colour, and that, combined with those startling eyes, had him almost permanently hard. It had rendered his restraint so thin it was friable. Last night, standing so close to her under that bright, white moon, with her intoxicating perfume spinning around him and her body heat rolling into his, it had all combined to demolish the tattered shreds of his self-control. All he'd known was that he'd ached to touch her, craved to taste her, and hungered to savour her.

So he had.

And she'd flooded him with unforeseen and unrestrained passion. Passion that had roared through him, feeding his desire with so much fuel that he'd almost combusted on the spot. His body had taken over, emptying his mind of everything except the white-hot pleasure of sex. And he'd revelled in it. It had been so long since he'd felt alive like that and nothing had existed except two hot bodies seeking each other.

Touch me. Her tremulous and breathy voice had sliced through him, penetrating his lust-fogged mind like a knife and dumping reality upon him as he'd realised who he'd been kissing.

Not Lisa. Hell, he'd had his tongue down the throat of

another woman and it hadn't been enough: he'd wanted so much more.

So he'd pulled away, despising himself for betraying Lisa.

What about betraying Poppy?

He stifled a groan and slugged more coffee. He hadn't seen her since she'd stormed away from him and he'd been in no state then to even try and call her back. Even if his mind and voice had worked, he knew she would never have stopped to listen and he'd been incapable of telling her the truth.

'Matt, ambulance is pulling in,' Jen called out as she hurried towards the ambulance bay.

Matt joined her, glad to be distracted from the mess he'd created, and he pulled on gloves, ready to treat the young man writhing in pain on the ambulance's stretcher. 'What happened?'

'His apprentice said he'd been lifting concrete slabs and went down screaming. I gave him some nitrous but he's still in pain.' Doug Finlay, the senior paramedic, gave a brief handover.

'Hernia?' Jen muttered, before moving to transfer the man onto the trolley, but as she reached his side she paused in surprise. 'Liam?'

Matt instantly recognised one of the town's builders and based on what the ambulance officer had said thought an abdominal or spinal disc hernia were very possible. 'Where does it hurt? Your back?'

Liam shook his head, his expression a combination of pain and embarrassment. 'It's *not* my back.'

Matt caught the look. 'Ah, Jen, can you go and start the paperwork.'

'Sure.'

As the door closed behind her, Liam started to dry-retch and Matt grabbed a kidney dish. 'As soon as I've examined you, I can give you something for the pain.'

'I remember being kicked in the balls when I was aa kid but this—' He seemed to have trouble breathing against the pain. 'This is absolute agony.'

Matt nodded sympathetically. 'I want to rule out a couple of other possibilities.' He palpated Liam's abdomen and groin but he couldn't feel a hernia. 'I need to examine your testicles.'

Liam barely nodded as his white-knuckled hands gripped the silver railing of the trolley.

'I think you've got a torsion of the testicle.'

Liam looked blank. 'What?'

'It's twisted.' He pulled the ultrasound over and examined the area. He pointed to the screen. 'There's the problem.'

Liam looked like he could hardly focus. 'It's absolute agony.'

'That's because the blood supply is being restricted.' He saved the picture, wiped the Doppler and returned it to its holder.

A knock sounded on the door and Matt tossed the modesty sheet over Liam as he called, 'Come in.'

Jen entered the room, followed by a woman who appeared to be a similar age to his patient. She rushed towards Liam, picking up his hand. 'I came as soon as Tim called me.'

Jen slung the clipboard over the end of the trolley and said quietly to Matt, 'Should I page Poppy?'

Matt tilted his head in agreement.

Jen returned it as she spoke. 'This is Emma Waterson—Liam's fiancée.'

Emma, still holding Liam's hand, looked up, her forehead creased with worry. 'What's wrong with him?'

Matt filled her in on his diagnosis and watched her face pale.

'Why...? I mean, how did it happen?'

'It's not an uncommon condition in men under twenty-five and I'd say Liam probably has a genetic or structural weakness. Combine that with heavy lifting, and it would be enough to cause the twist.'

She turned accusingly to her fiancé. 'You told me you were getting the bobcat in to lift that concrete.'

Liam blanched as another wave of pain hit him. 'Em, I'm sorry. I couldn't get it today and I was trying to get everything done so we could have a two-week honeymoon.'

Emma let out a wail. 'Oh, God, the wedding. Can you untwist it?'

Matt tried to suppress a shudder. 'Liam needs surgery. The good news is that we have a surgeon here.' *Good news for Liam, anyway.*

'Good news?' The soon-to-be bride swayed on her feet. 'That means there's bad news too. Will it mean we can't have children?'

'If the testicle has to be removed, the other one won't be affected.'

'And the honeymoon?' Liam grimaced as he moved.

Matt gave a wry smile. The guy was in agony but still thinking about sex. *It's all you've been thinking about today.*

He rubbed his temple. 'You'll be a bit tender for a day or so but the second week you should be just fine.'

Liam sunk back on the pillows. 'In that case, do your worst—just stop the pain.'

'I can do that.' Poppy strode into the room, her blue eyes flashing brightly.

With her green theatre scrubs floating around her and concealing the soft curves Matt knew nestled underneath, she gave him an almost imperceptible nod before studying the ultrasound screen.

Liam choked. 'You're the surgeon?'

Poppy gave a restrained smile. 'I understand you'd probably feel more comfortable with a man but think of it as taking one for all the women in the world who find themselves being treated by male gynaecologists.'

Emma laughed. 'I like her.'

'You're not the one going under the knife,' Liam grumbled.

'Poor baby, I'm sure she'll be gentle.'

Matt didn't disillusion either of them with his thoughts.

After Poppy had explained the procedure and obtained consent, he followed her out of the room, thankful they had a patient to discuss. 'I'll put in an IV, take some blood for FBC, U&Es and cross-matching, and then he's all yours.'

She raised her well-shaped jet brows. 'As long as you're sure. I'd hate it if you made a mistake.' Hurt shimmered around the sarcasm.

He swallowed a groan. It was time to make some sort of restitution. 'I wanted to talk to you this morning but you left before dawn.'

She folded her arms, scrunching the scrubs tightly over her breasts. 'Ah, the apology. No need, heard it before.'

Apology? What apology? But his gaze snagged on the outline of her bra and he swallowed, hard, forcing his mind to stay on track with the conversation. 'How can you have heard it before? I haven't ever apologised to you.'

She rolled her eyes, azure deepening to midnight. 'You're a man, I'm a woman. Believe me, I've heard it and I've heard every single excuse in the book of sorry. I don't have time for this, Matt. I'm due in surgery.'

He trapped his angry retort and watched her walk away. *Believe me, I've heard it.* What the hell did that mean? Did she think she could throw off some line and just keep walking?

Well, what did you really expect? He had no clue. Damn it, he hadn't actually planned on apologising. She'd been an equal participant in the kiss and this was 2011. Surely people had a right to change their minds.

You touched her breast; it had gone way past a kiss.

He tried to recall the sequence of events last night after his head had roared so loudly with the realisation of what he'd been doing—when betrayal and lust had collided and he'd pulled back.

This is a mistake.

That's what they all say.

Who the hell were 'they'?

This time Matt didn't cook. He didn't go to bed at 10:00 p.m. Or eleven. He opened the door to Poppy at eleven-fifteen.

Shocked surprise crossed her face and she quickly glanced towards her house before staring straight back at him. 'Two houses, both have rats.'

Anger scorched his intention to invite her to sit down and calmly talk this mess out. 'Oh, and that's really mature.' He ran his hand through his hair, trying to find the calm he'd once been known for. 'Look, we have to work together and right now we're sharing a house, so what do you need me to say so we can go back to being semi-civil with each other?'

'Nothing.' She tried to move past him.

He blocked her. 'That's rubbish. If it was nothing you wouldn't have left me out at the point last night to walk home.'

She shrugged. 'You told me you were planning on walking home anyway.'

'From the pub!' He heard his voice rise. 'Which is three minutes away, not three kilometres.'

Her stony expression wavered slightly with the tiniest mark of contrition, and he pounced on it as a sign of a chance at reconciliation. 'Do you want a drink?'

Her brows rose. 'Isn't that what got you into trouble last night?'

'I was *not* drunk.' For the second time that day, he ground out the indignant words. 'Six months ago you could have levelled that accusation at me but not last night.'

The faintest tremble wove across her bottom lip before she snagged it with her teeth. Teeth that had nipped at his lips last night in the frenzy of *that* kiss. The memory sent a bolt of heat through him and he realised he was staring at her mouth.

Her chin shot up. 'So you were sober. That makes it worse. I have to say, this is one hell of an apology.'

'I'm not apologising.' The yelled words shot around them both, loud and uncompromising.

She blinked and then spoke quietly. 'No, you're not.'

She walked past him, leaving him standing in the hall, stunned.

Your manners always made me feel special.

Lisa's voice chided him. He'd never yelled at a woman in his life so what the hell was wrong with him? He leaned against the wall and slowed his breathing before walking into the kitchen. Poppy had poured herself a glass of sauvignon blanc from the bottle he'd put in the fridge earlier, and was staring out into the night.

'I'm sorry, I shouldn't have yelled. I don't usually yell.'

She didn't turn round but her shoulders stiffened so much that balls could have bounced off them. 'Yeah, well, I've been known to have that effect on men. That and not being woman enough. Congratulations. You've gone two for two and you're up there with the best.'

He felt like the floor was tilting under his feet and he was left scrabbling for purchase while careering inexorably into a black sinkhole. 'What are you talking about?'

She spun to face him, her face pinched as conflicting emotions broke through her usually impenetrable armour. 'You want me to spell it out to you?' Her voice rose and she dragged in a breath. 'I'm an exceptional surgeon but a lousy kisser. I'm sorry it was such a disappointment for you.'

Her words hit with the velocity of a missile, stunning him. 'That's what you think?' He picked up his bottle of water, trying to assemble coherent thought. 'You think you're bad at kissing? Why on earth would you think that?'

A shudder whipped across her shoulders, round her

torso and down her long, long legs. 'Oh, let me see. It started at high school with my name scrawled all over the boys' toilets, then my ex-husband mentioned it as often as he could and, hmm, last night you told me it was a mistake.'

That's what they all say. Her words from last night lanced him and then all-encompassing anger at an unknown man erupted so fast it turned his breath fiery. 'Your ex-husband doesn't know squat.'

Her pupils dilated, drowning her shimmering cornflower-blue irises, and she swallowed, the ripple of movement centred in the hollow of her throat. The place he'd branded last night. The plastic bottle of water crunched loudly under his tightening fingers.

She shrugged. 'Yeah, well, let's not go there.'

'Poppy, believe me, you can kiss.' The husky words somehow passed through his tight throat and he downed some water, trying to douse his burning need for her.

She bit her lip as her hand crawled to her pendant. 'Don't do this, Matt. I'm not a child and you can't muddy the truth. It stands and it has done for a long time. It stood loud and clear last night out at the point. For whatever reason, you were moved to kiss me. I kissed you back and you pulled away. End of story. We'll both live.'

Despite everything, he knew their kiss had fired life into parts of his body that had been numb for a long time. Poppy had done that with her mouth, her tongue, her teeth and her taste. He couldn't let her continue to believe she was a lousy kisser. *So tell her why you pulled back.*

But he couldn't do it. He didn't want to have *that*

conversation, and see and hear her pity. With a growl he forced out, 'You've obviously been kissing the wrong men.'

She gave a derisive laugh, her face tight with the pain of her past. 'Yeah, well, last night was a case in point.'

No, it wasn't. In two strides he stood next to her, cupping her cheeks and pressing his mouth softly to hers. Taking a gamble to prove a point, a point she needed to understand.

She stiffened, her lips closed to him. Gently, his tongue ventured along the outline of those wondrous bee-stung lips, lips that drove him crazy on an hourly basis, and he tasted a hint of gooseberry and restraint born of hurt. But she didn't push him away so he slowly nibbled her generous bottom lip, coaxing it to open and unlock the ambrosia he knew waited within.

He heard a strangled moan and recognised the moment her inherent sexuality defeated her control. Her mouth—hot, moist and seeking—met his with a scorch of fire, lighting a blaze that tore though him, revisiting places and invading untouched parts of him. He buried his hands in her hair and her fingers dug into his scalp, as if it was the only way she could stay standing.

His skin, slick with sweat, tingled with something he barely recognised because the memory of it had faded to fuzzy faintness—hedonistic pleasure. He lost himself, amazed at how decadent yet occasionally sweet and tender her mouth could be. His tongue met hers in a dance of wonder that ignited into a fevered duel, each of them angling for control and driven crazy by need.

The power surge of her desire lit up the back of his mind.

When did you ever kiss Lisa like this in this house?

The thought shocked him so hard his mouth slackened and he almost fell.

Poppy's eyes, glazed with ecstasy's bliss, instantly focused. She pulled away, her breasts rising and falling with fast, shallow breaths. 'What the hell is happening? You're doing it again.'

This time, with the light of the room, he glimpsed raw and pulsating pain in the electric blue of her eyes before her steely control shut it down.

He closed his eyes against his own pain, shame, guilt and utter despair. *She doesn't deserve this.* Forcing himself to look at her, he knew with gut-wrenching certainty what had to come next. 'It's not you, Poppy, it's me.'

Poppy stared at him, barely able to catch her breath and hardly able to believe her ears. Her heart pumped desire-fuelled blood through her, making her skittish and demolishing her usually logical thought processes. It took more than effort to clear her head. She scraped her mussed hair out of her eyes and clamped it by tightening the now loose band, the action giving her precious moments to pull herself together. 'I don't understand.'

His hand ploughed through his hair as his expression became imploring. 'Please believe me when I tell you that you're not *just* an exceptional surgeon.'

A kernel of belief almost sprouted inside her, but words counted little against crystal clear actions. He'd pulled away from her twice and both times had ended the most bone-melting kisses she'd even known. He'd rejected her, like all the men in her life. 'I get the feeling there's a "but" coming.'

His eyelids hooded his dark eyes, masking his emotions, but his body betrayed him when his left hand fisted so tightly his knuckles gleamed white. When he finally spoke it sounded like it was coming from the depths of his soul. 'You're the first woman I've kissed since Lisa died.'

Poppy's legs gave way and she sat down hard on the couch. Oh, dear God, how had she been so dumb? She wanted to bury her face in her hands at her thoughtless and completely selfish neediness. Last night, when he'd stopped kissing her, her past had come rushing back so hard and fast it had obliterated any other possible reasons as to why he'd stepped back. By default, she'd made it all about herself, when in reality it was about him.

She had no idea what to say except the obvious. 'You loved her very much.'

'I do.'

And right then, with the blinding clarity of the hindsight, she understood. 'Kissing me is like cheating on Lisa.'

He sat down on the opposite end of the couch, his expression tinged with apologetic regret. 'Yeah.'

She wondered what it would be like to be loved by someone so much that they considered it an act of faithlessness to kiss someone else even when you were dead. Steven hadn't loved her enough in life to be faithful and yet she wasn't certain she'd want a lover to be racked with this much guilt after she'd gone. Had she done something to trigger memories? 'Do I remind you of her?'

'God, no!'

She took the hit, feeling it reverberate through her with a dull ache, which was dumb because of course he loved his wife.

Show no hurt. She tilted her head in irony. 'Just as long as you're sure.'

He had the grace to look abashed. 'Sorry.'

'Don't be.' She grabbed her wine and took a gulp, trying to dig down to find the mature adult. His emphatic reply spoke volumes: she was nothing like his wife and no matter how that made her feel it gave her the opening to ask the question that had been on the tip of her tongue from the moment she'd discovered he was a widower. 'So what was Lisa like?'

Her name. Matt stared at Poppy for a moment, realising that no one in town ever said Lisa's name to him any more. He turned away, doggedly looking out through the patio doors, uncomfortable about the comparison he was about to make. 'She was blonde to your black and short to your tall.' *Her mouth wasn't as full as yours.* He banished the thought by trying to focus on Lisa but his mental image of her face clouded around the edges. 'She had a way with people, an ability to find something uniquely special about them. It made you feel like you were the only person who mattered to her at that moment in time. She made friends easily but she also kept them. There was something about her that made you want to try and be the best person you could.'

'She sounds…exceptional.' Poppy's voice was strained and she cleared her throat.

'She was.' He kept staring out into the night as memories sucked at him, threatening to drown him, and he fought not to go to that dark place.

Poppy placed her glass on the side table and the noise of glass on wood brought him back to the present. She rose to her feet, the movement fluid yet extremely controlled, right down to the way the last hair on her head settled into place. He remembered the first time he'd met her and thought her all sharp angles and harsh lines. But that had been before he'd kissed her and discovered how wrong he'd been. Her air of command hid a raw sexuality that when unleashed had rocked him in ways he'd never imagined.

She jutted her chin in that precise way that meant she'd made up her mind about something. 'It's late.'

'It is.'

'See you in the morning, Dr Albright.'

He stared at her, realising she'd just played the colleague card, putting the boundaries firmly back in place, cutting the attraction off at the knees. Wasn't that what he wanted? Restoration of equilibrium? 'Coffee at seven, Ms Stanfield.'

'Seven it is.'

He ignored the scud of disappointment that gnawed at his gut.

CHAPTER SIX

'So HAS he put a foot wrong yet?' Poppy held her phone hard to her ear as she took the call in Matt's kitchen while making a late night 'catch-up' sandwich with chicken and salad.

Luke Davies, her favourite anaesthetist, filled her in on Alistair Roland, her competitor in Perth. She'd made the call after coming home from the first choir practice, needing to get her head firmly back in the game of her career rather than letting herself be sidelined by Bundallagong and a man with the smokiest gaze she'd ever encountered.

Not that it mattered that Matt could reduce her to a quivering puddle of need with one gaze, because he didn't want her. Her rational self didn't want him either but her body craved him so badly it sobbed continuously. If past history had taught her anything it was that she doomed relationships, familial and sexual. Even if she had any relationship skills, she couldn't compete with the memory of a dead woman who, unlike her, had made friends with ease and been admired by all she'd met. Matt had made that more than clear three nights ago.

So she'd been very sensible and pragmatic over the last few days, as had he. Whenever they consulted at work they were polite, professional and courteous. No one observing them would have any reason to think they'd once kissed each other senseless. As a result, it was getting easier with every day.

Is that so?

Yes!

You are so deluding yourself.

Luke's voice rumbled down the line, bringing her back to the point of her call. 'You might be in trouble. Alistair's got the nursing staff eating out of his hand.'

'That's not good news.' She opened the fridge, scanning the now considerable contents she'd purchased, and looked for her favourite mayonnaise.

'You wanted facts. I'm just the messenger.'

It was just the sort of information she didn't want to hear. 'Exactly how has he achieved that in such a short time?'

'Sorry, PICU is paging me. I have to go. Hang in there.'

The phone beeped as the call disconnected and Poppy felt the hitch in her gut. She didn't have the XY chromosome to make a predominantly female nursing staff 'eat out of her hand' but she'd always prided herself on being fair. Why didn't that ever seem to count for much?

Frustrated by the report and the paralysis of distance, she snapped her phone shut with one hand, grabbed the mayo with the other and bumped the door closed with her hip.

'What's not good news?'

The mayonnaise and her phone clattered onto the bench as her heart thundered hard and fast. *Matt.* She couldn't be certain how much of her reaction was due to fright and how much was the result of her body's natural response to seeing him.

Her heart hiccoughed.

Question answered.

It was a lot safer to hide behind fright and find indignation. 'First there's the goanna thundering in the roof at 3:00 a.m. whenever a cat disturbs it and now this.' She righted the mayonnaise bottle. 'Didn't anyone ever tell you not to sneak up on a person?'

He gave her a wry smile. 'Sorry. I thought you heard me call out when I came through the door. Is there a problem?'

Never show weakness, Poppy. Her father hadn't been around a lot but when he had, he'd hammered that message home hard, loud and clear. 'No.' *Deflect.* 'Well, there *is* the goanna. It's like an elephant in the roof. How do you sleep?'

His jaw tightened for a fraction of a second. 'The goanna and I have an understanding and you're changing the subject.' His perceptive gaze shone with questions. 'You're wearing a frown as deep as a mineshaft and it isn't goanna related.'

Admit nothing. 'I've got a lot on my plate, that's all.'

Matt lowered himself onto the stool by the bench, his manner interested but slightly detached, just like it had been at work ever since they'd buried the entire kissing incident. 'I'm happy to listen.'

'You wouldn't understand.' The words shot out, defensive and self-protective, with the intent of warning him off. Steven had never understood.

Instead of looking offended, Matt just shook his head

slowly as if he felt sorry for her. 'Try me. You might be surprised.'

His long fingers reached out and she watched mesmerised as he snagged a piece of chicken, tilted his head back and dropped it into his mouth. The mouth that had created such delicious havoc the other night and in the process had been branded on her memory for ever.

It had been years since she'd confided in anyone, having vowed never to again after the debacle with Steven. Usually she blocked people with snappy replies and if that didn't work, she crossed her arms. She didn't know if she was overtired, surprised by his interest or just a sucker for *chocolat-noir* eyes, but before she could second-guess her decision, she blurted out, 'I'm fighting for the chief of surgery job back in Perth.'

'Good.'

Indignation roared through her and she slapped mayo and mustard onto wholemeal bread. This was the sort of patronising response she'd got from Steven and the *exact* reason she never opened up to anyone. 'Good? Exactly *how* is it good?'

'You'd be great in that position.'

Surprise barrelled through her, dismantling her righteous anger and leaving behind a trail of confusion. 'Oh, um, thank you.'

Matt raised his brows as he sliced an avocado. 'Now, was telling me that so hard?'

Stop whining, Poppy, and just do the job. 'Yes.'

This time he laughed.

'Seriously, you have no idea.' She pushed her father's and Steven's voices out of her head but thoughts about work took their place. She waged a constant battle— emotionally and physically—to get the same deal as her male counterparts, which meant staying one step ahead at all times. She'd given up so much and she deserved the Perth job, but it was hard to keep fighting for it when she'd been taken out of her own work-place.

His laugh faded. 'Well, you did it, you told me, and life as we know it is still happening, so keep going. What's the specific problem?'

She loaded bread with moist chicken, avocado, thin slices of peppered tomato, fresh basil leaves and lettuce, before adding the top layer of bread and slicing the squares into neat triangles.

'Poppy?'

She knew she was stalling. She pushed one plate towards him and saw intense interest underpinned with support. 'My competitor is currently doing the job, shovelling charm by the bucketload and winning over the staff, while I've been sent up here to languish in the backblocks.'

'Ah.' He bit into the sandwich.

'Ah, what?' She pulled a piece of avocado out from between the slices of bread, her appetite vanishing.

'Who did you upset?'

Her hands hit her hips despite the truth. 'Why do you automatically assume I upset someone?'

'Come on, Poppy, you have to admit that sometimes you have a "take no prisoners" approach that steps on toes.'

She bristled at his criticism. 'You're not perfect yourself.'

'I'm very well aware of that, but right now we're talking about you.' A quiet smile wove through his dark stubble. 'Great sandwich, by the way.'

She leaned against the bench and sighed, partly at her

inability to withstand his smile but mostly because she realised she was totally unable to sidetrack him away from the topic. 'I was covering all bases and I applied elsewhere too and was unsuccessful. News got out and now it's being used against me.'

'But you want the job at Perth City?'

'I do. It's *my job*.' She tapped her chest vehemently. 'I've worked too hard for it to go to some interloper from the east.'

Understanding crossed his face. 'If it helps at all, everyone at the hospital is in awe at how much you've achieved in such a short time and I haven't heard too many grumbles about staff feeling overworked.' His cheeky wink softened his words. 'OK, you might not have the charm quotient like Mr East Coast but you've generated grudging respect.'

Her stomach clenched and she pushed her plate away, virtually untouched. 'Oh, fabulous—grudging respect. That good, huh? That's going to look sensational on my review…not! The only way I can counteract my competition is if I do an equal or better job so I need the staff to like me!'

'That will come with time, Poppy.'

She would have preferred simmering sexuality to this 'father knows best' air and she wanted to shake him. This was *her* career on the line and her voice rose in frustration. 'I don't have time on my side.'

His calm expression didn't change. 'So make it work for you instead of against you.'

'What the hell is that supposed to mean?'

'Be a surgeon at work and a person at play.'

'Play?'

'Yes, Poppy, play. Get out there and go fishing with

the theatre techs, call into the nurses' clothing and product parties, comment on the holiday photos of the clerks, cluck about the cleaner's new grandchild and make sure you show up to drinks at some point *every* Friday night.'

An unfamiliar sensation she didn't want to call panic zipped along her veins and her hand sneaked up to her pendant. 'But that's not me. That's not how I've *ever* done things.'

Matt's gaze showed no mercy. 'Do you really want that chief of surgery job?'

'Hell, yes.'

He grinned. 'And there's the drive we know and love.' He walked round the bench to plug in the kettle. 'Use your drive but redirect it. Show them there's another side to Poppy Stanfield.'

She'd spent years only showing the world the surgeon in charge because it was so much safer. The surgeon had steel-plated armour but the woman buried inside her did not. She crossed her arms in self-protection and her teeth snagged her lower lip. 'What if there isn't another side? What if what you see is all there is?'

'I don't believe that.' A husky edge clung to his voice and the collegiate mentor vanished under the heat-charged words.

Her stomach flipped. Memories of their kisses swirled and eddied around them, mocking everything she'd done to convince herself they were only colleagues. He stood so close to her she could smell the peppermint scent of his shampoo. She wanted his lips on hers, his arms around her waist and his body pressed hard against her, but when she glanced into his eyes, seeking the heat to match his voice, she could only find professional concern and perhaps a hint of friendship.

He doesn't want you. Men don't ever want you. She hated the empty feeling that settled over her and she ducked away from him, briskly covering the uneaten sandwich with cling wrap and covering her own irrational disappointment. 'By the way, I got the all-clear on the house. I'm moving in tomorrow as soon as the new furniture's delivered.'

A muscle close to his mouth twitched and he gave a brisk nod. 'I'm sure you'll be pleased to be in your own space.'

But Poppy read the subtext. He wanted her out and was pleased she was going. For her own peace of mind, she should be pleased too.

At 10:00 p.m. Matt saw the lights go on next door and tried to ignore them. Tried to ignore the fact Poppy was home. He tried to think about work, focus on how they'd both gone out of their way to be polite professionals, but all he could do was picture her in the kitchen, making one of her enormous 'catch-up' sandwiches after a day of grabbing food on the run.

Like the one she'd made him on the night he'd tried so hard not to let his hunger for her take over. The night she'd actually accepted some advice. It had been a good evening and they'd shared a companionable half-hour right up until the moment she'd nibbled her full, lush bottom lip.

He could have taken her right then—in the kitchen, on the bench, against the wall, anywhere. He had no idea how he'd managed not to. How he'd pulled himself back into line so she'd had no clue what he'd been thinking. Then she'd hit him with moving out.

God, he had to stop thinking about her, but the house was too quiet and offered up no distractions. Shadows danced across the walls and the strident, singing cicadas under the deck had gone silent on him. Even the goanna was undisturbed. The sensor light on the deck flickered on, probably triggered by a cat, and a slither of light caught something red behind the barbecue. He squinted and his heart cramped.

Annie's ball. He'd thought he'd collected all her toys but this one had refused to be found, lying in wait to layer on another fresh round of pain. He turned away from the glass and slumped down on the couch. Before Poppy's arrival he'd thought he was finally getting used to the emptiness of the house, if not the silence.

The huge silences were why he hadn't done anything about the goanna, because any sound was at least noise. But post-Poppy he'd realised that just by having another person in the place, even one who argued the point on almost every subject, had lessened the void that had taken over a home. Once it had known so much buzz but now silence had reduced it to a house. Four walls of loss.

Poppy had moved her two red suitcases out three days ago. Three long, quiet and lonely days. His loneliness had shocked him. Since Lisa's death he hadn't wanted company but tonight he ached for it. He'd spent the last three days arguing down every urge to go and visit her. He'd fought off the guise of the friendly neighbour bringing over a house-warming gift, wrestled down the doctor who thought he should 'follow up' on a case, and he'd shut up the eager mentor who kept insisting he should 'check up' and see how she was going with her campaign to warm up the staff.

So far he'd been successful at not going over, but it was consuming every moment of his day. And night. His phone beeped; a blessed distraction, and he read the reminder that flashed up on the screen. *Jen's b'day 2morrow bring food.* He smiled. Jen must have put the reminder in his phone when he'd left it at the nurses' desk.

He knew he hadn't contributed to a staff celebration in a long time and when he did he always bought something from the bakery, but right now, on this particular night, he wanted to make something, and the more he thought about it, the more it seemed like the perfect thing to do. He jumped to his feet and headed into the kitchen. He could only make one thing; a simple, no-cook chocolate slice his mother had taught him when he'd been a kid. She'd called it 'hedgehog'. Opening the kitchen cupboards, he reached to the very back and found a packet of plain biscuits. Amazingly, they were within the 'best before' expiry date.

He started whacking them hard with a rolling pin, enjoying the sensation of doing something normal and everyday. He rummaged through the drawer where Lisa had kept the spices and found cocoa and coconut and added them before opening the fridge for butter and eggs.

A cold, empty space greeted him.

Fresh ingredients? Who are you kidding?

Damn it, he hadn't shopped. *You never shop.* Had he lived in a city, he could have grabbed his keys and hit the supermarket at 10:00 p.m., but he didn't. He slammed the door closed, frustration licking along his veins. For the first time in for ever he'd actually wanted to make something and now he was stymied.

He turned slowly, looking out across the deck, and saw the lights next door were still on. *Poppy.* She'd have butter and eggs and, unlike all his created excuses to visit her, the ones he'd talked himself out of, this one was real. After all, Jen worked really hard and she deserved a birthday morning tea.

Oh, yeah, it's all about Jen's morning tea.

He ignored his sarcastic self. This visit was all about eggs and butter. He strode out of the house, across the garden and straight to Poppy's door, where he pressed the doorbell.

Waiting impatiently, he paced on the small porch. He pressed the bell again, this time holding his finger in place.

'Hang on, I'm coming.'

Poppy's voice sounded deep inside the house, followed by running feet slapping the bare floorboards. A moment later the door opened and Matt swallowed. Hard.

She stood in front of him, her long, black hair cascading over her shoulders like a silk shawl. His eyes followed the line of her hair, across shoulders almost bare except for the slash of the pink spaghetti straps of her camisole top. His gaze skimmed across her round breasts and down to the edge of the top. Here an expanse of tanned belly with the gentle swell of healthy roundedness was met by the band of a skimpy pair of royal-blue pyjama shorts, which clung low on her hips and high on her thighs. And then her legs; her long, long legs stretched on for ever.

He lost the power of speech.

'Matt?' Her blue eyes spun with confusion and concern.

Eggs and butter, remember? 'I need…' The words sounded way too husky. He cleared his throat. 'I need an egg and some butter.'

Her eyes widened and filled with surprise. 'You'd better come in, then.' She turned and walked towards her kitchen, the fabric of her pyjama shorts outlining the sweet curve of her behind.

Heat slammed through him, making him hard, and somehow, with superhuman effort, he managed to keep walking. *Talk about normal stuff.* 'It's to make something for Jen's birthday morning tea.'

'Oh.' She snagged her bottom lip with her teeth and disappointment sounded clear in her voice. 'I didn't know or I would have made something too.'

He stifled a groan. 'Seeing as you're donating the butter and egg, I'll say the hedgehog came from you.'

'You don't have to do that.' She opened the fridge, handing him an egg from the container in the door.

The egg felt thankfully cold in his hot and itchy palm. 'Sure I can. It's not like anyone's going to believe I cooked it.'

She laughed—a deep and throaty sound. 'Yes, but will I want to put my name to it?' She bent over, reaching for the butter, her pants riding up and exposing a glorious expanse of skin.

Heat fired through him, replacing air with all-encompassing need. He dropped the egg.

'Damn it.' He grabbed for a cloth and kneeled down at the same moment Poppy did, her hands filled with paper towel. Their foreheads banged.

'Ouch.' She laughed, her eyes sparkling with life.

Life. She was here, warm, real and, oh, so sexy. For months he hadn't wanted sex but every time he saw her he wanted her. Wanted her badly, and right now he couldn't think of anything else but sex.

Sex with Poppy.

He waited for the gut-wrenching guilt that had pulled him back every time but it didn't come and he didn't understand why but he wasn't going to question it. Poppy was nothing like Lisa and perhaps that was why it didn't feel like a betrayal. All he knew was that his hands burned to cup her bottom and her breasts, his mouth ached to trail kisses along her neck and across her glorious bare skin and he wanted to lose himself in her hair and breathe in her scent of being alive.

He slid his palm along her cheek, tilted her head and kissed her.

Poppy felt his hot lips on hers, felt her body melting, but the protective part of her brain screamed, *Stop!* Somehow she managed to grip his shoulders and pull back. 'Wh-what are you doing?'

Unfocused eyes, loaded with the haze of lust, stared at her. 'Kissing you.'

The words came out thick and hoarse, sending tingling need strumming through her and sucking at the edges of her control. 'What about the hedgehog?'

'I'll buy a chocolate cake.'

She wanted to smile but instead she rose slowly, dignity demanding she speak. 'You've kissed me twice before and pulled back.'

His face tensed and a sad smile curved his mouth. 'I promise you, I'm not going to stop this time. I want to keep kissing you until neither of us can stand.'

She bit her lip as she saw the turmoil of the lust of

now and the pain of the past in his eyes, and felt her own hurt. 'I'm not Lisa.'

His hand played in her hair and he spoke softly. 'This has *nothing* to do with Lisa.'

She didn't know if she should believe him or not. 'Then what is it to do with?'

'Us. This living, breathing "thing" that swirls constantly between us every time we're together, and even when we're not.' His eyes almost pleaded. 'You know what I'm talking about.'

She nodded silently. God help her, she did.

'So we need to have sex to defuse it and bring this "thing" back under control or we're both going to go insane over the next few weeks.' He pressed his mouth to the hollow of her neck.

Stars spun in her head and she clung to rational thought by a thread. 'Sex to defuse it?'

'Exactly.'

She could hardly think straight to follow his so-called logic. She had her own issues to face and she sucked in a deep breath. 'The thing is, I'm not very good at sex.'

'I don't believe that for one minute.' His mouth pressed nipping kisses along her jaw. 'I plan to show you just how good you really are.'

She swallowed hard, trying to stay strong against the delicious rafts of pleasure pouring through her, but she could feel herself slipping under the waves of desire and drowning in their headiness.

His finger tilted her chin so she looked directly at him. 'Sex for the sake of sex. No promises, no regrets, no future and no past, and absolutely no apologies.' His hands gripped her shoulders. 'Are you in?'

Just sex. Nothing more, nothing less.

Why not? It wasn't like she believed in 'happy ever after', and she knew she sucked at relationships and was never going down that torrid path again. She filled her life with work but right now her career hung in the balance, she was a hell of a long way from home and her body constantly hummed for this man. He wanted her body, which was more than any man ever had. Really, what did she have to lose?

Everything and nothing.

She circled his neck with her arms and sank into him with a moan that came all the way from her toes—the bliss of giving in to the longing that had consumed her for days and days. His mouth invaded hers: furnace-hot and with unleashed, potent desire that pulsated through her. She lost herself in his mouth, filling herself with his taste of mint and anticipation, exploring with teeth and tongue. With each foray he met her with one of his own, deepening the kiss, urging her to do the same until all thoughts vanished, the past imploded and nothing existed except his mouth and this kiss.

This time there was no holding back. This time Matt's hand sought her breast, slipping easily under her top, and while his thumb abraded her aching nipple his tongue sabotaged her mouth with bliss. The star-filled night sky had nothing on her body and mind as she lit up, every part of her igniting and burning for his touch. Gasping for breath, she pulled her mouth from his.

He groaned and could barely speak. 'Are you… changing…your mind?'

Her body screamed in protest that everything might come to an abrupt stop right now. 'God, no, but what about protection?'

Matt ran his hand through his hair as an expletive

hit the air. Then he kissed her hard and fast and came up laughing. 'Every hospital house has a medical kit. Where is it?'

Her brain spun with bliss and she fought to think. 'I put it in the bathroom.' He grabbed her hand and tugged her down the hall. 'Matt, it won't have condoms.'

He grinned. 'We're in the middle of nowhere and we have everything.' He flicked the latch and lifted the top tray.

Dipping her hand in, she pulled out a sheet of distinctive square foil wrappers. 'Plenty.'

'Speak for yourself.'

His eyes darkened, sending shivers of anticipation scudding through her. She tugged at his shirt, pulling it over his head, and her eyes feasted on a broad chest, slick with the sheen of the sweat of desire. Desire for her. She could hardly believe it as she reached out her hand, pressing it against hard muscle, feeling his heart thundering against it. 'You're magnificent.'

'So are you.' With a flick of his fingers the three silk-covered buttons of her top opened and he slid the material down her arms to the floor. 'That's so much better.'

His mouth closed over her breast and she cried out with sheer amazement as sensations cascaded over her. Sensations she didn't ever want to stop and she sagged against him as pleasure stole the strength from her legs.

He raised his head from her breast and trailed tantalising kisses back along her breastbone to the hollow in her neck. 'Time to move this to the bedroom. I want room to move and room to see you.' He linked his fingers through hers as he scorched her mouth with another kiss.

She sagged against him. 'I won't make the bed if you keep doing that.'

He tore his mouth away and grinned. 'Can't have that.'

He pulled her down the hall, stopping twice to kiss her. The second time she pressed her back against the wall, her body melting into a puddle of paradise as she clung to him, wrapping her legs around his waist.

He met her moan of need with one of his own and then staggered into the bedroom, carrying her. She fell backwards onto the bed, pulling him with her, never wanting to let him go, needing to feel his hands and mouth on her. She'd never known such rising pleasure, pleasure that tingled and taunted at the same time, and she wanted more of it.

He pulled back to unbuckle his belt and shuck his pants and she whimpered.

A moment or two later, condom in place, he leaned over her, his eyes as dark as rich chocolate, and slowly scanned her body, from her now burning cheeks across her aching pink-tipped breasts and down to her damp panties. He trailed a finger along the lace band before stroking downwards, inexorably slowly.

Her hips bucked as she throbbed with desperate emptiness and delicious promise, both of which were driving her insane. Her fingers gripped his wrist, trying to control his movements, trying to hurry him up before she spun out from unmet need.

'You're so amazingly hot.' His velvet-deep voice floated over her hot, flushed skin and then his mouth took hers for a moment before he slipped his finger under the lace and onto the one place that made her call out his name.

With delicious but maddening touches, he wove a path in ever-diminishing circles until she was beyond coherent thought and begging him. 'Now. Please, now.'

But he didn't do what she asked and instead slipped his finger inside her. She immediately tightened around him as her head thrashed against the pillow, and the tingling zeroed into one intense ball. She tried to pull him down, urge him inside her before she ruined everything, but the ball was soaring through her, sucking her with it, and she let go; let herself be carried into the whirling maelstrom until she was flung out in an explosion of wickedly wondrous and deliciously sweet convulsions that rained through her.

When the last wave ebbed away, leaving her limbs feeling like they were filled with molasses, she gazed up at him, not able to believe her body could do that. She almost sobbed. 'I'm sorry. I've never, that is, I mean…' But words couldn't explain it. 'Thank you.'

'Don't apologise or thank me.' His voice sounded rough and hoarse and he nuzzled her neck, his five o'clock shadow scraping gently on her skin. 'Watching you was almost as good as being there with you.'

She stared at him, studying him hard, trying to find the buried message that she'd done the wrong thing by climaxing before he'd entered her, but all she could see was heat and excitement. Heat for her. *You're so amazingly hot.* Was she? Really?

His tongue found her ear and her post-orgasm bonelessness instantly vanished. Flames licked at her again, building heat, building need, and this time she ached so much it hurt. She wanted to give to him what he'd given to her and she pushed at his shoulders, rolling him onto his back. 'Just lie there, I've got something for you.'

His hands gripped her arms. 'Don't even think about using your hands.'

She laughed and straddled him, her hair making a curtain around their heads. 'I wouldn't dream of wasting this.'

He grinned. 'And you thought you weren't good at this.'

She laughed as exhilaration poured through her and she eased herself over him, marvelling at his beauty. Then she closed her eyes and took all of him, almost crying with relief as he filled her. Moving in a rhythm as old as time, she opened her eyes and saw the combination of wonder and pain etched on his face.

She felt the jab right through to her solar plexus—he was thinking of his wife. *Just sex, no regrets.* She didn't want him to go to that dark place of grief so she kissed him with all she had and then threw her head back, gripping him hard. With more bravado than she felt, she hooked his gaze. 'I'm amazing, remember. Don't let me down now, Matt, or you'll put me in therapy for years.'

Lust drove every other emotion off his face and his hands gripped her buttocks. Rising with her, he drove them both higher and higher, taking them away from everything they'd ever known and hurling them out into a place free of pain and suffering, where they hovered until gravity pulled them back and reality encased them again.

CHAPTER SEVEN

'You look different.' Sarah gave Poppy a long, inter-rogating look when choir practice finished.

'It's just the hair. You're used to seeing it pulled back at work.' Poppy briskly tapped the pages of her music into a neat pile before sliding them into her folder.

Jen lowered the lid of the piano, smiling. 'No, it's more than that. You've had a secret smile for a few days now and we all know what a secret smile means.'

Poppy schooled her face into a blank expression despite the fact she was really starting to enjoy Sarah and Jen's company. However, she wasn't quite ready to confess to having had mind-blowing and universe-altering sex with Matt every night for a week, although she wasn't totally certain who she was protecting most by staying silent.

She threw her music satchel over her shoulder. 'Well, I did win the slab of beer for catching the biggest fish when I went out with the theatre techs the other day.'

'Oh, yeah, that would do it.' Sarah rolled her eyes and linked arms with Jen. 'I think she's holding out on us.'

'So do I. Especially given there's some new graffiti in the staff toilet that says, "P is a make-out bandit."'

Really? A ridiculous rush of gratitude rushed through her that Matt had actually done that. 'You so know that isn't me. That P has to be Penny Duffield.' Poppy didn't feel too bad about creating that rumour given she'd seen Penny locking lips with her anaesthetic registrar early last Wednesday morning.

Before Sarah could quiz her any more, Poppy's phone conveniently beeped and she checked the text message. *Hungry for food but hungrier for you. M.*

This time nothing could restrain her smile or the rush of anticipatory heat rising in a flush, racing up her neck and burning her cheeks.

'I knew it.' Sarah reached to grab the phone and Jen moved to corner Poppy.

But Poppy had played basketball and could weave and duck, so she used her height to hold the phone high and reached the door before they did. 'Have to go, girls, but great practice.' She stepped out of the door, using it as a barricade. 'Next week I think we'll start an *a capella* piece because the choir has been singing so well. Night.'

Good-natured jeers floated across the car park. 'You know we'll find out.'

'You can't hide for long—this is Bundallagong.'

'I'm not hiding, I'm flying high.' Laughing, Poppy got into her car as she heard Jen mention Damien's name. Hopefully her throwaway line would keep them off the scent for a bit longer.

She could hardly concentrate on driving for excitement. She and Matt didn't see a lot of each other during their workday, and today had been emergency-free so she hadn't seen Matt at all, but they always got together at night. Late at night. Both of them had kept the deal of no past, no future and no regrets. They were living for the moment and ignoring everything else. That was the way it had to be.

What if it could be different?

A tiny daydream started weaving its way through her mind but she immediately applied a wet rag to it, dismissing the thought. Once she'd let dreams of marriage and motherhood derail her and they'd taken her to the bottom of a very black pit. Now she knew that her job was the one thing she could rely on; unlike dreams, her career was concrete. She'd spent years sacrificing everything to climb the career ladder and now she was so close to the top job she couldn't let it go. *Your time here is just a minor detour.*

Five minutes later she parked in her carport and a fizz of surprise washed through her as she noticed that her interior lights were on. As she walked up the short path, her front door opened and Matt stood in the doorway, wearing a white-collared shirt with fine purple and green stripes. He looked neat, pressed and very much the eminent country doctor. But she knew appearances counted for little and the man in those clothes had more in common with his dishevelled hair that covered his collar and brushed his cheeks. Neat on the outside but anguished on the inside.

His aura of sadness didn't seem as dark as when she'd first met him but she wouldn't kid herself that if had anything to do with her. Both of them were conveniently forgetting their real lives for a few weeks and where was the harm in that? This was perfect. *Too perfect?* She banished the traitorous voice in her head, telling herself that with all the depressing news coming up daily from

Perth about how Alistair Roland was 'owning' her job, being with Matt gave her something fun to focus on.

She walked straight into Matt's strong, welcoming arms and breathed in deeply, loving his scent and still not quite believing she could hold him like this whenever they were alone. 'Hey.'

He smiled and kissed her thoroughly.

She lost herself in the pleasure of his mouth and her hands were reaching for the buttons on his shirt when he unexpectedly cupped her cheeks, kissed her on the nose and said, 'I thought we'd eat here.'

She leaned back slightly to focus on his face and at the same time focus on the change in their routine. Every other time she'd been the one to open the door to him and they'd kiss and that led to sex. Always. Granted, he normally arrived at around 11:00 p.m. because one of them had been caught up working, so tonight was unusual because it was only 8:00 p.m. and he was opening the door for her. *Her door.*

She tilted her head. 'By eating here, you mean my fridge has food in it. Food that's required to make something.'

He winked as they walked inside. 'That's part of it but I did bring wine.'

'So you've been waiting here for me to arrive home and cook?' A spurt of irritation washed through her and Steven's voice, which had faded to almost nothing recently, sounded deep and loud in the recesses of her mind. *Is it so unreasonable to expect you to cook?* She stomped towards the kitchen, annoyance growing into anger. She'd had a huge operating day followed by choir practice and the last thing she wanted to do was have to create a proper meal from scratch. The door swung

open and the two glasses of white wine and two plates
of salad with grilled chicken sat waiting on the bench.

She spun around to see him standing in the doorway,
eyebrows raised and a questioning look on his face. Her
hand shot to her pendant. 'Oh, God, I'm so predictable,
aren't I?'

He stepped in close and kissed her cheek. 'Actually,
you're not. Given any other combination of food in the
fridge and dinner wouldn't be waiting for you, but the
one culinary thing I can do is barbecue.'

'And supposedly make hedgehog, although I've yet
to see any.' She smiled, returning his kiss. 'I must remember to always stock meat, then, so you can grill.'
She glanced at the tiny kitchen table and then out the
window. The sun was dropping fast and the sky was
streaked in the vibrant colours of red and orange that
Bundallagong offered up almost every night, and that
she was coming to love. Right then she lamented the
fact she didn't have a deck. 'It's gorgeous out there. Why
don't we eat on your deck and enjoy the sunset?'

A tremor of tension rolled across his shoulders.
'The outdoor furniture's covered in bird poop and it
needs cleaning. Here's fine and we can enjoy the sunset
through the window.' He placed the plates on the set
table and then brought over the wine. 'Cheers.'

She tried to shrug off her disappointment. '*Salut.*'
She clinked his glass distractedly, realising with a start
that every time they'd been together it had been here, at
her place. Still deep in thought, she cut into the fragrant
and moist chicken and absently put a piece into her
mouth. They'd fallen into a routine of him arriving late
and usually leaving her bed around 3:00 a.m. to return
to his place. She understood that he wouldn't want to

have sex in the house he'd shared with his wife but did that preclude social stuff? Deep inside an ache sent out a niggle of distress that she could never compete with a dead woman.

You don't want to compete. This is short term, remember? You don't want long term. Steven burned you for that.

'Earth to Poppy?'

His words broke into her reverie and she jerked her head up to see his gaze full of questions. 'I'm sorry, what were you saying?'

'I was asking you about your pendant.'

'Oh.' Her hand automatically fingered the tiny diamonds at the bottom of the fine silver. 'It's a Tiffany P.'

'I gathered that.' He smiled. 'Who gave it to you? Family?'

She thought of her father and his endless array of trinkets that turned up by express post at birthdays, always with a note explaining why he couldn't visit. 'My father tried to give me a lot of jewellery but not this one.'

He frowned, his dark brows pulling down. 'Your husband, then?'

She flinched. 'My *ex*-husband and, no, he didn't give it to me. If he had, I wouldn't be wearing it.' She stabbed at her salad. 'Why would you assume someone gave it to me?'

'Because I've noticed you always touch it when you're feeling out of your depth.'

She stared at him, horrified. 'I thought we were just having sex, not analysing each other.'

He leaned in towards her. 'We're having fabulous sex

but that doesn't mean I don't notice things. And the fact you're getting defensive means I'm right, doesn't it?'

She took a large sip of her wine, wishing he wasn't perceptive and feeling like she was more exposed than when he gazed at her naked. 'I gave it to myself when I got divorced.'

'New start?' He drizzled balsamic dressing over his salad.

She shook her head. 'More of a reminder to be true to myself. My marriage, unlike yours, was very much a mistake.'

A pensive look crossed his face. 'How so?'

She sighed. 'For all intents and purposes, I married my father.'

He shrugged. 'Was that such a bad thing? I married my childhood sweetheart and statistically that shouldn't have worked either, but it did.'

Childhood sweetheart? It was the first time he'd voluntarily offered up any information about his marriage. She hadn't asked him any more about Lisa because this thing between them didn't mean spilling their guts to each other and dredging up painful memories.

Be honest, you're protecting yourself. You don't want to be held up against the perfect wife and citizen that you can never be. She wanted to put her hands against her ears to drown out the noise in her head or yell *I'm a damn good surgeon*, but both those options would have Matt doubting her sanity.

Instead she said, 'Given my relationship with my father, it was a bad move and not thought out at all. Very unlike me.'

He ran his finger around the base of his wine glass. 'Love is never rational.'

'Now, that *is* handy to know.' She heard the wasp-ish tone that came out automatically to close down the conversation but it only seemed to make him smile.

'OK, point taken. We'll change the subject. Tell me the story behind your name.'

She immediately relaxed. 'Stanfield?' We go back to the Norman Conquest.'

He grinned. 'How very apt. But I meant Poppy.'

Relaxation vanished. 'Of course you did.' She put her knife and fork together on the plate and decided to just blurt it all out and get it over with in one fell swoop. 'My father wanted a son and I was to be named Hugh after him, his father, his father before him and back another three generations. When I arrived and couldn't be Hugh, he gave the naming rights to my mother. She was a florist and my fate was sealed. I was Poppy to Mum, and Dad called me "mate".'

With a pang of immense sadness, Matt thought of his laughing Annie and all his affectionate pet names for her. He felt his brows draw down. 'Mate?'

Her shoulders rose and fell, and resignation rolled off her. 'He wanted a boy and, you know what? I did a damn good job trying to be a son for him. I learned pretty early on that if I played sport, he noticed me, so I became very good at tennis and basketball and I even got to the point where I occasionally beat him at one on one. Things got sticky when I started to develop breasts.' She refilled her glass. 'Around that time he also left my mother for his secretary and finally got the son he'd always wanted.'

Matt's parents had enjoyed a happy marriage so he could only imagine what losing her father's affection must have been like for her. 'Tough to compete with a baby boy?'

'Impossible. Even harder when a second son arrived.' Her usually firm voice cracked for a moment and then steadied. 'I sometimes wonder if it would have been better if Dad had cut himself off completely from my life but instead he'd send money and gifts for every birthday, every academic prize and sporting trophy, leaving me constantly hoping one day he'd actually turn up.'

Matt saw the remnants of a young girl's pain on her face, and caught the moment the steely, determined woman caught up.

She rolled her shoulders back. 'Still, the flip side is that I drove myself to impress him, which got me into medicine, and for *that* I can never have regrets.'

Her words illuminated her work ethic and the constant striving to win, and he realised what had started out as a bid for affection had become ingrained behaviour. 'And your husband was a father figure to you?'

His question shot out on an urge to find out more about the unknown man he actively disliked with an intensity that surprised him. He didn't really expect her to answer it.

Her amazing mouth formed into an ironic pout. 'Not that I was aware of at the time, although the counsellor I saw once post-divorce did point that out.' She took in a quick breath as if gearing up to get something nasty out of the way quickly. 'Steven was fifteen years older than me, divorced and an "empty-nester" with grown-up children. We met when I was a surgical registrar and his brother was one of my first solo procedures. Sadly, his presentation of a perforated bowel turned out to be undiagnosed cancer and he was riddled with secondaries. He died on the table.'

Poppy's fingers laced, her knuckles shining white. 'Perhaps it was my inexperience in dealing with relatives after losing a patient, perhaps it was his charm that was so similar to my father's, I don't know, but we started dating. For a few short weeks he made me feel like the centre of his world and when he proposed, I accepted. We hit the wall within weeks when he realised I wasn't going to be the sort of wife he'd expected. It got angry and ugly, and we divorced.'

Don't let me down: you'll put me in therapy for years. 'The ugly being him telling you that you weren't woman enough for him?'

Her head inclined slightly and then her eyes glittered with resolute grit. 'So, now you know all my sordid details. Aren't you lucky we're living in the moment and me and my emotional baggage will be heading back to Perth in a few weeks?'

He stood up and walked around to her, pulling her to her feet and into his arms, not really wanting to think about the fact her time here was finite. He stroked some inky-black hair back behind her ear. 'Did you happen to see the graffiti that you're a make-out bandit? I think we've managed to unpack and throw out the stuff about you not being woman enough.'

She smiled, a hint of hesitation spinning around her. 'Maybe.'

'Just maybe?' He thought about what they'd done in her bed, how every time the darkness threatened to suck him under she managed to keep him in the moment, and how losing himself in her kept the past at bay in a way hard drinking, exercise or work had never been able to. He wanted their sex to help her too.

'If it's only a maybe then you need to practise more because I know how much you like to be the best at everything.' He knew she could never resist a challenge but just in case he pressed his mouth to her ear, tracing the outline with his tongue, knowing that always made her melt against him and kiss him hard.

Her fingers reached for his belt buckle, unlacing the leather with expert ease, and then bluer-than-blue eyes shimmered with wicked intent. 'Prepare to be exhausted.'

He grinned. 'Sounds good to me.'

'Mr Simmonds, there's a spot on your lung that I want to do a biopsy on.' Poppy sat in a chair opposite the Vietnam veteran, watching his expression carefully.

'Cancer?' He sounded resigned. 'I've been waiting for the thing to catch up with me. Mates I served with have died from it.'

Poppy moved to temper the leap to that conclusion, although most of her agreed with him. 'Or it could be something else, which is why I want to do the biopsy so we know exactly what we're dealing with.'

'This cough's been with me for six months and the antibiotics haven't done a damn thing. Doc, I'm a realist. The war never leaves you and this is just another reminder.' The sixty-three-year-old's gaze stayed steady.

Poppy was the one who dropped her gaze first. 'I can only imagine what you went through and it probably doesn't come close.'

He shifted in his chair. 'Yeah, but I was one of

the lucky ones. Janice and the girls, they've kept me going.'

Poppy knew Janice from the choir. 'She's a delightful woman, your wife. Being able to share your experiences with her must have helped.'

He shook his head vehemently. 'I've never told her or the girls any of it. Why would I want to taint my home with horrors like that? No, that's what army mates are for. With Janice I can forget.'

His reply astounded her. How could he have been married for thirty-odd years and completely avoided a topic that had had such an impact on his life? 'And it's important to forget?'

'Yeah, love, it is.' His head dipped in reverie for the briefest of moments before he looked back at her. 'So when do you want to put me under the knife?'

Poppy showed her patient the thin, flexible broncho-scope, explained how he would be sedated and how the sample of tissue would be taken. 'I can do it tomorrow. See Sarah on your way out for the paperwork.'

Her pager bleeped loudly. *Need you in Emergency if you're not scrubbed. Jen.*

Mr Simmonds rose from his chair and extended his hand. 'Thanks, Doc. I'll let you get on with your day.'

She walked him to the door and then hurried towards Emergency. Jen met her as she pushed through the Perspex doors.

'Great, I was hoping you weren't in Theatre.'

'What's the problem?'

'There's a child in the resus room with a broken leg and the pain and stress has triggered an asthma attack.'

Poppy pulled on the proffered gown as she walked

towards the room, thinking the break must be pretty bad for Jen to call her. Usually young kids experienced greenstick fractures, which didn't require surgery. 'So, Matt's in with the patient already?'

Jen frowned and shook her head. 'No.'

Poppy's hand stalled on the doorhandle, thinking about her very first day in Bundallagong. 'But he's on his way, right?'

'No. I only called you.'

Poppy felt like she was missing something. 'I'm happy to consult but this is his department and you can't bypass him. You know how he hates that. You have to call him.'

Conflicting emotions played across the nurse's face. 'But the patient's the spitting image of Annie.'

OK, now it was definite. She was totally missing something. 'Who's Annie?'

Jen's eyes dilated in shock. 'You don't know? She was Matt's three-year-old daughter. Lisa and Annie died together.'

His daughter. A wave of nausea hit Poppy so hard she thought she'd vomit on the spot. *Oh, God!* She'd thought it bad enough that he'd lost his beloved wife but she'd no clue he'd lost a child too. Lost so much. No wonder the town had no idea how to behave around him. 'Page him.'

Genuine distress slashed Jen's face. 'But, Poppy, it will kill him.'

She shook her head, knowing that Jen's intentions were good but sadly misguided, and wouldn't help Matt one bit. 'It's not our place to make this decision for him. If he doesn't want to treat the child, that's fine. I can do it. But only he can make that choice.'

'You don't know him like we do or know what he's been through. Sure, he'll bark, but in this case, I know I'm right.'

The unfamiliar exclusion from Jen hit her with a chill, taking her straight back to high school, where she'd never fit in with the girls at school. Part of her wanted to side with Jen, to care for the fledgling friendship she was starting to value, but most of her knew this 'protection mode' was the worst thing in the world for Matt.

She tried to keep her voice even. 'That's very true. I don't know him like you do but this is a hospital, and protocol needs to be followed.'

'Protocol over people?' Jen muttered, before reluctantly picking up the phone.

Poppy bit her lip as she pushed open the door of the resus room, knowing she'd just lost a much-needed ally in Jen and, by default, the Perth job had taken another critical hit. But she'd worry about that later. Right now, she had a patient.

A distressed little girl rested against a bank of pillows with a vaporising mask on her face. Jen had correctly commenced a salbutamol nebuliser but the child was still visibly struggling to breathe, her chest heaving as she tried to force air into constricted and rigid lungs. Her left leg was encased in an air splint and a woman Poppy assumed was her mother sat next to her, holding her hands through the side bars of the emergency trolley.

'Hello, I'm Poppy Stanfield and I'm going to insert an intravenous drip into…' she picked up the chart '…Ashley's arm and give her some drugs that will help her breathe.'

'Thank you.' The worried mother wrung her hands. 'She hasn't been this bad in a long time.'

Poppy nodded her understanding and turned her attention to the little girl. 'Hey, Ashley.' She picked up a cuddle bear that Jen had provided. 'Can you give this bear a big hug for me? He's a bit scared and I know you can show him how to be brave while I put a needle into your arm, OK?'

The little girl's eyes widened in fear. 'Will it hurt?'

'Not as much as your leg does.' Poppy slid the brightly coloured tourniquet around the child's small, pudgy arm and prayed she could find a vein on her first attempt. Surgeons didn't insert IVs very often—that's what anaesthetists were for.

As she swabbed Ashley's arm with alcohol and popped the cover off the cannula, she heard raised voices outside. Matt's rough-voiced yell at Jen didn't surprise her in the least—that she could have predicted. What she couldn't foretell was how he'd react to Ashley.

Matt strode into the room with blind rage, boiling and ready for a fight. First Jen and now Poppy. Not since her first day had she made an arbitrary decision about a patient and he'd thought they'd worked all that out. So much for collegial respect. He couldn't understand it because just lately she'd actually been doing pretty well and gaining ground with the staff, but it was stunts like this that made him wonder if she'd ever learn.

Certainly, after hearing her talk about her father, he totally got why her need to win was so deeply ingrained and work was her world but, damn it, in this instance she knew better. He triaged and if she was required for a consult he called her. It didn't work the other way around.

Poppy's left hip rested on the edge of the trolley and her hair, which caressed his face every night when they had sex, cascaded down her back in a sleek, silky ponytail. She was leaning forward, deep in concentration, and he saw her hand reach for the pre-cut strips of tape on the dressing trolley. The angle of her body blocked his view of the patient but, no matter; he'd see him or her in a moment when he asked Poppy to step down.

'I'm sure you're required elsewhere, Ms Stanfield. I'll take over here.'

She turned and something in her cornflower-blue gaze sent a shiver of disquiet through him. He'd seen those eyes steely with the determination of a woman on a mission, shadowed by the memories of inflicted hurts, filled with the burning fires of lust, and sated with the fog of complete satisfaction. Not once had he ever seen sympathy in their depths, and although it made no sense that is exactly what he saw.

'Ashley, Beth, this is Matt Albright, our emergency specialist. I'm sorry he wasn't here to greet you—there was a slight miscommunication with the nursing staff.' She adjusted the flow of the IV and then moved aside.

His chest tightened so fast air couldn't move in or out of it. A little girl with a riot of blonde curly hair and clutching a hospital bear stared at him through huge, violet eyes.

Daddy, look! I've got a doctor bear with a white coat just like yours.

No. No! This isn't possible. His heart thundered hard and fast, pushing blood through a body that was both icily numb and throbbing in pain. Sweat dripped into his eyes and he blinked rapidly, as if that would help change the image in front of him. But when his eyes refocused, his daughter's double was still there on the trolley, struggling to breathe but, unlike his Annie, still breathing.

'I've started Ashley on IV methylprednisolone.' Poppy pulled a stethoscope out of her pocket and held it out towards him.

He snatched it like a lifeline. 'I'll page you if I need you.'

'I can stay.' The quiet tone of her voice matched her eyes.

His stomach churned and bile seared his gut. God, she knew. How the hell did she know? The town had gone silent, never mentioning the two people he'd loved as much as life itself, and he damn well hadn't told Poppy about Annie because he didn't want her to know. He'd never wanted to see 'that look' in her eyes.

'Get out.' He heard Beth's shocked gasp at the aggression in his voice but he didn't care. No way was he having Poppy in here with pity in her eyes, offering to take over or watching him struggle to keep it all together. Worse still, fall apart. He got enough of that from all the staff.

Her hand crept towards her pendant but stopped short. She rolled her shoulders back and stripped off her gloves. 'Ashley is in excellent hands, Beth, and hopefully the break is a clean one that only requires a cast.' She took a quick step forward and touched Ashley's hand with genuine caring. 'You look after that bear for me, won't you?'

The scared little girl nodded behind the mask as if she was petrified by the thought of Poppy leaving.

At that point Matt didn't know who he hated most—himself, Poppy or the universe.

CHAPTER EIGHT

ALTHOUGH Ashley didn't require surgery, a burns victim from the day before did, and that had tied Poppy up in Theatre until past six. She'd been thankful to have been kept busy because thinking about how much Matt was hurting was just too painful. She hurt too, even though she didn't want to, but the fact he'd never told her about Annie ate at her, making a mockery of everything they'd shared.

What did you expect? The deal you made was no-strings sex. That's want you want, remember, because it's safe.

Except you've been sharing meals and sharing stories, laughing together, and he's become a friend.

The thought chafed like a rash of doubt; hot, prickly and decidedly uncomfortable. Turning her doorhandle, she realised they probably weren't likely to be sharing anything any more. Not when he'd ordered her to leave ED in a voice that could have cut steel, and the look in his eyes had packed the velocity and damage of a bullet ripping through flesh. She stepped inside and the low glow of a lamp greeted her.

'Poppy.'

With a start she turned towards the sound of the deep

but expressionless voice and instantly recognised those familiar and tormented eyes. Surprise became tinged with concern and her heart beat faster. 'Matt? I didn't exp— Are you all—?' But his taut face stole her words, silencing her.

Go for neutral. 'You finished up earlier than I did.'

With his mouth grim and tense, he strode straight to her, his hands gripping the tops of her arms. Silently, he hauled her up onto her toes, pulled her against him, and then took her mouth in a kiss, plundering it with a frenzy close to desperation.

Surprise spun through her at the fact he was there at all, and intensified at the knowledge he still wanted her given what had happened in the ED. She opened her lips under his, wanting and trying to claim her place in the kiss and struggling to find it. She'd never been kissed quite like it, urgent need spinning together with what she guessed was misery.

With a gasp he pulled his mouth away and, still silent, grabbed her hand, tugging her up the hallway to the bedroom. Her feet stumbled at the speed and she should have been angry, perhaps even on one level scared, but all she could feel was his pain roaring through her like a hot wind.

Then his mouth was on hers again, hot, hard and frantic, and she was tumbling back onto the bed. 'This is in the way.' With clumsy movements he pushed her dress upwards but his hands fumbled with her bra.

'Let me do that.' She quickly undid the clasp and unbuckled his belt, and when the clothes were gone, she wrapped her arms tightly around him. Holding him close, trying to give him comfort, and then she kissed him. Softly.

He returned the kiss and for one brief moment his shuttered eyes opened and she saw ragged pain and torment. Her heart cramped so hard she felt the spasm tear clear through her, sending his searing hurt into every cell. She knew then he needed her to be there just for him.

His mouth pressed against her neck, marking a line of ownership as if she might vanish underneath him. Her hands soothed him by caressing his back while he kissed her, but it was like there was an invisible wall between them. But then his mouth took her breast in the way he knew she loved, and her body started to rise on a familiar stream of pleasure. As her mind slipped into bliss and her hips rose to meet his, he entered her, burying himself deeply.

Sensations built, spinning through her, and she wrapped her legs around him, feeling all of him and giving all of herself to him. She touched his face as she always did, seeking his gaze that filled her with joy. But like a man in a trance he looked right through her and all she could see was the reflection of a man trying to outrun his demons. A man who still loved his dead wife.

She swallowed her gasp of hurt. She wanted to wave a wand and change everything. For her. For him. She'd do anything to take away his pain and hurt but she had no power to do that. So she did the only thing she could. She held him tight and sheltered him until he sank with a sob against her, exhausted and spent.

Matt felt Poppy move under him and like a shock of electricity ripping through him he jolted back to earth, realising what he'd just done. He'd taken and not given much in return. He rolled off her, immediately stroking her hair. 'Hell, Poppy. I'm sorry.'

Her clear gaze hooked his and she put a finger against his lips. 'So you got it wrong once. Just don't make a habit of it.' She shot him a cheeky smile. 'Of course, if you're feeling guilty at not totally meeting my needs, you can always buy me flowers, chocolates, champagne and fill my freezer with delicious meals from Lizzie's Kitchen.'

An uncomfortable relief settled over him and he released a breath he hadn't realised he was holding. A breath of thanks. Pressing a tender and appreciative kiss to her forehead, he said, 'Is that all? Nothing in a pale blue box?'

She fingered her pendant. 'No, thanks, I buy my own.'

And that was Poppy to a *P*. Completely independent. Deep down something ached. He knew he owed her a full and detailed explanation about what had just happened but he couldn't do that until he'd made amends. He trailed a finger gently along the curve of her jaw. 'Can I start to make it up to you now?'

Black brows rose. 'What did you have in mind?'

'A neck massage. I know surgeons spend a lot of time looking down, which is tough on the neck muscles.'

She reached out and pressed her hand against his chest, in the same way she always did, with fingers splayed wide. 'Hmm, that might be nice, but I don't have any massage oil.'

Damn. Why hadn't he ever thought of buying some? He covered her hand with his. 'Well, I could massage you in the shower, using soap.'

'Perhaps.' She pouted, her lips slick with the sheen

of desire. 'Surgeons also get aching shoulders and backs.'

He grinned, loving the way this was heading. 'That's very true, not to mention all that standing takes its toll on your legs. I could massage those as well.'

'Could you?' She raised herself up; her pink nipples tightly budded against her creamy breasts. 'An entire body massage? Now, that might just go a long way towards clearing your tab.'

He kissed her with a rush of heat that tangoed with heady affection, and carried her into the shower.

The mattress moved underneath Poppy and a cool draught zipped in around her naked back. Barely awake, she rolled over as part of her brain accepted it was about 3:00 a.m., the time Matt always left her bed. The fact the room seemed lighter didn't really penetrate and sleep quickly pulled her back under. The next moment a shock of white light made her closed eyes ache and she moaned as her arm shot to her forehead to shield her eyes.

'Whoa.' She managed to crack one eyelid open and realised Matt was standing in the room, fully dressed. 'Is it morning?'

His hands circled her wrists and he gently pulled her into a sitting position before sitting down next to her. 'It is. Good sleep?'

She stretched languidly. 'It was an amazing sleep. Best one I've had since arriving.'

'Excellent.' He brushed his lips against her forehead. 'I got up half an hour ago and I've made breakfast.'

Half an hour ago? She could hardly believe it. Thirty minutes meant he'd stayed all night. She'd had her best sleep in—for ever, and he'd been in her bed all night.

She didn't want to let herself connect any dots about those two events but already her mind was doing it. 'Is there coffee with breakfast?'

'There is.' He tossed her a pair of shorts and a T-shirt.

She tugged the top over her head. 'Can't I have it in bed, seeing you've woken me up at...' she squinted at the clock '...stupid o'clock?'

'No. Breakfast is at my place.'

His place? She pulled up her sagging jaw as he walked out of her room. They never spent any time at his place. She fell into her shorts, wondering what was going on, and stumbled into the bathroom.

Five minutes later she slid, grumbling, into a chair at Matt's kitchen table and found herself in front of a steaming mug of coffee. 'You'd better have food as well as coffee.'

'Are you always this delightful first thing in the morning?' Matt sat down next to her, coffee in one hand and a photograph album in the other. 'I'm short on fresh food but I'll buy you something from the bakery on the way to work.'

'You're always short on fresh food because you never shop. Why are we here when I have fruit and yoghurt at my place?'

'Because my coffee's better and I need to show you this.' He put the album on her placemat and opened it up. A little girl with eyes the colour of grape juice stared up at her. 'I'd like you to meet my daughter.'

Her heart hiccoughed and she touched his hand as she continued to turn the pages of the album looking at photos of a loving wife and mother, a proud and loving husband and father, and a child they both clearly adored.

She wondered about that kind of love; a love that encompassed everyone in the family, the sort of love she'd never known. A bright green streak ricocheted through her. What sort of a shocking person was she to be jealous of a dead woman and child?

One that wants the same thing?

No. Thoughts of the dark days of her childhood and her marriage shored up her momentary lapse.

'All those curls. She's gorgeous.'

'Yeah.' He ran his hand through his hair, the strands falling back and masking his face, and then his body shuddered. 'Annie and Lisa died on a beach in Samoa when a tsunami struck. I was spending the day at an inland village and survived.'

She immediately wrapped her arms around him, resting her forehead on his, wishing she could take away all his pain and knowing she couldn't touch it. 'I can't even imagine what this is like for you.'

He absently kissed her cheek. 'I know.'

She needed him to really understand. 'I had no clue you had a daughter until yesterday when Jen and I argued over why she hadn't called you to the ED.' She tried to keep the hurt out of her voice. 'Why didn't you tell me, Matt?'

He shrugged. 'Perhaps I wanted *one* person not to define me by what I'd lost. One person who could stare me down, argue with me and treat me just like any other bloke.'

She bit her lip and tried not to tear up, tried to be the same person she'd been yesterday. 'I can argue the point.'

A quiet smile tugged at his lips. 'You can, and you do it very well.'

She thought of Mr Simmonds and how he'd never told his wife about the war because he didn't want to have to think about the horrors he'd been through when he was with his family. A shaft of clarity hit her and she realised why Matt was showing her photos of his family in his house and not hers. 'I still plan to argue with you.'

'I hope you do.' He dropped his head into her hair and sighed. 'Poppy, about last night. Seeing Ashley, who looks so much like Annie, and realising that you knew about her, well, I lost it. I haven't lost it in a long time. I'm truly sorry.'

She cupped his jaw and raised his head to hers, fighting an irrational sadness about her role in all of this, which was crazy. She had no reason to feel sad because she wasn't sticking around. She'd learned a long time ago that work was safer then relationships with all their inherent pitfalls and she knew Matt certainly wasn't looking for one. Yet she couldn't quite shake the feeling that perhaps together they could have something more. 'It's OK, I get it. Me and my house are a place for you to come and forget.'

Matt raised his head slowly and met Poppy's eyes filled with tacit understanding and something else he couldn't define. 'You're an amazing woman, Poppy.'

A ripple of tension shot along her mouth before she smiled. 'That's me. Brilliant surgeon and sex goddess.'

The quip reassured him that things hadn't changed between them, that their loose arrangement would continue while she was in town and she wasn't going to go all touchy-feely on him and want him to bare his soul even more. That was the beauty of Poppy: she didn't do emotions very well, either. With her he could still pretend his life hadn't been turned upside down and pulled sideways, and when that got too hard, he lost himself in her.

She drank more coffee. 'Have you been back to Samoa?'

He shook his head. 'I stayed there for a few months after it happened and then I thought it was time to come home.'

'How's that working for you?'

He didn't want to analyse that at all so he gave her the bare minimum. 'I think I mentioned the initial drinking binge but that's long over and now, well, I get through each day. I know I can treat children again, even ones who look like my daughter, so that has to be an improvement, right?'

A thumping noise sounded from the roof and Poppy's eye's rolled. 'And yet you let Rupert live in your roof?'

Unease shot through him that she was way too close to the truth. 'Why are you so obsessed by the goanna?'

'I'm not. I'm merely pointing out most people wouldn't want something like that living in their roof, causing damage to the house.' She stood up, taking her cup to the sink. 'Are you sure living here is the right thing for you?'

He gripped his coffee mug, hating that she'd just asked the question he often asked himself. 'Of course I'm sure. This is my home.'

Two small creases appeared at the bridge of her nose. 'This house or this town?'

'Both,' he said, but knew he lied. He stood up, knowing the exact way to cut this conversation off at the knees. 'You'd better hit the shower or you're going to be late for work.'

She yelped as she caught the time on the clock. 'Oh, hell, is it really seven-thirty? I've got pre-op consults in fifteen minutes.'

He saw a blur of colour, heard her feet on the bare boards and then the door slam. He grinned. 'Poppy has left the building.' He went to close the photo album and saw Lisa's face smiling up at him. He braced himself for the sear of guilt—guilt that he was still living, guilt that he'd found pleasure with another woman—but it didn't come. He released a long breath, left the page open and headed to the shower.

Sweat poured off Poppy as she gesticulated, controlling the choir with her arm movements, and backed up by her silent mouthing of the words. The clear, true sound of *a capella* rolled over her as the words of 'Amazing Grace' soared along with such a wave of feeling that she felt tears sting her eyes.

With her fingertips touching, she slowly drew her hands apart, holding the last note until she fisted her hands to indicate 'stop'. She grinned at the women's awestruck faces. 'Yes! You really did sound that fantastic. Well done. I think Sarah has posters about the concert she'd like you to put up so please take one with you before you leave, and on that note I'll call the formal part of choir over for the night. There's the usual tea and biscuits if you can stay.'

Shrieks of delight followed with the choir members breaking to give each other high-fives and Poppy turned as Sarah's hand touched her shoulder. 'Amazing.'

'Grace.' Poppy smiled.

'Take a compliment, woman!' Sarah hugged her. 'They're going to rock the town at the concert.'

'You mean the five people who might actually come out on a Sunday afternoon.'

'Yeah, well, there's that, but Justin's selling tickets at the surgery with the odd bribe, and I heard Matt Albright's reply to a recovering Daryl Jameson when he was trying to thank him for saving his life. He said that all the thanks he needed was Daryl attending the concert.'

Poppy groaned. 'These women deserve more than a pity audience.'

'You worry about the music and let us locals get the audience.'

Us locals. An odd feeling settled in Poppy's belly, and she tried to shake it off. It was ridiculous that she was letting two little words, two absolutely accurate words, make her feel uncomfortable. Sad almost. It didn't make a lot of sense—in fact, it made none at all because it wasn't like she planned on staying.

You're just tired and emotional. This is nothing a good sleep won't fix. Remember, this is a godforsaken place that's just a blip on your career radar.

A small voice protested. *The sunsets are amazing. So are the people.*

People like Matt.

Her stomach flipped, scaring her, and she dragged her mind back so fast from the man who was turning her world upside down that she risked mental whiplash. It was time to focus on the choir.

She'd met some incredible women out here, women whose lives were far from perfect but they kept going, trying to improve their situation and those of their families. Local or not, she wanted to honour them and be involved.

'I want this concert to be a success. How about we have a planning meeting at my place now? I got a hamper sent up from Perth yesterday with a fabulous Margaret River white wine, Swiss chocolate and a gorgeous runny Camembert that needs to be eaten.'

Sarah laughed. 'First of all you give me the "no-sex" talk and now this. Are you asking me out on a date?'

She smiled, enjoying the teasing. 'You found me out.'

Jen wandered over. 'Found out what?'

Things had been a bit strained between Jen and herself since the incident in the ED and perhaps this was a way of building bridges. 'Drinks at my place now—can you come?'

Jen visibly started. 'Really? OK, why not? Can I catch a ride with you?'

'Sure. We can ask Janice Simmonds to lock up, can't we?'

Sarah nodded. 'Janice will do anything for you now you've cured Harry. Your eyes were like saucers when you saw that sprouting pea in his lung.'

This time Poppy high-fived. 'Well, it was a pretty amazing find and so unexpected, but in a good way.' And not just for Harry Simmonds. The uniqueness of the case meant it had made it into the 'odd spot' in the Eastern papers and the Royal College of Surgeons had asked her to write it up for their journal. It was win-win for the patient and for herself, as well as a shot across the bows to Alistair Roland, William and the board. They might have sent her to the outer Barcoo but she was still a force to be reckoned with.

Sarah kept them entertained on the quick drive home with a story about a very tired Justin being called out of an antenatal clinic to stitch up a nasty wound when the patient had lost a battle with a bush saw. 'He was stitching John Ledger's hand.'

'I don't think Poppy's had the pleasure of meeting John,' Jen chimed in.

'If you think most of the blokes in this town are tough then John is reinforced steel. Anyway, Justin's going through the motions, asking all the important questions, but instead of asking John when he last had a tetanus injection, he asked the question he'd been asking all afternoon at the pregnancy care clinic, which was, 'When did you last have a pap test?''

Jen started to giggle. 'Poor Justin.'

'John gave him one of his famous "you're a moron" looks and said, "At the same time I had my last tetanus shot." John went straight from the surgery to the pub and Justin's never going to live it down.'

The laughs continued as they shared embarrassing work stories and Poppy poured wine and Jen opened chocolate and cheese.

'OK, how are we going to sell this concert as a "must attend" event?' Poppy tapped a pen against a note pad. 'Offer food?'

Jen sliced the cheese. 'Serve beer and the men will come.'

Sarah sat forward, wine glass in hand. 'Poppy, remember your first week here when you operated on the head of transport for the mining company?' She clarified, 'The bowel obstruction.'

Poppy nodded as his name came to her. 'Ed Papasoulis?'

'That's him. The miners who "fly in, fly out" get collected and taken to the airport. I'm sure with a word to him the bus could be early that day and come via the concert. It's only going to be half an hour and it would double our audience. Any unsupportive husbands who weren't planning on coming will be there on company time, and have the added benefit of being blown away by their wives' performances.'

Poppy stared at her. 'I'm in awe of your scheming.'

Sarah shrugged and gave her a grin. 'Perhaps I'm learning from you. By the way, great sound bite and visual on the Perth news the other night about Harry. So how's the battle for the Perth job going?'

'I wish I knew. It's just so hard being this far away and not being able to see my opposition in action and lobby.'

'He can't see you either so that levels the playing field a bit, doesn't it?' Jen remarked as she sipped her wine.

The support in the words both surprised and reassured Poppy. 'I guess I never really thought about it that way. Thanks.'

'No problem.' Jen paused for a moment. 'Listen, Poppy, I'm sorry about the other day with Matt. The thing is, just lately he seems to be coping better, looking less tormented and even cracking jokes and smiling, and I didn't want seeing Ashley to bring the trauma back again and send him backwards.'

An apologetic look touched her face. 'But you were right and I was wrong. He managed to hold it all together but I hated watching him have to do it.'

Poppy thought about how he'd fallen apart in her arms a few hours later. 'It was a tough day all round and no choice was easy, but it had to be his choice.' She offered the nurse a chocolate. 'Truce?'

Jen frowned. 'There was never a war, Poppy, we just differed in opinion. Friends can do that, you know, and then they talk it out.' She popped the ball of rich praline chocolate into her mouth and murmured a sound of delight. 'Oh, my God, Sarah, you have to try these.'

Sarah chose a chocolate and joined Jen in equal rhapsodising about the taste and texture, and Poppy leaned back and watched.

Friends. She realised with a start that these two strong women really did consider her a friend. The feeling settled over her like a new pair of shoes that fitted but would become truly comfortable with some extra wear. She was looking forward to it.

The front door opened with its usual squeak and Jen and Sarah looked up as Poppy's gut clenched. *Matt.* She'd been on such a high after the choir practice and enjoying herself with the girls, she'd forgotten to text him.

He walked in, talking. 'I thought we— Ladies, good to see you.'

The change in his conversation was almost seamless and if Matt was surprised to see Sarah and Jen, his face didn't seem to show it. He held up a bottle of wine. 'I brought wine for the choir meeting.'

Shock rendered Poppy speechless but Sarah stood up and accepted the bottle with a smile. 'Thanks, Matt. This is really thoughtful and will add to our spur-of-the-moment meeting. By the way, didn't know you were psychic.'

He didn't skip a beat. 'It's one of my many skills. I'll

leave you girls to it. Have a good night.' He closed the door behind him.

Sarah spun around with a squeal and pointed straight at Poppy. 'You are so having sex.'

Jen punched her gently on the arm and beamed. 'No wonder Matt's been looking better lately.' She looked at Sarah. 'How did we miss this?'

Sarah sat down. 'Because Poppy is cagey.'

Poppy tried to deny it, shaking her head. 'I'm not cagey and I'm not having sex.'

Sarah crossed her arms. 'The game's over, Poppy, and now it's time to spill. But before you do, can I just say thank you?'

'Thank you? I don't understand.'

'Matt and you as a couple—it's just so great after what he's been through.'

A ripple of panic set off through her and Poppy's hands flew up like stop signs. 'No, please, don't make that leap. I've been married once and never again. This is just sex. I'm only here for a few more weeks and, like you said that night in the bar, why not have some fun? See, I took your advice.' The words spoken with true conviction sounded strangely hollow.

Sarah frowned. 'Does Matt know?'

'It was *his* idea.' She moved to reassure their worried expressions, finding it harder than expected. 'Neither of us wants anything permanent and he still loves Lisa. We're both adults who've gone into this with eyes wide open. There's nothing for you to be concerned about.'

Liar.

The creases in Jen's brows faded slightly. 'Well, you have to admit, he's been a lot happier, so that's a good thing, right?'

Sarah didn't look quite so convinced but she smiled and leaned forward. 'Just sex, eh? So how good is it?'

Poppy leaned back, raised her glass to her friends, unable to stop a wicked smile racing across her face. 'Let's just say good is a far too prosaic adjective to describe it.'

CHAPTER NINE

POPPY kicked up from the depths of the water hole, breaking the surface, and felt Matt's arms wrap around her. She leaned back against him and stared up at the clear Outback sky. A strange feeling washed over her and she realised with surprise that this was what happiness felt like.

A while later, she lay in the shade cast by the massive, red-walled gorge, soaking in the unexpected coolness, when a mere forty steps away the sun was unrelentingly hot. 'It's so amazing that in the middle of all this arid, red-rocked, gibber-plain nothingness, there are ferns and a permanent water hole.' She rubbed her arms, flicking off the water from her swim, and laughed. 'I'm almost cold. How weird is that?'

Matt wrapped a towel around her shoulders. 'The Outback has its secrets, you just have to open yourself up to them.'

'And here I am.' She gave him an arch look. 'Although I thought the guy who asked the girl out did everything.'

He grinned. 'Division of labour. I drove and you arranged the picnic.'

She smiled against a looming frown. 'I'm not sure

that's actually a fair division, considering driving here happened on your day off and yesterday I had to shop and then put the food together.'

He winked. 'Yeah, but it made you finish work a bit earlier. Besides, you needed a day off and I've wanted to bring you out here for ages.'

She flicked him with the towel, half in jest and half serious as the scars of her marriage reddened. 'This week I've been home by eight three nights and no paper-work. I really think I've broken the back of the waiting list and things are getting more manageable and into a routine. Besides, you're the one who told me to go fish-ing and accept invitations to clothing parties, so today was my first totally free day.'

'How dumb was I? Still, that advice was before I got you into bed.' He kissed her on the nose. 'If you asked today, I might tell you something different.'

'I'm not so sure about that.' She looked hard into his eyes, trying to read more. She could see affection but it ran into something else. Something that prickled at her. 'All I'm saying is that I came here with a job to do, and I'm getting it done.'

'And all I'm saying is that *balance* in life is good.' He stretched out next to her. 'Your phone doesn't work out here and doesn't it feel good not to be obsessively checking emails?'

A defensive flicker clenched her gut. 'I don't obses-sively check emails.'

He cocked a knowing brow.

'OK, but to be fair, I've been sending William bi-weekly reports. How unreasonable is it to expect a reply?'

'Poppy, he holds the power in this so accept that he's toying with you and make it work for you.'

All her fears collided. 'This is my career you're so casually talking about. My life.'

He sighed. 'I know it's not easy for you to take advice but if I've learned anything in the last year and a half it's that life isn't all about work.'

She thought about how her father had consistently let her down, and how Steven had zeroed in on her need to be loved, turning it into a battlefield of 'you change and then I'll love you'. Now Matt was hinting along similar lines. The one constant in her life, the one safe thing that didn't let her down, was her career. 'And I've learned that my work is far more reliable than anything else.'

He opened his mouth to reply but she didn't want to spoil the day by arguing any more about work or workloads so she leaned over and pressed her mouth against his, kissing him deeply and hoping that was enough to distract him. 'Thanks for bringing me out here.'

He stroked her hair as she rested her head against his chest. 'You're very welcome. Walker's Gorge is always worth the drive. When I was a kid, Mum would choose the beach for picnics but Dad and I loved it out here. It was a favourite with Lisa's family, too. I remember getting into serious trouble when I was five after I pushed her into the water hole.'

Five! She could scarcely believe it. 'You really were childhood sweethearts.'

He crooked his free arm behind his head. 'It's hard to think of a time when she wasn't in my life.'

'What about uni?'

'Lisa came to Brisbane with me.'

It was spoken so casually, as if it was totally unremarkable that two people had lived all their lives together, but Poppy's surprise swooped to her toes. Had they never been apart until her death? 'So you were at uni together?'

'No, Lisa didn't want to go to uni. She was an artist and made the most amazing jewellery. She worked in the office of a law firm and made jewellery at night.' His mouth curved into a smile full of pleasant memories. 'We had a tiny flat with bookshelves made out of bricks and wood, beanbags for furniture, and it was decorated with Lisa's artwork. Her parents weren't happy about any of it and would visit often, mostly so her father could give me a really hard time about how I was a kept man because Lisa was earning more money than I was as a student.'

His chest rose and fell under her cheek. 'The moment I qualified we got married, and I took great delight at outearning her so she could quit her job and do jewellery full time. When Annie arrived, we moved back here and she cut back the jewellery to commission pieces only because she loved being a stay-at-home mum and being involved in the town, volunteering.'

He'd never talked so openly and Poppy knew she should be pleased for him that he'd now reached a place in his grieving where he could do this, only the green monster that had been slumbering of late raised its head. Lisa had been family-oriented and naturally giving, everything *she* wasn't.

Does it matter? It's not your future. Your future is Perth.

Is it? A hollow feeling filled her gut. The words so easily spoken when they'd first started their affair were getting harder and harder to believe, but her heart knew the alternative wasn't an option. Having it all—career, marriage and kids—was a big-time con and she'd learned that the hard way.

If he'd noticed her silence he didn't show it. 'If I'm honest, Lisa's choices made my life a lot easier because, given the hours I sometimes work, coming home to an oasis of calm was a gift.' He tensed. 'Ironically, it was her push to go to Samoa that changed everything.'

'No one was to know a holiday would end like that.'

He shook his head. 'We weren't there on holidays. Lisa had read about an organisation working with indigenous women to help them achieve sustainable futures and thought she could offer her skills and knowledge about turning crafts into income. She had it all worked out: we'd go for half a year and I could do medicine while she did business models.'

Poppy propped herself on an elbow and thought about how he'd mentioned staying in the Pacific for a while after the tsunami. 'So you stayed and fulfilled her vision?'

He frowned and the sadness that had left him returned. 'I stayed because I couldn't leave. I tried to leave, believe me, but I just couldn't separate myself from the island because it meant I had to accept Lisa and Annie were gone. Initially, I was part of the relief effort and the frantic pace kept the real world at bay, but once the Red Cross realised who I was, they pulled me out of the field because, as the paperwork described it, I was one of the victims.' His chest heaved. 'God, I hate that word.'

'So don't use it.' She pressed her hand to his chest, wanting him to see himself in a new light. 'You're someone directly affected by the event and it changed the direction of your life irrevocably. It's not OK that it happened but it doesn't make you a victim.'

Matt traced a finger down Poppy's cheek, marvelling at her inherent strength. 'I like that reframing.'

'It's yours. What brought you back to Bundallagong?'

'Time, and Lisa's father eventually came over and said the town needed me back.'

'Did you want to come back?'

He shrugged. 'I had to do something and coming home was at least familiar. Same town, same job.'

'Same house.' She wrinkled her nose. 'I think it must be unbelievably hard to try and live the same life you were living two years ago but without Annie and Lisa. I don't think it's really helping, is it?'

Her words echoed harshly yet truthfully in his head. He thought of the town's tentativeness around him, of how the only place he'd ever felt close to normal was at work and how he now hated a house he'd once thought was the only place he'd ever want to live.

'Nothing I do will bring them back so it really doesn't matter what I do or where I live.'

A shot of white anger sparked in the depths of her eyes, shocking him. 'That's not true. You have choices, Matt. You don't have to try and live the life you had before they died but why not finish the chapter you were living in when the tsunami hit? Lisa had a vision that she can no longer achieve but you can make it happen in her name.'

Fury, powerlessness and panic skittered through him. 'I know nothing whatever about jewellery, Poppy!'

She sat up straight, her face both earnest and irritated. 'But you probably know people who do, and if you don't, you can find them. Who you actually know are the people in this town who loved and cared for Lisa and Annie, so start there. Do some fundraising and create a foundation in their name so the work can be funded long into the future.'

A foundation? He tried to shrug off the thought, cross that Poppy was being her usual steamroller self, but it insisted on taking a tenuous hold. Why hadn't he thought of something like that? *Because the time wasn't right and you weren't ready for it.*

Was he ready now? The more he thought about it, the more the idea appealed. A foundation would do two special things—remember Lisa and help in a way she would have totally approved of.

And of all the people to think of this perfect idea, it had been Poppy, who hadn't even known Lisa. In a way it connected them and he found that oddly consoling. A tide of mixed emotions poured through him and when he spoke, his words came out roughly. 'Have you always been this damn bossy?'

She blinked and then a slow smile strolled across her cheeks before smouldering in her eyes. 'Yes. Bossy and in this case absolutely right.' She rummaged in her backpack. 'I'm sure I've got a pen and paper in here and you can start brainstorm—'

He shot his hand out to touch her arm. 'It's all about balance, remember. I can and I will do that later, on the long drive back. But right now we're on a day off and...' He pulled her into his arms, nuzzled his face against her neck and smiled as she relaxed against him. His blood hummed when he heard her delicious moan of consent.

'My dad does that to my mum.'

Poppy's eyes flew open in wild and shocked surprise as Matt's mouth trailed kisses along her collarbone while his hand caressed her left breast. She frantically leaned sideways to hide her partial nakedness and try and see who was talking. Matt almost toppled forward into the newly created space.

A little boy, who looked to be about five or six, stood in front of them, and she struggled to find a coherent reply as she pulled the shoulder strap of her bikini back into place. 'D-does he?'

The child gave a serious nod.

Matt, having righted himself, now squatted at eye level with the child, a smile on his face. 'Well, that's good to know because it means he loves your mum.'

Love? Panic and joy stalled Poppy's heart for a moment before common sense prevailed. Matt was merely explaining why he'd been more than just kissing her, in terms a child could understand.

'They close the bedroom door.'

'Obviously not always,' muttered Matt, throwing her a look that combined laughter with chagrin. 'I'm Matt. Who are you?'

'Lochie, and I five.'

'Five, hey? That's getting big. And where did you come from, Lochie?' He shielded his eyes with his hand and peered beyond the child and down the stony river bed, looking for people.

The little boy pointed behind him. 'There.'

Poppy, now decent, scrambled forward, wondering why this child was alone in the middle of nowhere. 'Where are Mummy and Daddy?'

'I runned here first.'

Matt's mind was obviously going to the same place

as hers and he put his hand out to the little boy. 'How about we go back the way you came and meet them? Because even though you know where you are, Mum and Dad don't.'

Lochie shrugged. 'OK.'

Poppy grabbed their towels and stuffed them inside the backpack. 'I'll come, too.'

Matt nodded, his face full of concern. 'Good idea. There are two water holes in this area so I've got no clue which one his parents are heading for. The track, if you can actually call it that, divides. Best bet is to return to the car park and we either meet them on the way or we wait there until they come back to sound the alarm.'

She touched his arm. 'Am I missing something about an Outback childhood or is the fact he's separated from his parents really dangerous?'

'No, you're right, but not everyone realises the dangers in this place until it's too late.'

They started walking and Lochie immediately streaked out in front, which was obviously what had got him separated from his parents in the first place.

Poppy called out, 'Hey, Lochie, slow down,' but the little boy didn't alter his pace.

Matt sprinted up to him, catching him by the back of his T-shirt, and Poppy caught up to them just in time to hear Matt say, 'Want to play a game, mate?'

Lochie's eyes lit up. 'What is it?'

'You stand between Poppy and I, and hold our hands. We all walk together counting out loud, and something special happens on three.'

'OK.' The child's warm hand slid into Poppy's as Matt mouthed over his head, 'We swing on three.'

Poppy knew Matt the lover, Matt the grieving

widower and the professional doctor, but this was the first time she'd seen the father in him. Deep down inside her an old, faded and discarded dream moved.

'Let's go.' Poppy started walking briskly to push away the unsettling feelings. *Chief of Surgery is what you want and where you belong. You gave up the dream of motherhood a long time ago. Work is far more reliable than men.* 'One, two…' she gripped Lochie's hand firmly in her own to avoid any slipping '…three!' Her arm swung forward, as did Matt's, and Lochie's legs swung sky high.

As the child's feet touched the ground again, he gave a whoop of delight. 'Again.'

Poppy laughed at his joy and looked across at Matt, knowing he would have done this very thing with Lisa and Annie, and a combination of concern for him and envy for herself sat heavy in her gut.

His expression was a revelation. Instead of the raw pain she'd seen so often in his eyes, his dark gaze held warm delight with a glimmer of resigned sadness. Sadness she knew would understandably stay with him for ever in some shape and form when he remembered his beloved daughter. Seeing him in action with Lochie, she knew he'd been a wonderful father.

The dream shifted again, tugging hard, morphing into something tangible and real. *You, Matt, a child on a picnic out here.* It tempted her so much that it terrified her. This time she deafened it with a loud yell of 'One, two…*wheeeeee!*'

The sun was dropping low in the sky and the air temperature dropped with it. Matt jogged back from the second water hole track, now seriously worried. He could see Poppy in the distance, wrapping Lochie up in one of the towels to keep him warm. Where the hell were his parents?

Relief filled Poppy's eyes when she saw him. 'Are they on their way back?'

'I didn't find them.'

Her face blanched and he gave her arm a squeeze. 'It's time to contact the police.' He leaned into the truck and got onto the radio as he heard Lochie asking for food.

'What about a lucky dip?' Poppy sounded overly bright as she opened the top of her backpack. 'Stick your hand in there and see what you can find.'

Lochie looked sceptical but Matt smiled, knowing Poppy had a secret stash of food in that pocket of her backpack. She had a natural affinity with children, which had been another surprise to him. It shouldn't have been. He'd learned over the past weeks that once people got past the smoke and mirrors of her no-nonsense, crisp façade that she hid behind, they found a woman with a huge capacity to give.

'Chocolate!' Lochie held up the distinctive purple-foiled bar.

'Jack, it's Matt Albright. We're at Walker's Gorge with a five-year-old and his parents are missing. Vehicle has New South Wales plates. We've been back at the car park for well over an hour and I've walked the two tracks the little bloke said he'd been on but there's no sign of them.'

'Five-year-olds are not that reliable, Matt.' The experienced police officer took the registration number and went on to suggest he break into the vehicle for any clues.

Cursing central locking, he yelled to Poppy and Lochie. 'We need a big rock to break a window.'

'Now, that's not going to be hard to find.' Poppy took two steps, picked one up and threw it through the driver's side window.

'You're really bad!' Lochie threw himself at Poppy's legs and she immediately bent down. 'Sweetie, I'm sorry but we need to see if Mummy or Daddy left a map or a plan of where they were going and they're not going to be cross, I promise.'

'I want Mummy.' The small boy's wail rent the air.

'I know you do, Lochie.' She gave him a quick hug and then opened the car door, carefully brushing away the shards of glass with a towel before looking for any identifying information.

Matt hung onto the radio, waiting for Jack. 'Have you found anything, Poppy?'

She held up a National Parks brochure. 'There's a map of the park and both water holes have been highlighted.'

'Matt.' Jack's voice crackled down the line. 'Car's registered to a Lance Wilkinson and we've just had a report that a personal location beacon's been activated in the area. Do you have a map?'

He leaned over and grabbed the laminated and detailed hiking map he always carried when he came out here. 'Got it.'

'Find your location. On the west side of the car park there's a rough side track that heads along the ridge. The GPS in the PLB is coming from there. You can get in by vehicle if you drive to Koonunga picnic ground.'

'How the hell did they end up there?' But it was a rhetorical question because to an inexperienced walker all scraggly gum trees and red rocks looked the same and taking the wrong direction was sadly far too easy. 'We're on it, Jack.'

He turned to call Poppy, only to find her sitting in the dirt by the other vehicle, cuddling a sobbing Lochie. Her right arm held him close and her left hand stroked his hair while the little boy clutched a well-loved soft toy bear she must have found for him in the car. Her dark hair rested against the boy's jet locks.

Mother and child. Poppy as a mother. The image stuck him hard in the solar plexus. He had to clear his throat before speaking. 'We've got co-ordinates, hop in.'

Half an hour later, after bouncing along a rocky escarpment no one in their right mind would call a road, and using their GPS, Jack's guidance and their eyes and ears, Matt stopped the truck for the fourth time and hopped out. Bringing his hands up to cup his mouth, he yelled, 'Cooee.'

Then he listened. He'd been straining to hear anything for so long that at first he thought the returning 'cooee' was his own voice.

'Did you hear that?' Poppy's face filled with hope.

He called again, and this time Lochie and Poppy joined in.

A male voice replied, 'Cooee. Help us.'

'We're on our way.' Matt grabbed the medical bag and was starting to walk in the direction of the voice when a bearded man, supporting a woman, stumbled into the clearing.

'Mummy, Daddy!' Lochie pulled out of Poppy's grasp and ran to them.

'Thank God, Lochie.' The woman sobbed out her

child's name as she was lowered to the ground, gripping her left arm close to her chest.

Lance grabbed his son, hugging him close until Lochie wriggled and said, 'Daddy, it hurts.'

Poppy ran to the distraught woman, and Lance, on seeing Matt, gripped his shoulder. 'Thank you. Thank you for finding him, for finding us.'

Matt suggested Lance sit down. 'Actually, Lochie found us and your PLB is how we found you.'

Lance rubbed his head, relief clear in his eyes. 'One minute we could see him and the next he was gone. Then I lost our bearings searching for him because all this red rock looks the same.'

'I'm just glad you're safe.'

'Matt, I need the medical bag.' Poppy was crouched down next to the woman, who was pale and sweaty and had removed her shirt. 'Joanne fell on an outstretched arm and she's got a shoulder separation, but you've probably seen more of these than me.'

Matt introduced himself to the patient. 'I'm going to be as gentle as I can but this will probably hurt.'

Joanne flinched. 'It can't be worse than it already is, can it?'

Matt didn't want to promise anything. His fingers explored the top of the humerus and then followed the clavicle. A red tinge flushed the skin, indicating bleeding, and a distinctive bump marred the normally smooth line over the AC joint. 'I'm going to treat this with a cuff and collar sling and give you some strong painkillers to keep you comfortable on the long trip back to Bundallagong. We'll X-ray and ultrasound it when we arrive at the hospital and check for any other fractures, displacement, muscle and ligament damage. Does it hurt anywhere else?'

'Just our pride that we did something so ridiculously stupid.' Joanne leaned her head against Lance's shoulder as Lochie nestled between them. 'I'm never letting this child out of my sight again.'

'Good idea.'

Matt and Poppy spoke at the same time and he caught her vivid gaze full of intense feeling. For the briefest moment he experienced a moment of pure simpatico unlike anything he'd ever known.

Poppy pulled her theatre cap off her head and dropped it in the bin, wondering what on earth was going on in Bundallagong on this particular Thursday with two middle-of-the-night emergencies. She'd only just finished removing a lacerated spleen from a young man after a car accident when Matt's registrar, who was on night shift this week, had rushed up a guy with a bleeding gastric ulcer. It had been touch and go, with the patient bleeding so much that the blood bank was now in dire straits.

As she created a reminder on her phone to ring the radio station's breakfast show at seven to get the word out so Bundallagong residents would make a special effort to give blood today, she saw the time and sighed. 6:00 a.m. It was a really lousy time to finish as there was no point going home to sleep because she'd barely have got settled when she'd have to get up again. Yet she had ninety minutes to fill before she could do pre-surgical rounds. She thought of Matt; gorgeous and rumpled, sleeping spread-eagled across her bed. Even though she knew she wasn't going home right now, the fact he was there, in her bed, waiting for her, wound around her heart.

Careful. She gave herself a shake and walked quickly to her office.

She turned on her computer and brought up the email program as she did routinely every morning now, since Matt had pointedly said that bed was a work-free zone. She'd tried to argue that point but had deliciously lost, conceding defeat as he'd brought her to the brink of orgasm and then suggested he needed to stop right there to go and check his emails.

She'd even amazed herself by not sending William the surgical report this week. It had taken considerable strength of will and she'd almost capitulated, especially when her secretary had reminded her, but Matt's suggestion had been worth a try, given that everything else she'd tried hadn't made much difference in getting any response from her boss.

As thirty emails downloaded, the ping of her 'countdown' widget alerted her to the blinking number fourteen at the bottom of her screen. Ten weeks down and two weeks remaining in Bundallagong. Two weeks left with Matt.

The thought screamed through like a missile. *You'll miss him*.

'Ms Stanfield?'

She looked up distractedly, her brain stalled on how fast her time in Bundallagong had flown and how soon it would be over. One of the cleaners stood in the doorway of her office, and with wobbly legs she stood up and greeted him. 'Morning, Joe.'

He pulled a photo out of his overalls front pocket.

'My Louisa, she had the baby, and my son-in-law, he email me this.'

She'd been hearing about this long-awaited baby who'd been very slow to put in an appearance for ten days now, and as she stared down at the photo of a black-haired baby with fathomless eyes, her throat tightened. 'Congratulations, she's adorable.'

Joe beamed. 'Maria and I, we fly to Perth today to visit, but don't you worry. Franco will be looking after your office and I tell him to start your coffee at seven.'

A prickle of embarrassment made her feel uncomfortable. 'That's very kind, Joe, but, really, I can make my own coffee.'

The cleaner nodded as he put the photo back in his pocket. 'Yes, but if we look after you, perhaps you stay here in Bundallagong.'

Two and a half months ago Poppy would have scoffed at such a suggestion, but with every patient she'd treated, with every staff member she'd got to know and with every choir meeting, tiny roots had sprouted, connecting her to the community. She'd enjoyed her time here.

And if you don't get the job, would you stay?

The unexpected thought spun around her heart like the silky strands of a web, tying her to Bundallagong. Tying her to Matt.

A spasm hit, freezing her muscles, making it hard to breathe and hard to stand. Somehow she managed to smile, wish Joe a safe trip to Perth and sink back into her chair. She pushed her hands against her forehead and up into her hair.

No, no, no. You can't be that stupid.

Panic skittered through her, sending her reeling.

Falling for Matt, a man who still loved his dead wife, would be beyond dumb—it would be her worst nightmare. She sucked at relationships at the best of times but there was no way she could compete with Lisa, who'd been perfect alive and was now immortalised as a saint.

Have you learned nothing from your disastrous relationships? Her guiding Amazon rose up to her full height and brandished her sword and shield. *Woman up!*

Poppy pulled up memories of her father and Steven—betrayal, hurt, rejection—each recollection shoring up her resolve, but every time she thought of Matt she could only picture him laughing with her, teasing her, talking, listening and wrapping his arms around her each night until she fell into a deep sleep.

You love him.

Oh, God, no.

No, not love, please, not love. She dropped her head into her hands as the thought branded her with its full impact. She loved him. Little by little, day by day, she'd fallen in love with him so slowly she hadn't even realised it.

How had she left herself so unprotected?

She knew better than this. She knew from bitter experience that love wasn't enough and never had been. Love left a girl open to hurt and heartache, and to being let down in the worst way. Nothing good could ever come from being in love, and exploring this bit of self-realisation was pointless.

No promises, no regrets, no past and no future.

Matt's words rose up in her mind. She'd made a complete mess of something that should have been fun and short term. Once again, she'd let herself fall in love with a man who wasn't able to love her. She was too foolish for words.

Biting her lip, she welcomed the jolt of physical pain and rolled back her shoulders, pushing the feelings down deep to languish with the other relationship mistakes in her life and the ashes of her ill-fated marriage.

She tuned into work like she always did, keeping all her emotions at bay, and ploughed through the list of mail, deleting, forwarding and replying as required, while she sipped coffee and listened to the cacophony of sound that came with the dawn. She smiled as the sky filled with pink and grey as the native parrots rose from their sleep—another Bundallagong ritual she'd come to enjoy.

As she hit Send on the last email, her phone beeped its reminder. 7:00 a.m. She silenced it and immediately heard a ping from her computer, heralding a new email.

William.

A chill ran through her as her gut rolled on a wave of acid. She put her phone down and her hand hovered over the mouse for a few seconds before she moved the cursor over his name and clicked.

CHAPTER TEN

MATT woke with a start and stretched out to feel for Poppy but his arm and hand only connected with cool sheets. A vague memory slowly formed and he recalled Poppy's phone ringing, her quietly murmured conversation, his grunted 'Do you need me?'

And her lips on his cheek as she'd said, 'Go back to sleep.'

But now he was awake and the green light of the bedside clock said 5:00 a.m. With a groan, he closed his eyes and as his head hit the pillow he gratefully accepted that at least it wasn't three. He hated 3:00 a.m., when there was still so much night left and no more ability to sleep. It became a long slog, waiting for the dawn, and so as not to disturb Poppy, he'd get up and go and pace the floors at his house.

His eyes shot open so abruptly that the muscles ached. He hadn't woken up at 3:00 a.m. all this week. *It's been longer than that.* He worked backwards and realised with a start that he couldn't recall an early wake-up since he'd told Poppy about Annie, and that had been three weeks ago.

With a contented sigh, he rolled over, tugging at the sheet, intending to grab one extra precious hour of sleep, but his brain, already jolted awake, buzzed with ideas for the foundation. He accepted defeat, got up, walked into the pre-dawn chill—the only time Bundallagong was cool—and let himself into his house.

The long hallway echoed as he walked towards the kitchen and the house smelled musty, like it needed a good airing. He filled the kettle and then picked up the folder marked 'Lisa's Way', which he'd left on the table next to his laptop two nights ago. Grabbing a pen, he quickly scrawled down the name of Lisa's bead supplier that had been eluding him, along with some ideas to run past Sarah for a fundraising night at the neighbourhood centre. That done, he made coffee and set the plunger to rest on the top of the carafe while it brewed, and then opened the fridge for the milk.

A malodorous scent greeted him, the milk having become yoghurt and a lone lettuce now a ball of slime. He hastily dumped both in the bin and searched the pantry all the way to the back for some long-life milk. There was none. How could that be? He knew he was a poor shopper, but UHT milk was a staple that even in his darkest days he'd always had.

You're virtually living with Poppy.

The thought rocked him. He poured sugar into his coffee, stirring it fast as he grappled with his thoughts. Running back over the events of the last few weeks, the truth stared him in the face. He'd hardly been here. The reality was that he'd only been using his place to shower, change clothes, do laundry, and when Poppy was held up at work he'd come back here to do some foundation work.

Not even then.

He sat down hard in a chair as his legs trembled.

Last week he'd spent an evening at her place working on Lisa's Way while Poppy had been at choir practice because being over there was so much more pleasant than being here.

He heard the dawn thumping of Rupert but instead of being much-needed noise, he suddenly saw in his mind's eye the damage the reptile was likely inflicting on the roof. He looked around the room as if seeing it with new eyes, and for the first time the house didn't seem to be mocking him with its silence or its memories. He stood up and slowly walked the length and breadth of the house. Starting by opening the door to Annie's room, he systematically visited every other room in the house until he stood in the stripped-bare master bedroom. A room he'd avoided with the exception of the night Poppy had arrived.

He girded himself for the expected onslaught of pain, sadness and grief, the way it had been when he'd first arrived home from the Pacific, and the reason he'd moved to the guest room. But the house no longer spoke to him about loss—it didn't really speak to him at all.

Lisa and Annie were no longer part of the house.

The news should have broken his heart but instead it soothed it and an odd peace settled over him. His love for Lisa now resided in the creation of the foundation and his love for Annie poured into his work whenever he had scared and sick kids in the ED.

He ran his hand through his hair. He was no longer part of the house, either.

It's time.

He blew out a long breath laden with relief. He'd loved his wife and daughter dearly but now the time had come for him to move on with his life. Shoving his hands in his pockets, he glanced out the window at the house he'd come to think of as Poppy's place, despite the fact many people had lived in the house over the years.

Poppy.

Her lips matched her name and she was a bright spark of colour in what had been a very black time of his life. God, he enjoyed being with her. She made him laugh, she challenged him and at times frustrated the hell out of him, but she was the first person he thought of when he woke up in the morning and the last person he thought of when he closed his eyes at night.

That's love.

His chest tightened on his sharp intake of breath and he gripped the architrave. *Love.* The spasm faded, followed by a wave of warmth and the tendrils of belonging.

It *was* love.

He loved her.

He started to grin like a fool, his cheeks aching with happiness. She'd stormed into his life all attitude and vibrant energy and turned his grieving world upside down. Somewhere along the way he'd moved into her house and she'd moved into his heart. Now he couldn't imagine his life without her.

With a plan forming in his mind, he stepped out of the house and gently closed the door behind him.

Poppy stepped out of the theatre change rooms into the main hospital corridor and suddenly found herself being twirled around, pulled into strong arms and kissed so soundly her legs gave way.

Matt's sparkling brown eyes stared down at her as his fingers caressed her cheek. 'Hello.'

'Hel—' Her mouth stalled as her brain received the image from her eyes. Her hands flew to his hair, her fingers unaccountably aching as they tried unsuccessfully to lose themselves in the now short strands 'Oh. Your hair, it's...' She finally found her voice. 'You've had it cut.'

He grinned. 'I have. It was time.'

She'd always loved the way his hair reached his jawline, reminding her of a pirate. 'Why?'

But instead of replying, he just gave her a secret smile and pulled her into the on-call room and locked the door. A small white-cloth-covered table held a platter of freshly made sandwiches along with two bottles of fruit juice and a plate of what looked like peppermint slice. 'Lunch for two, courtesy of the kitchen.'

She smiled and kissed him, reminding herself of her plan to treasure every last moment with him. 'Lovely idea. I'm starving.' She greedily picked up a sandwich and started eating. 'Hmm, this is so good. Why haven't we done this before?'

'I guess we didn't have a reason to celebrate before.'

Her hand fell from her mouth and she stared at him in surprise. How did he know William had offered her the post of Chief of Surgery at Perth City? She hadn't told anyone. She'd read the email five times and had waited for the rush of joy that she'd finally got the job of her dreams, the one she'd been working towards for years. But instead of a rush it had been more of a slow trickle, as if she couldn't really believe she'd finally nailed it. But she had. The job was hers and the endpoint to her time in Bundallagong had arrived, as she'd always known it would. What hadn't arrived was the excitement she'd expected to experience on leaving the dust-filled town.

Matt stood in front her, his face full of warmth, friendship and pleasure for her, and the fact she'd achieved her long-held dream. Nothing about him showed that he was in any way sad about her leaving.

Why would you expect that? He still loves Lisa.

No promises, no regrets, no past and no future, remember?

But given all that, he'd thought to organise this lunch so they could celebrate now rather than waiting until the end of the day. No one had ever done anything like that for her before and she swallowed around the lump in her throat.

'Thank you.' She threw her arms around his neck with such enthusiasm that he staggered backwards, falling onto the bed. She lay against him and kissed him the way she knew made his head spin and his body hard.

He rolled her over. 'Had I known you were this easy to impress, I'd have done lunch a long time ago.' He stroked her hair. 'Marry me.'

Her gut went into freefall and she sat up fast, not able to believe what she thought she'd just heard. 'I beg your pardon?'

He sat up too, gently cupping her cheeks with his hands. 'Marry me.'

He knows about the job, he told you weeks ago you'd be great at it, and he still wants to marry you. Say yes.

But the question was so unexpected that she searched his face, his eyes, even the line of his mouth for clues.

Although everything seemed familiar, *nothing* was the same. A tremor of panic scuttled through her, mirroring her feelings early that morning when she'd realised she loved him. 'Are you sure you really want to marry me?'

'I do. I love you. I was floundering but you've changed everything and brought me back into the world. With you there's light.' His sincerity wrapped around her. 'I want to live with you until we're old and grey, and running around after ten grandchildren.'

Grandchildren. The aching longing that had been part of her since their day at the gorge surged and she let her head fall onto his shoulder, feeling the security of his breadth and the protection of his arms. *I love you.* The marvel of his words wove through her, tempting her with a promise of an amazing future. 'You see us with children?'

He kissed her hair. 'Why sound so surprised? You're great with kids and you'll be a sensational mother.'

She let the dream float over her and dared herself to believe. This wonderful man loved her and wanted to be the father of her children. *This time love and marriage will be different.* Her heart expanded, bursting open the self-imposed lock she'd chained to it years ago. 'We *will* be great parents.'

His lips touched hers with an almost reverent kiss, the touch imbued with a promise of things to come. 'Children are amazing and they change your life. I can picture a house, a garden, a deck, a pool. *Our* home.'

She could see it too and her hand pressed against his chest, feeling the beat of his heart. 'Somewhere by the river.'

His fingers played in her hair. 'I think you mean the beach.'

'No, I don't want to live in Fremantle because it's too far from the hospital. I suppose we could look at Cottlesloe if you think you'll miss the sea too much, but you might be surprised—the river's really pretty.' Still talking, she hugged him hard, excitement finally hitting her, bubbling through her like the bubbles of champagne. She had it all. It really was possible to have a man who loved her, a top job and in the future a family of her own.

'I wanted to tell you in person but somehow you found out and then you did this special and amazing thing for me and—' She stopped babbling, realising he'd gone completely still and was staring at her intently.

'What are you talking about?'

She joke-punched him on the arm. 'Don't be such a tease. You know exactly what I'm talking about.'

Confusion lay heavily on his cheeks and he shook his head slowly.

'But the celebration lunch…' And she realised the lunch wasn't connected with her new job at all but with his proposal. He didn't know her news. She grinned, loving how much pleasure it gave her to be the one to tell him as she'd originally planned. 'You're not only looking at your fiancée, you're also looking at Perth City's new Chief of Surgery.'

She opened her arms, expecting congratulations and an enormous embrace, but he just stared at her, his expression both stunned and surprised.

'You got the job?'

His words came out quietly without any acknowledgment of her massive achievement. The young Poppy who'd always strived yet failed to impress her father stirred deep inside her, sending out an aching ripple. 'William emailed me early this morning and followed up with a phone call. The board has been really impressed by the work I've done, especially with the way I had the full support of the staff.'

She reached out her hand, needing to touch him, needing to see some sign from him that he was happy for her. 'I couldn't have done it without your advice and support.'

Finally he smiled and hugged her tightly before kissing her gently on the cheek. 'Congratulations, I'm so proud of you.'

She breathed again, not realising she'd stopped.

His warm and loving gaze turned serious. 'But now we're engaged, are you certain this is the job you want?'

Every muscle in her body clenched. 'It's been everything I've worked towards for the last ten years.'

'Absolutely.' He nodded, his expression sincere. 'But things have just changed, haven't they? It's best if we live, work and raise our family here in Bundallagong.'

Steven's voice rose up like a spectre from the past, taunting her with pain and bitter memories. *Poppy, we're living at my place. It's really not up for discussion.*

When Annie arrived, Lisa and I moved back here.

Her heart quivered and her voice sounded overly bright. 'So we just relocate and do it all in Perth instead.'

He frowned. 'We move to Perth and you take the job?'

'Of course I take the job.' She smiled. 'Ten years, remember? All that hard work and now this is the reward. It's incredibly prestigious.'

He sighed, a long, low, ominous sound. 'In Bundallagong your surgical hours are almost workable, but how on earth are you going to balance family life with being Chief of Surgery?'

You're never home and I only asked you to do one thing—to collect my dry-cleaning and you couldn't even manage to do that.

It made you finish work a bit earlier.

Nobody has ever loved you without wanting to change you. First your father, then Steven and now Matt. A surge of anger obliterated her sob. She should have realised, she should have known this was all too good to be true. She should have recognised the massive signs from their conversation at Walker's Gorge.

She crossed her arms to stop herself from shaking. 'Worried you're going to have to learn how to shop and cook, are you?'

His jaw tightened. 'Believe me, cooking and shopping are the least of my concerns.'

Fool, fool, fool! He's no different. 'Oh, and let me guess what those concerns might be. You hate it that I won't be home every night before you, that I'll earn more than you, and that I'm not going to be barefoot and pregnant when you come home from a hard day at work.'

He threw up his hands. 'Now you're just being ridiculous.'

For heaven's sake, Poppy, you're my wife so act like one. Steven's voice faded as Matt's moved over it.

Lisa's choices made my life a lot easier. She remembered so clearly Matt saying that out at the water hole.

Her world tilted sideways, tipping out the fantasy of marriage and a family that she'd foolishly allowed herself to believe in for a few deluded moments. She so wanted to trust that he loved her for who she was but, like her father and Steven, he could only love her if she changed for him. If she gave up everything for him. Her chest tightened so much she could barely breathe as the past choked her.

Matt didn't really love her, he just thought he did. He only wanted a replacement for Lisa. His love, just like that of the men before him, came with conditions that would destroy them both. She stood up, moving away from him, and forced herself to do what she should have done the moment he'd proposed.

'I can't marry you, Matt. I can't make your life easier by being a stay-at-home wife. I can't be Lisa's replacement and live in the same house and help you live the life you had with her.'

Poppy's words plunged into Matt's heart like a knife, leaving him completely bewildered. 'God, Poppy, this has *nothing* to do with Lisa.' But he could tell by the look on her face she didn't believe him.

He tried to explain it. 'Lisa *chose* to stay at home and I supported her in doing that. I'm not asking you to give up working—of course you need to work. I want you to work. All I'm asking is that we live and work *here* so we can protect what we have.'

The starchy Poppy he hadn't seen in weeks materialised, her voice sharp and brisk. 'What we *have* is a short-term affair with an end date. We've been in this sensual bubble where it's just been us and the sex, but that isn't real life.' Her hand touched her pendant. 'Today real life intruded and already it's tearing us apart and it's only going to get worse.'

'It doesn't have to.' He walked towards her, wanting to touch her, wanting to remind her that what they had was worth saving. 'I'd consider moving to Perth if you took another job there. Look, if we compromise, we can make this work.'

Her eyes flashed. 'Not when one of us wants something at the expense of the other.'

'I'm not stopping you being a surgeon!' Trying to rein in his frustration, he ploughed his hand through his hair, only to discover with a shock just how unsatisfying it was with short hair. 'Give me some credit here, Poppy. I know how much time it takes to make a relationship work and if you become Chief of Surgery, you'll disappear into that job and it will kill us.'

She shook her head, her lips compressed into a thin line. 'Obviously I can't be married to you and be the surgeon I want to be.'

His heart slammed against his ribcage and slithered down, a bleeding, battered mess. 'You really believe that? You're going to walk away from this amazing thing we share for a job?'

'A job?' Her eyes glittered with a collage of emotions that swirled together with no defined edges. 'You really don't get it at all.'

Anger born of desperate hurt spewed bile. 'Oh, I get it. I get it loud and clear. My God, I thought you'd grown while you were here. I thought you'd worked out what was important in life, that it was people and relationships and love that counted, not pushing yourself to win at any cost. You're putting this job ahead of everything else. You really don't have a clue, do you?'

She tilted her chin up, her eyes flashing and her shoulders sharp, reminding him of the very first time he'd met her. 'I have more of a clue than you do, Matt. This conversation is just the start of what will happen to us if we get married, and the arguments will only get worse until we're tearing each other apart and wondering why the hell we once thought we loved each other. I'm doing this for us.'

'That's total garbage, Poppy. You're doing it for yourself and I only hope being Chief of Surgery keeps you warm at night.'

She flinched. 'I think we're done now. Goodbye, Matt.'

The door slammed behind her, shattering his hopes and dreams and leaving him devastated and alone.

CHAPTER ELEVEN

'MAIL for you, Ms Stanfield.'

Poppy glanced up from her spreadsheet to see the Perth City internal postwoman holding out a sheaf of mail. 'Thanks, Leanne. By the way, how did that biology assignment go?'

Surprise raced across the young woman's face before she smiled shyly. 'Wow, I can't believe you remembered that I was doing the course. I got an A.'

Poppy smiled as she picked up her outbound mail from the tray. 'Of course I remembered. It sounds like you're well on the way to getting the mark you need to get into nursing.'

'Hope so.' Leanne took the proffered mail. 'See ya, Ms Stanfield.'

'Bye, Leanne.'

As she walked out, William walked in, clutching a manila folder. 'First-name terms with the clerks, Poppy?' His brows rose. 'What the hell happened to you in that godforsaken place?'

'And hello to you too, William.' She pasted a smile on her face for her acerbic boss. 'Perhaps you should visit Bundallagong one day.'

He either missed or ignored the jibe. 'Harrumph. Far too busy for that and so are you.'

He wasn't wrong. She'd thought her first two weeks in Bundallagong had been long and arduous but they'd been almost relaxed in comparison to her start at Perth City. Not that she minded working hard, she didn't, which given her current circumstances was a good thing. But unlike in the past, when work had excited her, now a lot of it seemed like a chore.

When she'd first arrived back in Perth she hadn't cared how busy she was because work had filled her brain to capacity, leaving no space to think about Bundallagong, Matt and heartache. But just recently, when most nights she was only home for barely enough time to sleep, she'd started to think William's expectations of his department heads might be excessive. For the first time in her life she was pining to sit on her couch and just 'be'. Yesterday afternoon she'd even found herself wondering who she knew in Perth who might want to catch up for a drink and a chat, and much to her surprise she'd checked the notice-board for any posters about product parties. *You're lonely.*

William dropped the file on her desk. 'Applications for the surgical registrars and consultant operating rights. You also have to pick someone to go to Bundallagong next month. Interviews start at seven on Thursday evening. Happy reading.'

She stifled a groan. She'd been determined to have one night at home reading this week but job applications didn't count. 'I can't do Thursday.'

He fired her one of his penetrating looks. 'You *are* full of surprises today. I thought your life was the hospital but don't tell me you actually have a private life?'

She bristled, even though he was pretty much correct. 'I've organised a movie night fundraiser in the hospital auditorium for that night. I can interview earlier in the day.'

'Oh, yes, I think I saw a poster about that—something to do with women in Samoa? Can't you just do your speech at the start and then leave?'

Somehow she held onto her temper. 'No, William, I can't. I need to be there, sell raffle tickets, answer questions and thank people for their support.'

He nodded slowly, as if absorbing the news. 'I'll get my secretary to contact you with the new interview date but, Poppy, next time you act out of character, let me know.'

Quietly seething, she watched his retreating back and pictured daggers. Just because she wanted to have *one* night off, it didn't mean she'd changed.

You never got involved in anything out of work before Bundallagong.

True, but just because she was raising money for a worthy cause, it didn't mean she'd changed. *Lisa's Way is not just any worthy cause, though, is it? You're doing it to feel close to Matt.*

Blocking the perceptive voice in her head and throwing off her William-induced ill humour, she started flicking through her mail and her hand stalled on a small square box. She sliced open the tape with her letter knife and drew out a CD and a card written in Sarah's bold script.

Hi! Wanted you to have the first copy of the choir's CD, recorded at the concert! Sorry it's taken this long to get it into the mail! Choir's going great and Jen's conducting. Justin and I in Perth 8th-9th for a childless weekend, but can't have sex all the time ;-) so can you do Sunday brunch?

Poppy laughed as she read the words, able to hear Sarah's voice in her head, and a fizz of anticipation bubbled inside her at the thought of seeing her. They'd shared some laughs at choir, the pub and at their respective houses and it would be wonderful to kick back over a leisurely brunch and hear all the Bundallagong news.

Matt sold his house and is in Samoa doing work for Lisa's Way. Still no replacement surgeon here and we miss your bossy but motivating ways.

A leaden feeling settled in her belly, overriding the excitement. She hadn't done anything fun since she'd got back to Perth. With shocked surprise, she realised exactly how much she missed Sarah and Jen's company.
You miss Matt.
You know you miss Matt. Every. Single. Day.
A fresh wave of pain washed through her. *Call him.*
The idea had her reaching for the phone but as her fingers started dialling she dropped the handset back into the cradle like it was on fire. Exactly what was she going to say? 'I miss you.' But then what? Nothing had altered; the impasse still stood. At least this time she'd found out before getting married that the man she loved wanted to change her.
So why are you so miserable?

Distracting herself, she shoved the choir's CD into her computer and while it loaded she read the last bit of the note.

Hope Perth is worth it. Sarah xx

She pushed the note aside and then pulled it back, her gaze fixated on five words. *Hope Perth is worth it.*

Deep in the recesses of her mind a small voice asked a question. *Are you sure this job is what you want?* The question scared her witless and she stomped on it hard and fast. *Of course it's what I want. I can depend on it.*

OK, if you think so. But the reply didn't sound all that convincing.

The CD finally started playing and her throat tightened as the choir's voices filled the air. She closed her eyes and Bundallagong moved into the office. She could smell the dust and the salt, see the smiling faces of her staff, visualise the old choir hall and feel the camaraderie of the women. She heard the pride in their voices and she knew how much more than just music the choir meant to its members; how much it had come to mean to her. An aching lethargy came over her, dragging at every muscle like flu. She ached for the connection she'd shared with the women.

You ache for Matt.

And she couldn't deny it. She pictured him lying in her bed with his arms around her, sitting at the kitchen bench, listening to her talk about her day and offering advice, and laughing as they swung Lochie between them.

But he wanted you to give up something that was

vitally important to you. She bit her lips to stop tears spilling. She loved him but, like her father and Steven, he just didn't love her enough.

Get fresh air and coffee. Coffee will help. She pushed back her chair and left her office, walking across the road to the park and the coffee vendor. Families sat under trees, having picnics, and children on school holidays charged around kicking footballs.

She joined the queue, enjoying the sunshine on her skin after too many weeks of being inside. *You saw more of the outside world in Bundallagong.*

Yeah, red-dust dirt.

Walker's Gorge was red dust and dirt but it had a rugged beauty.

'Poppy, good to see you.'

With a start she pulled her attention away from memories of Bundallagong to the present, and the outstretched hand in front of her. 'Oh, Alistair, you're still in Perth?'

She'd met Alistair Roland once, soon after she'd returned, and she'd assumed he'd gone back east. 'Sorry, obviously you're here and not in Sydney.'

He laughed. 'We moved to Perth lock, stock and barrel five months ago. So, how's the new job and workaholic William treating you?'

She scanned his face, looking for signs of resentment that she'd got the job over him, but all she could see was genuine interest. She thought about the punishing hours. 'You know, like any new job, it takes a while to get a handle on it.'

'The surgery's the easy bit, right?'

She blinked at his insight and relaxed. 'I have days I

want to hide in Theatre and not come out in case there's another manila folder on my desk.'

He nodded in understanding. 'You're lucky you're single.'

Irritation and sadness buffeted her. 'Why do you say that?'

A boy ran over. Alistair stretched out his arm and the boy snuggled in against him. 'Hey, Dad, can I have a strawberry smoothie?'

'Sure.'

'Thanks.' The boy tore off again.

Alistair shook his head, his expression full of affection. 'That streak was Jake and...' he pointed to another boy chasing a football '...that's Lucas. My wife Deanna is reading under the tree. They came down to meet me for lunch because I had a cancellation, and that's the beauty of Perth over Sydney. Lifestyle.'

'Exactly.' This was what she and Matt could have had if he'd been prepared to leave Bundallagong. 'It's just what I was trying to explain to someone not that long ago and it's great you've been doing this sort of thing since you arrived.'

A light frown creased his forehead. 'The whole time I was working for William, I hardly saw the boys.'

'Oh, why was that?'

'Seriously? You're working for William as Chief of Surgery and you're asking me that? How many evenings have you been home since you became Chief?'

None.

But that's because I want to be busy.

Not totally.

Alistair nodded, taking her silence as an answer. 'Which is why that job defeated the point of us moving here. Deanna's amazing but she didn't marry me to become a sole parent and that's what was happening. I want to be involved in my kids' lives.' Passion and love shone on his face. 'The stress of trying to do the job and be a dad and a husband, well, it was crazy stuff so I pulled out of the running. Only a single surgeon can do that job.'

She stared at him, stunned. 'Wasn't it hard to walk away from the sort of job you spent your entire career aiming for?'

He gave a wry smile. 'You know, I really thought it would be, but at the end of the day I realised you can't have the one hundred per cent best career and a real family. So I'm not Chief but I get to see my kids most evenings. It's all about balance.'

If we go to Perth you'll disappear into that job and it will kill us.

Her gut rolled with nausea and she almost gagged. Alistair Roland with a supportive stay-at-home wife had walked away from the top job to protect his family.

'Poppy, are you OK?' Alistair looked concerned.

She tried to rally as her head swirled with thoughts and she managed a sort-of smile. 'Nothing a coffee won't fix. So what are you doing job-wise now?'

He moved up with the queue. 'It's been a huge step but I've gone into private practice and it's giving me the flexibility with the boys I could never have as Chief of Surgery. Being a parent is one big juggling act and I guess it's always going to be a work-in-progress but Southgate's given me operating rights and I'm really hoping you'll approve my application for City.'

Somehow she managed to nod, give her assurances that she would support his application and then finished the conversation with a promise of meeting his wife at a later date. Somehow her legs carried her back across the park to the reflection room at the hospital. In the cool quiet of the sanctuary, her heart thundered loudly and her stomach sizzled with acid that spilled into her throat.

Give me some credit, Poppy. I know how much time it takes to make a relationship work.

But she hadn't, she hadn't given Matt any credit at all. She'd seen his love and care for them as a couple as a direct attack on herself, and had lumped him in with her father and Steven. But Matt was nothing like them. He hadn't been trying to change her. Not wanting her to take this job hadn't been lack of support at all. He'd been trying to create the opportunity so they could try and have it all—love, marriage, career and a family. And she'd let her past control her and had completely messed it up.

Her head fell into her hands as everything she'd thought she believed in came crashing down around her. She'd risen to the top of her career ladder in the job of her dreams and she had absolutely nothing else. Five months ago it wouldn't have mattered that work was all she had, but William was right. She'd changed. Bundallagong had changed her. Matt had changed her. Being Chief of Surgery was no longer enough.

She wanted more.

She wanted Matt.

She'd put her trust in the wrong basket and made the most horrendous mistake of her life. She'd been so deluded, so busy playing the blame game, but it was all her own fault she was alone and miserable—she'd brought it on herself.

So stop whining and do something about it.

For the first time ever, her father's words actually helped.

She pulled out her phone and hesitated. She might be risking everything for nothing.

Just do it. Deal with any regrets later.

Matt sat contemplatively in the airport lounge at Perth airport. His flight from Apia had been late, making him miss his connection to Bundallagong, and now his only option was to sit out the two hours until the next flight. He texted the new flight details to Sarah, who was now on the Lisa's Way board, explaining his delay, and then let out a long sigh. The funny thing about travel was that the moment the date for returning arrived, the brain raced ahead and took up residence at home while the body still had to undertake the journey.

Home. He shifted in his chair. He didn't actually have one.

He'd sold the Bundallagong house fully furnished, as he'd planned to do before he'd proposed to Poppy, and had stowed a few boxes in storage before heading to Samoa to set up Lisa's Way. Two months later, with a fantastic young woman on the ground in the village, and the connections in Australia all set up it was time to go back to Bundallagong or even think of working somewhere else.

Perhaps he'd look at the jobs online while he was waiting but first he'd finish up his Lisa's Way financial report. Using the wireless internet in the lounge, he checked the foundation's bank balance and saw with pleasant surprise a new and sizeable deposit. He read the transfer note. Stanfield PCFR.

Poppy.

Stunned to see her name, he stared at the cryptic PCFR, trying hard to work out what the other four letters meant. His brain finally clicked in. Perth City Fund Raiser.

His heart beat faster. He couldn't believe that despite everything, despite how much she'd hurt him and the harsh way they'd parted, Poppy had organised a fundraiser.

Did it mean anything?

His wounded heart said, *No. Don't even go there.*

He ordered a coffee and a Danish pastry then turned his attention back to the financial statement and the rows of figures.

'Here's your coffee.'

Thinking that being in Perth was really doing his head in because the voice sounded just like Poppy's, he looked up abruptly. Ice and heat tore through him as his gaze met those unforgettable vivid blue eyes.

'Hello, Matt.'

She handed him a coffee and he noticed she held a cup, too. A thousand thoughts sprinted though his head but his anger won, coming out as sarcasm. 'It's a Wednesday morning. I would have thought you'd be at work.'

She shuddered slightly and he watched the movement roll down her body. *Irreconcilable differences.* He didn't regret for a moment that he'd just highlighted the reason they'd parted so acrimoniously. If she thought she could just sit down and 'chat' like old friends, she was wrong. Very wrong.

He caught sight of a familiar red suitcase and things fell into place. 'Ah, it's conference season.'

'Here's your pastry, sir. Sorry for the delay.' The smiling attendant put down a plate and looked at Poppy. 'I brought you one as well as a thank-you for helping me out back there with the coffee disaster.'

Poppy smiled warmly. 'No problem.'

As the attendant walked away, Poppy turned back to Matt, her hand creeping towards the silver P. Half of him wanted to pull her hard against him but the other half demanded he stay cool and aloof so that there was no danger of his heart ever being battered by her again.

'Can I sit down?'

He shrugged. 'Suit yourself.'

She sank onto the couch and crossed her long legs. 'Sarah said you've been in Samoa.'

Her perfume enveloped him, threatening to take him back to a time when he'd thought they'd be together for ever. He fought the memory by flicking the collar on his shirt. 'Two months. I'm on my way back to Bundallagong.'

'How's Lisa's Way going?'

He sighed. 'Poppy, do you really want to make polite chitchat?'

She rolled her lips inwards. 'I'm enquiring about it because I'm a contributor and a friend.'

'You're a *contributor*.'

She flinched at the harshness in his voice but he didn't care. Did she really think she could sit there next to him in her tailored black suit and pretend they hadn't shared anything? Did she think he'd overlook the fact that she'd put a job ahead of everything? A job she'd left him for?

The black heart of his pain spluttered.

She gave a grim smile. 'Matt, I don't—'

He held up a hand. 'I don't want to argue, either. I don't think I even want to talk to you. I'm not going to ask you how the job's going because I'm not interested.'

She breathed in, seeming to hold her breath. 'I've quit.'

Shock made him gape. 'You've what?'

'I've quit and I have a new job.'

His gaze returned to her red suitcase and he immediately recalled the prestigious job he'd seen advertised soon after she'd left. It carried more kudos than the job she had, and Poppy didn't like to lose. He couldn't keep the bitterness out of his voice. 'Ah. St Stephen's in Sydney. Of course, that makes total sense.' He couldn't bring himself to offer congratulations.

'Ah, no, not St Stephen's.' She twisted her hands in her lap in an unusual display of unease. 'The last decision I made as Chief of Surgery was to appoint a permanent surgeon to meet the needs of the growing population of Bundallagong. I have firsthand experience of how much one is needed.'

Every word she spoke reminded him of what they'd lost and he struggled to sound enthusiastic. 'Well, that's good news for the town. Who is it?'

'I'm the new surgeon in Bundallagong.'

Her words slammed into him and a glimmer of hope sprouted in a sea of pain, but the memory of how much she'd hurt him made it struggle.

Poppy watched Matt, knowing this was the moment of truth, and it petrified her. Everything about him, from the strands of his long hair to the tips of toes shod in leather boat shoes, emanated anger. Had she really been so naive as to think he'd welcome her with open arms?

You hurt him so much. From the moment she'd got Sarah's text telling her Matt was in the airport lounge, and from the second she'd seen him, she'd wanted to throw her arms around his neck and tell him what a fool she'd been and beg for his forgiveness. But she had to do it this way and now she was dying inside, waiting for him to speak.

He sat perfectly still, his body almost as rigid as a statue, and the only movement was the complex map of emotions on his face, with hurt shining the brightest. When he finally spoke his voice sounded strained. 'Why?'

She swallowed hard, knowing this conversation was never going to be easy, and tried a touch of levity. 'Because Bundallagong needs a kick-ass surgeon.'

Not even a hint of a smile hovered on his lips but his eyes sought hers. 'Is there another reason?'

This time she went for honesty. 'Yes. I love you.'

A flicker of something flared in his eyes and faded. 'You once said you loved me but you left me, putting a job ahead of us.'

She swallowed against the lump in her throat. 'I know and I'm sorry. I got it all horribly wrong.'

'Yeah, you did.'

His ice-cool voice made her heart hammer hard against her ribs, and she could hear the tremble in her voice but she knew she was fighting for the most important 'job' of her life. 'I was scared. I thought you were trying to make me a different person, just like my father and Steven, trying to make me more like Lisa, and my fear got in the way. I let it screw everything up.' Her hands twisted together. 'I now know you weren't trying to change me. You were making sure we'd make it by creating a wonderful life for us. You saw what I couldn't see, that being Chief of Surgery would consume me and destroy us.'

His expression gave nothing away. 'And yet you didn't believe me. Exactly when did you work this out?'

His quiet but drilling words made her sweat and she pressed her damp palms against her black skirt. Everything she held dear rode on her explanation. 'I missed you every day like a part of me had been lost.'

His jaw tensed. 'I find that hard to believe. You didn't even call.'

The accusation stung but she wore the pain like a badge. 'I know. I've made a mess of everything. When I first came back to Perth I thought I was returning to my life, slipping back into a familiar and secure groove. But it didn't feel right, and it isn't a life I want any more.'

She gulped in a breath and pushed on, exposing her heart like she'd never exposed it before. 'I came to Bundallagong thinking it was a waste of my time, but without me realising, it changed my life. *You* changed my life. I'd always believed that work kept me safe and gave me everything I needed but then I met you. You opened up my world, showed me that life is to be lived, not hidden from. No job, no matter how much I sacrificed to get it, is worth it if I lose you.'

He swallowed hard and his voice wavered. 'The Poppy I met when she first arrived in Bundallagong would never have admitted she was wrong but I need to ask you one thing. Are you absolutely certain this is what you want?'

She nodded. 'It's what I want most in the world. I want to be a surgeon, not an administrator. I want time with friends and girls' nights out. I want a family, but most of all I want you.'

Extending her hand, she let it hover between them. Trying to hold back tears, she sent up the wish of her life. 'I know I need to prove to you that I've changed, and I know at times I can be difficult and that I'm nothing like Lisa, but I need to ask you one thing. Do you want me?'

Matt's fingers bypassed her hand and cupped her cheek. 'Lisa was the love of my boyhood and what we shared will always be part of me but, Poppy, *you're* the love of my manhood. You're my future.'

She fell apart, tears streaming down her face. He pulled her into his arms, burying his face in her hair. 'I want you because you're you. Passionate, giving and full of wonderful flaws, just like me.'

She sniffed. 'I can be stubborn with workaholic tendencies but I'm working on that. I'm going to block out non-work time in the week and stick to it, plus having a new surgical registrar is going to help.'

Surprise lit his face and he grinned. 'The last chief of surgery at Perth City *was* very proactive for Bundallagong.'

She laughed. 'Someone has to look out for rural communities.'

He stroked her hair. 'I hate shopping and housework and I can't cook, but I'll pay Lizzie to keep the freezer full of healthy meals and I'll grill on the weekends.'

She snuggled in against him, pressing her hand against his heart. 'Who's cleaning the house?'

'Mrs Ferguson.'

'I can live with that.'

'And I can't wait to live with you.' He smiled, his face

radiating love. 'So you'll want a year in the job before we start a family?'

Her heart swelled with so much love and adoration that it almost burst. He'd always known work was important to her and he still did, and she couldn't believe how she'd almost lost him. 'You're forgetting I've already had three months in the position and with an experienced registrar starting next week I think he'll be able to fly solo in about nine months.'

The delight on his face mirrored her own. 'I can't wait to start practising.'

'Will you marry me, Matt Albright?'

'I most certainly will, Poppy Stanfield.'

She grinned and ran her fingers through his hair. 'How do you feel about keeping this longer?'

His eyes took on a familiar smoky hue that made her weak with longing. 'Ms Stanfield, do you have a thing for guys with long hair?'

'No, just for you.'

He cupped her face and kissed her long and hard, his lips infusing her with his love, support, caring and passion.

'Passengers on Flight 273 to Bundallagong, your flight is boarding now. Please make your way to gate seventeen.'

Matt stood up and extended his hand. 'Let's go home.'

Home.

To the red dust of Bundallagong with the man she loved. She couldn't wait.

A DOCTOR TO REMEMBER

JOANNA NEIL

CHAPTER ONE

SO, HERE SHE was at last. Saffi stretched her limbs and walked across the grass to the clifftop railing, where she stood and looked out over the bay. After several hours on the coach, it was good to be out in the fresh air once more.

From here she could see the quay, where fishermen stacked their lobster pots and tended their nets, and for a while she watched the brightly coloured pleasure boats and fishing craft as they tossed gently on the water. Seagulls flew overhead, calling to one another as they soared and dived in search of tasty tidbits.

In the distance, whitewashed cottages nestled amongst the tree-clad hills, where crooked paths twisted and turned on their way down to the harbour. This little corner of Devon looked idyllic. It was so peaceful, so perfect.

If only she could absorb some of that tranquillity. After all, wasn't that why she was here, the reason she had decided to leave everything behind, everything that had represented safety and security in her life—even though in the end that security had turned out to be something of a sham?

A small shiver of panic ran through her. Was she doing the right thing? How could she know what lay ahead? Had she made a big mistake in coming here?

She pulled in a shaky breath, filling her lungs with sea air, and then let it out again slowly, trying to calm herself. She'd been living in Hampshire for the last few years, but this place ought to be familiar to her, or so she'd been told, and it was, in a way, in odd fragments of memory that drifted through her brain, lingered for a moment, and then dissolved in mist as quickly as they'd come.

'Perhaps it's what you need,' her solicitor had said, shuffling the freshly signed papers into a neat bundle and sliding them into a tray on his desk. 'It might do you some good to go back to the place where you spent your childhood. You could at least give it a try.'

'Yes, maybe you're right.'

Now the warm breeze stirred, gently lifting her honey-gold hair and she turned her face towards the sun and felt its caress on her bare arms. Maybe its heat would somehow manage to thaw the chill that had settled around her heart these last few months.

A lone seagull wandered close by, pecking desultorily in the grass, searching for anything edible among the red fescue and the delicate white sea campion. He kept an eye on her, half cautious, half hopeful.

She smiled. 'I'm afraid I don't have any food for you,' she said softly. 'Come to think of it, I haven't actually had anything myself since breakfast.' That seemed an awfully long time ago now, but she'd been thinking so hard about what lay ahead that everything else, even food, had gone from her mind. Not that forgetfulness was unusual for her these days.

'Thanks for reminding me,' she told the bird. 'I should go and find some lunch. Perhaps if you stop by here another day I might have something for you.'

She felt brighter in herself all at once. Coming here had been a big decision for her to make, but it was done. She was here now, and maybe she could look on this as a new beginning.

She moved away from the railing, and glanced around. Her solicitor had made arrangements for her to be met at the Seafarer Inn, which was just across the road from here. It was an attractive-looking building, with lots of polished mahogany timbers decorating the ground-floor frontage and white-painted rendering higher up. There were window-boxes filled with crimson geraniums and trailing surfinias in shades of pink and cream, and in front, on the pavement, there were chalkboards advertising some of the meals that were on offer.

There was still more than half an hour left before her transport should arrive, plenty of time for her to get some lunch and try to gather her thoughts.

She chose a table by a window, and went over to the bar to place her order. 'I'm expecting a Mr Flynn to meet me here in a while,' she told the landlord, a cheerful, friendly man, who was busy polishing glasses with a clean towel. 'Would you mind sending him over to me if he asks?'

'I'll see to it, love. Enjoy your meal.'

'Thanks.'

The solicitor had told her Mr Flynn had been acting as caretaker for the property these last few months. 'He'll give you the keys and show you around. I think he's probably a semi-retired gentleman who's glad to help out. He seems very nice, anyway. When I wrote and told him you don't drive at the moment he offered to come and pick you up.'

So now all she had to do was wait. There was a fluttery feeling in her stomach, but she went back to her table and sat down. She felt conspicuous at first, being here in a bar full of strangers, but now that she was tucked away in the corner she felt much more comfortable, knowing that she was partially shielded by a mahogany lattice.

For her meal, she'd chosen a jacket potato with cheese and a side salad, and she had only just started to eat when a shadow fell across her table. She quickly laid down her fork and looked up to see a man standing there.

Her eyes widened. Was this Mr Flynn? He wasn't at all what she'd been expecting, and her insides made a funny kind of flip-over in response.

Her first impression was that he was in his early thirties, tall, around six feet, and good looking, with strong, angular features and a crop of short, jet-black hair. He was definitely no elderly caretaker, and seeing such a virile young man standing there came as a bit of a shock.

He, in turn, was studying her thoughtfully, a half-smile playing around his mouth, but as his dark grey glance met hers it occurred to her that there was a faintly guarded look about him.

'Saffi?'

'Yes.' She gave him a fleeting smile. 'You must be… You're not quite what I expected…um, you must be Mr Flynn…?'

He frowned, giving her a wary, puzzled glance. 'That's right. Matt Flynn.' There was an odd expression around his eyes and in the slight twist to his mouth as he watched her. He waited a few seconds and then, when she stayed silent, he seemed to brace his shoulders and said in a more businesslike fashion, 'Your solicitor wrote to me. He said you wanted to look over the Moorcroft property.'

'I… Yes, that's right…' She hesitated, suddenly unsure of herself. 'I was hoping I…um…' She glanced unseeingly at the food on her plate. 'I…uh…' She looked up at him once more. 'I didn't mean to keep you waiting. Do you want to leave right away?'

He shook his head. 'No, of course not—not at all. I'm early—go on with your meal, please.' He seemed perplexed, as though he was weighing things up in his mind, but she couldn't imagine what was going on in his head. Something was obviously bothering him.

'Actually,' he said, after a moment or two, 'I'm quite hungry myself. Do you mind if I join you?' He smiled properly then, the corners of his eyes crinkling, his mouth making a crooked shape. 'The food here's very good. The smell of it's tantalising as soon as you walk in the door.'

'Yes, it is.' She began to relax a little and waved him towards a chair. 'Please…have a seat.'

'Okay. I'll just go and order, and be back with you in a minute or two.'

Saffi nodded and watched him as he walked to the bar. His long legs were clad in denim and he was wearing a T-shirt that clung to his chest and emphasised his muscular arms and broad shoulders, causing an unbidden quiver of awareness to clutch at her stomach. Her heart was thudding heavily.

It was strange, acknowledging that she could have such feelings. For so long now it had seemed she'd been going through life on autopilot, stumbling about, trying to cope, and feeling her way through a maze of alien situations. She didn't know where men fitted into all that.

He came back to the table and sat down opposite her, placing a half-pint glass of lager on the table. He studied her thoughtfully. 'Your solicitor said you've been mulling over your options concerning Jasmine Cottage. Are you planning on staying there for a while?' He looked around. 'Only I don't see any luggage, except for a hold-all.'

'No, that's right, I'm having it sent on. I thought it would be easier that way. There's quite a lot of stuff—I'll be staying for a while until I make up my mind what to do…whether to sell up or stay on.'

'Uh-huh.' There was a note of curiosity in his voice as he said, 'I suppose it would have been easier for you if you had a car, but your solicitor said you sold it a few weeks ago?'

'I… Yes. I was… I…' She faltered momentarily. 'It was involved in a rear-end collision and I had it repaired and decided I didn't need a car any more. I lived quite near to the hospital where I worked.'

It was a fair enough excuse, and she didn't want to go into the reasons why she had suddenly lost her confidence behind the wheel. All sorts of daily activities had become a challenge for her in the last few months.

'Ah, I see…at least, I think I do.' He gave her a long, considering look. 'Are you worried about driving for some reason?'

He hadn't believed her lame excuse. She winced. 'Perhaps. A bit. Maybe.' She hoped he wasn't going to ask her any more about it.

He sat back for a moment as the waitress brought his meal, a succulent gammon steak and fries. He was quiet, absorbed in his own thoughts, as though he was troubled by something. Whatever it was, he appeared to cast it aside when the girl had left and said, 'Are you planning on working at a hospital here in Devon?' He sliced into the gammon with his knife.

She shook her head. 'No, at least, not right away. I'm going to take a break for a while.'

It still bothered her that she had to say that, and as she lifted her iced drink to her lips she was dismayed to see that her hand shook a little. She put the glass down and took a deep breath, hoping that he hadn't noticed.

'What about you…what do you do? I'm guessing you're not a semi-retired caretaker, as my solicitor suggested.'

A variety of conflicting emotions crossed his face and Saffi gazed at him uncertainly. He seemed taken aback, somehow, by her question.

His dark brows lifted and his mouth made an ironic twist. After a moment, he said, 'No, actually, caretaking is just a minor part of my week. I'm an A and E doctor, and when I'm not on duty at the hospital I'm on call as a BASICS physician, weekends and evenings mostly.'

Her eyes grew large. 'Oh, I see. We have something in common, then, working in emergency medicine.'

Being a BASICS doctor meant he worked in Immediate Care, as someone who would attend injured people at the roadside, or wherever they happened to be. These doctors usually worked on a voluntary basis, so it was up to the individual doctor if they wanted to take a call.

'Yes, we do.' He nodded, and then looked her over once more, a sober expression on his face. He seemed… resigned almost. 'You don't remember me at all, do you?'

Saffi's jaw dropped in consternation. 'Remember you? Should I?' No wonder his manner had seemed so strange. Her stomach was leaden. So much for a new beginning. Even here it seemed she had come face to face with her vulnerabilities. 'Have we met before?'

'Oh, yes. We have.' He said it in a confident, firm voice and she floundered for a second or two, thrown on to the back foot. Of course there would be people here she had known in the past.

'I'm sorry.' She sent him a worried glance. 'Perhaps it

was some time ago?' She was desperately hoping that his answer would smooth away any awful gaffe on her part.

'We worked together at a hospital in London.'

'Oh.' Anxiety washed over her. 'Perhaps you were working in a different specialty to me?'

He nodded. 'That's true, I was working in the trauma unit. But I definitely remember you. How could I forget?' His glance moved over her face, taking in the soft blush of her cheeks and the shining hair that fell in a mass of soft curls around her face. His eyes darkened as though he was working through some unresolved torment.

She exhaled slowly, only then realising that she'd been holding her breath. 'What were the chances that we would run into each other again here in Devon?' she said, trying to make light of things, but she looked at him with troubled blue eyes.

'I guess it was bound to happen some time. After all, we both knew your aunt, didn't we? That's another thing we have in common, isn't it?'

She hesitated. 'Is it? I…I don't know,' she said at last on a brief sigh. He'd taken the trouble to come here, and said they knew one another—perhaps she owed him some kind of explanation.

'The thing is, Matt, something happened to me a few months ago…there was an accident, and I ended up with a head injury. I don't remember exactly what went on, only that I woke up in hospital and everything that had gone before was a blank.'

He made a sharp intake of breath. 'I'm sorry.' He shook his head as though he was trying to come to terms with what she had told him. 'Your solicitor mentioned you had some problems with your memory, but I'd no idea it was so profound.' He reached for her, cupping his hand over hers. 'What kind of accident was it? Don't you remember anything at all?'

'Not much.' His hand was warm and comforting, enveloping hers. He was a complete stranger to her, and yet she took heart from that instinctive, compassionate action.

'They told me I must have fallen down the stairs and banged my head. I shared a house with another girl—my flat was on the upper floor—and apparently my friend found me when she came home at the end of her shift at the hospital. She called for an ambulance, and they whisked me away to Accident and Emergency.'

She went over the events in her mind. 'It turned out I had a fractured skull. The emergency team looked after me, and after that it was just a question of waiting for the brain swelling to go down, so that they could assess the amount of neurological damage I had been left with. I was lucky, in a way, because there's been no lasting physical harm—nothing that you can see.' She gave a brief smile. 'Except for my hair, of course. It used to be long and shoulder length, but they had to shave part of my head.'

'Your hair looks lovely. It suits you like that.'

'Thank you.' She moved restlessly, and he released her so that she was free to take another sip of her cold drink. Her throat was dry, aching. 'I remember bits and pieces. Some things come back to me every now and again, and I manage to keep hold of them. Other memories seem to float around for a while and then disappear before I can picture them clearly.'

'I'm so sorry, Saffi. I can't imagine what that must be like.' His grey eyes were sombre and sympathetic. 'You must be taking a leap in the dark, coming here, away from everything you've known for the last few years. Or perhaps you remember Devon, and Jasmine Cottage?'

She frowned. 'No. I don't think so. Some of it, perhaps.' Her lips flattened briefly. 'I'm hoping it'll all come back to me when I get to the house.'

He nodded. 'I was really sorry when your aunt died. She was a lovely woman.'

'Yes.' She said it cautiously, unwilling to admit that she couldn't remember very much about the woman who had left her this property in a picturesque village situated near the Devon coast. Everyone told her they'd been very close, but the sad truth was she simply had no clear recollection of her benefactor. It seemed wrong to come here to take up an inheritance in those awful circumstances, but all those who knew her back in Hampshire had persuaded her it was the right thing to do. Only time would tell.

'Apparently she died before I had my accident, and I'd been to her funeral. All this business with the property had to be put to one side while I was recovering in hospital.' She glanced at him. 'Had you known my aunt for a long time?' She was suddenly keen to know how he was connected to her relative, and how he came to be caretaking the property.

He appeared to hesitate before answering and she wondered if this was something she ought to have known, some part of the way they'd known one another. 'We met a few years back, but then I went to work with the air ambulance in Wales, so I didn't see much of her until I came to work in Devon last summer. After that, she called on me from time to time to help fix things about the place.'

'I'm glad she had someone. Thanks for that.' She smiled at him, and made light conversation with him while they finished their meals. Her emotions were in a precarious state and she didn't want to enquire right then into how she'd known Matt in the past. Perhaps he understood that, or maybe he had his own reasons for not bringing it up. He seemed concerned, and clearly he had been thrown off balance by her loss of memory.

They left the inn together a short time later and went to his car, a fairly new rapid-response vehicle equipped with a blue light, high-visibility strips and badges.

He held open the passenger door for her and she slipped into the seat. The smell of luxurious soft leather greeted her, and she sat back and tried to relax.

Matt set the car in motion and started along the coast road, cruising at a moderate pace so she had the chance to take in the scenery on the way.

She gazed out of the window, watching the harbour slowly recede, and in a while they left the blue sweep of the bay behind them as he drove inland towards the hills. The landscape changed to rolling green vistas interspersed with narrow lanes lined with clusters of pretty cottages decorated with hanging baskets full of bright flowers.

He sent her a quick, sideways glance. 'Is this meant to be a kind of holiday for you—a chance to recover from everything that has happened? Or are you more concerned with sorting out your aunt's estate?'

'I suppose it's a bit of both, really. I was beginning to feel that I needed a break, a change of scenery at least, and although it was a sad thing that my aunt passed on, it gave me an opportunity to get away. I...' She hesitated momentarily, then went on, 'There's no one else left in my family, so it's down to me to sort out what's to be done with the property.'

Perhaps she'd managed to come to terms with all that before the accident, but since then she'd felt her isolation keenly. Being unable to remember people around her meant that she was cut off from all that was familiar, and it left her with an acute sense of loneliness.

'And do you think you'll manage all right?' he said, cutting in on her thoughts. 'If you're not working, I mean?' He saw her hesitation and pulled a wry face. 'Am I overstepping the mark? You'll have to let me know if I do that—I'm afraid I tend to get carried away and say what's on my mind. '

She shook her head. 'That's all right. I appreciate you being open with me.' She frowned. 'I'm not sure how I'd handle going back to medicine just yet. But I have enough money to keep me going for now, until I find my feet. After my parents died some years ago, it seems that

I sold the property and invested what they left me. So at least I don't have any worries on that score.'

'Perhaps that's just as well. It looks as though you have more than enough on your plate right now.'

He concentrated on the road for a while as he negotiated a series of bends, and then, after following a winding country lane for about half a mile, Saffi suddenly became aware of an isolated farmhouse coming into view. It was set back from the road amidst fields, a little gem in the surrounding greenery.

'That's the house, isn't it?' she said, excitement growing inside her as they drew closer. It was a long, rambling property, with a couple of side-on extensions that had been added to the main house over the years, giving it three different roof elevations. It was pleasing on the eye, with the traditional white rendering throughout and slate roofs over all. The window-frames were mahogany, as was the front door. A trailing jasmine shrub sprawled over the entrance wall, its bright, yellow flowers making a beautiful contrast to the dark evergreen leaves.

'Do you remember it?'

'No. But my solicitor showed me a photograph. It's lovely, isn't it?'

He nodded, and parked the car on the drive. 'Here, you'll need the keys.'

'Thank you.' She stood for a moment or two, gazing at the house, and then she slowly walked up to the front door. The scent of jasmine filled the air, sweetly sensuous, instantly calming. Saffi breathed it in and suddenly she was overwhelmed as her mind captured the image of a dear, slender woman, a nurturing, gentle soul.

'Oh…Annie…Annie…'

Her eyes filled with tears, the breath caught in her throat, and she heard Matt saying urgently, 'What is it, Saffi? What's wrong? Have you remembered something?'

She was shaking. 'My aunt…it was just as though she was here…I could feel her… But she's gone, and I don't think I can bear it…'

He hesitated momentarily, and then wrapped his arms around her. 'It's all right, Saffi. I know it's hard, but it's good that you remember her.'

She didn't move for several minutes, overtaken by grief, but secure in his embrace, glad of the fact that he was holding her, because but for that she might have fallen. Her legs were giving way as emotion wreaked havoc with her body, leaving her fragile, helpless.

'I'm sorry,' she said after a while, ashamed of her weakness and brushing away her tears with her fingers. 'The memory of her just came flooding back. I wasn't expecting it.'

'Do you remember anything else?' he asked cautiously. 'About the house, your work…your friends?' He was looking at her intently, and perhaps he was asking if she had begun to remember anything at all about him and the way they'd known one another.

She shook her head. 'All I know is that I was happy here. I felt safe. This is home.'

He let out a long breath, and then straightened up, as

though in that moment he'd come to some sort of decision. 'Well, that's good. That's a start.' He didn't add anything more, didn't try to tell her about the past, or give any hint as to what their relationship might have been. Instead, he seemed to make an effort to pull himself together, reluctantly releasing her when she felt ready to turn back towards the door.

'I should go in,' she said.

'Do you want me to go in with you? You might still be a bit shaky…and perhaps I ought to show you around and explain what needs to be done with the animals. I mean, I can look after them till you find your feet, but maybe you'll want to take over at some point.'

She stared at him. 'Animals?'

'You don't know about them?'

She shook her head. 'It's news to me.' She frowned. 'You're right. Perhaps you'd better come in and explain things to me.'

They went into the house, and Saffi walked slowly along the hallway, waiting in vain for more memories to come back to her. Matt showed her into the kitchen and she looked around, pleased with the homely yet modern look of the room. The units were cream coloured and there were open shelves and glass-fronted cabinets on the walls. A smart black cooker was fitted into the newly painted fireplace recess, and an oak table stood in the centre of the room.

'I bought some food for you and stocked the refrigerator when I heard you were coming over here,' Matt said. 'Your solicitor said you might need time to settle in before you started to get organised.'

She smiled. 'Thanks. That was thoughtful of you.' She checked the fridge and some of the cupboards and chuckled. 'This is better stocked than my kitchen back in Hampshire. We were always running out of stuff over there these last few months. I had to write notes to remind myself to shop, because my flatmate was worse than me at organisation.'

'I can see I'll need to keep an eye on you,' he murmured. 'We can't have you wasting away.' His glance ran over her and a flush of heat swept along her cheekbones. She was wearing jeans that moulded themselves to her hips and a camisole top that outlined her feminine curves, and she suddenly felt self-conscious under that scorching gaze.

'I…uh…I'll show you the rest of the house if you like,' he said, walking towards a door at the side of the room. 'Unless it's all coming back to you?'

She shook her head. 'It isn't, I'm afraid.' She followed him into the dining room, where the furniture followed the design of the kitchen. There was a cream wood Welsh dresser displaying patterned plates, cups and saucers, and a matching table and upholstered chairs.

'The sitting room's through here,' Matt said, leading the way into a sunlit room where wide patio doors led on to a paved terrace.

She glanced around. It was a lovely room, with accents of warm colour and a sofa that looked soft and comfortable.

'I think you'll find it's cosy of an evening with the log-burning stove,' he murmured.

'Yes.' She had a fleeting image of a woman adding logs to the stove, and a lump formed in her throat.

'Are you okay?'

She nodded. 'I guess I'll need a plentiful supply of wood, then,' she said, getting a grip on herself. 'Where did my aunt get her logs from, do you know?'

'There's a copse on the land—your land. It should supply plenty of fuel for some time to come, but your aunt did a lot of replanting. Anyway, I've filled up the log store for you, so you won't need to worry about that for quite a while.'

'It sounds as though I owe you an awful lot,' she said with a frown. 'What with the groceries, the wood and…you mentioned there were animals. I don't think I've ever had any experience looking after pets—none that I recall, anyway.' Yet no dog or cat had come running to greet them when they'd first entered the house. It was very puzzling.

'Ah…yes. We'll do a quick tour upstairs and then I'll take you to see them.'

There were two bedrooms upstairs, one with an en suite bathroom, and along the corridor was the main bathroom. Saffi couldn't quite work out the layout up here. There were fewer rooms than she'd expected, as though something was missing, but perhaps her senses were off somehow.

'Okay, shall we go and solve the mystery of these pets?' she murmured. Maybe her aunt had a small aviary outside. She'd heard quite a bit of birdsong when they'd arrived, but there were a good many trees around the house that would have accounted for that.

They went outside to the garden, and Saffi caught her breath as she looked out at the extent of her property. It wasn't just a garden, there was also a paddock and a stable block nearby.

'Oh, no. Tell me it's not horses,' she pleaded. 'I don't know anything about looking after them.'

'Just a couple.' He saw her look of dismay and relented. 'No, actually, Annie mainly used the stable block as a store for the fruit harvest.'

She breathed a small sigh of relief.

Fruit harvest, he'd said. Saffi made a mental note of that. On the south side of the garden she'd noticed an archway in a stone wall, and something flickered in her faulty memory banks. Could it be a walled garden? From somewhere in the depths of her mind she recalled images of fruit trees and glasshouses with grapes, melons and peaches.

They walked by the stable block and came to a fenced-off area that contained a hen hut complete with a large covered wire run. Half a dozen hens wandered about in there , pecking the ground for morsels of food.

'Oh, my...' Saffi's eyes widened. 'Was there anything else my aunt was into? Anything I should know about? I mean, should I ever want to go back to medicine, I don't know how I'll find the time to fit it in, what with fruit picking, egg gathering and keeping track of this huge garden.'

He laughed. 'She was quite keen on beekeeping. There are three hives in the walled garden.'

Saffi rolled her eyes. 'Maybe I should turn around right now and head back for Hampshire.'

'I don't think so. I hope you won't do that.' He gave her a long look. 'I don't see you as a quitter. Anyway, it's not that difficult. I'll show you. Let's go and make a start with the hens.'

He led the way to the coop. 'I let them out in the morning,' he explained. 'They have food pellets in feeders, as well as water, but in the afternoon or early evening, whenever I finish work, I give them a mix of corn and split peas. There's some oyster shell and grit mixed in with it, so it's really good for them.' He went over to a wooden store shed and brought out a bucket filled with corn. 'Do you want to sprinkle some on the ground for them?'

'Uh…okay.' This had all come as a bit of a jolt to her. Instead of the peace and quiet she'd been expecting, the chance to relax and get herself back together again after the trauma of the last few months, it was beginning to look as though her days would be filled with stuff she'd never done before.

She went into the covered run, leaving Matt to shut the door and prevent any attempted escapes. An immediate silence fell as the birds took in her presence.

'Here you go,' she said, scattering the corn around her, and within seconds she found herself surrounded by hens. Some even clambered over her feet to get to the grain. Gingerly, she took a step forward, but they ignored her and simply went on eating. She shot Matt a quick look of consternation and he grinned.

'Problem?' he asked, and she pulled a face.

'What do I do now?'

He walked towards her and grasped her hand. 'You just have to force your way through. Remember, you're the one in charge here, not the hens.'

'Hmm, if you say so.'

He was smiling as he pulled her out of the run and shut the door behind them. 'They need to be back into the coop by nightfall. As long as their routine isn't disturbed, things should go smoothly enough. They're laying very well at the moment, so you'll have a good supply of eggs.'

'Oh, well, that's a plus, I suppose.'

He sent her an amused glance. 'That's good. At least you're beginning to look on the positive side.'

She gritted her teeth but stayed silent. Now he was patronising her. Her head was starting to ache, a throbbing beat pounding at her temples.

'And the beehives?' she asked. 'What's to be done with them?'

'Not much, at this time of year. You just keep an eye on them to make sure everything's all right and let them get on with making honey. Harvesting is done round about the end of August, beginning of September.'

'You make it sound so easy. I guess I'll have to find myself a book on beekeeping.'

'I think Annie had several of those around the place.'

They made their way back to the house, and Saffi said

quietly, 'I should thank you for everything you've done here since my aunt died. I'd no idea the caretaking was so involved. You've managed to keep this place going, and I'm very grateful to you for that.'

'Well, I suppose I had a vested interest.'

She frowned. 'You did?'

He nodded. 'Your aunt made me a beneficiary of her will. Didn't your solicitor tell you about it?'

She stared at him. 'No. At least, I don't think so.' She searched her mind for details of her conversations with the solicitor. There had been several over the last few weeks, and maybe he'd mentioned something about another beneficiary. She'd assumed he meant there was a small bequest to a friend or neighbour.

The throbbing in her temple was clouding her thinking. 'He said he didn't want to bother me with all the details because of my problems since the accident.'

He looked at her quizzically and she added briefly, 'Headaches and so on. I had a short attention span for a while, and I can be a bit forgetful at times…but I'm much better now. I feel as though I'm on the mend.'

'I'm sure you are. You seem fairly clear-headed to me.'

'I'm glad you think so.' She studied him. 'So, what exactly did you inherit…a sum of money, a share in the proceeds from the livestock…the tools in the garden store?' She said it in a light-hearted manner, but it puzzled her as to what her aunt could have left him.

'Uh…it was a bit more than that, actually.' He looked a trifle uneasy, and perhaps that was because he'd assumed she'd known all about it in advance. But then he seemed to throw off any doubts he might have had and said briskly, 'Come on, I'll show you.'

He went to the end extension of the property and unlocked a separate front door, standing back and waving her inside.

Saffi stared about her in a daze. 'But this is… I didn't notice this before…' She was completely taken aback by this new discovery. She was standing in a beautifully furnished living room, and through an archway she glimpsed what looked like a kitchen-diner, fitted out with golden oak units.

'Originally, the house was one large, complete family home, but your aunt had some alterations made,' he said. 'There's a connecting door to your part of the house and another upstairs. They're locked, so we'll be completely separate—you'll have a key amongst those I gave you.'

She looked at the connecting door, set unobtrusively into an alcove in the living room.

'I'll show you the rest of the house,' he said, indicating an open staircase in the corner of the room.

She followed him up the stairs, her mind reeling under this new, stunning revelation. No wonder she'd thought there was something missing from the upper floor when he'd taken her to look around. The missing portion was right here, in the form of a good-sized bedroom and bathroom.

'You're very quiet,' he murmured.

'I'm trying to work out how this came about,' she said

in a soft voice. 'You're telling me that my aunt left this part of the house to you?'

'She did. I'd no idea that she had written it into her will or that she planned to do it. She didn't mention it to me. Does it bother you?'

'I think it does, yes.'

It wasn't that she wanted it for herself. Heaven forbid, she hadn't even remembered this house existed until her solicitor had brought it to her attention. But her aunt couldn't have known this man very long—by his own account he'd only been in the area for a few months. And yet she'd left him a sizeable property. How had that come about?

All at once she needed to be on her own so that she could think things through. 'I should go,' she said. 'I think I need time to take this in. But…thanks for showing me around.'

'You're welcome.' He went with her down the stairs. 'Any time you need me, Saffi, I'll be here.'

She nodded. That was certainly true. His presence gave a new meaning to the words 'next-door neighbour'.

She'd come here expecting to find herself in a rural hideout, well away from anyone and anything, so that she might finally recuperate from the devastating head injury that had left her without any knowledge of family or friends. And none of it was turning out as she'd hoped.

Matt had seemed such a charming, likeable man, but wasn't that the way of all confidence tricksters? How could she know what to think?

Her instincts had been all over the place since the accident, and perhaps she was letting that trauma sour her judgement. Ever since she'd woken up in hospital she'd had the niggling suspicion that all was not as it seemed as far as her fall was concerned.

She'd done what she could to put that behind her, but now the question was, could she put her trust in Matt, who seemed so obliging? What could have convinced her aunt to leave him such a substantial inheritance?

CHAPTER TWO

SAFFI FINISHED WEEDING the last of the flower borders in the walled garden and leaned back on her heels to survey her handiwork. It was a beautiful garden, filled with colour and sweet scents, just perfect for the bees that flew from flower to flower, gathering nectar and pollen. Against the wall, the pale pink of the hollyhocks was a lovely contrast to the deep rose colour of the flamboyant peonies. Close by, tall delphiniums matched the deep blue of the sky.

'You've been keeping busy, from the looks of things,' Matt commented, startling her as he appeared in the archway that separated this part of the garden from the larger, more general area. 'You've done a good job here.'

She lifted her head to look at him, causing her loosely pinned curls to quiver with the movement. He started to walk towards her, and straight away her pulse went into overdrive and her heart skipped a beat. He was overwhelmingly masculine, with a perfect physique, his long legs encased in blue jeans while his muscular chest and arms were emphasised by the dark T-shirt he was wearing.

'Thanks.' She viewed him cautiously. She hadn't seen much of him this last week, and perhaps that was just as well, given her concerns about him. In fact, she'd wondered if he'd deliberately stayed away from her, giving her room to sort herself out. Though, of course, he must have been out at work for a good deal of the time.

It was hard to know what to think of him. He'd said they'd known one another before this, and she wanted to trust him, but the circumstances of his inheritance had left her thoroughly confused and made her want to tread carefully where he was concerned. What could have led her aunt to leave the house to be shared by two people? It was very odd.

To give Matt his due, though, he'd kept this place going after Aunt Annie's death—he'd had the leaky barn roof fixed, her closest neighbours told her, and he'd made sure the lawns were trimmed regularly. He'd taken good care of the hens, too, and she ought to be grateful to him for all that.

'I see you've made a start on picking the fruit.' He looked at the peach tree, trained in a fan shape across the south wall where it received the most sunshine. Nearby there were raspberry canes, alongside blackberry and redcurrant bushes.

She gave a wry smile. 'Yes…I only had to touch the peaches and they came away from the branches, so I guessed it was time to gather them in. And I had to pick the raspberries before the birds made away with the entire crop. Actually, I've put some of the fruit to one side

for you, back in the kitchen. I was going to bring it over
to you later today.'

'That was good of you. Thanks.' He smiled, looking
at her appreciatively, his glance wandering slowly over
her slender yet curvaceous figure, and making the breath
catch in her throat. She was wearing light blue denim
shorts and a crop top with thin straps that left her arms
bare and revealed the pale gold of her midriff. All at
once, under that all-seeing gaze, she felt decidedly un-
derdressed. Her face flushed with heat, probably from a
combination of the burning rays of the sun and the fact
that he was standing beside her, making her conscious
of her every move.

She took off her gardening gloves and brushed a stray
tendril of honey-blonde hair from her face with the back
of her hand. 'There's so much produce, I'm not quite sure
what my aunt did with it all. I thought I might take some
along to the neighbours along the lane.'

'I'm sure they'll appreciate that. Annie sold some of
it, flowers, too, and eggs, to the local shopkeepers, and
there were always bunches of cut flowers on sale by the
roadside at the front of the house, along with baskets of
fruit. She trusted people to put the money in a box, and
apparently they never let her down.'

'That sounds like a good idea. I'll have to try it,' she
said, getting to her feet. She was a bit stiff from being
in the same position for so long, and he put out a hand
to help her up.

'Thanks.' His grasp was strong and supportive and
that unexpected human contact was strangely comfort-

ing. Warm colour brushed her cheeks once more as his gaze travelled fleetingly over her long, shapely legs.

'You could do with a gardener's knee pad—one of those covered foam things...'

'Yes, you're probably right.' She frowned. 'I'm beginning to think that looking after this property and the land and everything that comes with it is going to be a full-time job.'

'It is, especially at this time of year,' he agreed. 'But maybe you could get someone in to help out if it becomes too much for you to handle. Funds permitting, of course.'

She nodded, going over to one of the redwood garden chairs and sitting down. 'I suppose, sooner or later, I'll have to make up my mind what I'm going to do.'

She waved him to the seat close by. A small table connected the two chairs, and on it she had laid out a glass jug filled with iced apple juice. She lifted the cover that was draped over it to protect the contents from the sunshine. 'Would you like a cold drink?'

'That'd be great, thanks.' He came to sit beside her and she brought out a second glass from the cupboard beneath the table.

She filled both glasses, passing one to him before she drank thirstily from hers. 'It's lovely out here, so serene, but it's really hot today. Great if you're relaxing but not so good when you're working.' She lifted the glass, pressing it against her forehead to savour the coolness.

'How are you coping, generally?'

'All right, I think. I came here to rest and recuperate but the way things turned out it's been good for me to keep busy. I've been exploring the village and the sea-side in between looking after this place. The only thing I've left completely alone is anything to do with the bee-hives. I think I'm supposed to have equipment of some sort, aren't I, before I go near them?'

'There are a couple of outfits in the stable block. I can show you how to go on with them, whenever you're ready.'

She nodded. 'Thanks. I'll take you up on that. I'm just not quite ready to tackle beekeeping on my own.' She drank more juice and studied him musingly. Despite her reservations about him, this was one area where she'd better let him guide her. 'Did you help my aunt with the hives?'

'I did, from time to time. She needed some repairs done to the stands and while I was doing that she told me all about looking after them. She said she talked to the bees, told them what was happening in her life—I don't think she was serious about that, but she seemed to find it calming and it helped to clear her thoughts.'

'Hmm. Perhaps I should try it. Maybe it will help me get my mind back together.'

'How's that going?'

She pulled a face. 'I recall bits and pieces every now and again. Especially when I'm in the house or out here, in the garden…not so much in the village and round about. I was told Aunt Annie brought me up after my parents died, and I know…I feel inside…that she loved me as if I was her own daughter.'

Her voice faltered. 'I…I miss her. I keep seeing her

as a lively, wonderful old lady, but she was frail towards the end, wasn't she? That's what the solicitor said…that she had a heart attack, but I don't remember any of that.'

'Perhaps your mind is blocking it out.'

'Yes, that might be it. Even so, I feel as though I'm grieving inside, even though I can't remember everything.' She was troubled. Wouldn't Matt have been here when she had come back to see her aunt, and again at the time of the funeral? Everyone told her she'd done that, that she'd visited regularly, yet she had no memory of it, or of him.

She straightened her shoulders, glancing at him. 'Anyway, I'm glad I came back to this house. I was in two minds about it at first, but somehow I feel at peace here, as though this is where I belong.'

'I'm glad about that. Annie would have been pleased.'

'Yes, I think she would.' She studied him thoughtfully. 'It sounds as though you knew her well—even though you had only been back here for a short time.'

She hesitated for a moment and then decided to say what was on her mind. 'How was it that you came to be living here?' She wasn't sure what she expected him to say. He would hardly admit to wheedling his way into an elderly lady's confidence, would he?

He lifted his glass and took a long swallow of the cold liquid. Saffi watched him, mesmerised by the movement of his sun-bronzed throat, and by the way his strong fingers gripped the glass.

He placed it back on the table a moment later. 'I'd started a new job in the area and I was looking for a place to live. Accommodation was in short supply, it being the height of the holiday season, but I managed to find a flat near the hospital. It was a bit basic, though, and after a while I began to hanker for a few home comforts...'

'Oh? Such as...?' She raised a quizzical brow and he grinned.

'Hot and cold running water, for a start, and some means of preparing food. There was a gas ring, but it took forever to heat a pan of beans. And as to the plumbing—I was lucky if it worked at all. It was okay taking cold baths in the summer, but come wintertime it was bracing, to say the least. I spoke to the landlord about it, but he kept making excuses and delaying—he obviously didn't want to spend money on getting things fixed.'

'So my aunt invited you stay here?'

He nodded. 'I'd been helping her out by doing repairs about the place, and one day she suggested that I move into the annexe.'

'That must have been a relief to you.'

He smiled. 'Yes, it was. Best of all was the home-cooked food—I wasn't expecting that, but she used to bring me pot roasts or invite me round to her part of the house for dinner of an evening. I think she liked to have company.'

'Yes, that was probably it.' Her mouth softened at the image of her aunt befriending this young doctor. 'I suppose the hot and cold running water goes without saying?'

'That, too.'

She sighed. 'I wish I could say the same about mine.

I would have loved to take a shower after doing all that weeding, but something seems to have gone wrong with it. I tried to get hold of a plumber, but apparently they're all too busy to come out and look at it. Three weeks is the earliest date I could get.'

He frowned. 'Have you any idea why it stopped working? Perhaps it's something simple, like the shower head being blocked with calcium deposits?'

'It isn't that. I checked. I've a horrible feeling it's to do with the electronics—I suppose in the end I'll have to buy a new shower.' Her mouth turned down a fraction.

'Would you like me to have a look at it? You never know, between the two of us, we might be able to sort it out, or at least find out what's gone wrong.'

'Are you sure you wouldn't mind doing that?' She felt a small ripple of relief flow through her. He might not know much at all about plumbing, but just to have a second opinion would be good.

'I'd be glad to. Shall we go over to the house now, if you've finished what you were doing out here?'

'Okay.' They left the walled garden, passing through the stone archway, and then followed the path to the main house. Out in the open air, the hens clucked and foraged in the run amongst the patches of grass and gravel for grain and food pellets, and ignored them completely.

'So, what happened when you tried to use the shower last time?' Matt asked as they went upstairs a few minutes later.

'I switched on the isolator switch as usual outside the bathroom and everything was fine. But after I'd switched off the shower I noticed that the isolator switch was stuck in the on position. The light comes on, but the water isn't coming through.'

'I'll start with the switch, then. Do you have a screwdriver? Otherwise I'll go and get one from my place.'

'The toolbox is downstairs. I'll get it for you.'

'Thanks. I'll turn off the miniature circuit-breaker.'

He went off to disconnect the electricity and a few minutes later he unscrewed the switch and began to inspect it. 'It looks as though this is the problem,' he said, showing her. 'The connections are blackened.'

'Is that bad? Do I need to be worried about the wiring?'

He shook his head. 'It often happens with these things. They burn out. I'll pick up another switch from the supplier in town and get someone to come over and fix it for you. I know an electrician who works at the hospital—I'll ask him to call in.'

'Oh, that's brilliant…' She frowned. 'If he'll do it, that is…'

'He will. He owes me a favour or two, so I'm sure he won't mind turning out for this. In the meantime, if you want to get a few things together—you can come over to my place to use the shower, if you like?'

'Really?' Her eyes widened and she gave him a grateful smile. 'I'd like that very much, thank you.'

She hurried away to collect a change of clothes and a towel, everything that she thought she would need, and then they went over to his part of the house.

She looked around. The first time she had been here

she'd been so taken aback by his revelation about the inheritance, and everything had been a bit of a blur, so she hadn't taken much in.

But now she saw that his living room was large and airy, with a wide window looking out on to a well-kept lawn and curved flower borders. He'd kept the furnishing in here simple, uncluttered, with two cream-coloured sofas and an oak coffee table that had pleasing granite tile inserts. There was a large, flat-screen TV on the wall. The floor was golden oak, partially covered by an oriental patterned rug. It was a beautiful, large annexe—what could have persuaded Aunt Annie to leave him all this?

'I'm afraid I'm on call today with the first-response team,' he said, cutting into her thoughts, 'so if I have to leave while you're in the shower, just help yourself to whatever you need—there's tea and coffee in the kitchen and cookies in the jar. Otherwise I'll be waiting for you in here.'

He paused, sending her a look that was part teasing, part hopeful. Heat glimmered in the depths of his grey eyes. 'Unless, of course, you need a hand with anything in the bathroom? I'd be happy to help out. More than happy…'

She gave a soft, uncertain laugh, not quite sure how to respond to that. 'Well, uh…that's a great offer, but I think I'll manage, thanks.'

He contrived to look disappointed and amused all at the same time. 'Ah, well…another day, perhaps?'

'In your dreams,' she murmured.

She went upstairs to the bathroom, still thinking about his roguish suggestion. It was hard to admit, but she was actually more than tempted. He was strong, incredibly good looking, hugely charismatic and very capable…he'd shown that he was very willing to help out with anything around the place.

So why had she turned him down? She was a free spirit after all, with no ties. The truth was, she'd no idea how she'd been before, but right now she was deeply wary of rushing into anything, and she'd only known him for a very short time.

Or had she? He'd said they'd known one another for quite a while, years, in fact. What kind of relationship had that been? For his part, he was definitely interested in her and he certainly seemed keen to take things further.

But she still wasn't sure she could trust him. He was charming, helpful, competent…weren't those the very qualities that might have made her aunt want to bequeath him part of her home?

She sighed. It was frustrating to have so many unanswered questions.

Going into the bathroom, she tried to push those thoughts to one side as she looked around. This room was all pearly white, with gleaming, large rectangular tiles on the wall, relieved by deeply embossed border tiles in attractive pastel colours. There was a bath, along with the usual facilities, and in the corner there was a beautiful, curved, glass-fronted shower cubicle.

Under the shower spray, she tried to relax and let the

warm water soothe away her troubled thoughts. Perhaps she should learn to trust, and take comfort in the knowledge that Matt had only ever been kind to her.

So far, he had been there for her, doing his best to help her settle in. She had been the only stumbling block to his initial efforts by being suspicious of his motives around her aunt. Perhaps she should do her best to be a little more open to him.

Afterwards, she towelled her hair dry and put on fresh clothes, jeans that clung to her in all the right places, and a short-sleeved T-shirt the same blue as her eyes. She didn't want to go downstairs with wet hair, but there was no hairdryer around so she didn't really have a choice. Still, even when damp her hair curled riotously, so perhaps she didn't look too bad.

Anyway, if Matt had been called away to work, it wouldn't matter how she looked, would it?

'Hi.' He smiled as she walked into the living room. 'You look fresh and wholesome—like a beautiful water nymph.'

She returned his smile. 'Thanks. And thanks for letting me use the shower. Perhaps I ought to go back to my place and find my hairdryer.'

'Do you have to do that? I'm making some lunch for us. I heard the shower switch off, so I thought you might soon be ready to eat. We could take the food outside, if you want. The sun will dry your hair.'

'Oh…okay. I wasn't expecting that. It sounds good.'

They went outside on to a small, paved terrace, and he set out food on a wrought-iron table, inviting her to sit down while he went to fetch cold drinks. He'd made pizza slices, topped with mozzarella cheese, tomato and peppers, along with a crisp side salad.

He came back holding a tray laden with glass tumblers and a jug of mixed red fruit juice topped with slices of apple, lemon and orange.

'I can bring you some wine, if you prefer,' he said, sitting down opposite her. 'I can't have any myself in case I have to go out on a job.'

'No, this will be fine,' she told him. 'It looks wonderful.'

'It is. Wait till you taste it.'

The food was good, and the juice, which had a hint of sparkling soda water in it, was even better than it looked. 'This has been a real treat for me,' she said a little later, when they'd finished a simple dessert of ice cream and fresh raspberries. 'Everything was delicious.' She mused on that for a moment. 'I don't remember when someone last prepared a meal for me.'

'I'm glad you enjoyed it.' He sent her a sideways glance. 'Actually, Annie made meals for both of us sometimes—whenever you came over here to visit she would cook, or put out buffet-style food, or occasionally she would ask me to organise the barbecue so that we could eat outside and enjoy the summer evenings. Sometimes she would ask the neighbours to join us.' He watched her carefully. 'Don't you have any memory of that?'

'No…' She tried to think about it, grasping at fleeting images with her mind, but in the end she had to admit defeat. Then a stray vision came out of nowhere, and she said quickly, 'Except—there was one time… I think I'd been out somewhere—to work, or to see friends—then somehow I was back here and everything was wrong.'

He straightened up, suddenly taut and a bit on edge. Distracted, she sent him a bewildered glance. 'I don't know what happened, but the feelings are all mixed up inside me. I know I was desperately unhappy and I think Aunt Annie put her arms around me to comfort me.' She frowned. 'How can I not remember? It's as though I'm distracted all the while, all over the place in my head. Why am I like this?'

It was a plea for help and he said softly, 'You probably feel that way because it's as though part of you is missing. Your mind is still the one bit of you that needs to heal. And perhaps deep down, for some reason, you're rejecting what's already there, hidden inside you. Give it time. Don't try so hard, and I expect it'll come back to you in a few weeks or months.'

'Weeks or months…when am I ever going to get back to normal?' There was a faint thread of despair in her voice. 'I should be working, earning a living, but how do I do that when I don't even know what it's like to be a doctor?'

He didn't answer. His phone rang at that moment, cutting through their conversation, and she noticed that the call came on a different mobile from his everyday phone. He immediately became alert.

'It's a job,' he said, when he had finished speaking to Ambulance Control, 'so I have to go. I'm sorry to leave you, Saffi, but I'm the nearest responder.'

'Do you know what it is, what's happened?'

He nodded. 'A six-year-old boy has been knocked down by a car. The paramedics are asking for a doctor to attend.' He stood up, grim-faced, and made to walk across the terrace, but then he stopped and looked back at her. He made as if to say something and then stopped.

'What is it?' she asked.

He shook his head. 'It's nothing.'

He made to turn away again and she said quickly, 'Tell me what's on your mind, please.'

'I wondered if you might want to come with me? It might be good for you to be out there again, to get a glimpse of the working world. Then again, this might not be the best call out for you, at this time.' He frowned. 'It could be bad.'

She hesitated, overwhelmed by a moment of panic, a feeling of dread that ripped through her, but he must have read her thoughts because he said in a calm voice, 'You wouldn't have to do anything. Just observe.'

She sucked in a deep breath. 'All right. I'll do it.' It couldn't be so bad if she wasn't called on to make any de-cisions, could it? But this was a young child...that alone was enough to make her balk at the prospect. Should she change her mind?

Matt was already heading out to the garage, and she hurried after him. This was no time to be dithering.

They slid into the seats of the rapid-response vehicle, a car that came fully equipped for emergency medical situations, and within seconds Matt had set the sat nav and was driving at speed towards the scene of the accident. He switched on the flashing blue light and the siren and Saffi tried to keep a grip on herself. All she had to do was observe, he'd said. Nothing more. She repeated it to herself over and over, as if by doing that she would manage to stay calm.

'This is the place.'

Saffi took in everything with a glance. A couple of policemen were here, questioning bystanders and organising traffic diversions. An ambulance stood by, its rear doors open, and a couple of paramedics hid her view of the injured child. A woman was there, looking distraught. Saffi guessed she was the boy's mother.

Matt was out of the car within seconds, grabbing his kit, along with a monitor and paediatric bag.

With a jolt, Saffi realised that she recognised the equipment. That was a start, at least. But he was already striding purposefully towards his patient, and Saffi quickly followed him.

Her heart turned over when she saw the small boy lying in the road. He was only six…six years old. This should never be happening.

After a brief conversation with the paramedics, Matt crouched down beside the child. 'How are you doing?' he asked the boy.

The child didn't answer. He was probably in shock. His eyes were open, though, and Matt started to make a quick examination.

'My leg…don't touch my leg!' The boy suddenly found his voice, and Matt acknowledged that with a small intake of breath. It was a good sign that he was conscious and lucid.

'All right, Charlie. I'll be really careful, okay? I just need to find out where you've been hurt, and then I'll give you something for the pain.'

Matt shot Saffi a quick look and she came to crouch beside him. 'He has a fractured thigh bone,' he said in a low voice so that only she could hear. 'He's shivering— that's probably a sign he's losing blood, and he could go downhill very fast. I need to cannulate him, get some fluid into him fast, before the veins shut down.'

He explained to Charlie and his mother what he was going to do. The mother nodded briefly, her face taut, ashen.

Saffi could see that the boy's veins were already thin and faint, but Matt managed to access one on the back of the child's hand. He inserted a thin tube and taped it securely in place, then attached a bag of saline.

The paramedics helped him to splint Charlie's leg, but just as they were about to transfer him to the trolley the boy went deathly pale and began to lose consciousness.

Matt said something under his breath and stopped to examine him once more.

'It could be a pelvic injury,' Saffi said worriedly, and Matt nodded. He wouldn't have been able to detect that through straightforward examination.

'I need to bind his pelvis with a sheet or something. He must have internal injuries—we need to get more fluids into him.'

One of the paramedics hurried away to the ambulance

and came back with one of the bed sheets. Matt and the two men carefully tied it around the child's hips to act as a splint, securing the suspected broken bones and limiting blood loss. Saffi noted all that and moved forward to squeeze the saline bag, trying to force the fluid in faster.

Matt glanced at her, his eyes widening a fraction, but he nodded encouragement. She'd acted out of instinct and he must have understood that.

A minute or two later, the paramedics transferred Charlie to the ambulance, and Matt thrust his car keys into Saffi's hands. 'I'm going with him to the hospital,' he said. 'Do you think you could follow us? I'll need transport back afterwards. Are you still insured to drive?'

She stared at the keys. She'd not driven since the accident, not because she didn't know how but because, for some reason, she was afraid to get behind the wheel. It didn't make sense—her accident had been nothing to do with being in a car.

'Saffi?'

'Y-yes. I'll follow you.' She had to know if the boy was safe.

He left her, and she went to the car, opening the door and sliding into the driver's seat. She gripped the wheel, holding onto it until her knuckles whitened. She couldn't move, paralysed by fear. Then she saw the ambulance setting off along the road, its siren wailing. Charlie was unconscious in there, bleeding inside. His life was balanced on a knife-edge.

Saffi wiped the sweat from her brow and turned the

key in the ignition. She had to do this. Her hand shook as she moved the gear lever, but she slowly set the car in motion and started on the journey to the nearest hospital.

Matt was already in the trauma room when she finally made it to her destination. 'How is he? What's happening?' she asked.

'It's still touch and go. They're doing a CT scan right now.'

'Do you want to wait around to see how he goes on?'

'I do, yes.'

'Okay.' She thought of the boy, looking so tiny as he was wheeled into the ambulance. Tears stung her eyelids and she brushed them away. She was ashamed of showing her emotions this way. Doctors were supposed to be in control of themselves, weren't they?

It had been a mistake for her to come here. She wasn't ready for this.

Matt put his arm around her. 'It'll be a while before we know anything,' he said. 'We could go and wait outside in the seating area near the ambulance bay. They'll page me when they have any news.'

She let him lead the way, and they sat on a bench seat next to a grassed area in the shade of a spreading beech tree.

He kept his arm around her and she was glad of that. It comforted her and made her feel secure, which was odd because in her world she'd only known him for just a few days.

She was confused by everything that was happening and by her feelings for Matt. Her emotions were in chaos.

CHAPTER THREE

'ARE YOU OKAY?' Matt held Saffi close as they sat on the bench by the ambulance bay. 'It was a mistake to bring you here. I shouldn't have put you through all that—it's always difficult, dealing with children.'

He pressed his lips together briefly. 'I suppose I thought coming with me on the callout might spark something in you, perhaps bring back memories of working in A and E.'

'It did, and I'm all right,' she said quietly. 'It was a wake-up call. Seeing that little boy looking so white-faced and vulnerable made me realise I've no business to be hanging around the house feeling sorry for myself.'

'I don't think you've been doing that. You've had a lot to deal with in these last few months, first with your aunt's death and then the head injury coming soon afterwards. Your aunt was like a mother to you, and losing her was traumatic. No one would blame you for taking time out to heal yourself.'

'You'd think I'd remember something like that, wouldn't you?' She frowned. 'But I do keep getting these images of how she was with me, of moments we shared.

The feelings are intense, but then they disappear. It's really bewildering.'

'It's a good sign, though, that you're getting these flashbacks, don't you think? Like I said, you should try not to get yourself too wound up about it. Things will come back to you, given time.'

'Yes.' She thought of the little boy who was so desperately ill, being assessed by the trauma team right now. 'I can't imagine what Charlie's parents must be going through. This must be a desperate time for them. What are his chances, do you think?'

'About fifty-fifty at the moment. He lost a lot of blood and went into shock, but on the plus side we managed to compensate him with fluids and we brought him into hospital in quick time. Another thing in his favour is that Tim Collins is leading the team looking after him. He's a brilliant surgeon. If anyone can save him, he's the man.'

He sent her a thoughtful glance. 'You came up with the diagnosis right away, and knew we had to push fluids into him fast. That makes me feel a bit less guilty about bringing you out here, if it was worth it in the end.'

She gave him a faint smile. 'It was instinctive…but there was no pressure on me at the time. I don't know how I would cope by myself in an emergency situation. There's been a huge hole in my life and it's made me wary about everything. I doubt myself at every step.'

He nodded sympathetically. 'At least it was a beginning.' He stretched his legs, flexing his muscles, and glanced around. 'Shall we go and walk in the grounds for a while? It could be some time before they page us with the results.'

'Okay. That's a good idea. Anything would be better than sitting here, waiting.'

They walked around the side of the hospital over a grassed area where a track led to a small copse of silver-birch trees. There were wild flowers growing here, pinky-white clover and blue cornflowers, and here and there patches of pretty white campion.

Beyond the copse they came across more grass and then a pathway that they followed for several minutes. It led them back to the hospital building and they discovered an area where wooden tables and bench seats were set out at intervals. Saffi looked around and realised they were outside the hospital's restaurant.

It was late afternoon, and there were few people inside the building, and none but themselves outside. They chose a table on a quiet terrace and Saffi sat down once more.

'I'll get us some drinks,' Matt said, and came back a few minutes later with a couple of cups of coffee. 'This'll perk you up a bit,' he murmured. 'All you need is a bit of colour in your cheeks and you'll soon be back to being the girl I once knew.'

'Will I?' She looked at him, her eyes questioning him. 'You don't think she's gone for ever, then?'

He shook his head. 'No, Saffi. The real you is there, under the surface, just waiting to come out.'

He sat beside her and she sipped her coffee, conscious that he was watching her, his gaze lingering on her honey-coloured hair and the pale oval of her face.

After a while, she put down her cup and said thoughtfully, 'How well did you and I know one another?'

He seemed uncomfortable with the question, but he said warily, 'Well enough.'

His smoke-grey glance wandered over the pale gold of her shoulders and shifted to the pink, ripe fullness of her lips. Sudden heat flickered in his eyes, his gaze stroking her with flame as it brushed along her mouth, and despite her misgivings an answering heat rose inside her, a quiver of excitement running through her in response.

He was very still, watching her, and perhaps she had made some slight movement towards him—whatever the reason, he paused only for a second or two longer, never lifting his gaze from her lips, and as he leaned towards her she knew instinctively what he meant to do. He was overwhelmingly masculine, achingly desirable, and she was drawn to him, compelled to move closer, much closer to know the thrill of that kiss. Yet at the same time a faint ripple down her spine urged caution as though there was some kind of hidden danger here, a subtle threat to her peace of mind.

A clattering noise came from inside the restaurant, breaking the spell, and she quickly averted her gaze. She'd wanted him to kiss her, yearned for it, and that knowledge raced through every part of her being. Through all her doubts and hesitation she knew she was deeply, recklessly attracted to him.

She took a moment to get herself together again, and

when she turned to him once more she saw that there was a brooding, intent look about him, as though he, too, had been shaken by the sudden intrusion.

'You didn't really answer my question,' she said softly. '"Well enough" hardly tells me anything. Why are you keeping me in the dark?'

He looked uncomfortable. 'I…uh…I think it's probably better if you remember for yourself—that way, you won't have any preconceived ideas. In the meantime, we can get to know each other all over again, can't we?'

She stared at him in frustration, wanting to argue the point. Why wouldn't he open up to her about this? But his pager went off just then and he immediately braced himself.

'They're prepping Charlie for surgery,' he told her after a moment or two. 'I'll go and find out what came up on the CT scan.'

'I'll go with you.'

'Are you sure you're ready to do this?' He looked at her doubtfully.

'Yes. I'm fine.' She'd now recovered from her earlier bout of tearfulness and she should be more able to cope with whatever lay ahead. Perhaps she just hadn't been ready to face that situation… It was one thing coming back to medicine, but quite another to find herself caught up in the middle of one of the worst possible incidents. No one, not even doctors, wanted to come across an injured child.

'Hi, boss,' the registrar greeted Matt as they arrived back in the trauma unit.

Saffi looked at Matt in astonishment. He was in charge here? That was another shock to her system. No wonder he exuded confidence and seemed to take everything in his stride.

'Hi, Jake. What did they come up with in Radiology?'

Jake showed them the films on the computer screen. 'It's pretty bad, I'm afraid.'

Saffi winced when she saw the images, and Matt threw her a quick glance and said quietly, 'You know what these show?'

She nodded. 'He has a lacerated spleen as well as the leg injury, and there's definitely a fracture of the pelvis.'

'He's lost a lot of blood but he's stable for the moment, at any rate,' Jake said. 'We don't know yet if he'll have to lose the spleen. Mr Collins will take a look and then decide what needs to be done. The boy's going to be in Theatre for some time.' He hesitated. 'You know, there's nothing more you can do here. You'd be better off at home.'

'I know, you're right,' Matt agreed with a sigh. 'Thanks, Jake.'

He walked with Saffi back to the car park a few minutes later. 'You weren't too sure about driving here, were you?' he said. 'How did it go?'

'It was difficult at first, but then it became easier.' She pulled a face. 'I suppose I should have persevered a bit more before getting rid of my car.'

He opened the passenger door for her. 'I suspected there was more to it when you sold your car…some kind of problem with driving. It might not be a bad idea to get

yourself some transport now that you've made a start...
keep up the good work, so to speak. It would be a shame
if you were to lose your nerve again.'

She studied him thoughtfully as he slid behind the
wheel and started the engine. Then she said in a faintly
accusing tone, 'You did it on purpose, didn't you—giving me the keys? What would have happened if I'd refused? How would you have managed to get home?'

'Same way as always. I'd have cadged a lift back with
the paramedics or hailed a taxi. Sometimes the police
will drive the car to the hospital for me.' His mouth
twitched. 'I was pretty sure you could do it, though.
You're not one to give up easily.'

She frowned. 'That makes two trials you've put me
through in one day—I suppose I can expect more of this
from you? Do you have some sort of interest in me getting back on form?'

He thought about that. 'I might,' he said with a smile.
'Then again...' He frowned, deep in thought for a second
or two. 'Perhaps it would be better if...' He broke off.

'If...?' she prompted, but he stayed annoyingly silent,
a brooding expression around his mouth and eyes. What
was it that he didn't want her to remember? What had
happened between them that he couldn't bring himself
to share? It was exasperating not being able to bring
things to mind in an instant. Would she ever get to know
the truth?

An even darker thought popped into her head...he had
grown on her this last week or so, but would she still feel

the same way about him if she learned what was hidden in their past? Perhaps that was what haunted him.

He parked up at the house, and she left him to go back to the annexe alone. It had been a long, tiring day for her so far, and she needed to wind down and think things through.

'Will you let me know if you hear anything from the hospital?'

'Of course. Though I doubt they'll ring me unless there's any change for the worse. No news is good news, so to speak.'

'Okay.'

She hadn't expected to remember so much of her work as a doctor, but it had started to come back to her when Charlie's life had hung in the balance. What should she do about that? Was she ready to return to work? Would she be able to cope on a day-to-day basis?

Anyway, she wasn't going to decide anything in a hurry. For the moment she would concentrate on getting back to normality as best she could. She would do as her doctor had suggested, and take advantage of her time here in Devon to recuperate, by doing some gardening, or wandering round the shops in town, and exploring the seashore whenever the weather was good.

The very next day she made up her mind to go down to the beach. They were enjoying a few days of brilliant sunshine, and it would have been sheer folly not to make the most of it.

The easiest way to get there from the house was via a

crooked footpath that ended in a long, winding flight of steps and eventually led to a small, beautiful cove sheltered by tall cliffs. She'd been there a couple of times since her arrival here, and she set off again now, taking with her a beach bag and a few essentials…including sun cream and a bottle of pop.

The cove was fairly isolated, but even so several families must have had the same idea and were intent on enjoying themselves by the sea.

She sat down in the shade of a craggy rock and watched the children playing on the smooth sand. Some splashed at the water's edge, while others threw beach balls or dug in the sand with plastic buckets and spades. Her eyes darkened momentarily. This was what Charlie should be doing, enjoying the weekend sunshine with his family.

There'd been no news from the hospital about the little boy, and she'd thought about giving them a call. But she wasn't a relative, and none of the staff at the hospital knew her, so she doubted they would reveal confidential information. She had to rely on Matt to tell her if there was anything she needed to know. He would, she was sure. She trusted him to do that.

She frowned. He was so open with everything else. Why was he so reluctant to talk about their past?

A small boy, dressed in blue bathing trunks, came to stand a few yards away from her. He was about four years old, with black hair and solemn grey-blue eyes, and he stood there silently, watching her. There was an empty bucket in his hand.

She smiled at him and put up a hand to shield her eyes from the sun. 'Hello. What's your name?'

'Ben.'

'I'm Saffi,' she told him. 'Are you having a good time here on the beach? The sand's lovely and warm, isn't it?'

He nodded, but said nothing, still staring at her oddly, and she said carefully, 'Are you all right? Is something bothering you?'

He shrugged his shoulders awkwardly and she raised a questioning brow. 'You can tell me,' she said encouragingly. 'I don't mind.'

'You look sad,' he said.

Ah. 'Do I?' She smiled. 'I'm not really. It's too lovely a day for that, isn't it?'

He nodded, but his expression was sombre, far too wise for a four-year-old.

'Are you sad sometimes?' she asked, prompted by a vague intuition.

He nodded again. 'It hurts here,' he said, putting a hand over his tummy.

Saffi watched him curiously, wondering what could be making him feel unhappy. Being here on the beach and being out of sorts didn't seem to go together somehow.

'Do you feel sad now?' she asked.

He shook his head. 'I did, a bit, 'cos I don't see Daddy every day, like I used to. But it's all right now.'

'Oh. Well, that's good. I'm glad for you. Are you on holiday here with your daddy?'

He shook his head. 'We live here.'

She looked around to see if his father was anywhere nearby, and saw a man just a few yards away, in rolled-up jeans and tee shirt, kneeling down in the sand, putting the finishing touches to a large sandcastle. When he stood up and looked around, Saffi's throat closed in startled recognition.

Matt came towards them. 'What are you up to, Ben? I thought you were coming down to the sea to fill up your bucket. Or have you changed your mind about getting water for the moat?'

Then he looked at Saffi and his eyes widened in appreciation, taking in her curves, outlined by the sun top and shorts that clung faithfully to her body. 'Hi...I wondered if I might see you down here some time.'

She nodded vaguely, but inside she was reeling from this new discovery. Matt had a son? That meant he was married—or at least involved with someone. It was like a blow to her stomach and she crumpled inside. Was this what he'd been trying to keep under wraps? No wonder she'd been guarded about her feelings towards him... her subconscious mind had been warning her off...but weren't those warnings all too late?

Ben was looking at Matt with wide-eyed innocence. 'I do want to finish the moat. I was just talking to the lady.'

'Hmm.' Matt studied him thoughtfully. 'You know what we've said about talking to strangers?'

The boy nodded. 'But she's not a stranger, is she? I know her name. She's Saffi.'

Matt made a wry face, trying unsuccessfully not to smile at that marvellous piece of childish logic.

He shook his head, looking at Saffi. 'I guess I don't need to introduce you to one another. Ben seems to have taken care of all that for me.' He lightly ruffled the boy's hair. 'He's going to be staying with me for a week or so.'

'Oh, I see,' she said slowly, and then with a dry mouth she added quietly, 'I didn't realise you had a child. You didn't say anything about him.'

He raised his brows in surprise. 'You think I have a child? Heavens, no—that's not going to happen any time soon. I'm not planning on getting involved in any deep, long-term relationships.' He frowned. 'Once bitten, as they say…'

Saffi stared at him, feeling a mixture of relief and dismay at his words. He wasn't married. That was something at least. But as to the rest, she didn't know what to think. He'd spoken quickly, without giving the matter much thought, but it was clear his feelings were heartfelt. Once bitten, he'd said. Who had hurt him and made him feel that way?

Matt seemed to give himself a shake to get back on track and said, 'Ben's my nephew, my sister's child. I should have told you right away, but I think I was a little bit distracted with this talking-to-strangers business. I barely took my eyes off him while I finished off the drawbridge, yet he managed to wander off. I could see him, out of the corner of my eye, talking to someone, but you have to be so careful… It can be a bit of a nightmare, taking care of children.'

'Well, yes. I can see that it must be worrying.' She was still caught up in his comment about long-term relationships. So, when he flirted with her it was nothing more than a bit of fun, a light-hearted romance. Of course it was. Why would she have expected anything more? She barely knew him.

At least it was out in the open, though, and she would be on her guard even more from now on. She didn't think she was the sort of woman who would be content with a relationship that wasn't meaningful. Or was she? Her mind was a blank where past boyfriends were concerned.

Matt turned to Ben once more, crouching down so that he was at the boy's level. 'I think you and I need to have another serious chat some time, Ben. Do you remember we talked about strangers?'

Ben nodded.

'That's good. So, what would you say if a stranger came up to you and asked if you'd like a sweet?'

Ben thought about it. 'Um… Yes…please?' he answered in an overly polite voice, and Matt groaned.

'I've a feeling it's going to be a long conversation,' he murmured, getting to his feet. 'Do you want to sort through those pebbles in the other bucket, Ben? See if you can pick out the smallest.'

'Okay.' Ben went to do as Matt suggested.

Saffi smiled. 'How is it that you're looking after him?'

'Gemma's ill—my sister, that is. She hasn't been well for some time, but late last night she rang me and said she was feeling much worse. I went over there and decided she needed to be in hospital. She didn't want to go, and kept saying it was just stress, but I insisted. At the very least, I thought she needed to have tests.'

Saffi sucked in a quick breath. 'I'm sorry. That must have been upsetting—for you and for Ben—for all of you.'

'Yeah, it was a bit of a blow.'

'How has he taken it? He must miss his mother.'

'He's not doing too badly. I explained that she was poorly and needed to rest, and he thinks he's spending time with me so we can have fun together.' He looked at Ben once more. 'Why don't you put some of those pebbles on the wall of the sandcastle, while I talk to Saffi?'

The boy nodded, his eyes lighting up with anticipation. 'Okay.'

'What's wrong with her?' Saffi said, once the boy was absorbed in his new pursuit. 'Do you mind me asking?'

He shook his head. 'No, that's all right. We're not sure what the problem is, exactly. She's been feeling tired and nauseous for a few weeks now, with a lot of digestive problems, and yesterday she was vomiting blood.'

He glanced at Ben, to make sure he couldn't hear. 'That's why I took her to the hospital, so that the doctors can find the source of bleeding and cauterise it. They'll start doing a series of tests from tomorrow onwards to find out what's causing the problem.'

'It's good that your sister can rely on you to take care of things,' Saffi said. 'But how is it going to work out, with you looking after Ben? You have to be on duty at the hospital throughout the week, don't you?'

'Yes, but he'll be at day nursery some of the time, and

for the rest he'll be with a childminder until I'm free to look after him. We'll muddle through, somehow.'

He smiled at her. 'Anyway, it's good to see you here. Do you want to help us finish off this sandcastle? Ben's been nagging me to bring him down here and get on with it since breakfast this morning. Of course, he's not satisfied with plain and simple. The bigger, the better.'

She went over to the castle. 'Wow. It looks pretty good to me.' There were towers and carved windows and walls that surrounded different levels. 'It's fantastic,' she said, and Ben beamed with pleasure at her praise.

She looked at Matt. 'You must have been working on this all afternoon.'

'Pretty much,' Matt agreed. 'There's no slacking with this young man. He knows exactly what he wants.'

She watched the little boy arrange small pebbles on top of the castle's main wall. He did it with absorbed concentration, placing each one carefully.

'Shall I make some steps just here, around the side?' Saffi asked, kneeling down, and Ben nodded approvingly.

Matt knelt down beside her and added some finishing touches to the drawbridge. After a while he sat back on his heels and surveyed his handiwork.

'That's not looking too bad at all,' he mused, wiping the beads of sweat from his forehead with the back of his hand.

Saffi smiled at his boyish satisfaction. 'You look hot. Do you want a drink?'

He nodded and she rummaged in her canvas beach

bag until she found the bottle of pop. 'Here, try some of this.'

He drank thirstily, and when he had finished she offered the bottle to Ben. He took a long swallow and then went back to work with the pebbles.

She glanced at Matt, who was studying the castle once more. 'Has there been any news from the hospital?' she asked, having a quick drink and then putting the bottle back in her bag.

He nodded. 'I rang the hospital just before we left the house. Tim managed to repair Charlie's spleen, and stabilised the pelvis. He'll be non-weight-bearing for a while, and he'll have to wear a spica cast for a few weeks, while the fractures in his leg and pelvis heal, but he should gradually return to his normal activities. He came through the operation all right and Tim thinks he should recover well.'

'I'm so glad about that.' Saffi gave a slow sigh of relief. 'I don't suppose you found out how he is in himself?'

'He's obviously frail and shocked right now, but children are very resilient. They seem to get over things far quicker than we expect.'

He glanced at Ben. 'It all makes me thankful that it didn't happen to my own family. Though I guess I have Gemma to worry about now.'

Kneeling beside him, Saffi laid a comforting hand on his arm. 'You did the right thing, taking her to hospital. I'm sure they'll get to the root of the problem before too long.'

'Yes, I expect so.' He looked at her hand on his arm and overlaid it with his own. His fingers gently clasped hers and his gaze was warm as it touched her face softly. 'You're very sweet, Saffi. It's good to have you here.'

She smiled in response, but they broke away from one another as Ben urged them to look at his creation.

'That's great,' Matt told him. 'I think we can say it's actually finished now, can't we?'

'It's wonderful,' Saffi said.

She sat back and watched Matt and Ben, their heads together, admiring their handiwork.

A tide of warmth ran through her. What was not to love about Matt? She was drawn to him despite her misgivings. He was everything any woman could want… and yet instinct told her she had to steel herself against falling for him.

Didn't she have enough problems to contend with already? He wasn't the staying kind, he'd more or less said so, and the last thing she needed was to end up nursing a broken heart.

CHAPTER FOUR

SAFFI HEARD A rustling sound behind her and turned around to see that Ben had come into the garden. He stood, solemn faced, just a few yards away from her.

'Hello,' she said with a smile. 'You're up and about bright and early. Are you ready for school?'

He nodded, not speaking, but watched as she tended the flowers at the back of one of the borders. It was breakfast-time, but she'd wanted to get on with the work before the sun became too hot.

'I'm putting stakes in the ground so that I can tie up the gladioli,' she told him, guessing that he was interested in what she was doing but unwilling to talk to her. 'See? I've wrapped some twine around the stem.'

He stayed silent but seemed content to stay and watch her as she worked, and she wished there was some way she could bond with him, or at least reach out to him. What could be going on inside his head? Of course, he must be missing his parents. The disruption going on in his family was a lot for a four-year-old to handle.

'Sometimes the flower stems get too heavy and fall over,' she told him, trying to include him in what she was doing, 'or they might bend and break. Tying them like this keeps them standing upright.'

He nodded almost imperceptibly, and they both stood for a while, looking at the glorious display of flowers on show. There were half a dozen different colours, and Saffi was pleased with the end result of her work.

'It's time we were setting off for nursery school, Ben.' Matt came to find his nephew and smiled at Saffi. 'Hi.' His gaze was warm and in spite of her inner warnings her heart skipped a beat as her glance trailed over him.

'Hi.'

He was dressed for work in his role as the man in charge of A and E and the trauma unit, wearing a beautifully tailored suit, the jacket open to show a fine cotton shirt and subtly patterned silk tie.

'It's looking good out here,' he said, glancing around. 'You definitely have green fingers.'

Saffi glanced down at her grimy hands and made a face. 'In more ways than one,' she said with a laugh. 'I suppose I'd better go and clean up. I need to make a trip to the shops to get some food in. The cupboard's bare.'

'Uh-huh. That won't do, will it?' His glance drifted over her, taking in her dark blue jeans and short-sleeved top. There was a glint in his dark eyes. 'We can't have you fading away and losing those delicious curves.'

Her cheeks flushed with heat, but he added on an even note, 'I can give you a lift into the village if you like. But we need to leave in ten minutes.'

'Oh…' She quickly recovered her composure. 'Okay, thanks. I'll be ready in two ticks.'

She hurried away to wash her hands, and met up with Ben and Matt at the front of the house a short time later. They were waiting by the rapid-response vehicle, and as she slid into the passenger seat she asked softly, 'Are you on call again today?'

He nodded. 'Just this morning.'

She was puzzled. 'How does it all fit in with you working at the hospital?'

'Well enough, most of the time. There are some mornings or afternoons when I'm in the office, or attending meetings, rather than being hands on, so to speak, like today, so I fit in outside jobs when I can. Otherwise the call centre has to find other people who are available.'

He smiled. 'At least it means that this morning I can take Ben to nursery, rather than handing him over to Laura, his childminder. His routine's already disturbed, so I want to make things easier for him as best I can. He's been a bit unsettled, with one thing and another.'

'I noticed that,' she said softly. She glanced behind her to see Ben in his child seat, playing with an action figure. 'He's very quiet this morning. I suppose that's understandable, in the circumstances.'

Matt nodded. He parked up outside the day nursery and Saffi went with him to see where Ben would be spending the next few hours. The school was a bright, happy place with colourful pictures on the walls and stimulating puzzles and craft activities set out on the tables for the children.

The staff were friendly and welcoming, and one of

the women took Matt to one side to speak to him while Saffi helped the boy with his coat.

Matt came back to Ben a moment or two later. 'All being well, your daddy will be coming to fetch you at lunchtime,' he said, bending down to give him a hug. Ben's face lit up at the news. 'If he can't make it for some reason, Laura will come as usual. Anyway, have a good time…we'll see you later.'

Saffi and Matt waved as they left the school and went from there to the village store, where Saffi stocked up on essentials like bread, eggs and cheese. Later, as they walked back to the car, she talked to him about Ben's father.

'Does he work away from home a lot of the time?' she asked as they stowed her groceries in the boot alongside all the medical equipment. 'Only, the other day when we were at the beach, Ben told me he feels upset sometimes about not seeing his father so much.'

'Mmm…that's a difficult one. He *is* away a lot of the time…he works for a computer company and goes out to set up systems or resolve problems for business clients in the banking industry or health services. Sometimes it means he has to travel to Scotland, or Wales, or wherever the customer happens to be based. If their systems go down for any reason, he has to sort it out and recover any lost data.'

'Is that why Ben gets anxious—because his father's working life is unpredictable?'

'Possibly. Though he and Gemma have been going through a bad patch lately. That might be something to do with it. They decided to separate, and I think Ben has picked up on the tension. They haven't told him about the split, but most likely he's sensed some of the vibes.'

'I'm sorry. It must be really difficult for everyone.'

'It is, but at least James is home right now. I haven't actually spoken to him, but apparently he called the day nursery to let them know, and he also left a message for Gemma to say he would pick up Ben today—up to now I've tried calling him to let him know that Gemma is ill, but I haven't been able to reach him. I think he must have changed his number.'

'Oh, I see.' She sent him a quick glance. 'It's a bad time for you just now, having to look after Ben and with your sister in hospital. How is she? Is there any news?'

He grimaced. 'Not too much as yet. They're still trying to find what's causing her problems—they've done blood tests, and an endoscopy to check out her stomach and duodenum, and they've taken a biopsy. They're keeping her in hospital because she's very anaemic from loss of blood, and she's lost a lot of weight recently. Obviously, they want to build up her strength.'

'From what you've told me, I'd imagine she must have stomach or duodenal ulcers.'

'Yes, that's right, but the tests have shown they aren't due to any bacterial infection.'

His grey eyes were troubled and she said softly, 'It's worrying for you…if there's anything I can do to help, you only have to ask. I could watch over Ben for you any time you want to go and visit her.'

'Thanks, Saffi.' He squeezed her arm gently. 'I appreciate the offer…but Ben wants to see his mother whenever possible, so I'll probably take him with me.'

She nodded. 'Well, the offer still stands…if there's anything I can do…if you want to talk… A trouble shared is a trouble halved, as they say.' She waited while he closed the boot of the car. 'Do you have any other family?'

'Only my parents, but they don't live locally, and, like me, they're both out at work during the week, so they're not really able to help. And Gemma was desperate to have Ben stay close by.'

'It's good that you were able to look out for him.'

He nodded. 'The other alternative was foster-care, and I didn't want that for him.' His mobile phone trilled, and he quickly took the call, becoming quiet and alert, so she guessed it was the ambulance control centre at the other end of the line.

He cut the call and glanced at Saffi. 'Looks like you get to come along for the ride once again,' he said, a brow lifting questioningly.

She pulled in a quick breath, doubts running through her. Was she up to this? What if it was another child, like Charlie, whose life stood on the brink? Part of her wanted to pull out, to shut herself off from anything medical, but another, more forceful, instinct urged her to face up to her demons.

She nodded. 'Where are we going?' she asked, easing herself into the passenger seat a moment later.

'A riding stables—or, at least, an area close by them. A girl has been thrown from her horse.'

Saffi winced. 'That could be nasty.'

'Yeah.' He hit the blue light and switched on the siren and Saffi clung on to her seat as they raced along the highway, heading away from town towards the depths of the countryside.

A few minutes later, he slowed down as they turned off a leafy lane on to a dirt track that ended at a wide wooden gate, bordered on either side by a rustic fence and an overgrown hedgerow.

Saffi saw a small group of people gathered around a young woman who was lying on the ground. Someone was holding the reins of a horse, and a little further away two more riders stood silently by their mounts. Everyone looked shocked.

Matt stopped the car and removed his jacket, tossing it onto the back seat. He grabbed his medical kit and hurried over to the girl, leaving Saffi to follow in his wake. There was no sign of the ambulance as yet.

'What happened here?' he asked. 'Did anyone see how she fell?'

'The horse reared,' one of the bystanders said, her voice shaking. 'Katie lost her hold on him and fell. Then Major caught her in the back with his hoof as he came down again.'

'Okay, thanks.'

Matt kneeled down beside the injured girl. 'How are you doing, Katie?' he asked. 'Do you have any pain anywhere?'

'In my neck,' she said in a strained voice. 'It hurts if I try to move.'

Saffi could see that she was completely shaken, trau-matised by finding herself in this situation. For Saffi, it was heart-rending, knowing how serious this kind of in-jury could be. If there was a fracture in any of the neck bones, causing spinal-cord damage, this young woman might never walk again.

'All right,' Matt said in a soothing voice. 'It's best if you try to keep as still as possible, so I'm going to put a neck brace on you to prevent any further injury. Once that's in place I'll do a quick examination to make sure everything's all right. Okay?'

'Yes.' The girl was tight-lipped, ashen-faced with pain. She was about seventeen or eighteen, a slender girl with long, chestnut hair that splayed out over the grass.

Saffi helped him to put the collar in place, carefully holding Katie's head while Matt slid it under her neck. Then he fastened the straps and began his examination, checking for any other injuries.

'Shall I start giving her oxygen through a mask?' Saffi asked. Any damage or swelling in the area could eventually deprive the tissues of oxygen and add to the problem.

'Yes, please.' He went on checking the girl's vital signs. 'Heart rate and blood pressure are both low,' he murmured a short time later, glancing at Saffi. 'We need to keep an eye on that. I'll get some intravenous fluids into her to try and raise her blood pressure.'

She nodded. 'She's losing heat, too. Her skin's flushed and dry. We should get her covered up as soon as pos-sible.'

'Yes, it's most likely neurogenic shock. But first we need to get her on to a spinal board. I'll go and fetch it from the car.' He gave a brief smile. 'Last time I saw it, it was underneath a large sack of chicken feed.'

She pulled a face. 'Oops.'

He was soon back with the board, and quickly enlisted a couple of onlookers to help him and Saffi logroll their patient onto the board. 'We need to do this very carefully, no jolting. Is everyone ready?'

On a count of three they gently laid Katie on the board and then Matt covered her with a blanket before securing the straps.

As if on cue, the ambulance finally arrived, and Saffi sighed with relief.

Matt made sure the transfer into the vehicle went smoothly, and once Katie was safely inside, a paramedic stayed beside her to watch over her. The driver closed the doors and then walked round to the cab. Matt spoke to him briefly and a few seconds later Katie was on her way to the hospital.

'I'll follow her and see how she gets on,' Matt said. 'Do you want to come with me or should I call for a taxi to take you home?'

'I'll go with you,' Saffi said quickly. 'I want to know what the damage is.'

'Come on, then. I'll ask the paramedics if they can drop you off at home when they've finished at the hospital.'

He was as worried as she was, she could tell, from the way his mouth was set in a grim line. When they were almost at their destination, though, he relaxed enough to ask, 'How are you coping with all this…coming with me on callouts?'

'All right, I think. It's like stepping into the unknown…I'm a bit scared of what I'll find.'

'But you decided to come along anyway. That must have been hard for you…I could see you were in two minds about joining me.' He sent her a sideways glance. 'So what made you do it in the end?'

'I felt I had to see things through.' Her lips made a flat line. 'After all, this was my career before I fell down the stairs and lost my memory. I need to know if I can go back to it at some point.'

'Do you think that will happen?'

She sighed. 'I don't know. It's one thing to stand to one side and watch, but it's a whole different situation making decisions and holding someone's life in your hands.'

He nodded agreement. 'Yes, I can see how that would be difficult.'

He turned his attention back to the road, pulling up at the hospital a few minutes later. They hurried into the trauma unit.

'Hi, there,' Jake greeted him at the central desk, and smiled at Saffi. 'Are you here to find out about the girl from the riding accident?'

'We are,' Matt said. 'What's been happening so far? Have you been in touch with her parents?'

'They're on their way…should be here in about half an hour. She's been down to X-Ray and right now the neurologist is examining her reflexes. Her blood pressure's still low, so we're giving her dopamine to improve cardiac output.'

'And the heart rate? Has that improved?'

'It's getting better. She's had atropine, two milligrams so far.'

'Good. That's something, at least. Now, these X-ray films—'

'Coming up.' Jake brought up the pictures on the screen and Matt sucked his breath through his teeth.

'That's a C7 fracture. She'll need to go for surgery to get that stabilised. See if Andrew Simmons is available to come and look at her.'

'I will. I think I saw him earlier in his office.'

'Okay. She'll need her pain medication topped up and steroids to bring down the inflammation.'

'I'll write it up. Gina Raines is her specialist nurse. I'll let her know.'

Matt's head went back. 'Gina?'

Saffi frowned. It was clear he was startled by this information for some reason.

'Yes, she generally works at the community hospital, but she transferred over here a couple of days ago on a temporary contract. She's pretty good at the job, from what I've seen.'

'Oh, yes,' Matt said. 'She's certainly well qualified. She was always keen to get on.' His expression was guarded and Saffi wondered what had brought about this sudden change in him. Had he worked with Gina before this? From the sound of things, he knew her fairly well.

'It's all right, Jake,' he said briskly, getting himself back on track. 'I'll go and speak to her myself. Perhaps you could concentrate on chasing up Andrew Simmons.'

'I'll do that.'

Matt turned to Saffi, laying a hand lightly on her elbow. 'Are you okay to go home with the paramedics? They have to go through the village on the way to the ambulance station.'

'Yes, that's fine, as long as they don't mind helping me transfer my groceries from your car.'

'I'm sure they'll be okay with that.'

He seemed concerned about her and Saffi smiled at him. 'Don't worry about me. I know you want to see to your patient and I understand that you're busy.'

He relaxed a little. 'They'll be in the restaurant, getting coffee, I imagine, but I asked them to page me when they're ready to go.'

She walked with him to the treatment bay where Katie was being looked after by a team of doctors and nurses. The girl was still wearing the rigid collar that protected her cervical spine, and she looked frightened, overwhelmed by everything that was happening. A nurse was doing her best to reassure her. Was this Gina?

The nurse's glance lifted as Matt entered the room and there was an immediate tension in the air as they looked at one another.

'Well, this is a surprise,' she said. There was a soft lilt to her voice. She was an attractive woman with green eyes and a beautifully shaped mouth, and dark brown hair that was pinned up at the back in a silky braid. 'It's been quite a while, Matt.'

'It has. I—uh—wasn't expecting to see you here.'

'No. I'm standing in for the girl who went off on maternity leave.'

'Ah.' He cleared his throat, and Saffi guessed he was more than a little disturbed by this meeting. 'So, how's our patient doing?'

'She's very scared.'

'That's only natural.' He walked over to the bedside and squeezed Katie's hand gently. 'Your parents are on their way, Katie. They should be here soon.'

He spoke in a calm, soothing voice, comforting her as best he could and answering her questions in a positive manner. After a while, the girl seemed a little less tense.

Gina looked at him in quiet satisfaction as they walked away from the bedside. 'You were always good with the patients,' she murmured. 'You seem to have the magic touch.'

'Let's hope her faith in me isn't misplaced,' he said, his mouth making a taut line.

Gina glanced at Saffi, and her eyes widened a fraction. 'Saffi. I thought you were based in Hampshire? Are you working here now?'

'Um. No. I'm just visiting.' She was flummoxed for a while after Gina spoke to her. It seemed that the nurse knew her, as well as Matt, and that made her feel more confused than ever. How many more people would she come across that she didn't recognise?

'Saffi's been in an accident,' Matt said, giving the

nurse a strangely intent look. His pager bleeped and he quickly checked it, before adding, 'She has amnesia and she's here to recover.'

'Oh, I'm sorry.'

'It's all right.' Saffi was suddenly anxious to get away, her mind reeling with unanswered questions. Just how well did Matt and Gina know one another? Quite closely, she suspected, from the way Gina looked at him. Would they be getting back together again?

Her mind shied away from the thought. She realised she didn't want to think of Matt being with another woman, and that thought disturbed her and threw her off balance.

'I'd better leave you both to your work,' she murmured. 'I should be going now, anyway.' She turned to Matt. 'Was that the paramedics paging you a moment ago?'

He nodded. 'They're waiting by the desk. I'll take you over to them.'

'No, don't bother. You stay here and look after your patient.'

He frowned. 'If you're sure?'

'I am.'

'Okay, then. Bye, Saffi.'

'Bye.' She nodded to Gina and hurried away. More than ever she felt as though she needed to escape. How was it that Matt had crept into her heart and managed to steal it away?

The paramedics were a friendly pair, making up for the stress of the job they were doing with light-hearted humour. Word of the exchange between Matt and Gina must have travelled fast, because they were chatting about it on the journey home.

'Is she another conquest in the making, do you think?' the driver said with a smile.

His partner nodded. 'I wouldn't be surprised. I don't know how he does it. I could do with a bit of his charisma rubbing off on me.'

They both chuckled, and Saffi kept quiet. Heaven forbid they should see her as yet another woman who had managed to fall for the good-looking emergency doctor. Just how many girls had fallen by the wayside where Matt was concerned?

The paramedics dropped her off at the house and then left, giving her a cheerful wave.

She started on some chores, desperate to take her mind off the image of Matt and Gina being together. It bothered her much more than she liked to admit. She'd wanted to stay free from entanglements, but somehow Matt had managed to slide beneath her defences and now she was suffering the consequences.

Some time later, she glanced through the local newspaper, studying the advertisements for cars. One way or another, she had to steer clear of Matt before she became too deeply involved with him. She could finish up being badly hurt, and she'd been through enough already, without adding that to her troubles. Having her own transport would be a start. But was she ready to get back behind the wheel? That one time she'd driven Matt's car was still seared on her brain.

Around teatime, she went out into the garden to feed the hens. She filled up a bucket with grain from the wooden shed but as she was locking the door a huge clamour started up, coming from the chicken run. Filled with alarm, she hurried over there. Had a fox managed to get in? But hadn't Matt told her there was wire mesh under and around the base of the pen to keep scavengers out? Besides, there were solid walls and fences all around the property.

The hens were squawking, making a huge din, scurrying about, flapping their wings in distress, and she was startled to see that, instead of a fox, it was Ben who was behind the disturbance.

He was running around, shouting, waving his arms and shooing the hens from one end of the compound to the other. How had he managed to get in there? She looked around and saw an upturned plastic flower tub by the side of the gate. He must have climbed on it to reach the door catch.

'Ben! Stop that right now.' Matt strode towards the enclosure as though he meant business.

Ben stood stock-still, his face registering dismay at being caught doing something wrong, swiftly followed by a hint of rebellion in the backward tilt of his head and in the peevish set of his mouth.

Matt opened the door to the run and he and Saffi both went inside.

'I know you think it's fun to get the hens running about like this,' Matt said, 'but they're not like you and me…they could die from fright. You have to be careful around them.'

Ben's brow knotted as he tried to work things out in his head, and Saffi wondered if he actually knew what it meant to die from fright. He certainly knew from Matt's tone of voice that it wasn't a good thing. In the meantime, the hens went on squawking, still panicked.

'I'm sorry about this, Saffi,' Matt said. 'He's been fractious ever since I fetched him from the childminder.'

'It's not your fault.' She frowned. 'I thought he was supposed to be with his father this afternoon?'

'He was, for a while, but apparently James was called away again.'

'Oh, I see.' She made a face. 'That can't have helped.'

'No. Anyway, I'll take him away and leave you to get on.' He turned to Ben and said firmly, 'Come on, young man, we're going back to the house.'

The boy went to him as he was told, but there were tears of frustration in his eyes and Saffi's heart melted. He was obviously upset about his father and over-whelmed at being in trouble, and maybe all he needed was some kind of distraction therapy.

She cut in quietly, 'Perhaps it would help him to learn how to look after the hens instead of scaring them. I could show him how to feed them, if you like.'

Ben looked at him with an anxious expression and Matt smiled, relenting. 'That's a good idea. Thanks, Saffi.' He looked at Ben. 'You know, it's kind of Saffi to do this, so make sure you behave yourself.'

Ben nodded, the tears miraculously gone, and Saffi

showed him how to grab a handful of corn and scatter it about. He watched as the hens started to peck amongst the sand and gravel and giggled when they nudged his feet to get at the grain.

'You're doing really well,' Saffi told him. 'Your dad would be proud if he could see you now.'

'Would he?' He looked at her doubtfully, and then at Matt.

'Oh, yes,' Matt agreed. 'He would. Shall I take your picture? Then you can show him next time you see him.'

'Yeah.' Ben threw down some more grain, showing off and smiling widely at the camera, and Matt snapped him on his mobile phone. He showed him the photo and the little boy grinned in delight.

'I want to show Mummy.' Ben's expression sobered instantly and tears glistened in his eyes once more. 'I want Mummy.' His bottom lip began to tremble.

Matt put an arm around him and gave him a hug. 'I know you do. We'll go and see her at the hospital after tea.'

'We could pick some flowers for her,' Saffi said. 'I think she'd like that, don't you?'

'Yeah.' Ben rubbed the tears from his eyes and looked at her expectantly. 'Can we do it now?'

'Okay. Let me finish up here and we'll find some for you.'

They made sure the hens were contented once more and then Matt locked up and removed the flower tub from the gate while Saffi went with Ben into the walled garden, carrying a trug and scissors.

'I wonder what your mummy would like?' Saffi said, looking around. 'What do you think, Ben?'

'Those ones.' He pointed to a trellis that was covered with delicate sweet-pea blooms, and Saffi nodded.

'That's a good choice, Ben. I think she'll love those.' She started to cut the flowers, frilly pink-edged blooms along with pale violet and soft blues, placing them carefully in the trug on the ground. The four-year-old went down on his knees and put his nose against them, breathing in the scent.

She smiled. 'These were Aunt Annie's favourites. She planted them every year.' She put down the scissors and handed him the basket. 'I think that's enough now. Why don't you take them into the kitchen and I'll find a ribbon to tie round the stems?'

'Okay.' Ben hurried away, taking extra care with his treasure trove.

'You remembered…' Matt was looking at her in wonder, and Saffi stared at him, not knowing what he was talking about. 'Your Aunt Annie,' he prompted, 'planting sweet peas.' She gasped, stunned by the revelation.

She laughed then, a joyful, happy laugh, full of the excitement of new discovery. 'I remember her showing me how to grow them when I was a small child,' she said, suddenly breathless with delight. 'And then we picked them together and made up little wedding baskets for some children who were going to be bridesmaids.' She laughed again, thrilled by the memory and the unlocking of part of her mind that she had thought was gone for ever.

Matt put his arms around her. 'I'm really glad for you, Saffi.' He hesitated, then asked on a cautious note, 'Has it all come back to you?'

She shook her head. 'No, but I do remember living here when I was a child. She was a wonderful woman. She always had time for me and I loved her to bits.' There was sadness with the memory, and as he heard the slight shake in her voice, Matt held her close, knowing what she was going through.

'I think you've absorbed a lot of her qualities,' he said softly. 'You were so good with Ben just now. I'm not sure I would have handled the situation as well as you did. But now you've given him something to look forward to.'

She smiled up at him. 'He's not a bad boy, just over-whelmed with what's going on in his life right now. He's bewildered by what's happening to him. I feel the same way sometimes, so I think I understand something of what he's going through. His world has turned upside down.'

He sighed, gently stroking her, his hand gliding over her back. 'I know. I wish I could make things right for him…and for you. It was great just now to see you laugh. It lights up your face when you do that,' he said hus-kily, 'and when you smile, I'm helpless… I tell myself I must keep away, and not go down that road but, no matter how much I try to hold back, I just want to kiss you…I'm lost…'

Inevitably, the thought led to the action, and slowly he bent his head and brushed her lips with his. It was a gentle, heart-stopping kiss that coaxed a warm, achingly sweet response from her. As her lips parted beneath his, he gave a ragged groan as though he couldn't stop himself, and he held her tight, drawing her up against him so that her soft curves meshed with his long, hard body and her legs tangled with his muscular thighs.

She ran her hands over him, loving the feel of him. Elation was sweeping through her, the ecstasy of his kisses sending a fever through her blood and leaving her heady with desire—a desire that seemed altogether familiar all at once. She needed him, wanted him.

Had she been wrapped in his arms this way at another time? Her feelings for him were so strong... She loved being with him this way, feeling the thunder of his heartbeat beneath her fingers—could it be that she simply couldn't help falling for him? He'd been so caring, so supportive and understanding of her. Or was there more to it...had she felt this way for him long before this, before her memory had been wiped out?

'You're so beautiful, Saffi,' he whispered, his voice choked with passion. 'It's been so tough, being with you again after all this time, longing to hold you...and yet...I just can't help myself...'

He broke off, kissing her again, his hands moving over her, tracing a path along her spine, over the rounded swell of her hip, down the length of her thigh. It felt so good to have him touch her this way. It felt right...as though this was how it should be.

Her hand splayed out over his shoulder, feeling the strength beneath her palm. 'I want you, too,' she said. She ached for him, but her mind was suddenly spinning with unanswered questions. 'What happened to us, Matt? After all this time, you said…were we together back then?'

A look of anguish came over his face. 'In a way,' he said.

'In a way…?' She broke away from him, looking at him in bewilderment. 'What do you mean? What kind of answer is that?'

'I can't…' He seemed to be waging some kind of inner battle, struggling to get the words out, and finally he said in a jerky, roughened voice, 'I can't tell you how it was. I'm sorry, but…' he sucked in a deep breath '…I think this is something you need to remember for yourself.'

His eyes were dark with torment. 'I shouldn't have kissed you. I don't want to take advantage of you, Saffi… and perhaps for my own self-preservation I should have held back. I should have known better.'

She stared at him in bewilderment. What did he mean when he talked about self-preservation? What was so wrong in them being together—was he so determined against commitment? What was it he'd said before— *once bitten*? Had he been so badly hurt in the past that he didn't want to risk his heart again? But as she opened her mouth to put all these questions to him, his phone began to ring.

At the same time Ben came out of the house, looking indignant. 'I thought we were going to the hospital to see Mummy?' he said crossly. 'You've been ages.'

Matt braced his shoulders. 'We'll go soon,' he told the little boy.

'Do you promise?'

'I promise.' He looked at Saffi and held up the phone, still insistently ringing. 'I'm sorry about this,' he said on a resigned note. 'It might be about the girl in the riding accident.'

'It's all right. Go ahead.' She was deeply disappointed and frustrated by the intrusion, but she took Ben's hand and started towards the house.

The moment of closeness had passed. He might not be forthcoming about what had gone on between them before, but whatever his reasons one thing was for sure... it was much too late now for her to guard against falling for him. She had so many doubts and worries about him, but he'd grown on her and she didn't want to imagine life without him. She was already in love with him.

He pressed the button to connect his call. 'Hello, Gina,' she heard him say, and her heart began to ache.

CHAPTER FIVE

'CAN I DO that?' Ben watched Saffi as she picked runner beans, carefully dropping them one by one into a trug. It was the weekend and the sun was shining, and the only sounds that filled the air were birdsong and the quiet drone of bees as they went about their business. A warm breeze rippled through the plants, making the leaves quiver.

'Of course you can. Here, let me show you how to do it. We snap them off where the bean turns into stalk—like this, see?' He nodded and she added, 'Why don't you try picking some of the lower ones and I'll do these up here?'

'Okay.'

They worked together amicably for a while, with Ben telling her about his visits to the hospital. 'Mummy's still poorly,' he said. 'She's got lots of…um…acid…inside her, and it's hurting her. They don't know why she's got it.'

'I'm sorry to hear that, Ben. But the doctors are looking after her, and I'm sure they'll soon find out what's causing her to be poorly.'

'Yeah.' His eyes grew large. 'Uncle Matt says they're going to take some pictures of inside her tummy.'

'That's good. That should help them to find out what's wrong.' Saffi guessed he meant they were going to do a CT scan. She winced inwardly. That sounded as though they suspected something quite serious was going on.

'Hi, Saffi.' Matt came to join them in the garden, and immediately she felt her pulse quicken and her stomach tighten. He was dressed in casual clothes, dark chinos and a tee shirt in a matching colour, and it was easy to see why women would fall for him. His biceps strained against the short sleeves of his shirt and his shoulders were broad and powerful. He looked like a man who would take care of his woman, protect her and keep her safe.

'Hi.' She tried to shut those images from her mind, but even so her heart turned over as she recalled the meeting between him and the nurse. They'd known each other for a long time, and from the tension that had sparked between them she guessed there was still a good deal of charged emotion on the loose.

'It's a beautiful day,' she said, trying to get her thoughts back onto safer ground. 'Do you have plans for today, or are you on call?'

He shook his head. 'I don't have any plans. It's not really possible to make any while I'm looking after Ben.' He sent her a thoughtful, hopeful glance. 'I suppose we could all go down to the beach after breakfast, if you'd like to come with us?'

'Yay!' Ben whooped with excitement. 'Come with us, Saffi.'

Saffi smiled at the four-year-old. He hadn't said a lot to her over these last few days, being quiet and intro-spective, but if he wanted her to go with them, that was a heartening sign. It made her feel good inside to know that he had warmed to her.

'I'd like that,' she said. She sent Matt a questioning glance. 'What would you be doing if you didn't have to look after Ben? How do you usually spend your week-ends?' She didn't know much about his hobbies or inter-ests, but from the looks of him he must work out quite a bit at the gym.

He shrugged. 'Sometimes I swim—in the sea, or at the pool—or I might play squash with a friend. I go to the gym quite often. On a day like this, when there's a breeze blowing, a group of us like to go kite-surfing at a beach a bit further along the coast. There's a good southerly wind there and a decent swell.'

'Kite-surfing? I'm not sure if I know what that is.'

'You go out on the sea on a small surfboard, and with a kite a bit like a parachute. The wind pulls you along. It's great once you've mastered the skill.'

Her mouth curved. 'It sounds like fun. Why don't you join your friends? I'll look after Ben on the beach. We can watch the surfing from there. What do you think, Ben?'

'Yeah.' He was smiling, looking forward to the trip.

Matt frowned. 'I can't do that. It's too much to ask of you.'

'No, it's fine, really.' She started to move away from the vegetable garden, but at the same time Ben went to Matt to tug on his trousers and claim his attention.

'I want to see the kites…please, Uncle Matt,' Ben pleaded.

Saffi sidestepped him, trying to avoid a collision, and caught her heel against one of the bean canes.

'Ouch!' She felt a stab of pain as she untangled her foot from the greenery.

'What is it? Have you twisted your ankle?' Matt looked at her in concern, reaching out to clasp her arm as she tried to look behind her at her calf.

She shook her head. 'No. It's a bee sting.'

'Come into the house. I'll have a look at it.' He turned to Ben, who was watching anxiously. 'She'll be fine, Ben. Bring the trug, will you? Can you manage it?'

'Yes, I'm strong, see?' The little boy picked up the basket and followed them into the house.

'Sit down.' Matt showed her into the kitchen and pulled out a chair for her at the table. He reached for a first-aid kit from a cupboard and brought out a pair of tweezers. 'Let's get that sting out. Put your leg up on this stool.'

She did as he suggested. She was wearing cropped cargo pants, and he crouched down and rolled them back a little to expose the small reddened, inflamed area where the bee had stung her. Then he carefully pulled out the sting with the tweezers. Ben watched every move, his mouth slightly open in absorbed concentration.

'Okay, now that's out, we'll get something cold on the leg to help take down the swelling.' He fetched a bag of frozen peas from the freezer and laid it over the tender area. 'Are you all right?'

'I'm fine.' She made a wry face. 'It's not a good start to my beekeeping, is it?'

He smiled. 'I expect you disturbed it. They don't usually sting if you're calm with them and keep your movements slow. When you're working with the hives it might help if you go to them between ten o'clock and two in the afternoon, when most of the bees are busy with the flowers…and make sure you always wear protective clothing. That's what Annie told me.'

He looked at her leg, lifting the frozen plastic bag from her. 'That's not quite so inflamed now. I'll rub some antihistamine cream on it, and it should start to feel easier within a few minutes.'

'Thanks.' She watched him as he smoothed the cream into her leg, his head bent. He was gentle and his hands were soothing, one hand lightly supporting her leg while he applied cream with the other. She could almost forget the sting while he did that. She studied him surreptitiously. His black hair was silky, inviting her to run her fingers through it.

'How are you doing?' He lifted his head and studied her, and she hastily pulled herself together. She felt hot all over.

'I'll be okay now. Thanks.'

'Good.' He held her gaze for a moment or two as though he was trying to work out what had brought colour to her cheeks, and then, to her relief, he stood up. 'Do you want to stay and have breakfast with us, and then we'll head off to the beach? I'm not sure what we're having yet. Toast and something, maybe.'

'That sounds good.' She straightened up and made herself think about mundane things. It wouldn't do her any good to think about getting close up and personal with Matt. Look what had happened last time. He was fighting his own demons, and she was worried about all the other women who might try to take her place.

'I could take Ben with me to collect some eggs. How would that be?' She stood up.

'Dippy eggs and toast soldiers!' Ben whooped again and licked his lips in an exaggerated gesture. 'I love them.'

'Sounds good to me,' Matt agreed. 'But are you sure you don't want to rest your leg for a bit longer?'

'I'll be fine. Why don't you ring your friend and make arrangements to do some kite-surfing? We'll be back in a few minutes.'

She collected a basket from her kitchen and took Ben with her to the hen coop. There she lifted the lid that covered the nesting boxes and they both peered inside.

'I can see two eggs,' he said happily, foraging amongst the wood shavings. 'And there's some more.' He looked in all the nest boxes, carefully picking out the eggs and laying them in the basket. He counted them, pointing his finger at each one in turn. 'There's six.'

'Wow. We did well, didn't we?' Saffi closed the lid on the coop and made everything secure once more.

'Let's go and wash these and then we'll cook them for breakfast.'

'Yum.' Ben skipped back to the house, more animated than she'd seen him in a while.

Over breakfast they talked about kite-surfing for a while, and about how Saffi was coping with the day-to-day running of the property.

'It's fine,' she said. 'It's quite easy once you get into a routine—but, then, I'm not going out to work at the moment, so that makes a big difference.'

Thinking about that, she looked over to Ben. Keeping her voice low she said, 'At least you must be able to see your sister every day, with working at the hospital. How is she? Have they managed to find out what's causing her problems? Could it be anything to do with stress, with the marriage problems, and so on?'

'It's always possible, I suppose. But they're still doing tests—she'll be going for a CT scan on Monday.'

'It must be a worry for you. Do you manage to get together with your parents to talk things through?'

He nodded. 'They've been coming over here to visit her as often as they can. I think my mother will have Ben to stay with her next weekend.'

'That should give you a bit of a break, at least, and I expect Ben will look forward to staying with his grandmother for a while.'

She glanced at the boy, who was placing the empty top piece of shell back onto his egg. He was getting ready to bang it with his spoon.

'Humpty Dumpty,' he said, and they both smiled.

Still dwelling on news from the hospital, Saffi asked, 'Have you heard anything more about the girl who fell from her horse? How's she doing?'

'She's had surgery to stabilise the neck bones, and she's on steroids to bring down the inflammation, as well as painkillers. They'll try to get her up and about as soon as possible to make sure she makes a good recovery. I think she'll be okay. She's young and resilient and she has a lot of motivation to get well again.'

'That's a big relief.'

'Yes, it is.' He seemed pensive for a second or two, and Saffi wondered what was going through his mind.

She glanced at him and said tentatively, 'At the hospital, you seemed quite surprised to see the nurse…Gina. I had the feeling…were you and she a couple at one time?'

Perhaps they still were, or maybe he was planning to resume their relationship… Her mind shied away from the thought.

His mouth flattened. 'We dated for a while.'

'Oh.' She absorbed that for a moment or two. Wasn't it what she had expected? 'Did something happen to break things up? I suppose you moved to different parts of the country?' And now they were reunited once more in Devon…what was there to stop them taking up where they had left off? A shiver of apprehension ran down her spine.

'Gina wanted to take things to a more serious level.' He grimaced. 'I wasn't looking for anything more than a fun time.'

She winced inwardly. Was this the way he treated all

women? Hadn't he admitted as much? As far as she and Matt were concerned, at least he'd had the grace to say he didn't want to take advantage of her.

'That must have been upsetting for her.'

'Yes, I guess it was.'

She frowned. She couldn't see him simply as a man who played the field without any consideration for the feelings of the girls he dated. But if he did, there must surely be a reason for his behaviour. She didn't want to see him as a man who was only interested in seducing women with no thought for the consequences.

They finished breakfast and cleared away the dishes, and Matt started to get his kite-surfing gear together.

'I hope you're all right with this,' he said. 'We're usually on the water for about an hour.'

'I can keep Ben amused for that long, I'm sure.' She smiled. 'Are we about ready to go? I think the waiting's too much for him. He's running around like a demented bee.'

Matt laughed, and a few minutes later he crammed his kite and small surfboard into the back of the rapid-response car and they set off.

'How can you answer an emergency call if you're out on the water?' she asked with a quizzical smile as he drove along the coast road.

'I can't. I'd have to turn them down, and ask them to find someone else to go in my place, but if anything should happen when I'm back on dry land I'll be prepared. Usually I get to enjoy my weekends, but you never know.'

They went a few miles down the road until they arrived at the surfers' beach, a sandy cove, bound by rugged cliffs that were covered with lichens and here and there with moor grass and red fescue.

Matt parked the car and Saffi looked out over the sea as he changed into his wetsuit. He was wearing swimming shorts under his clothes, but it was way too distracting, seeing his strong, muscular legs and bare chest with its taut six-pack. 'From the looks of those people surfing, it must be an exhilarating experience,' she said.

'It is,' Matt agreed. 'If you're interested, I could teach you how to do it—just as soon as we get a day on our own. Do you do any water sports?'

'Um…I've a feeling I do. I know I can swim, anyway, and I think I might like to learn kite-surfing. It's mostly men who do the sport, though, isn't it?'

'Not necessarily. A lot more women are getting into it nowadays. You'd start with a trainer kite and learn simple techniques first of all.' He looked at her expectantly and she nodded.

She was getting her confidence back now, feeling stronger day by day, and maybe it was time to accept some new challenges.

'Maybe I'd like to try,' she said, and he gave her a satisfied smile. She breathed in the salt sea air. It was good to be with him out here, and to look forward to more days like this, but didn't she know, deep down, that she was playing with fire? She was getting closer to him all the time, when the sensible thing would be to keep her distance. It was quite clear he wasn't looking for any serious involvement.

He introduced her to his friends and she and Ben watched from the beach as they went out onto the water. Saffi walked along the sand with the contented little boy, helping him to collect shells in a plastic bucket, looking up every now and again to see the surfers wheeling and diving, letting the wind take them this way and that.

Ben kicked off his shoes and splashed in the waves that lapped at the shore, while Saffi kept a close eye on him, and then they walked back to the base of the cliff where he could dig in the sand.

She saw the surfers moving over the sea at a fast pace, some of them lifted up by the kites from the surface of the waves, skilfully controlling their movements and coming back down again to ride the water. The wind was getting up now, gusting fiercely, and she rummaged in her beach bag for a shirt for Ben.

'Here, put this on. It's getting a bit chilly out here.'

He stopped digging for a while to put on the shirt and then he gazed out at the sea. 'I can't see Uncle Matt,' he said. 'He's too far away.'

'There are two of them in black wetsuits…I'm not sure, but I think that might be him coming in to the—' She broke off, clasping a hand to her mouth in horror as she saw one of the surfers lifted up by a sudden squall. Was it Matt? His kite billowed, the fierce wind dragging him swiftly towards the cliffside so that he was powerless to do anything to stop it. He was hurtling towards the craggy rock face at speed, and Saffi's stomach turned over in sheer dread. As she watched, he hit the jagged rocks near the foot of the cliff and crumpled on to the sand below.

She saw it happen with a feeling of terror. Was it Matt? It couldn't be Matt…she couldn't bear it.

She sprang to her feet. 'Ben, come with me,' she said urgently. 'That man's hurt and I have to help him. We need to get the medical kit from the car.'

He didn't argue but left his bucket and spade behind as they hurried up the cliff path to the car. 'Is it Uncle Matt?' he asked.

'I don't know, sweetheart.' She rummaged in her bag for her phone and called for an ambulance.

'Will you make him better?'

She gently squeezed his hand. 'I'll do everything I can. But you must stay with me, Ben. You can't wander off. I need to know you're safe. Promise me you'll stay close by me.'

'I promise.'

'Good boy. It might not be very nice to see the man that's hurt, so you'll probably need to look away.' Heaven forbid it should turn out to be Matt. She studied him. 'Okay?'

He was solemn-faced, taking in the enormity of the situation. 'Okay.'

She whipped open the boot of the car, thankful that Matt had left the keys with her. She pulled out the heavy medical backpack and the patient monitor and then locked up the car once more and hurried back down the path as fast as she could go, with Ben by her side.

They had to make their way carefully over rocks to get to the injured man and all the time she was praying that it wasn't Matt who was lying there. Whoever it was, he was screaming with pain. A small crowd had gathered around him and she said, 'Let me through, please. I'm a doctor.'

People moved aside and she saw that two lifeguards were already by the man's side. One of them, white-faced, said quietly, 'His foot's twisted round at an odd angle. It's like it's been partly sheared off.'

Saffi pulled in a quick breath. Not Matt, please don't let it be Matt.

'I'll look at him,' she said, shielding Ben from what was going on. 'Would one of you keep an eye on the little boy for me?' She glanced around. 'Perhaps he'd be better over there, out of the way, but where I can still see him.' She pointed to a sheltered place in the lee of the cliff where there was enough sand for him to dig with his hands.

'Sure. I'll do it.'

'Thanks.' She looked down at the kite-surfer and a surge of relief washed through her as she realised it wasn't Matt lying there. It was his friend, Josh. She laid down her pack and knelt beside him.

'Josh, I'm a doctor…I'm going to have a look at you and see if I can make you more comfortable before we get you to hospital. Okay?'

'Okay.' He clamped his jaw, trying to fight the pain, and Saffi went through her initial observations. The foot was purple, with no great blood loss, and he was able to wiggle the toes on his other foot, as well as move his leg.

She didn't think there was any spinal injury but she needed to take precautions all the same, so she asked the lifeguard to help her put a cervical collar around Josh's neck.

Josh's pulse was very fast and his blood pressure was high, most likely because of the excruciating pain. That was going to make it difficult to move him. He might also have other, internal injuries, so the best thing to do would be to administer pain relief.

She asked both lifeguards to help her. 'I'm going to give him drugs to reduce the pain. As soon as I've given him the medication, we'll have to carefully roll him on to his back and set him up with an oxygen mask. Are you all right with that?'

'Yeah, that's okay.'

She glanced at Ben to make sure he was staying put, and then prepared to go on with the procedure. Thankfully, it wasn't likely that he could see much of what was going on, while three people were gathered around Josh. She made sure Josh was as comfortable as possible, looping the oxygen mask over his head.

There was a movement on the periphery of the crowd and she saw that Matt had gone to stand with Ben. She looked at him and he gave her a nod of support.

At the same time, the ambulance siren sounded in the distance, getting nearer.

'Thanks for your help,' she said to the lifeguards as she connected the oxygen cylinder to the tube. 'One last thing…I need one of you to help me get his foot back into the proper position.' If they didn't do that, the circulation could fail and the foot would be useless.

One of the lifeguards hesitantly volunteered. 'I don't know what to do,' he said.

'It'll be all right,' she said, reassuring him. 'I'll talk you through it. We need to give it a tug.'

He swallowed hard, but a few minutes later the foot pinked up, and she could feel that the pulses were present.

She sat back on her heels. The paramedics would help with splinting the foot and getting Josh onto a spinal board. Her work was almost done.

Matt came over to her, holding Ben by the hand, as they transferred his friend to the ambulance a short time later. He'd rolled down the top half of his wetsuit and Saffi couldn't take her eyes off him. He was hunky, perfectly muscled, his chest lightly bronzed. Her heart began to thump against her rib cage and her mouth went dry.

Together, they watched the ambulance move away, and as the crowd dwindled and people returned down the path to the beach Matt drew her to him, putting his free arm around her.

'You were brilliant,' he said. 'I thought about coming over to you to help, but I could see you had everything under control, the whole time. You were amazing. How did it feel?'

'Feel?' She stared at him blankly for a moment, not understanding what he was saying, and then realisation came to her in a rush. Without any conscious thought she'd acted like a true A and E doctor.

'I didn't think about what I was doing,' she said, her eyes widening. 'All I know is I was terrified it might be you who was injured, and I was desperate to make sure you were all right. I couldn't think beyond that. The adrenaline must have taken over.'

'That's my girl.' He hugged her close and kissed her swiftly on the mouth.

His girl? Her heart leapt and she returned his kiss with equal passion, a fever beginning to burn inside her. How did he manage to do this to her every time, to make her want him more than anything, more than any other man?

Where had that thought come from? She didn't remember any other man in her life before this. There must have been, surely? But somehow she was certain that Matt was the one man above all who could stir her senses and turn her blood to flame.

Ben started tugging at Matt's wetsuit. 'Can we go down to the beach? I want to make another sandcastle.'

Matt gave a soft groan and reluctantly broke off the kiss. 'Perhaps I should never have started that,' he said raggedly. 'Wrong place, wrong time.' He frowned. 'It's always going to be like that, isn't it?' he added with a sigh. 'I have to keep telling myself I must stay away, but when I'm with you it's so hard to resist.'

And she should never have responded with such eagerness, Saffi reflected wryly. She knew what she was getting into, and going on his record so far it could only end in sorrow, so why couldn't she keep her emotions firmly under lock and key?

CHAPTER SIX

'HAVE YOU THOUGHT any more about going back to work in A and E?' Matt asked. He'd popped home from the hospital to pick up his laptop, and Saffi was glad to see him, and even more pleased that he'd stopped to chat for a while. She missed him when he wasn't around.

It was lunchtime and she was hosing down the chicken run, a chore she did once a week to make sure the birds' living quarters were scrupulously clean. The hens were out on the grass, exploring the pellets of food she'd scattered about.

Matt seemed keen to know what she planned to do workwise, and she guessed it was because he cared enough to want her to be completely well again. Being able to do the job she'd trained for was a big part of that recovery process.

'I think it would do you good to go back to working in a hospital,' Matt said. 'It could help to bring back some memories.'

She nodded. 'I've been thinking the same thing. I'm just not sure I'd cope with the responsibility—what if I've forgotten some of the techniques I knew before?'

'I know it would be a huge step for you after you've spent the last few months getting yourself back on track, but you did so well looking after Josh—I think you proved yourself then.'

'Maybe.' She was hesitant. Was she really ready for it? He seemed to have a lot of faith in her.

'How is Josh?' she asked, switching off the hose and laying it on the ground. 'His foot was in a pretty bad state, wasn't it?'

'Yes, but he went up to Theatre and Andrew Simmons pinned it with plates and screws, and did a bone graft. It'll take a while to heal, and he'll need physiotherapy, but I think he'll be all right eventually.' He gave her a look of new respect. 'You saved his foot, Saffi. If you hadn't restored the circulation he could have been looking at an amputation.'

'I'm just relieved that he's all right.' She was thoughtful for a second or two. 'One thing I'll say—it's definitely put me off kite-surfing. Are you sure you want to go on doing it? I was worried sick when I thought you might have been hurt.'

'Were you? I'm glad you care about me.' He ran his hands down her arms in a light caress. 'I understand how you feel about trying it out. That's okay. And as for the other—I'm always careful to avoid going close to cliffs or rocks. You don't need to worry about me.'

'That's a relief.'

He studied her briefly. 'So what do you think about going back to work?'

'I don't know. Perhaps I could do it…but I always

thought I would know when the time was right because I'd have recovered all of my memories. It doesn't seem to be happening that way, though, does it?'

'Amnesia can be strange,' he murmured, 'but, actually, you've been doing really well. You've remembered your aunt and your career, and all the time, day by day, you're getting small flashes of recall. Perhaps by going back to your job things will begin to come back to you more and more.' He shooed a hen out of the flower border, where she'd been trying to eat one of the plants. 'Go on, Mitzi, back with the others.'

'You could be right. I don't know why it matters so much to me…but I feel…it's like I'm only half a person.' She looked at him in despair, and he took her into his arms.

'I can't bear to see you looking so forlorn,' he said. 'You mustn't think like that—anyway, you look pretty much like a whole person to me,' he added in a teasing voice. 'So much so that I think about you all the time…I can't get you out of my mind. You're beautiful, Saffi… and incredibly sweet. Look how you coaxed Ben to come out of himself.'

He gave her a gentle squeeze, drawing her nearer, and his words came out on a ragged sigh. 'It's getting more and more difficult for me to keep my resolve. Every time I look at you I want to show you just how much I want you.'

Having his arms around her was a delicious temptation but she couldn't give in to it, could she? Much as she wanted to believe every word he said, she had to make a strong effort to resist. At least, she had to do better than she'd managed up to now.

'Hmm…' She looked into his smoke-grey eyes. 'From what I've heard, that's what you say to all the girls.'

He pressed a hand to his heart as though she'd wounded him. 'It's not true. Would I do that? Would I?'

'I think that's open to debate,' she murmured.

He gave her a crooked smile. 'You're gorgeous, Saffi, and that's the truth, and I feel great whenever I'm with you. I have to keep pinching myself to believe that I'm actually living right next door to you.'

He was saying all the things she wanted to hear, but did she really want to end up as just another conquest? She couldn't get it out of her head what the paramedics had said. He had a way with women.

'You certainly do live next door—and that's another thing about you that confuses me,' she commented on a musing note, trying to ease herself away from him. 'I still haven't figured out why my aunt would leave part of the house to you. It doesn't make any sense to leave a house to be shared by two people who aren't related.'

She rubbed her fingers lightly over her temples in a circling motion to get rid of a throbbing ache that had started up there. Having him so close just added to her problems. She couldn't think straight.

'It's just another of those mysteries that I can't solve…' she murmured, 'but perhaps one day I'll get to the bottom of it. At the moment my mind's like a jigsaw puzzle with lots of little bits filled in.'

He became serious. 'I'm sure things will come back

to you if you start to live the life you once had. I mean it. Going back to work at the hospital could be the best thing for you. I need another doctor on my team, and you would be perfect. You could work part time if it suits you—in fact, that would probably be the best option to begin with.'

'You need someone? You're not just trying to find a job for me?'

'We're desperately short of emergency doctors. I'd really like you to say yes, Saffi, not just for me but also for your own well-being. We'll get clearance for you to work again from the powers that be, and maybe arrange for someone to work with you for a while. I'd keep an eye on you to begin with until you get your confidence back.'

He looked so sincere she knew he would watch over her, and part-time work did seem like the ideal solution for her at the moment. It would give her the best of both worlds and allow her time to adjust.

She swallowed hard. 'Okay,' she said. 'I'll do it.'

'Yay!' He swooped her up into his arms once again and kissed her firmly, a thorough, passionate kiss that left her breathless and yearning for more.

'That's wonderful, Saffi.' He looked at her, his grey eyes gleaming, his mouth curved in a heart-warming smile. 'We should celebrate. Let me take you out to dinner this evening.'

She smiled back at him. 'I'd like that,' she said, 'except…' she frowned '…I'm expecting a visitor at around nine o'clock. He's bringing some stuff I left behind in Hampshire—a few books, my coffee-maker, glassware, things like that. My flatmate has been looking after them for me, but Jason offered to bring them here. Apparently he's coming to Devon to take a few days' holiday.'

Matt frowned. 'Jason? You know this man? I thought you didn't remember anyone from where you lived?'

'No, I don't know him. I mean, I did, apparently, according to my flatmate. She's the only one I recalled after the accident, but even that was just bits and pieces that came back to me before I left Hampshire. Jason's a complete blank in my mind.'

'It seems odd that he's coming over so late in the evening?'

'I suppose it is, but he told Chloe he has to work today. He'll head over here as soon as he's finished.'

'That makes some kind of sense, I suppose.' He was still doubtful, a brooding look coming into his eyes as though he was already weighing up Jason as some kind of competition. His dark brows drew together. 'He must be really keen to see you if it can't wait till morning. Did your flatmate tell you anything about him?'

She could see he was suspicious of the man and his motives. 'No, she didn't, not really…not much, anyway. She mentioned something about us dating a few times. I remember he came to see me when I was in hospital, but I was getting distressed whenever I had visitors—they were all strangers to me and I was a bit overwhelmed by everything that was happening to me. I think the doctors advised her to let me remember things in my own time.' A feeling of unease washed through her. 'I feel bad about it…all those people I was supposed to know…'

'It wasn't your fault, Saffi.' He held her tight. 'Look, how about this—we could go for an early dinner. What do you think? I really want to spend some time with you. I'll make sure you're back here in time to meet up with this Jason...' he pulled a face '...even though I'd rather you weren't going to see him.' His eyes darkened. 'I don't like the idea of him taking up where you left off.' Once again, he was at war with himself. 'I hate the thought of you dating someone else.'

'I'm not dating him. I don't even know him.' She nodded thoughtfully. 'An early dinner sounds like a good compromise. But what will you do about Ben...or will he be coming with us? I don't mind, if that's what you want.'

He shook his head. 'His father's going to look after him. He's back from sorting out the latest crisis, and he says he's going to stay home for a few days.'

'Oh, that's good news.' She smiled. 'Ben will be really happy to see him.'

'Yeah. Let's hope he doesn't get unsettled again when James has to leave.'

She winced. 'You're right, he's really come out of himself this last couple of weeks. Do you think James will take him to see Gemma in hospital?'

'He said he would. He wants to know the results of the CT scan they're doing.'

Of course...they would be doing the scan today. Matt had told her about it. He must be worried sick about what it might reveal.

He checked his watch. 'I have to go. It's almost time

I was back on duty. I'll see you later. Dinner for about seven o'clock? Would that be all right?'

She nodded. 'I'll look forward to it.'

'Good. I'll book a table.'

It was only after he'd left for work that she realised she'd done it again—that she'd agreed to spend time with him when she should be putting up some barriers between them. Did she really want to end up like Gina, still hankering after him years later, when their relationship had run its course? And how would she get on with Gina if they had to work together? Had she made a mistake in agreeing to it?

She shook her head. It was done now, and she may as well throw caution to the wind and look forward to the evening.

What should she wear? After she'd showered and started her make-up later on in the day, she hunted through her wardrobe and picked out a favourite wine-coloured dress, one that she'd brought with her from Hampshire. It was sleeveless, with a V-shaped neckline and pleated bodice, a smooth sash waist and a pencil-line skirt. She put the finishing touches to her make-up, smoothing on a warm lip colour and adding a hint of blusher to her cheeks.

When Matt rang the doorbell at half past six, she was finally ready.

'Hi,' she said. 'I wasn't sure you'd make it here on time. I know how things can be in A and E. It isn't always easy to get away.'

'I handed over to my registrar.' He gazed at her, his

eyes gleaming in appreciation as he took in her feminine curves, outlined by the dress, and her hair, which was a mass of silky, burnished curls. 'You look lovely, Saffi. You take my breath away—you're the girl of my dreams.'

Her cheeks flushed with warm colour at the compliment. He looked fantastic. He must have showered and changed as soon as he had got home from work because his black hair was still slightly damp. He wore an expensively styled suit that fitted perfectly across his broad shoulders and made him look incredibly masculine.

They went out to the car and he drove them along the coast road to the restaurant. He was unusually quiet on the journey, a bit subdued, and she wondered if something had happened at work to disturb him. Was it something to do with his sister? Or perhaps he was simply tired after a stressful day. She remembered feeling like that sometimes after a bad day at work.

It might not be a good idea to bombard him with questions right away, though. If he wanted to talk to her about whatever it was that was bothering him, he would be more likely to do it after he had relaxed into the evening a little.

He took her to a pretty quayside restaurant, and they sat at a table by the window, from where they could look out at the boats in the harbour.

'It's lovely in here,' she said, looking around. 'It's very peaceful and intimate.' There were screened alcoves with candlelit tables, a glass-fronted display cabinet showing mouth-watering desserts, and waiters who hovered discreetly in the background. 'It makes me want to skip the meal and go straight for the dessert,' she said, eying up the assortment of gateaux and fruit tarts.

He laughed. 'You always did go for the dessert.'

'Did I?' Her brow puckered. 'Have we done this before?'

He nodded cautiously. 'Don't worry about it,' he said. 'Just relax and enjoy the food.'

She tried to do as he suggested, but at the back of her mind she was trying to work out why, if they had been a couple at one time, they had drifted apart, with her working in Hampshire and Matt here in Devon. What wasn't he telling her?

Through the starter of freshly dressed crab served with asparagus spears and mayonnaise they talked about her starting work in a week's time, and then moved on to generalities, but Matt said nothing about what might be troubling him. They chatted and she could tell he was making an effort, being as considerate and thoughtful as ever.

He ordered a bottle of wine, and Saffi took a sip, studying him as the waiter brought the main course, sirloin of beef with red wine sauce. 'You're not yourself this evening,' she said softly, when they were alone once more. 'What's wrong?'

He blinked, and then frowned slightly. He wasn't eating, but instead he ran his finger around the base of his wine glass. 'I'm sorry. It's nothing. I'm just a bit preoccupied, that's all, but I didn't mean to spoil the evening.' He smiled at her. 'You were saying you were thinking of buying a new car?'

'Well, I'll need one if I'm going to start work. But that's not important right now. I want to know what's wrong, Matt. Something's troubling you. Is it your sister?'

He sighed heavily and then nodded. 'I've seen the results of the tests and the CT scan. They've diagnosed Zollinger-Ellison syndrome.'

She pulled in a quick breath. 'Oh, no...no wonder you're feeling down... I'm so sorry, Matt.' It was bad news. She laid her hand over his, trying to offer him comfort, and he gave her fingers an answering squeeze.

She really felt for him. Zollinger-Ellison syndrome was an illness caused by a tumour or tumours in the duodenum and sometimes in the pancreas, too. They secreted large amounts of the hormone gastrin, which caused large amounts of stomach acid to be produced, and in turn that led to the formation of ulcers. It was a very rare disease and there was around a fifty per cent chance that the tumours might be malignant. 'How is she? Does she know about it?'

'Yes, she knows. Obviously, it was a huge shock for her, but she was trying to put on a brave face for Ben.'

'Will they try surgery?'

He nodded. 'As a first stage of treatment, yes. The Whipple procedure would be the best option, but it's difficult and very specialised surgery, as you probably know. If the tumours have spread to other parts of her body they won't even consider it. We'll just have to take things one step at a time.'

'It's hard to take in. I've heard it might go better if

the patient has chemotherapy before surgery as well as afterwards.' She reflected on that for a while, knowing just how terrible it must be for Gemma and Matt to have to go through all this heartache.

She said, 'If there's anything I can do…does Gemma want any more books, or magazines, anything that will help to take her mind off things? I could perhaps find her some DVDs if she'd prefer?'

'Thanks, Saffi. I think she still has some of the magazines you sent last week. Maybe some comedy DVDs might help to take her mind off things for a while. Perhaps we can sort something out between us? I tried taking her fruit and chocolates but, of course, she has to be careful what she eats. Some things disagree with her.'

'We'll find something.'

They went on with their meal for a while, but somehow the pleasure in tasting the perfectly cooked meat and fresh vegetables had waned. She said quietly, 'Do your parents know?'

'Yes, I phoned my mother this afternoon. She was at work—she's a vet up in Cheltenham. She was so upset she said she was leaving everything and coming over right away.'

'I expect that will be good for Gemma.'

He nodded. 'My father's a GP in Somerset. He's going to try and get a locum to cover his practice for a while.'

'Your parents are divorced, then? I hadn't realised. Did that happen a long time ago?'

'When I was a child, yes.' His eyes were troubled. 'I was about eight years old when they broke up. Gemma

was younger. It was fairly traumatic for both of us…
though I suppose it often is for the children if it's a fairly
hostile split.'

He leaned back in his seat as the waiter came to clear
the dishes and take their order for dessert. He swallowed
some of his wine, and then refilled Saffi's glass.

'We chose to stay with my mother—Gemma and I.
My father could be distracted by work and we didn't always get to see much of him.' He pulled a face. 'Then
about three years later my mother had a sudden illness
that affected her kidneys and we were taken into foster-
care for a while.'

Saffi sucked in a breath. 'Is she all right now? It must
have been a double blow to go through the break-up of
your family and then to have that happen.' She frowned,
trying to imagine what it would have been like to endure
such an emotional upset.

'I think she's all right. While she was in hospital,
they managed to prevent the worst of the kidney damage, but she has to take medication now to control her
blood pressure and cholesterol, to make sure there aren't
any further problems. She sees a specialist once a year,
and things seem to be going well for her, as long as she
follows the dietary advice he's given her.' He was quiet
for a moment. 'I think she's the reason I wanted to study
medicine.'

The waiter brought dessert, a pear tatin with vanilla
ice cream, and Saffi ate, almost without knowing what
she was eating. 'I'd no idea you had such a troubled

childhood,' she said. 'But I suppose it was better for you once your mother was out of hospital?'

'Yes, it was.' He toyed with his food. 'Gemma and I had been in separate foster-homes for quite a long time, and that was tough. We were taken away from everything that made us feel safe.' He lifted his glance to her. 'But I don't suppose it was much worse than what you went through. After all, your parents died, didn't they?'

'They did, but I was quite young when that happened. And I had Aunt Annie. She stepped in right away and was like a mother to me. My uncle was there as well until two or three years ago, so he became a father figure for me.'

She dipped her spoon into the tart and savoured the taste of caramelised fruit on her tongue. 'Did you see much of your father back then?'

'Quite a bit. We'd spend time with him whenever he had a free weekend, but then he married again and his wife already had children of her own. We didn't get on all that well with them. We tried, of course, but they were older than me and Gemma and I think they resented us.'

'Oh, dear. That doesn't sound good. It must have been awkward for you.'

He smiled. 'Probably, as children, you take these things more or less in your stride. It's only when you get to adulthood and you look back that you realise it could have been a lot better, or maybe that you could have handled things differently. I was more or less okay with my father getting married again, but when my mother did the same thing I wasn't too happy.' He pulled a face. 'I was quite rebellious for a time.'

Saffi studied him thoughtfully as he signalled to the waiter and ordered two cappuccinos. 'Do you think it's had an effect on you?' she asked when the waiter left. 'Now, I mean, as an adult.'

He mused on that for a while. 'Possibly. I suppose it makes you cautious. But it's probably worse when you're an adolescent. Your emotions are all over the place anyway then. At one time I began to think I didn't really belong anywhere. I looked out for Gemma—that was the one thing that was constant.'

'Maybe that's why you can't settle into relationships now—the reason you bale out when things start to get serious—because deep down you think it could all go wrong and then it would be heart-wrenching for you all over again.'

He looked startled for a second or two, but he mused on that for a while, and then he frowned. 'I hadn't thought of it that way,' he said. He gave a crooked smile. 'I think you could be right. Men are supposed to be tough, but even they can have their hearts broken.'

She stirred brown sugar crystals into her coffee and stayed silent, deep in thought. *Once bitten?* Had some woman broken his heart in years past? Perhaps that had reinforced his conviction that he must steer clear of getting too deeply involved. Was it the reason he seemed to have so much trouble dealing with his feelings for her?

Maybe it might have been better if she'd never worked out the cause of his reluctance to commit long term. If he started going over past decisions in his mind, would he soon start to have second thoughts about seeing Gina again?

When they left the restaurant, it was still fairly early, and they walked along the quayside for a while, looking at the yachts in the harbour. He put his arm around her bare shoulders and said softly, 'I'm sorry for weighing you down with my problems. I wanted this to be a pleasant evening.'

'It was. It is. Perhaps we should do it again some time.' Her face flushed a little as she realised how pushy that sounded, and she added hurriedly, 'I mean, when you're not so troubled and you can relax a bit more.'

He smiled. 'I'd really like that.' They stopped by a railing and looked out over the bay in the distance, formed by tall cliffs and a long promontory. Waves lapped at the shore and splashed over the rocks. Further out, a lighthouse blinked a warning to any passing ships.

After a while, he checked his watch and said soberly, 'I suppose we should start heading for home. I wish we didn't have to break up the evening like this. I want to be with you...' He smiled wryly. 'I'm beginning to resent this Jason before I've even met him.'

He linked his fingers in hers as they started to walk back to the car. It felt good, just the two of them, hand in hand, and she, too, wished the evening didn't have to end.

It was still well before nine o'clock when they arrived home, but Saffi was dismayed to find that there was a black car parked on the drive. As she and Matt approached the house, the driver's door opened and a man stood up and came to greet them. He was tall, with crisply styled brown hair and hazel eyes. He wore a beautifully tailored dark suit.

'Saffi, it's so good to see you again.' Before she could guess his intention, Jason had put his arms around her and drawn her to him in a warm embrace. Beside her, she felt Matt stiffen.

Saffi froze. Jason was a virtual stranger to her and she had no idea how to react. She had the strong feeling he would have kissed her, too, but he seemed to gain control of himself just in time and released her. Maybe he realised she wasn't responding to him as he might have expected.

She felt bad about her reaction. 'I…uh…Jason…hello. I don't think you know Matt, do you? He lives in the annexe over there.' She waved a hand towards the end of the building. 'He's been really helpful to me, one way and another, these last few weeks.'

Jason frowned, and it seemed like an awkward moment, but Matt nodded a guarded acknowledgement of him and said, 'She's been through a bad time, so I've been looking out for her. I mean to go on doing that.'

Something in the way he said it made Saffi glance at Matt. Perhaps he'd meant it as a subtle warning, but Jason didn't seem put out.

She said, 'Thanks for coming over here, Jason. It was good of you to do that.'

'I was glad to. I wanted to see you again.'

'You came to see me in hospital, didn't you?'

He nodded. 'I'd have visited more often, but the nurses wouldn't let me. Then your flatmate kept sending me away, saying you weren't up to seeing people. Can you believe it—after all we meant to one another? I'm just so glad that we can finally be together.'

She heard Matt's sudden intake of breath and she made a shuddery gasp. It was no wonder he was alarmed by what Jason was saying. It had come as news to her, too.

Her cheeks flooded with sudden heat. How could she tell Jason that she didn't know him? He seemed to think things were exactly as they had been before—that they could go back to whatever relationship they'd had before she'd suffered her head injury.

'I...I'm still having trouble remembering things, Jason,' she said in a soft voice. 'I'm sorry, but I still don't know who you are and I don't think we can go back to how we were. It's not possible.'

Jason shook his head. 'I know it was a bad thing that happened to you, Saffi, but I'm not going to give up on what we had. Even if you've lost your memory, we can start again.'

Saffi looked at him, a feeling of apprehension starting up in her stomach. 'I don't think that's possible, Jason. Things are different now. I'm not the same person I was back then, back in Hampshire.'

'I don't believe that's true, Saffi. People don't change, deep down. And I won't give up on you. How can I? I won't rest until things are back to how they should be. You mean everything to me, Saffi. We love one another. We were practically engaged. It'll be the same again, you'll see.'

Saffi stared at him in disbelief. Engaged? Was it true? Matt was looking stunned by the revelation and she felt as though the blood was draining out of her. A feeling of dread enveloped her. How could she even consider being with another man when in her heart she knew she wanted Matt?

But wasn't that the worst betrayal of all, wanting to have nothing at all to do with a man she was supposed to have loved?

Distraught, she looked at Matt. She was shattered by everything Jason had said.

'Let's not get ahead of ourselves,' Matt said, his gaze narrowing on Jason. 'Whatever was between you two before this has to go on the back burner. She's in shock. She doesn't know you. You have no choice but to let it go for now.'

CHAPTER SEVEN

MATT HELPED JASON to unload the boot of his car, and between the three of them they carried Saffi's belongings into the house. The men seemed to have come to a mutual agreement that there would be no more talk of what had gone on in the past, and gradually Saffi felt the shock of Jason's announcement begin to fade away. Had they really been on the point of getting engaged?

After a while she managed to find her voice once more and she tried to make general conversation, wanting to ease the tension that had sprung up between the two men.

Neither of them said very much, but when they had finished the work, they both followed her into the kitchen. Matt was making no attempt to return to the annexe, and she suspected he had no intention of leaving her alone with Jason.

'My coffee-maker,' she said with a smile, unpacking one of the boxes. 'I've really missed it. Who's for espresso?'

She spooned freshly ground coffee into the filter and added water to the machine. It gave her something to do, and helped to take her mind off the awfulness of her situation. She'd been thoroughly shaken by events, so much so that her hands were trembling. Turning away, she tried to hide the tremors by going to the fridge and pouring milk into a jug.

Matt was frowning, his dark eyes watching Jason, assessing him. 'How long will you be staying in Devon?' he asked, and Saffi was grateful to him for taking over the conversation for a while. She felt awkward, out of her depth and she had no idea what to do about it.

'A couple of weeks,' Jason answered. 'I've booked into a hotel in town.'

Saffi handed him a cup of coffee. 'Chloe said you were taking some time off work…' She pulled a face. 'I don't even know what it is that you do.'

'I'm a medical rep. I generally work in the Hampshire area, and sometimes further afield if an opportunity crops up.'

'And you were working near to here today?'

'That's right, but I'd already made up my mind to come and see you. I just wanted to be near you, Saffi.' His gaze was intent, his hazel eyes troubled. 'We were so close before the accident. I want to be with you and make it like it was before. We can do that, can't we?'

She looked away momentarily, unable to face the yearning in his expression. He seemed to be in such an agony of emotion—how was it that she could have forgotten him, feel nothing for him, and yet apparently they had been so close? She was overwhelmed by guilt.

'I don't know what to say to you, Jason. I don't know

what to do.' She frowned, trying to work things out in her mind. Why did this have to happen…especially now, when she cared so much for Matt? But how could she simply turn Jason away? That would be heartless, like a betrayal of whatever relationship they'd once had. Was she the kind of person who could do that?

She said quietly, 'I know this must be very difficult for you. Perhaps we could get to know one another again…take it slowly…but I can't make any promises. I don't know how things will turn out. Things have changed. I'm not the same person any more.'

'What are you trying to say to me?' Jason's mouth made a flat line. 'Are you telling me you feel differently because you're with him?' He looked pointedly at Matt, a muscle in his jaw flicking.

She closed her eyes for a second or two, a tide of anxiety washing through her. 'Yes, I think I am.' She let out a long, slow breath. She'd said it. Admitted it. She'd known what the consequences might be when she couldn't stay away from Matt. She'd flirted with danger. Matt didn't want a long-term relationship, he had been clear on that, but she'd gone ahead anyway, getting herself in deeper and deeper.

Standing beside her, she saw Matt brace his shoulders. His lips were parted slightly as though on a soft sigh…of relief, or was he concerned now because she might want their relationship to be more serious? He didn't say anything, though, but looked fixedly at Jason.

Jason's mouth was rigid. 'You don't love her,' he said. 'You can't possibly care for her as I do. You've only known her for five minutes…how can that compare with what Saffi and I have shared?'

Matt pulled a wry face. 'Actually, you're wrong about that. I've known Saffi for years. The irony of it is that she doesn't remember me either.'

Jason looked stunned. After a second or two he recovered himself and said briskly, 'So, we're on an even footing. We'll see who comes out of this the winner, won't we?'

'True.'

Saffi stared at both of them, a wave of exasperation pulsing through her. 'Have you both finished discussing me as though I'm some kind of commodity to be shifted from one place to another as you please?' she enquired briskly. 'I think it's time for you both to leave.'

Stunned by her sharp rebuke, they did as she asked, albeit with great reluctance. Jason said goodbye, stroking her arm in a light caress, hesitant, as though he wanted to do more, perhaps to take her in his arms. Finally, he went to his car and drove off towards town.

Matt stood on the drive, watching him turn his car onto the country lane.

Saffi raised her brows questioningly. 'You're still here,' she said.

He gave her a wry smile. 'I'm just making sure you're safe,' he murmured, and then with a gleam in his eyes he added, 'If you begin to feel anxious in the night, or you want some company, you only have to bang on the wall and I'll be there in an instant.'

'Hmm…thanks for that, I appreciate it. But don't hold your breath, will you?' she murmured.

His mouth made an amused twist. 'You think I'm joking. Believe me, I'm not. Are you sure you don't want me to stay? After all, a few minutes ago you admitted you had feelings for me.' He moved closer as if to take her in his arms but she dragged up a last ounce of courage and put up a hand to ward him off.

'I can't do this, Matt,' she said huskily. 'I want to, but I can't. Not now. My whole life has been turned upside down and I don't know what to do or what to think. I need some space.'

He laid his hands lightly on her shoulders. 'I'm sorry. It's just that I hate to think of you being with that man— with any man. Seeing him with you has come as such a shock it's making me reassess everything.' He frowned. 'I don't mean to put pressure on you, Saffi, but you must know I want you…I need you to know that. I want you for myself. I want to protect you, to keep you from harm, in any way I can.'

'I'm not sure you would feel the same way if I hadn't lost my memory.' She shook her head. 'It makes a difference, doesn't it?'

'I don't know. All I know is I've always wanted you, Saffi. I've tried to fight against it, but I can't help myself. It seems like I've longed for you for ever and a day.'

Wanting wasn't the same as loving, though, was it? She daren't risk her happiness on a man who couldn't settle for one woman in his life. More and more she was growing to understand that it was what she wanted above all else—to have Matt's love and to know that it was forever.

'Things are all messed up,' she said softly. 'I don't know who I am or how to respond any more.'

Briefly, he held her close and pressed a gentle kiss to her forehead. 'Just follow your instincts,' he said, 'and know that I'm here for you, whenever you need me.'

He was still watching her as she went back into the house and closed the door. Alone once more, Saffi leaned back against the wall and felt the spirit drain out of her. Everything that she was, or had been, was locked up inside her head. Why didn't she know what had happened between her and Jason? Why had she and Matt parted company all those years ago? If only she could find the key to unlock the secrets hidden in her mind.

Jason came to call for her the next day, after Matt had left for work, and they spent time walking in the village and exploring the clifftop walks nearby. Perhaps he'd had time to think things through overnight, because he seemed to be doing everything in his power to help ease her mind. He made no demands of her, so that after a while she was able to relax a little with him. He told her about his job as a representative for a pharmaceutical company, and how it involved meetings with hospital clinicians, GPs and pharmacists.

In turn, she told him about her love for the house she'd inherited, the time she spent in the garden or looking after the hens and the beehives.

'I'll have to collect the honey soon,' she told him.

'You could help if you want. I could find you some protective clothing.'

'I could never have imagined you doing such things,' he said with a grin. 'You were always so busy, working in A and E. You loved it. It was your passion.'

'Was it?' She couldn't be certain, but it felt as though he was right. 'I'll be doing it again in a few days' time.'

He frowned. 'You will? Are you sure you're up to it? How are you going to manage things at the house if you do that? The garden's huge. That's a full-time job in itself, without the hassle of looking after the hens.'

'It's not so bad. Matt helps with everything, especially the bigger jobs around the place, like repairing fences or painting the hen coop. He's been keeping the lawns trim and so on. Besides, I'll only be working part time to begin with.'

'Even so, you don't need all this bother. You've been ill, Saffi. Why don't you sell up and come back to Hampshire? Life would be a lot easier for you there, and you would have friends around you.'

She shook her head. 'I don't remember anyone back there and I wasn't getting better. I was frightened all the while, and I didn't know why. It's different here. I love this house. It's my home, the place where I spent my childhood and where I felt safe.'

Jason wasn't happy about her decision, and she knew he wanted her to return to Hampshire with him, but he said no more about it. She saw him most days after that, while Matt was out at work, and he was always careful not to push things too far. Perhaps he was hoping her memory would return and they could take up where they had left off, but that didn't happen.

Although she knew Matt hated her being with Jason, he didn't try to persuade her against seeing him. Instead, he was there every evening, helping her with whatever needed to be done about the place. She discovered one of the hens, Mitzi, had a puncture wound in her leg and he cleaned it up while she gently held the bird to stop her from struggling.

'I think she might have broken the leg,' he said with a frown. 'I'll use some card as a splint and bind it up. Then we'll take her along to the vet.' He looked around. 'It's hard to see how she's managed to hurt herself—unless she was panicked in some way and fell against the timbers.'

'Perhaps we should keep her separate from the others for a while?'

He nodded. 'I'll sort out something for her. I think there's an old rabbit cage in the shed. I'll scrub it out and make it as good as new and it should make a good place for her to rest up.'

'Okay. Thanks.' She smoothed Mitzi's feathers. 'You'll be all right,' she said soothingly. 'We'll look after you.'

The vet prescribed antibiotics, a painkiller and splinted the leg properly. 'Keep her quiet for a few days, away from the other hens. She should heal up in a few weeks. Bring her back to me next week so that I can see if the leg's mending okay.'

'We will, thank you.' They went back to the house and settled her down in her new home.

'Maybe we could let her out on the grass on her own when she's feeling a bit more up to it?' Saffi suggested. She went over to the garden table and poured juice into a tumbler.

'Yes, we can do that. If it looks as though she's going to flap about too much, we'll pop her back in the cage.'

He sat down on one of the redwood chairs and she slid a glass towards him. He stared into space for a while, unseeing, and she guessed his thoughts were far away.

'Are you all right? Are you thinking about your sister? Have they operated on her? You said they were deciding on the best course of treatment.'

'That's right. They had to find out how far the disease had gone...whether it had spread beyond the pancreas and duodenum, but it seems she's in luck as far as that goes. They're bringing in a specialist surgeon to perform the Whipple procedure.'

She stood at the side of him and reached for his hand, wanting to comfort him as best she could. It was major surgery, a complicated procedure where part of the pancreas and the small intestine were removed, along with the gall bladder and part of the bile duct. After that had been done, the remaining organs would be reattached.

'When will they do it?'

'Next week. She's having a course of chemotherapy first to try and make sure it goes no further than it already has. They're going to do minimally invasive surgery, through laparoscopy, so there should be less chance of complications.'

Saffi bent down and put her arms around him. 'If you hadn't insisted on taking her to hospital, things could have been much worse. You've done everything you can for her, Matt.'

'Yeah.' He sighed. 'It just doesn't seem like nearly enough.'

'You're looking after Ben again, aren't you? Has his father gone back to work?'

He nodded. 'James is worried sick about Gemma and about the effect it's having on Ben. He was at the hospital all the time, but now he has to go away on an urgent callout. He's going to make sure he's back here when she has the surgery. I think this illness has really shaken him up.'

'I don't suppose Ben's reacting too well to all the changes going on in his life. Perhaps he can help me with the honey—not the collecting of it but afterwards, when I put it into jars?'

'I think he would enjoy that. When are you planning on doing it?'

'At the weekend.' She made a wry face. 'I thought I would open up the hives on Saturday, around lunchtime, when, like you said, most of the bees would be out and about.'

'Good idea. I'll give you a hand.'

She smiled at him. 'Thanks. I wasn't looking forward to doing it on my own for the first time.' Jason had said he had to be somewhere else on that particular morning, and she wondered if he had a problem with bees, or was worried about being stung. He still maintained she ought to sell up and leave everything behind.

Matt shot her a quick glance. 'How do you feel about going into work next week?'

Her mouth made a brief downward turn. 'I'm a bit apprehensive, to be honest. I'm worried that being able to help Josh might have been a once-only thing, and that I was working purely on instinct. I feel pretty sure I know what I'm doing, but I'd hate to come across something that I couldn't handle.'

'I don't think that's going to happen, because the way you were with Josh everything you did seemed skilful and automatic, as though it was part of you. And after talking to you the hospital chiefs are confident that you'll be fine. But if you're worried, you could come to the hospital with me tomorrow, just to observe and help out… if you want to. There's no pressure.'

'That's probably a good idea. I might get to know one way or the other if it's going to work out.'

'Okay. That's a date.' He grinned. 'Not the sort I'd prefer, but I guess it'll have to do for the time being.'

He picked her up in the morning after breakfast and drove her to the hospital. 'I'll introduce you to everyone, and after that you can just watch what's going on, or you can work alongside me,' he said as they walked into A and E. 'If you feel uncomfortable at any time, just let me know.'

She looked around. Everything seemed familiar to

her, and perhaps that was because she'd been here before with the little boy, Charlie, who had broken his leg
and pelvis in the road accident. He was doing well now,
by all accounts. She hadn't taken it all in then, but now
she saw the familiar layout of an emergency unit.

'I think I'd like to work with you,' she said. 'If you'll
show me where everything is kept.'

He put an arm around her shoulder and gave her a
quick hug. 'Brilliant. I know you can do it, Saffi. It'll be
as though you've never been away, you'll see.'

She wasn't so sure about that to begin with, but gradually, as the morning wore on, she gained in confidence,
standing by his side as he examined his patients and
talking to him about the problems that showed up on
X-ray films and CT scans. It was a busy morning, and
they finally managed to take a break several hours after
they had started work.

'It's finally calmed down out there,' she said, sipping
her coffee. 'It's been hectic.'

He nodded. 'You seem to be getting on well with Jake,
our registrar, and the nurses on duty.'

'They've been really good to me, very helpful and
kind.' Except that Gina Raines had come on duty a short
time ago, and straight away Saffi had become tense. She
wasn't sure why, but she had a bad feeling about her.
Maybe it was because she knew she and Matt had been
involved at one time, but that was over now, wasn't it?
So why should that bother her now? As soon as she had
seen her, though, a band of pain had clamped her head
and her chest muscles had tightened.

She frowned. 'They all know about my head injury. I know we talked about telling them, but it feels odd.'

'I thought it best to be straight with everyone from the start, to explain what we're doing and why you're here. They're a good bunch of people. You'll be fine with them.'

'Yes. I think it will work out.' She took another sip of coffee and all of a sudden her pager went off. Matt checked his at the same time, and stood up, already heading towards the door. Saffi hurried after him.

'A five-year-old is coming in with her mother,' the triage nurse said. 'The little girl had just finished eating a biscuit at a friend's house when she felt dizzy and fainted. Now she can't get her breath.'

Matt and Saffi went to meet the mother in the ambulance bay, and quickly transferred the child to a trolley. It was clear to see that she was struggling to get air into her lungs, and a nurse started to give her oxygen through a mask.

'She's been saying her tummy hurts,' the distressed mother said, 'and she's been sick a couple of times in the car. She's getting a rash as well.'

They rushed her to the resuscitation room and the child's mother hurried alongside the trolley, talking to her daughter the whole time, trying to soothe her.

'Has Sarah had any problems with fainting before, or with similar symptoms?' Matt asked.

'She's never fainted, but she does have asthma, and she had a bit of a reaction to peanuts once.'

'Did she see her GP about the reaction?'

The woman shook her head. 'It was quite mild, so we didn't bother.'

'All right, thanks,' Matt said. 'You can stay with us in Resus. The nurse will look after you—if you have any questions, anything at all, just ask her.' He indicated Gina, who went to stand with the mother as they arrived in the resuscitation room.

It looked very much as though Sarah was having a reaction to something she'd eaten. Her face was swollen, along with her hands and feet. Saffi handed Matt an EpiPen, an automatic injector of adrenaline, and he smiled briefly, knowing she had intercepted his thoughts.

'Thanks.' He injected the little girl in the thigh, and Saffi handed him a syringe containing antihistamine, which he injected into the other leg. Then he began his examination, while a nurse worked quickly to connect the child to the monitors that gave readings of heart rate, blood pressure and blood oxygen. Everyone was worried about this little girl who was fighting for her life.

'Blood pressure's falling, heart rate rising. Blood oxygen is ninety per cent.'

'Okay, let's get a couple of lines in to bring her blood pressure up. I'll intubate her before the swelling in her throat gets any worse. And we need to get her legs up to improve her circulation—but be careful, we don't want to cause more breathing problems.'

After five minutes the child was still struggling with the anaphylactic shock. 'I'll give her another shot of adrenaline,' Matt said, 'along with a dose of steroid.'

The medication was already in Saffi's hand and she quickly passed it to him. They had to work fast. This was a life-threatening condition and they had to do everything they could to bring down the swelling and restore her life signs to a safe level.

Matt looked concerned, anxious for this small child, but he followed the treatment protocol to the letter.

'Her breathing's still compromised,' Saffi murmured. 'Should we give her nebulised salbutamol via the ventilator circuit?'

'Yes, go ahead. It should open up the air passages.'

A short while later they could finally relax and say that the child was out of immediate danger. They were all relieved, and Matt took time out to talk to the girl's mother and explain the awful reaction that the girl had experienced.

'We'll send her to a specialist who will do tests,' he said. 'We need to know what caused this to happen. In the meantime, we'll keep her here overnight and possibly a bit longer, to make sure that she's all right. We'll give you an EpiPen and show you how to use it so that you can inject Sarah yourself if anything like this happens again. You'll need to bring her straight to Emergency.'

He took the woman to his office so that he could talk to her a bit more and answer any of her questions.

Saffi went home later that day, satisfied that she had managed a successful day at work. She felt elated, thrilled that she was back on form, workwise at least.

Matt came to find her in the garden the next day when she was getting ready to open up the beehives. She'd brought out the protective clothing and laid it down on the table in preparation.

'Two new skills in one week,' he said with a smile. 'You're really up for a challenge, aren't you? You did really well yesterday. How did it feel to you, being back in a hospital?'

'It was so good,' she said, returning the smile. 'Like you said, it felt as though I'd never been away. I remembered everything about medicine, and how much I love being a doctor, the way Jason said I did.'

His brows drew together at the mention of Jason. 'How are you getting on with him?' he asked cautiously. 'Have you remembered how it was with you two before the accident?'

She shook her head. 'From time to time I get flashbacks, of places we've been, or brief moments we've shared, the same as I do with you and me, when we were once together, but they're so fleeting that I can't hold onto them.' Her glance met his. 'You still don't like him being here, do you?'

He winced. 'It shows? I thought I was doing a pretty good job of hiding it.' He moved his shoulders as though he was uncomfortable with the situation. 'Of course, he's been quite open about the fact that he wants you back, and I can scarcely blame him for that. You're a special kind of woman, and who wouldn't want to be with you? But I wish he'd stayed back in Hampshire.'

She studied him for a moment or two, frowning. 'It's more than that, isn't it? You really don't like him.'

'I think it's odd that he hasn't come to find you before this. I would have moved heaven and earth to find you if I was in his shoes.'

His brow furrowed. 'He's putting pressure on you—subtle pressure, but it's there all the same. He says you were practically engaged, but "practically" isn't the same as having a ring actually on your finger, is it? I can't help wondering if he's exaggerating.'

'Does that matter? Wouldn't you do the same if you really cared about someone?'

'I do care about someone—I care very deeply for *you*, Saffi. I've never felt this way before—you can't imagine how badly it hurts to see you with someone else.'

She pressed her lips together. She didn't want to hurt him. It grieved her to see the pain in his eyes, but she was torn. She loved Matt, deeply, intensely, but didn't she owe Jason something, too?

To turn her back on him would be a betrayal. He would feel she hadn't even given him a chance. She didn't want to hurt anyone, but she desperately wanted Matt.

She lifted her arms to him, running her palms lightly over his chest. 'Isn't that a kind of pressure you're using, too? I don't want to see you hurting, Matt. That's the last thing I want.'

He gave a ragged sigh, the last of his willpower disintegrating as her hands trailed a path over his chest and moved up to caress the line from his neck to his shoulders.

He pulled her to him and kissed her fiercely, all his pent-up desire burning in that passionate embrace. His hands smoothed over her, tracing every feminine curve, filling her with aching need.

She clung to him, her fingers tangling in the silk of his hair, loving the way his body merged with hers, the way his strong thighs moved against her, and longing for him to say to her the one thing she wanted to hear.

She wanted his love, needed it more than anything in the world, but would it ever be hers?

'Saffi, I'm lost without you... What am I to do?' His voice was rough around the edges and she could feel his heart thundering in his chest.

The sun beat down on them and she felt heady with longing, fever running through her as his hand cupped her breast and his thumb gently stroked the burgeoning nub. A quivery sigh escaped her, and she looked up at him, her gaze meshing with his. More than anything, she wanted to give in to her deepest desires, to have him make love to her without any thought for the consequences.

But she couldn't do that. Not until she knew the truth about her past, about what had happened to spoil their relationship and send her headlong into Jason's arms.

Slowly, she came down to earth, and began to gently ease herself away from him.

Even as she did so, a small voice called in the distance, 'Uncle Matt, I finished my picture. Come and see.'

Matt gave a soft groan, releasing her and gazing at her with smoke-dark eyes full of regret.

'We have to sort out this thing with Jason,' he said huskily. 'I'm not going to share you with any man, in body or in spirit.'

CHAPTER EIGHT

'HEY, YOU'VE BEEN out and bought yourself a new car!' Matt looked admiringly at Saffi's gleaming silver MPV. 'It looks great, doesn't it?'

'I'm pleased with it,' Saffi said, glad that he liked her choice. 'I need one so that I can get to and from work, so I went ahead and took the plunge yesterday.'

'I wonder how I managed to miss that? You must have put it straight in the garage while I was busy with something else.'

'Yes, I did. I was a bit overwhelmed by the time I arrived home—getting back behind the wheel and so on.'

Frowning, he put an arm around her. 'I would have gone with you if you'd said. Did you have any problems finding what you wanted?'

She shook her head. 'Actually, Jason went with me to the showroom.'

She felt Matt stiffen, and added hastily, 'I didn't have much choice in the matter. He came to see me and insisted on going along with me.'

'How can he insist on anything? He's not your keeper.'

She winced. 'True. But I feel so guilty about forgetting him... I'm finding it hard to make him understand that I need some space.'

'He's playing on your emotions.'

'Maybe. Anyway, he wasn't too happy with my choice of car. He thought I should have gone for something smaller, but I like the flexibility of this one. You can fold down the seats to create more storage space. That might come in useful if I ever have to carry medical equipment around with me.'

He smiled. 'Do you think you might want to try your hand at being an immediate care doctor?'

She chuckled. 'Perhaps I'd better not try to run before I can walk. But you never know.'

'Hmm.' He sobered. 'How does it feel to drive? I mean, you said you were a bit worried about it.'

'It's okay, I think. I didn't actually have a problem bringing it home, anyway.'

'That's good. One more hurdle out of the way.'

'Let's hope so. I thought I could drive us to the vet's with Mitzi after work today, if that's all right with you? Unless you'd like me to go on my own?'

'No, I'll go with you. I want to hear what the vet has to say. It's good to see other professionals at work, and it's useful to get their advice. You never know when it might come in handy. Besides, I like spending time with you. You know I do.' He frowned. 'I'd do it a lot more if it wasn't for Jason hanging around.'

He turned to go back into the house to get ready for work. 'I'll see you at the hospital in two ticks.'

'Okay.' She set off for the hospital, still smiling at

what he'd said. He liked spending time with her. It made her feel warm inside.

They met up in A and E a short time later, and even though this was her first official day at work, everything went smoothly. She treated a child who had come in with a broken collarbone after playing football at school and a girl who had dislocated her shoulder in a fall. There was also a tricky diagnosis where a boy had fallen and felt disorientated…it turned out to be a case of epilepsy.

Matt left her to get on with things pretty much on her own, but she was aware he was keeping an eye on her all the while. He needn't have worried, though, because she was absolutely sure of what she was doing, and after a while the whole team relaxed and treated her as one of themselves, as if she'd been there for years.

At lunchtime Matt disappeared, and she guessed he'd gone to check up on Gemma. She was having her surgery today, and although Matt had been as calm and as efficient as ever as he went about his work, she knew that he was worried about her.

When he returned to A and E after about half an hour, he said quietly, 'Shall we go and get a coffee?'

'That would be good. I'm ready for one.' She walked with him to the staffroom. 'How is Gemma?'

'She's still in Theatre, but everything's going well so far. Her vital signs are okay, which is good.' He fetched two coffees and they went to sit down. 'James is in the waiting room. He's in bad shape. He's terrified something might go wrong.'

'Whatever happened to break them up, it seems as though he really cares about her.'

He nodded. 'I think he does. I'm fairly sure it's his job that's the trouble, because he's away from home so often.'

'Can't he get some other kind of work?'

'That would be the best answer, and I think he realises it now. He says he's applying for posts close to home. His qualifications are good, so he shouldn't have too much trouble finding something suitable.'

She sipped her coffee. 'It's been a scary time for both of you.'

'Yeah.'

'Even so, I envy you, having a family, having someone close. I sometimes wish I'd had a brother or a sister. My aunt wasn't able to have children, so there weren't even any cousins.'

He looked at her, his eyes widening a fraction. 'Is that a new memory?'

'Oh!' She gave a laugh. 'Yes, it was. Perhaps you were right about me coming back to work. It must be opening up new memory pathways.'

They went back to A and E a few minutes later, and Saffi became engrossed once more in treating her patients.

She left for home a few hours before Matt, and spent the afternoon getting on with chores. Jason had wanted to meet up with her, but she'd put him off as she needed to make a trip to the grocery store.

'I could go with you,' he'd said. 'I just want to be with you.'

'I know, Jason, but I'd sooner do this on my own. Anyway, I'm going to the hairdresser and then to the vet's surgery later.' She didn't want to be with him for too long. She'd much rather be with Matt, and she suspected Jason knew that.

After Matt arrived home, she gave him time to grab a bite to eat and then she put Mitzi into a carrier ready for the journey to see the vet.

'Is there any news of Gemma?' she asked as they went over to her car. She slid into the driver's seat and Matt climbed in beside her.

'Well, she's out of surgery and in Intensive Care. Her blood pressure's very low and she's had several bouts of arrhythmia—they're obviously concerned. She's in a lot of pain, too, so they're giving her strong drugs.'

'At least she came through it, Matt.' She laid her hand on his arm. 'She's young, and that's in her favour.'

'Yeah, there is that.' He breathed deeply. 'And James is at her bedside. If she wakes up, she'll see him right away.'

She started the engine. 'Where's Ben today?'

'He's with my mother. She's staying at Gemma's house so that he's in familiar surroundings.'

'That's good. This is bound to be upsetting for him.'

A few minutes later she turned onto the tree-lined road where the vet's surgery was situated. They didn't have to wait long before they were called into his room and he examined Mitzi's leg once more.

'That seems to be healing up nicely,' he said. 'Sometimes the leg becomes crooked, but it looks as though she's doing really well. I'll give you some more antibiotics for the wound, and a few painkillers, although I think she probably won't need them for too long.'

Mitzi's ordeal was over in a few minutes and they put her in the carrier once more then went back to the car.

Saffi drove back to the village. There was a fair amount of traffic on the main road at this time of the evening, and she checked her rear-view mirror regularly along the way.

After a while, she noticed that a black car was edging into view, coming close up behind her. She frowned. Whoever was driving it had been following her for some time, getting nearer and nearer, and now she was beginning to feel uneasy. Because of the shadows she couldn't see the driver's face clearly, but seeing that car had sparked something in the darker regions of her mind. She was sure something like this had happened to her before, that she'd been followed along a busy road.

She indicated to turn off the main road, and breathed a soft sigh of relief as the black car made no signal to do the same. It had all been in her imagination. The car wasn't following her. It was going straight on.

She drove onto the country lane, and after a while she glanced into her rear-view mirror once more. The car was there again, right behind her. She gripped the steering-wheel tightly. Her heart was thudding heavily.

'Saffi, what's wrong?' Matt's voice sounded urgent. 'You're as white as a sheet.'

'I'm not sure,' she managed, 'but I think I'm being followed.' She pulled in a shaky breath. 'It's probably nothing. It's just that…'

She broke off, switching on her indicator and carefully bringing the car to a halt in a lay-by. Beads of sweat had broken out on her brow.

She looked in the mirror once more. The black car had slowed down, too, as though the driver was unsure of himself, but then at the last moment he pulled away and went on down the country lane.

Saffi leaned back in her seat and let the fear drain out of her. The image of that black car was imprinted on her mind.

'Can you tell me what happened?'

'I don't know. Perhaps I made a mistake.'

'You were frightened, Saffi. What was it that scared you? Is it because you were in a collision once before? Did it happen because someone was following you?'

She swallowed hard. 'I think so. I can't remember clearly. It was a dark-coloured car. Something happened…I think I was rammed from behind…then a man stepped out of the car and came over to me.' She searched her mind for anything more, but the image faded and she couldn't bring it back. 'All I know is I was terrified.'

He undid his seat belt and leaned towards her, wrapping his arms around her. 'No wonder you were scared. It would be a bad experience for anyone.' He stroked her hair. 'Did you report it to the police?'

She frowned. 'I don't think so. I don't know what happened after he came over to me.'

They sat for a while with Matt holding her until her heart stopped thumping and she felt as though she could go on.

'Would you like me to drive the rest of the way?'

She shook her head. 'No, thanks. I'll do it. I'll be all right now.' She wanted to stay in his arms, but at the same time she needed to overcome her fears. Slowly, she eased away from him.

He frowned. 'Okay…if you're sure.' He fastened his seat belt once more and she started the car, driving cautiously until they arrived home.

'If you want me to be a passenger in the car over the next few weeks until you're over this, that's fine by me,' Matt said after she'd settled Mitzi back in her cage.

'Thanks.' She smiled at him. 'I think I'll be okay.'

Somehow knowing what it was that had caused her worries about driving was enough to ease her mind. Whatever had happened was in the past and not something that she need be concerned about now. It was like a weight off her mind, and it meant that when she drove to work the next day she was calm and the journey was uneventful.

'You seem to have settled in here well,' Gina said, as she assisted her with a young patient who needed sutures in a leg wound. 'Are you getting to know your way around?'

'I think so,' Saffi answered. 'Everyone's been very helpful.'

'Yes, I found that, too.'

'Ah, of course—you came here just a few days before I started, didn't you?' She glanced at Gina, who was wearing her brown hair loose this morning, so that it fell in soft waves to the nape of her neck. 'You're covering for a maternity leave? What will you do when that contract finishes?'

'I'll go back to the community hospital. They let me do this as a way of gaining experience in other departments. The nursing chief is good like that. She thinks variety will make for better nursing, so she was willing to allow the transfer.'

'She's probably right.'

Saffi tied off the last suture and gave her small patient a smiley-face badge. 'You were very brave,' she said.

Gina stayed behind to clear the trolley while Saffi went off to examine a six-year-old who had breathing difficulties and a barking cough. The nurse seemed friendly, and she hadn't anticipated that. She'd wondered if there might be some tension between them since Gina had dated Matt, but working with her had been much easier than she'd expected.

Matt had gone to see his sister before coming into A and E this morning, and Saffi busied herself going about her work. Whenever she had a brief free moment she thought about the dilemma she was in, and what she should do about Jason. He'd been easygoing, good company, and she could perhaps see some small reason why they might have been a couple before the accident that had blighted her life.

She didn't have any feelings for him, though, and she was fairly certain that even if she were to spend several more weeks in his company she still wouldn't feel anything for him. Was that because something inside her had changed after her head injury, or was it because she had fallen in love with Matt?

What could she say to him? He would be going back to Hampshire in less than a week and he was begging her to go with him.

And what should she do about Matt? Emotionally, she was totally bound up in him. He wanted her and they were good together, but there was no future in the relationship that she could see. Wasn't she inviting heartache?

Matt walked briskly into A and E, breaking into her thoughts, and quickly glanced through the list of patients who were being treated. 'Any problems so far?' he asked, and the registrar shook his head.

'It's all under control.'

Saffi glanced at Matt, trying to gauge his mood. His expression was serious, and she wondered if everything was all right with his sister.

'How is she?' she asked.

His mouth flattened. 'She's feeling pretty awful at the moment. There are all sorts of tubes that have to be left in place for a while, as you know, and one of the insertion points is infected. They've taken swabs to find out what bacteria are involved, and put her on strong antibiotic cover in the meantime.'

'I'm sorry.'

The triage nurse cut across everyone's conversation just then, saying, 'Red alert, people. We've a child coming in by ambulance. Suspected head injury after a fall on a path at home. Estimated arrival ten minutes.'

Everyone was immediately vigilant, ready to do their designated jobs.

When the boy, Danny, was brought into the resuscitation room, Saffi's heart lurched. He was about the same age as Ben, and he looked so small and vulnerable, white-faced, his black hair stark against the pillows.

'He's been vomiting on the way here,' the paramedic said, but by now the child had slipped into unconsciousness.

Immediately, Matt began his assessment, while Saffi quickly set up a couple of intravenous fluid lines. A nurse connected Danny to monitors and Matt began a thorough examination of his small patient.

Once his vital signs had stabilised and Matt was satisfied there were no other major injuries, he said, 'Okay, let's get him over to Radiology for a CT head scan.'

Matt and Saffi went with the child. She was apprehensive, dreading what the scan might reveal. Head injuries like this were always serious and could be life-threatening. Danny's parents must be frantic with worry.

Seeing the results of the scan on the computer screen, Matt's jaw tightened. Saffi was filled with anxiety.

'Call Theatre,' Matt told Gina, who was assisting. 'Tell them I'm on my way with a four-year-old who has a subdural haematoma.'

'Are you doing the surgery?' Gina asked.

He nodded. 'There's no one else available right now. Prep the child and I'll go and scrub in as soon as I've spoken to the parents.' He looked at Saffi. 'Do you want to come and scrub in as well?'

'Yes. I'd like to.'

Everything happened very quickly after that. He explained to the parents that blood was leaking into the tissues around their child's brain and because it had no way of escaping it was building up dangerous pressure inside Danny's head. Left untreated, it could cause brain damage.

To prevent that, Matt had to make a hole in the boy's skull in order to release that pressure and remove any blood clots that had formed.

The boy's parents were stunned, and obviously terrified about what was happening to their child, but they signed the consent form and soon Danny was on his way to Theatre.

As soon as Danny had been anaesthetised, Matt worked quickly and carefully, aided by computer monitoring, to make a burr-hole in the child's skull. Saffi suctioned the wound to remove a huge clot that had formed, and then Matt controlled the bleeding with cauterisation and finished the procedure, inserting a drainage tube into the operation site.

Danny was still in danger, as Saffi knew only too well from her own experience of head injury, but at least he could be treated with drugs now to keep him sedated and bring down the swelling on the brain. The worry was whether he would have suffered any brain damage, but that might not become clear for some time.

Afterwards, Danny was taken to the recovery room where he was to be cared for by a specialist nursing team. Matt supervised the transfer. 'We'll send him over to Intensive Care just as soon as they're ready to receive him.'

He and Saffi started back down to A and E, and Matt said quietly, 'Are you due to go off home now? It must be about time for your shift to end.'

'Yes, it is. Why? Do you want me to stay for a bit longer?'

'I wondered if you have time for a coffee in my office. I need to record my case notes, but we could talk for a while.'

'Okay.' She followed him into the office and watched as he set up the coffee-machine in a small alcove.

He passed her a cup a few minutes later, and she stood with him, sipping the hot drink and admiring his strong, wonderfully capable hands and his long, powerful body as he leaned back against the worktop. They talked for a while, about his sister, their work, and the way her memory was coming back in fits and starts.

He put his arm around her, and she looked up at him.

'I'm glad I came to work with you,' she murmured. 'You're very good at what you do. Everyone here respects you and would do anything for you. And you were so efficient, so quick at getting Danny up to Theatre and then operating on him.'

'Sometimes you have to work fast.'

She nodded. 'I thought you were brilliant.'

He pretended to swagger. 'Well, I do my best.'

She smiled up at him, settling into his embrace, gazing at him in love and wonder. 'I mean it. You're a good teacher, too…I've watched you show junior doctors how to carry out difficult procedures. You're very patient.'

'You do realise this is all going to my head, don't you? I shall be too big for my boots at this rate.' He gave that some consideration. 'Hmm. Perhaps I'd better stop you from saying any more.' He drew her towards him and bent his head, capturing her lips with his own.

His kiss was gentle at first, exploring the sweetness of her mouth with such tenderness that it seemed he was brushing her lips with fire. Her body tingled with exhilaration. And all the time he was coaxing her to move in closer, his hand smoothing over the base of her spine and urging her against him. 'You're everything I want in a woman, Saffi,' he said in a roughened voice. 'I don't think you know what you do to me.'

'What do I do to you?' she asked mischievously, revelling in the way her soft curves were crushed against his hard body.

'Ahh…' he groaned, as though he was in pain. 'You know exactly what it is.' His dark gaze moved over her, and the breath snagged in his throat. 'I need you, Saffi. It makes my heart ache to think of you with another man.'

'I'm not with another man.'

'You are. You know who I mean…Jason.' He sucked in a shuddery breath. 'Will you be seeing him this afternoon?'

'Oh.' She gave a small sigh. 'Yes. He said he wanted to take me to a place along the coast.'

His eyes closed briefly as though he was trying to shut out the picture that formed in his mind. 'Promise me you won't fall for him, Saffi.'

'I'm not dating him, Matt. I'm just trying to help him…it must have been such a shock for him, knowing he was like a stranger to me. I thought, if we got to know one another, he might realise we have nothing.'

'Things don't quite work out like that, though, do they…the way we expect? You might suddenly remember what it was you had before.'

'Matt…'

He kissed her again, quelling the words before she could get them out, and her mind spun in a heady vortex of desire and longing, and all the while mixed up with it was a spiralling fear that uneasy suspicions might tear them apart.

She loved him. How could she ever leave him for another man? But, on the other hand, would he eventually tire of her and leave her for someone else? Someone like—

The image of a dark-haired temptress with sultry green eyes swam into her vision. In her mind, the girl was standing in a bedroom doorway, one hand resting on the doorjamb. She was dishevelled, her shirt falling open to show her bra and a skirt that was unbuttoned at the waist. Saffi recoiled as though she'd received a blow to the stomach. 'No…oh, no…'

'Saffi?' Matt looked at her in consternation. 'What

is it? Has something happened?' He stared at her, trying to work out what was going through her mind. 'Is it another memory?'

'I...she...yes...she was there...she was with you...' She broke away from him, aghast at the images that had swirled through her mind.

The colour drained from Matt's face. 'Saffi, it's not what you think. You have to believe me.'

She shook her head, as though that would shake off the picture that was splashed across her vision like the pages of a magazine.

She stared at him, shocked to the core. 'You know what I'm seeing, don't you?' His words were like an admission of guilt, even though he was denying it. 'No wonder you wouldn't tell me what had happened between us.'

He moved towards her, reaching out to hold her, but she backed away.

'You...you ch-cheated on me... Oh, no...'

She felt sick, her stomach was churning, her chest heaving. The image, once forgotten, was now burned on her mind.

'How could you? We were in love and you cheated on me with Gina.'

Matt looked agonised. 'I tried to explain, but you wouldn't listen. I didn't cheat on you, Saffi. I know it must have looked that way, but I didn't.'

'She told me...she said you wanted her...that it was all over between you and me. How can I believe you when she told me herself what was going on?' She turned away from him and rushed to the door. 'I have to get out of here.'

She heard him calling after her, but she ignored him and kept on going, out of the door, desperate to get away. The department's emergency phone began to ring, and as she stepped into the main area of the emergency unit she heard Matt's pager bleep. She knew he couldn't come after her now, and she fled to the car park, thankful that she had been able to make her escape.

CHAPTER NINE

'YOU'RE VERY QUIET today. Has something happened between you and Matt?'

Jason watched Saffi keenly, but she tried to avoid his gaze. They were sitting on the grass in a picnic area high up on the moor, overlooking a magnificent bay. 'I noticed that you keep trying to avoid him by going into the house whenever he's around in the garden. You did that yesterday and again this morning.'

'I'd rather not talk about it,' she said. 'Could we finish up here and go back to the house, do you think?' She hadn't wanted to come out at all this afternoon, but he'd persuaded her to come with him on a picnic and now she was regretting it. Her heart simply wasn't in it. She needed to be on her own, to think things through.

'But it's beautiful out here, don't you agree? It might help you to relax if we stay for a little longer. I picked this spot especially…it's peaceful and shaded from the sun, and we can see over the moor for miles.'

'I know. I'm sorry.' It was true that this was a lovely place to spend an afternoon, and for the most part she'd appreciated the peaceful riverside walk. They'd followed the path through the woods and come to this idyllic place, where they could sit and look at the coastline in the distance.

But she didn't want to be here with Jason. She wanted to be with Matt, but every time she thought about him her stomach turned over and she felt panicky and sick inside. How could he have let her fall in love with him all over again only to have the beautiful bubble of illusion burst in her face?

'Have some food,' Jason suggested, rummaging in the hamper and bringing out a pack of sandwiches. 'You've hardly eaten anything.'

'No, I'm not hungry. Thanks all the same.'

He held up a plastic container. 'How about a jellied fruit pot?'

'No, really. Thanks. You thought of everything, the food was excellent and this place is perfect, but I want to start back now.' Her head was hurting as the blood pounded through her veins and her forehead was hot.

He frowned. 'But I thought we could—'

She started to pack away the paper plates and packaging. 'Stay here, if you like,' she said, unable to cope any longer with his prevarication, 'but I'm going home.'

'Ah, come on, Saffi, don't be like that. I thought we might stay here for a bit and then wander down to the inn later on. We could head down that way now, if you want.'

She stood up. 'You're not listening to me, Jason. We've already been out for a few hours, when I didn't want to come here at all. It's my fault, I should never have agreed. But now I'm going home.'

She started to walk across the moorland, taking a short cut to where they'd left the car. Jason caught up with her and fell into step beside her.

'You've fallen out with him, haven't you?' he guessed, and when she didn't answer he said with quiet satisfaction, 'Well, I can't say I'm sorry. I'm glad he's out of the picture.' He gazed at her, his eyes filled with longing. 'You and I belong together, Saffi. I knew we were right for each other the moment we met.'

'I don't know about that,' she said. 'I still don't remember how it was before I hurt my head.'

He smiled. 'Perhaps if I kissed you, it would all come flooding back.'

A faint tremor ran through her. 'No,' she said, perhaps a little too firmly. 'That's not a good idea.'

He was quiet after that, walking along with her to the car, making desultory conversation.

It was a huge relief finally to be back at the house and when he asked if he could come in, she said softly, 'I want to be alone for a while, Jason. I think I'll go and lie down for a bit.'

She had a sick headache, and perhaps it was a result of the strain of these last few days, or maybe it was because everything was coming unglued inside her head and her memories were returning thick and fast. She'd longed for that to happen these last few months, but now she wished she could go back to her state of blissful ignorance.

At work in A and E it took a real effort not to let her unhappiness show. She spoke to Matt about their patients or anything medical, but whenever he tried to talk about what had happened between them she cut him off.

'I don't want to hear it, Matt,' she said in a fractured voice. 'We've been through this before. It's over.' Even though she'd managed to say it, inside she was falling apart. His expression was tortured, and she guessed he was full of regret for the way things had ended all over again. Her stomach churned to see the pain in his features, but it was all of his own doing, wasn't it? She couldn't be with a man who had cheated on her. Wasn't there always the chance he might do it again? Hadn't his love for her been strong enough to overcome temptation?

She finished her shift at the hospital and hoped Jason would stay away from her. She hadn't exactly been good to him the day before. But he turned up again a couple of hours after she returned home, full of plans for where they might go.

'We could drive over to Rosemoor and look around the garden,' he suggested. 'You'd love it there. There's an arboretum and a cottage garden—all the things you like.'

She shook her head. 'Not today, Jason. I think I'll just stay here and potter in the garden. There's quite a lot of tidying up to do.' She could see he was disappointed and she added gently, 'I know this is your holiday and you want to be with me, but I'm not in the best of moods. Perhaps you'd do better to look up old friends or go out and about by yourself.'

'No. I'll stay with you,' he said, and her heart sank. Sooner or later, she would have to tell him it would never work out for them. Perhaps she'd seen something in him at one time and they'd been good together, but, whatever it was, it had gone. It had taken her less than a fortnight to discover that they weren't suited.

She doubted she'd ever find love again. Matt had ruined her for that. For her, he was the one and only, but it looked as though he hadn't felt the same way about her. What had gone on between him and Gina was in the past, of course, but it could well happen again when he tired of her and she couldn't handle that.

Jason sat on the rustic bench and watched her as she carried out everyday gardening tasks, dead-heading flowers and pulling up the occasional weed. They talked as she worked, and he told her more about his job as a rep, and how they'd met up when he'd come to the hospital pharmacy back in Hampshire as she had been fetching medication for a patient.

She'd started to gather seed pods from the aquilegia when Ben wandered into the garden. 'Hi,' he said, giving her a big smile. 'What are you doing?'

'I'm collecting these pods from the flowers,' she said, showing him. 'They're full of seeds, see?' She shook some out into a small bowl. 'I'll put them into envelopes so that they can dry out, and then next year I can plant them in the ground. They'll grow into flowers.'

'Can I have some? When Mummy comes home, we can put them in the garden.'

'That's a good idea. I'll give some to your Uncle Matt to keep for you.' She didn't want him deciding to see what they tasted like. 'How is your mother? Have you been to see her?'

He nodded vigorously. 'We're going in a little while—
me and Uncle Matt. She's feeling a bit better. She was
sitting in a chair when we went to see her yesterday.'
His eyes shone with excitement. 'My daddy's coming
back home to live with us.'

'That's great, Ben.' She gave him a hug. 'I'm so
pleased for you.'

Jason cleared his throat noisily, drawing her attention
away from Ben, and when she turned towards him he
said, 'All this talk about planting seeds—surely you're
not thinking of staying here?'

She frowned. 'Yes, of course. I thought you realised
that's what I wanted to do. I wasn't sure what I was going
to do when I first came back here, but now I know it's
what I want more than anything.'

'But I thought you would go back with me to Hampshire. You know that's what I want. We talked about it.'

She stared at him, aghast. How could he have assumed so much? She searched her mind for anything she
might have said that could have given him the idea she
had agreed to his suggestion, and came up with nothing.

'I'm not leaving here,' she said.

Ben tugged on her jeans. 'Can we go and look for
some eggs?'

'Yes, okay.' She glanced at Jason and saw that he
was scowling at the boy. He obviously didn't like the
interruption.

'Jason,' she murmured, 'it looks as though I'm going
to be spending some time with Ben now, and then I plan
to have a quiet evening. Like I said, I'm not the best

company today. Perhaps it would be best if you went back to your hotel.'

'We haven't had much time together,' he complained, 'with you working, and people dropping by.'

'People?' she echoed.

'All these distant neighbours that come by for flowers or vegetables—it wouldn't be so bad if they took the stuff and went away, but they stay and chat. And now the boy's come along to take up your time.'

Ben looked confused, sensing that something was wrong. Saffi put a comforting arm around the child and said, 'I like chatting with my neighbours, and I want Ben to feel that he can come round here whenever he wants.'

She hesitated, bracing herself for what had to be said. 'I think you should go, Jason. This isn't going to work out the way you hoped. I don't know how it was before, but I can't care for you the way you want. We're just not suited.'

'You feel that way because you've been ill, you suffered a bad head injury and it's taking time for you to get things back together again. We'll be fine. Give it time, Saffi.'

She shook her head. 'I'm sorry, Jason. I don't mean to hurt you, but you're so keen to see things the way they were that you're not giving any thought to the way I am now and what I feel and think.'

'We could work it out. You just have to give it time.'

He couldn't accept what she was telling him, and he countered everything she put to him with an argument of his own.

In the end, she said sadly, 'I can't do this any more, Jason. Please, go.'

Ben tugged once more at her jeans and she nodded, looking down at him. 'Yes, we'll go and see the hens.'

Jason left in a huff, and Saffi winced. Could she have been a bit more tactful or given him more time? Maybe, from his point of view, he had good reason to feel put out.

She went with Ben to the hen house and helped him to collect the eggs from the nesting boxes. 'Shall we see if Mitzi's left any for us?'

He nodded and they went over to the rabbit hutch. Matt had attached a wire run to the cage so that she could stretch her legs, and Ben was gleeful when he found two large brown eggs nestling in the wood shavings.

Matt came over to them as they started back towards the house. 'You've been busy,' he said, looking at the basket.

'We found six!' Ben said gleefully. 'They're for tea.' He thought about it. 'I could eat them all.'

Matt chuckled. 'You must be hungry. Do you think you could take them into the kitchen? Be careful.'

'I will.' Ben went off, holding the basket very still so as not to disturb the eggs.

Matt looked at Saffi, searching her face for some clue as to how she was feeling. 'How are you?' he asked.

She shrugged. 'I'm okay.'

He grimaced. 'I'd have done anything not to upset you.'

'Then perhaps you should have told me what happened before I started to care for you all over again,' she said sharply. 'You should have thought about it in the first place before you decided to two-time me with Gina. Or perhaps you imagined I wouldn't find out?'

His face was contorted with grief and regret. 'It didn't happen, Saffi—it wasn't what you thought.'

'Wasn't it?' Her eyes widened in disbelief. 'It seemed pretty straightforward to me. I dropped by your place one night when you weren't expecting to see me, and Gina came out of the bedroom. What am I supposed to make of it?'

'She was trying to get back with me. When you came by after your shift finished she took advantage of the situation and made it seem as if we'd been together.'

She was scornful. 'You've had a long time to think that one up, haven't you? There's no future for us, Matt. I told you at the time, I believe what I saw, and what she said. She told me you were getting back together. Why would I think differently?'

'Because you know me, and I'm telling you that's how it was.' His eyes darkened with sorrow. 'Or perhaps I'm wrong about that, and you never really knew me at all.'

'Obviously you're right about that.' There was pain in her eyes as she flung his words back at him. 'I thought I knew you, but you deceived me and I was devastated— twice over. I don't know how you could do that to me.' Her mouth tightened. 'And why *didn't* you tell me what had happened between us when we met up again instead of letting me find out weeks later?'

His brows shot up. 'Are you kidding? If I'd done that

I would never have had the chance to show you who I really am all over again. You wouldn't have had anything to do with me.' His mouth flattened. 'You can't imagine how difficult it's been for me to stay silent, or how hard it was for me to watch and wait for your memory to return, knowing all the while that you might cut me out of your life all over again.'

'You were right,' she said stiffly. 'That's exactly what I'd do. I couldn't be with anyone who played around.'

'I told you I didn't do that. I tried to explain, but you wouldn't listen and instead you left within the week and started a new life in Hampshire.' His grey eyes were bleak. 'You wouldn't take my calls, you wouldn't see me when I went over there—you wouldn't even speak to me at your aunt's funeral. Where does trust come into all this, Saffi?' There was an edge of bitterness to his words as though he was finally coming to accept what had happened to them.

He said nothing for a while, deep in thought as though he was trying to work things out in his head. Then at last he said, 'You're right. There's no future for us, because it seems to me that without trust there's nothing at all. I knew I should never have allowed myself to get close to you all over again. I was just setting myself up for heartbreak, wasn't I?'

She turned away from him as Ben came out into the garden once more. Her throat was aching and her eyes burned with unshed tears. She couldn't answer him, and she escaped into the house, her heart pounding, her throat constricted.

She wished she'd never remembered how he'd cheated on her. Then she could have gone on loving him in blissful ignorance instead of having to suffer this awful heartache. More than anything, she wanted to be with him, but how could their relationship ever work out with that awful betrayal hanging over them? How was she even going to cope with working alongside him?

Back in A and E the next day she was busy with her patients and managed for the most part to stay out of Matt's way. At lunchtime she went over to the intensive care unit to look in on Danny and find out how he was doing.

'His intracranial pressure is down,' the nurse told her, 'and we've done another CT scan, which shows everything's going along nicely. There's no sign of the blood clot building up again.'

'So you'll be removing the drainage tube soon?'

'In a day or so, I should think. He's doing really well. We're very pleased with him.'

Saffi was relieved. Danny was sitting up in bed, talking to his parents, and it looked as though his mother was showing him pictures in a story-book. She said cautiously, 'Is there any sign of brain damage?'

The nurse shook her head. 'Thankfully, no. He's a very lucky boy.'

'He is.' Smiling, Saffi went back down to A and E to finish her shift. She was glad Danny was doing so well. Things could have turned out so differently if it hadn't been for Matt's prompt action.

'Shall I help you with the patient in Room Three?'

Gina asked, cutting in on her thoughts. 'It's an infant with a bead lodged in her ear. You might need me to distract her while you try to get it out.'

'Yes, okay. Thanks, Gina.' Saffi frowned. It was an uncomfortable feeling, working with this woman, now that she'd remembered everything that had happened between her and Matt. She had to dredge up every ounce of professionalism she possessed in order to do her job properly, without letting her emotions get in the way.

'Are you all right?' Gina was studying her closely. 'Matt said you were recovering new memories all the time. Has it upset you?'

Saffi closed her eyes briefly. 'It has. It was bound to, don't you think?' She looked at Gina, beautiful, green-eyed, her hair shining with health. Was it any wonder that Matt's head had been turned, especially if Gina had made a play for him?

'There's nothing going on between us, you know,' Gina said quietly. 'I'm engaged to be married—look.' She held out her left hand, showing her sparkling diamond ring.

'Oh, I see.' Saffi's brows drew together. 'Congratulations.' She hesitated. 'That wasn't actually what was bothering me.'

'No.' Gina's voice was flat. 'Matt said you'd remembered me being in his bedroom.' She winced. 'I wanted to get back with him after he'd finished with me, so I went to see him when I knew you were busy at work. He was friendly enough, but he didn't want anything to do with me as a girlfriend and wanted me to leave, so

I said was feeling ill…a bit sick, faint, and so on. I lied
to you, Saffi.'

Saffi stared at her, shock holding her still, rooted to
the spot. Had she made a terrible mistake?

'I was desperate to make him want me. He said perhaps I should lie down for a while, undo my skirt to ease
the pressure on my waist, and I did as he said. Only I
undid a few more buttons on my blouse than was necessary. He just drew the curtains and left me alone. After
a while, he came to see if I was all right.'

She swallowed hard. 'I wanted him to love me, but he
just saw me as a friend. I felt so unhappy, and when you
turned up after your shift had ended, I wanted to finish
things between you, the way he'd finished things with
me. I thought, maybe, if he didn't have you, he might
turn to me after all.' She pressed her lips together. 'He
never did.'

Saffi let out a long, shuddery breath. 'It was all a lie?
All of it?'

Gina nodded. 'I'm sorry. I know what I did was stupid, hurtful. It's just that I was hurting too, inside.'

Saffi's head was reeling. All this time she'd refused to
listen to Matt. She'd believed what Gina had said at the
time, and she'd sent Matt away. Without trust, he'd said,
there was nothing at all. He would never forgive her.

'Saffi, I really am sorry.'

Saffi nodded. It took everything she had to keep
going and she said now, 'I'm glad you told me.' She
took in several long breaths to steady herself. What was
she to do?

She gazed around her without seeing for a moment or two. Then gradually, the sights and sounds of the hospital came back into view and she said dully, 'We'd better go and see what we can do about this bead.'

She made herself go into the room and talk soothingly to the little girl and her mother. 'I'm going to look inside your ear with this,' she said to the two-year-old, showing her the otoscope. 'It won't hurt, I promise.'

When she could see the shiny object, way down in the ear canal, she tried to gently remove it using special forceps, but when that didn't do the trick, she asked Gina for suction equipment. After a few seconds, much to the mother's relief, she'd retrieved the bead.

She left the room a few minutes later, leaving Gina to talk to the patient and her mother and clear away the equipment. The only thing on her mind was to find Matt and talk to him, though how she was going to persuade him to forgive her lack of trust was beyond her right now. He'd seemed to have made up his mind, finally, that there was no point any longer in trying to win her back. He'd decided she wasn't worth the effort.

'He went out on a call,' Jake told her, 'and I think he's going to be tied up in meetings all afternoon. Do you want me to pass on a message?'

'No, that's all right, Jake. Thanks. I'll catch up with him later.'

She arrived home feeling washed out and dreadful. How could she have been so blind, so certain that she'd had things right all this time?

She was pacing the floor of her living room when

Jason turned up at the house, and she groaned inwardly. This was the last thing she needed, but some part of her insisted that even though he would never win her round she should let him say his piece. Wasn't that where she'd gone wrong with Matt, by not listening to him?

They went back into the living room.

'I'm going back to Hampshire tomorrow,' Jason told her.

'So soon? I thought you had another couple of days here?'

'No.' He shook his head. 'I have to go and see the head of a regional pharmacy service. It's a new contact for me, and my bosses didn't want me to miss it.'

She smiled. 'It sounds as though your job is going really well. You must be pleased.'

He shrugged. 'I work hard and make a lot of contacts, but I could have done without that one right now. I need more time here to persuade you that we belong together.'

'It's never going to happen, Jason,' she said, unhappy because she had to hurt him yet again. 'I don't know how it was before, but I can't see how we were ever a couple, to be honest. I don't think I've changed so much from how I was before the accident.' She still felt the same way about Matt as she'd always done, so how could it be any different with Jason? Something had to be wrong somewhere.

'You're being very cruel to me, Saffi. How can you say these things to me?'

She sent him a troubled look. 'I don't mean to be

cruel. I'm trying to be straightforward with you, so that you don't have any illusions as to how it will be.'

'But I love you, and you loved me. How can that all have changed?'

Her expression was sad as she tried to explain, 'I don't think it was ever that way. It feels to me as though you've conjured something up in your mind and made it into something that never was. It's what you want to believe.'

He moved closer to her. 'You're my blonde, beautiful, blue-eyed angel,' he said. 'How could I not love you?'

'It isn't love, Jason. You're infatuated with someone you can't have. Don't you see that?'

'All I see is you and me, together.'

He slid an arm around her and pulled her to him. 'I'm not letting you go, Saffi. You're mine, and sooner or later you'll see that I'm right.'

He tried to kiss her and she pushed him away. 'No, Jason, stop it.'

'It'll all come right, you'll see.' He ignored her protests and backed her up against the wall, clasping her wrists and pinning her there with his body.

'I said no, Jason. Get off me. Let go of me.' She struggled, trying to wriggle free, and as they tussled he somehow knocked over a stool. It fell against the wall with a crash, and it made her realise how determined he was. 'Jason, this is crazy,' she said. 'Let me go.'

He tightened his grasp on her wrist and she stared up at him, frightened, afraid of what he might do. A startling image flashed across her mind, of another place, another time, when he'd grabbed her wrist in that very same way.

'Oh, no…no…' she cried. 'This can't be happening, not again.' The last time he'd held on to her this way they'd been at the top of a flight of stairs. She'd tried to get away from him, and the next thing she'd known she'd been tumbling down and down and then there had just been blackness until she'd woken up in hospital.

'You're the reason I fell down the stairs. You were trying to stop me from breaking up with you.' Her voice was rising with panic. 'Please, Jason. Think about what you're doing. Do you want it to happen all over again? Are you deliberately trying to hurt me?'

He didn't get the chance to answer because all at once there was the sound of a key scraping in a lock, and Matt came rushing into the room through the connecting door.

'Let go of her,' he said in an ominously threatening voice. His jaw was clenched in anger and there was the fierce promise of retribution in his grey eyes.

Jason paled with fright. 'What are you doing here?'

'Never mind that. Do as I said. Let her go.'

Jason hesitated for a few seconds too long, and Matt was on him right away, putting an arm around his neck and yanking him backwards, while at the same time hooking his leg from under him.

Matt gave him a push and Jason fell to the floor. Standing over him, his foot firmly placed over Jason's arm, Matt glanced at Saffi.

'Are you all right?'

Saffi resisted the urge to rub her sore wrists, and nodded. She was winded, breathing hard after the skirmish, and her heart was pounding as she wondered what she would have done if Matt hadn't intervened. Perhaps a knee to the groin would have done the trick?

'Let me up,' Jason said, struggling to get to his feet.

Matt pushed him back down with his other foot. His balance and his strength were incredible, and Saffi realised his sessions at the gym had definitely paid off.

'What do you want me to do with him? Do you want to call the police?' Every time Jason made a move, Matt pushed him down again.

'I don't know,' she said, filled with anxiety. 'Do you think he'll come back and try again?'

'I won't. I won't do that.' Jason's voice shook as he became more desperate.

Matt ignored him. 'I don't think it's very likely,' he said, looking at Saffi. 'If he does, he'll certainly regret it, because I'll do more than drag him off you next time. He'll wish he'd never been born.'

'I just want him out of here,' she said, and Matt nodded.

He grasped Jason by the collar of his sweatshirt and dragged him to his feet. 'You heard what she said. Get out of here, and don't come back.'

He pushed him towards the front door and pulled it open wide. 'Get in your car and don't come within twenty miles of her, don't phone her, don't email, don't write to her. If you try to contact her in any way, we'll get an injunction against you. Are you clear on all that?'

Jason nodded, his face ashen. He must have realised

he didn't stand a chance against Matt, who was so much fitter and stronger than he was. He didn't say another word but hurried over to his car and drove away as though he was terrified Matt would come after him.

'Thank you for coming in and rescuing me,' Saffi said when Matt returned to the living room. 'I thought you would be out all day. I thought I was completely alone with him.' The after-effects of her ordeal suddenly kicked in and she began to tremble. Feeling behind her for a seat, she sank down into the sofa and clasped her hands in her lap.

Matt came to sit beside her. After a moment of hesitation, as he appeared to be at war within himself, he wrapped his arms around her and held her until the trembling stopped. Then he said softly, 'I'll make you a hot, sweet drink. That should help you to feel better.'

She nodded silently. She would have gone after him, but her legs were weak and all the energy had drained out of her. The shock of Jason's assault and the memory of how her fall down the stairs had come about were too much for her to take in. She started to shake all over again.

'Here, drink this.' Matt handed her a cup of tea and helped her to clasp her hands around it. He sat with her as she tried to gain control of herself.

'Thank you for this.' She swallowed some of the reviving tea and then slid the cup down onto the coffee table. 'I can't tell you how glad I am that you came through that door when you did.' She sent him a puzzled look. 'But I don't understand how you were there, how you knew to come to me.'

'I was afraid something like this might happen. Ben told me that you were talking in the garden yesterday. He said Jason was cross when you said you weren't leaving here and he was angry when you asked him to go, and that started warning bells in my head.' He grimaced. 'I cancelled all my meetings so that I could be here, just in case I was needed.'

'You did that, even though I'd been so awful to you?' She clasped his hand, needing that small contact.

'I was already watching out for trouble after you were followed the other night.'

'By the black car?'

He nodded. 'I'm fairly sure it was Jason in the car. He must have thought you were on your own—perhaps the headrests obscured his vision. Did you tell him you were going to the vet's surgery?'

She frowned, thinking about it. 'I don't remember. I was busy and then… Oh, yes…he wanted to take me out and I said I couldn't go with him because I had to take Mitzi to the vet.'

'He must have been waiting there, ready to follow you home.'

'But why would he do that?'

'He's obsessed with you. He must have followed you before. How was your other car damaged in a rear-end collision? Do you have any recollection of it?'

She nodded slowly, covering her face with her hands as the incident came back to her in bits and pieces. Getting herself together after a minute or so, she said, 'It was when I wanted to finish things with him…he took to following me. When I wouldn't stop the car, he drove me off the road.' She looked at Matt. 'He's out of his mind, isn't he? Perhaps we should have called the police after all, or tried to persuade him to get treatment?'

'I doubt the police would do anything without proof. Were there any witnesses?'

She shook her head.

'And when you fell down the stairs?'

'No.' It came out as a whisper, and she began to shake all over again. 'He must have left me there at the foot of the stairs, knowing I needed help. But he did nothing. Apparently, it was Chloe who called for the ambulance when she arrived home from work. I don't know how long I was lying there.'

He put his arms around her and drew her to him, gently stroking her silky hair. 'It's over now, Saffi. He won't trouble you again.' They stayed together that way for some time, and eventually he said softly, 'It looks as though your memory's come back in full force.'

She gave him a tremulous smile. 'It does, doesn't it?' She gazed up at him, her brow puckering. 'But why did I lose it so completely? I can understand partial amnesia because it was a bad head injury, but such a total loss is unusual—people don't often recover their memories after such a loss.'

'There's probably a combination of reasons. The head injury is one, as you say, but your mind could have been shutting out the bad things, all the emotional trauma that you didn't want to face…like your relationship with Jason.'

'And the end of my relationship with you. That has been the worst of all.' She looked at him anxiously, passing her tongue lightly over her dry lips. 'Matt—I spoke to Gina before I left work today. She told me that she'd lied to me.' Her gaze meshed with his. 'I'm so sorry I doubted you. You were right all along—I should have trusted you.'

'We'll have to start again, won't we…and make a pact to always trust one another?'

'Does that mean you forgive me?' She looked at him in wonderment. 'Do we have some kind of a future together?'

He looked into her blue eyes. 'We'd better have a future. I'm not going to lose you again, Saffi. It's been hell on earth for me these last few days…these last few years, even.'

'But you don't believe in long-term relationships, do you? Wasn't that why you finished things with Gina, because you didn't want any kind of commitment?'

'I thought that was the reason at the time. It was what I told myself. But the truth is, Gina and I were never right for one another. She wanted to get serious, but I knew it would never work.'

He hesitated. 'I never looked for commitment. But then I met you, and I could feel myself getting in deeper and deeper, knowing that you were the one woman I could love. But all the time I was afraid that it would go wrong, that it would end the way it always did with people I cared about…my parents, even my sister was lost to me when we ended up in separate foster-homes. I was afraid to love you in case I lost you. And then the very worst happened. You thought I'd cheated on you.'

He drew in a shuddery breath. 'It made me even more wary of getting involved. When I met up with you again, here in Devon, I was so afraid of being hurt all over again. I told myself I needed to keep my distance, but it was too difficult and I ended up not being able to stay away. And after you remembered what had happened with Gina, I was devastated all over again. It was like my worst nightmare. I thought I'd lost you for ever.'

She lifted a hand to his face and stroked his cheek. 'You haven't lost me. I love you, Matt. I think I knew it almost from the first.' She gently drew him towards her until their lips touched, and he gave a ragged groan, kissing her fiercely, with all the longing and desperation that had built up inside him.

'Will you marry me, Saffi?' His voice was husky with need. 'I couldn't bear to lose you again.'

'Yes…yes, I will…' She wrapped her arms around him, loving the way he ran his hands over her body, over every dip and curve. She kissed him because she loved him, because she wanted him, because she needed him to know that she would be his for evermore.

When they at last stopped to gather breath, she said softly, 'Aunt Annie thought we were meant for each other, you know. She knew how much I loved you and she always had faith in you, even when I was floundering. That must be the reason she left you part of the house. She wanted us to be together, and she knew we'd have to find some way of making it work if we both lived here.'

He chuckled. 'Yes, I'd worked that one out. She was right, wasn't she? I know she couldn't have expected it to happen so soon, but her plans were all intact. She didn't leave anything to chance.'

She snuggled into him, nuzzling his neck and planting soft kisses along his throat. 'I love you so much.'

'And I love you, beyond anything. That's why I came to work in Devon. I knew, sooner or later, you would come to visit Annie and I would do everything I could to win you round. I just had to see you again.' He gave a wry smile. 'And then when you turned up and hadn't a clue who I was, I thought maybe here was my chance to get you to love me all over again.'

'Well, you managed that all right.'

'I did, didn't I? That must say something about true love lasting for ever.' He kissed her again. 'Are we too late for a summer wedding, do you think?'

She smiled up at him. 'I shouldn't think so. I'm sure we'll manage to sort something out.'

'That's good…that'll be perfect.' He gently pressured her back into the cushions and eased himself against her, and after that neither of them had any inclination to move apart for a long, long time.

* * * * *

FLIRTING WITH DR OFF-LIMITS

ROBIN GIANNA

This one's for you, Meta, as you well know!

Whether I just need your great advice or I'm
seriously panicking, you're always there for me.
I can't thank you enough for that.
You're the best!   xoxo

CHAPTER ONE

KATHERINE PAPPAS HOPED with all her heart that she'd been abducted by aliens. And that an extraterrestrial scientific experiment had sucked her brain dry.

After all, she'd much rather believe that the blankness of her mind throughout the night had been due to interplanetary interference and not because she'd just plain forgotten everything she'd ever learned in medical school. Exactly three weeks after she'd graduated. With a new job as a first-year intern at the same well-respected hospital as her hotshot surgeon brother.

Katy sucked in a calming breath. *You know this stuff. Just quit with the nerves and do the job you've been dreaming of doing forever.* She moved into a corner so no one, hopefully, would notice her until she felt ready to head to the first patient's room for morning rounds. After wiping her sweaty hands on her scrubs, she began to organize cards on each patient she'd be seeing that morning,

The shrill sound of her phone made her nearly jump out of her skin, and her stomach somehow both sank and knotted as she answered. The words that had been so wonderful to say just a week ago seemed to stick in her throat and choke her. "Dr. Pappas."

"Paging Dr. Katherine Pappas, world's best surgical intern on her way to becoming world's best family practice physician. Is she available?"

Hearing the voice of her closest friend in med school, Rachel Egan, made Katy relax and even conjure a small grin. "Dr. Pappas is available, except more likely she's on her way to becoming the first intern booted out of Oceancrest Community Hospital only hours after arriving."

"Uh-oh," Rachel said. "Bad night on call?"

"The nurses are probably referring to me as Dr. Dolittle. As in do very little." She sighed. "All night when they asked me questions, the right answer seemed to take a minute to percolate in my brain. I was sure I could do this, but now I'm worried."

"You're being ridiculous. Who had a straight four-point GPA in both undergrad and med school, like any human can do that? Who got the Alpha Omega Alpha award when we graduated? You're brilliant, Katy, and you're the only one who doesn't realize it."

"Then why doesn't the perfect answer pop instantly into my 'brilliant' brain?"

"Because we're nervous newbies, that's why. We crossed that med-school finish line, and all of a sudden we have the word 'Doctor' in front of our names and have to answer to it. Who wouldn't be scared? I know I am."

"Really? You are?" Rachel had always been the calm and confident student, the one who'd earned smiles and praise from professors and attending physicians for her cool and collected demeanor. In stark contrast to Katy's often ruffled one.

"Heck, yes, I am! I wish we'd ended up training at the same hospital. Maybe we'd both feel less freaked out if we had each other to lean on."

"I know. But you're happy to be back in your hometown, and I'm thrilled to be in San Diego. Plus I think it's good that I moved in with Nick. He's going through a hard time right now."

"Still pretty depressed about his divorce, huh?"

"Actually, the divorce isn't final yet. But, yeah, he's very glum compared to his usual self." Katy didn't know what had gone wrong in her brother's marriage, but it was sad that, after just a year, it hadn't worked out. She wished she could blame his wife, Meredith, except Katy had always liked her a lot—and, as the saying went, it took two to tango. Whatever their problems, both of them had probably contributed to them.

"It'll be good for him to have you there, I'm sure, though I hope nobody gossips about favoritism since you're his sister."

Favoritism? Katy hadn't even thought about that, and hopefully no one else would either.

"So, tell me—"

Katy's hospital call system buzzed and her belly tightened. "Gotta go, Rachel." She punched the button and swallowed hard before she tried to talk. "Dr. Pappas."

"Mrs. Patterson's potassium is at three point zero, and I need to know what you want me to do."

Okay, so that was low. She should order a potassium IV—probably four mil. No, wait. Maybe she should give it orally? A nervous laugh bubbled up in her throat as she wondered how the nurse would react if she prescribed a banana to bring up the patient's potassium.

She swallowed. "You know, I'll have to call you right back."

"Are you serious?" the nurse said in an annoyed and condescending tone. "Fine. I'll be waiting."

"Okay." Katy's face burned as she turned off her phone and wiped her hands, which were somehow sweaty and icy cold at the same time, on her scrubs again. She fumbled in her pocket for her Scut Monkey book. Rachel made fun of her that she infinitely preferred using it over trying to look things up on the internet. But her little book had helped her more than once, and she was determined to get this right.

Katy gnawed her lip and studied the little book. Based on the patient's age, weight, and kidney function, it looked like she was right. Four ml potassium to drink would be the safest, most effective approach. Okay, good. As she tried to call the nurse back she dropped her phone on the hard floor, sending the plastic cover soaring across the room.

She groaned as she grabbed up the phone, relieved to see it was still working. Klutzy Katy. Why had she been plagued with some pitiful clumsiness gene, and why did it get worse when she was nervous? Graceful under fire she was not.

She called the nurses' station, surprised that a different nurse answered to take the oral potassium order. How many staff worked in this hospital? The number must be mind-boggling.

Right, time to get to rounds!

The patient card on the top of her pile read "Angela Roberts, Room 1073." She went to knock on the door, pausing to inhale a deep breath. This was it! Seeing her very first patient in person as a real doctor! Yes, she'd inherited all of them from the resident who'd already seen them, but still. The thought was nerve-racking but thrilling, too, and a big, spontaneous smile came on her face.

"Hello, Mrs. Roberts. I'm Dr. Pappas, your intern. How are you feeling?"

"I'm all right, dear. Wishing they could figure out my spells so I can get the gall-bladder surgery over with."

"We're working hard to figure that out." She warmed her stethoscope against her palm before examining the woman. "We're in the process of ruling out things like seizures or transient ischemic attacks, which are little mini-strokes."

"Strokes? I'm sure I would know if I'd had a stroke, dear."

"TIAs are so tiny you might not notice." Katy smiled, her chest a little buoyant as she thought about this puzzle they were solving.

"Well," Mrs. Roberts said, waving her hand, "I trust Dr. Armstrong to know what he's doing. Whatever he figures out is right, I'm sure. He's a lovely man."

Katy felt her smile slip and she forced it back up, at the same time avoiding rolling her eyes. "No doubt Dr. Armstrong is an excellent surgeon."

And excellent at other things, too. Like giving fake excuses for not being with someone—breaking hearts in the process—then turning around and doing exactly that with someone else. Like having inappropriate hospital affairs that got other people fired. Fooling everyone who used to think he was wonderful in every way.

The old embarrassment and anger filled her chest again when she thought of how many years she'd hero-worshipped the man who didn't deserve it.

"And handsome! So good looking, like a doctor on TV. I'm sure a young thing like you can hardly resist a handsome surgeon like Dr. Armstrong."

"He's my superior here at the hospital, Mrs. Roberts."

Long ago, she'd agreed. She'd thought everything about him gorgeous—his football-player physique, his warm amber eyes, his thick dark hair. Funny and smart, with a teasing grin that was irresistible.

But no more. A man had to be beautiful on the inside as well as the outside to appeal to her. Not that she appealed to him anyway, which he'd made abundantly clear.

"I'm feeling a little tired." The woman snuggled down into her bed as Katy continued her examination. "Can you come back later?"

"I'm almost done for now, Mrs. Roberts. May I pull your sheet down a little? I just want to take a listen to your belly."

Katy glanced up when she didn't respond and was startled to see that her head had lolled to one side of the pillow, her mouth slack and her eyes closed. Had she fallen asleep, just like that?

"Mrs. Roberts?" Katy's heart sped up and she spoke louder, shaking the woman's shoulder. "Mrs. Roberts?"

The monitor the patient was hooked up to began to screech and Katy looked at the screen. Her oxygen level was dangerously low, but there was no change in her heart rate. That couldn't be right, could it? Quickly, she rubbed her knuckles against Mrs. Roberts's sternum.

Nothing. No response. Katy put shaky fingers against the woman's carotid artery. Her pulse was so slow and faint Katy knew this was beyond serious. Heart pounding in her ears now, she leaped up and smacked the red code button on the wall then ran back to the bedside.

"Okay, Katy, you've got this," she said out loud to herself as her mind spun through the advanced cardiac life support protocol she'd finished during orientation just yesterday. "It's as easy as ABC, right? Airway, breathing, circulation."

Her own breath seriously short and choppy, she shoved the pillows from the bed to get Mrs. Roberts lying flat and lifted her chin to open her airway. The woman's chest still barely moved.

Damn it! Katy knew she had to get a bag valve mask on her immediately, then noticed the EKG wires had been disconnected, probably when she'd gone to the bathroom. Stay calm here, you know what to do, she reminded herself, sucking in a deep breath to keep from fainting along with Mrs. Roberts.

Fumbling with the equipment, she managed to stay focused as two nurses ran into the room. "We need to get her back on the monitor. I need to bag her. Can you get me a bag valve mask? And another IV." She could practically smell their alarm and forced down her own. *Do not panic, Katy. This woman's life could depend on you.*

The loud sound of a cart rumbling down the hall and into the room made Katy sag in relief. The cavalry had arrived.

"Give me the patient's history," a guy said, as he moved from the crash cart to the head of the bed, quickly getting a bag on Mrs. Roberts to provide the oxygen she desperately needed. He was probably from the ICU team, but Katy wasn't about to waste time asking questions.

"Patient is eighty-two, with cholecystitis, her surgery is on hold until she's medically cleared by Cardiology." Katy gulped as she stared at the still-unresponsive Mrs. Roberts and forged on. "She was talking to me and just kind of collapsed. She has fainting spells and we're trying to figure out why."

She stared at the monitor as the ICU guy attached the

last EKG lead. Involuntarily, Katy let out a little stressed cry when she saw the heart rate was alarmingly slow at only thirty-five beats per minute. "Sinus bradycardia," she said. "Atropine point five milligrams and we need pads for transcutaneous pacing."

Had all that really come right out of her mouth? No time to give herself a pat on the back as the ICU guy barked to the nurse, "Get Cardiology on the line. You, Doctor, get her paced as I intubate."

Katy blinked and a touch of panic welled in her chest that she resolutely tamped down. He'd just called her "Doctor". She was part of this team, which would hopefully save this woman's life. Concentrating intently on getting the pads placed amid a flurry of activity by the nurses, she didn't even notice the tall, broad form that came to stand next to her.

"I'll take over now," a familiar deep voice said. "Good job, Dr. Pappas."

Alec Armstrong brushed past her as she moved to one side, allowing him to deliver the electricity to Mrs. Roberts's heart. Katy stood there, stunned, her hands now shaking like a tambourine. Beyond glad it wasn't her trying to get the pacing finished and giving orders to the nurses.

Which wasn't the right attitude, she scolded herself, since she wanted to be a doctor—was a doctor. But, dang it, how many newbies had to deal with their very first patient coding on them?

She watched Alec work, and couldn't help but notice how different he was, and yet somehow the same as when she'd known him years ago. As a boy and teen, he'd practically lived in their house as Nick's best friend. While he'd been as fun and adventurous as anybody she'd known, he'd always become calm and focused when there had been an important task at hand, his eyes intent, just like they were now. His hands moved swiftly and efficiently, as they had during all the crazy science experiments they'd done together. All the times he and Nick had worked on projects with her, teasing about her endless quest to learn new things and solve weird problems.

Her hero-worship of Alec was over. But the moment that thought came into her head, as she watched him work, she knew it wasn't true. How could she not admire how capably he dealt with a critical situation? But she didn't have to like him as a person to admire how good he was as a doctor and doubtless as a surgeon.

In a short time the frantic flurry of activity was over and the ICU guy began to wheel Mrs. Roberts from the room. As he left, he said over his shoulder, "I'll dictate my procedure note. You got the code note?"

"I've got it," Katy and Alec said at the same time. Their eyes met, his the amused, warm amber she remembered so well, and she felt her face flush. How could she have thought the guy was talking to her when attending surgeon extraordinaire Alec Armstrong had taken over?

"So, Katy-Did." His lips curved as he folded his arms across his chest. "What the hell did you do to my patient to make her code like that?"

"Please call me Katherine or Katy. I'm not a kid anymore," she said with dignity. Which he should know after her ill-advised behavior at her brother James's wedding five years ago. Her cheeks burned hotter at the memory.

"Fine, Dr. Katherine Pappas." His smile broadened, showing his white teeth. "How did you almost kill her?"

"I didn't almost kill her, and you know it. I didn't do anything." Katy's voice rose to practically a squeak on

the last word and she cleared her throat, forcing herself
to sound somewhat professional. "I was talking with her
and giving her an exam, and she just fainted. I think she
probably has sick sinus syndrome, which is why she's
sometimes fine and other times faints."

"Do you, now?" He laughed. Actually laughed, and
Katy felt her face heat again, but this time in annoyance.

"Yes, I do. I may be a total newbie, but I'm allowed
to give my opinion, aren't I? Isn't it part of my training
to form an opinion, even if it's wrong?"

"It is. And you are. Right, I mean, not wrong. And
why am I not surprised that on your first day you've
figured out this woman's likely diagnosis?" He stepped
closer, touching his fingertip to her forehead and giving it a few little taps. "Some things never change, and
one of them is that amazing, analytical brain of yours."

Some things never changed? Wasn't that the unfortunate truth? In spite of him making clear he had no interest in her as a woman, in spite of everything she knew
about the kind of man he was, being so close to Alec
made her breath a little short, which irritated her even
more. How was it possible that the deepest corners of her
brain still clung to the youthful crush she used to have?
But being on Dr. Playboy's teaching service for the next
month would most definitely squelch the final remnants
of that for good. She was sure of it.

His fingertip slipped to her temple then dropped away.
"Teaching rounds begin in an hour. Not too many people
get to brag about dealing with a code on their very first
day." That crooked grin stayed on his mouth as he gave
her a little wink. "You did great. Welcome to Oceancrest, Katy-Did."

He turned and walked from the room, and she found

herself staring at his back. Noticing that his thick dark hair was slightly longer than the last time she'd seen him. Noticing how unbelievably great his butt looked in those scrubs, how his shoulders filled every inch of the green fabric.

Noticing how horribly unkempt she herself looked at that moment. She looked down at her own wrinkled scrubs before she glanced in Mrs. Roberts's bathroom mirror at circles under her eyes the size of an IV bag. Ridiculously messy hair that had been finger-combed at best and now looked like it had been tamed by an egg-beater. Sleeping in the on-call room—if you could call the few hours her eyes had been closed sleeping—did not exactly lend itself to looking pulled together and rested.

She sighed and ran her fingers through her hair. Why did it have to be that the first time Alec saw her at the hospital, she looked like a wreck?

And why did she care, anyway? The man was a player through and through.

Never would Alec have guessed he'd someday have Katy Pappas on his surgical teaching service. The cute but clumsy little girl who'd bugged the hell out of him and her brother Nick when they'd been young, tagging along on their adventures and asking nonstop questions, for some reason believing they'd know the answers.

The worshipful gaze of her blue eyes had always made his chest puff up a little with pride. Despite how much he and Nick had complained about her hanging out with them, he'd always secretly liked it when she had. That someone had thought he was smart and worthy of that kind of adulation had felt damned good, since it had been in very short supply in his own home.

The nonstop criticism his father had doled out had made Alec want to live up—or down—to his father's expectations of him. He'd worked as hard at partying as he had at football, and probably the only reason he hadn't gone down in flames had been because he'd had the steady support of the Pappas family, and Dr. George Pappas in particular.

After he and Nick had headed off to college and medical school, he hadn't seen the Pappas clan again until five years ago at a family wedding. Gobsmacked that Katy, awkwardly geeky child and studious teenager, had morphed into a drop-dead gorgeous twenty-one-year-old woman, he remembered standing stock-still, staring at her in disbelief. Shocked that he'd found her attractive in a way that was *not* at all brotherly.

He'd been even more shocked when, standing in a quiet corner at the reception, a champagne-tipsy Katy had grabbed his face between her hands and pressed her mouth to his. A mouth so warm and soft and delectable that every synapse in his brain had short-circuited and he'd found himself kissing her back. Their lips had parted and tongues had danced as he'd sunk deeply into the mind-boggling pleasure of it.

Then sanity had returned and he'd practically pushed her away, horrified. No way could he have anything like that with Katy Pappas, little sister of his best friend. She was totally off-limits. Period.

He'd tried to make a joke of it. Katy, however, hadn't thought it was remotely amusing when he'd told her he didn't feel that way about her, and that it would be all wrong if he did.

If she'd been pressed closer against him, she would

have known part of that statement was a lie. But appropriate? Hell, no.

He sighed. From that moment on his friendship with Katy had been pretty much over. She'd been cool at other family functions since then. Aloof, even.

Alec had shoved down his feelings of disappointment that she was no longer the Katy who'd thought he was great. Hell, after the mess he'd made of some things in his life, he shouldn't expect anyone to feel that way.

Then he'd walked into the coding patient's room and seen her, wrinkled, messy, and nervous. Beautifully messy and nervous, yes, but so much like the Katy he'd once known he hadn't been able to help but want that old friendship back.

And just like the old Katy, in the midst of all the chaos she'd still shown what a brainiac she was. That she was good at figuring out what to do in any circumstances, despite being brand new at the art and science of doctoring.

Maybe it was absurd, pathetic even, but he wanted to see again the Katy who used to like and admire him, who had tolerated and even enjoyed his teasing.

Alec remembered well the feel of her lips against his. But a woman like her no doubt had so many boyfriends that a little kiss five years ago would have been completely forgotten.

CHAPTER TWO

As Alec strode down the hall, he could see the residents and interns waiting for him at the end of it, but his gaze stuck fast on Katy.

She'd changed into street clothes and a lab coat, and had obviously found a minute to brush her hair, which was no longer in a tangle but instead covered her shoulders in lustrous waves. He remembered that thick hair of hers always falling into her eyes and face as they'd studied things together, and he'd gotten into the habit of tucking its softness behind her ears so she'd been able to see whatever he and Nick had been showing her.

Her hands waving around as she spoke—another thing that was such a part of who she was—Katy was talking intently to the young man next to her, a frown creasing her brows, which made Alec smile. If he had to guess, she was regaling the other new intern with details about some condition or patient she was wondering about, because that brain of hers never rested.

"Good morning, everyone. I'm Dr. Alec Armstrong, as most of you know." He forced his attention from Katy to look at the young man she was speaking with. "You must be Michael Coffman, one of our new interns. We're glad you're here. Please tell us about yourself."

"I'm going into general surgery, planning to special-ize in urology."

"Excellent. Our other intern here is Katy Pappas." He smiled at her, but she just gave a small nod in return. "Tell us about your intended specialty."

"I'm going into family practice medicine. I really enjoyed working with all kinds of people during med school." She looked at the group around her and her ex-pression warmed. "Older folks and little ones and ev-erybody in between. Figuring out what their medical problems are, when sometimes it can be a bit of a mys-tery, fascinates me. Knowing I'm helping individuals and families alike. I'm going to love doing that kind of work."

She spoke fast, her blue eyes now sparkling with the enthusiasm he remembered from their childhood when-ever she had been tackling a puzzle or been deep into a science project, and his own smile grew.

"I'm glad you've discovered your calling. Figuring that out is sometimes the hardest part of medical school." He found himself wanting to keep looking at her, wanting to hear her speak and see her smile, but he made himself turn to the rest of the group.

"So let's continue our introductions. This is our fifth-year surgical resident, Elizabeth Stark, who performed some of the surgeries on the patients we'll see this morn-ing. You met our second-year surgical resident, Todd Ei-terman, this morning on work rounds."

Alec finished the spiel he always gave new interns, hoping they actually listened. "Beyond the nuts and bolts of diagnosis and surgery I want to teach you how to talk to people, to ask questions and listen carefully to the answers, which is the only way to truly learn their histories. Conclude what you think the working diagnosis might be then order tests based on those conclusions."

"Excuse me, Dr. Armstrong, but last month Dr. Hillenbrand said the opposite, so I'm confused," Todd, the second-year resident, said with a frown. "I thought we were to order tests then, based on those tests, come up with a working diagnosis."

"Technology is an amazing thing, Todd. But it can't replace hands-on doctoring, which is the single most important thing I want you to learn on my rotation." Alec studied the expressions on the faces before him. Smug understanding from Elizabeth, who'd heard it more times from him than she wanted to, he was sure, and also liked to play suck-up to the doctor evaluating her. Skepticism from Todd. Bewilderment and confusion from Michael. And avid concentration and focus from Katy's big blue eyes, which made him wish he could pin a gold star on her before rounds had even begun.

The thought sent his gaze to the lapels of her coat and the V of smooth, golden skin showing above her silky blouse, and he quickly shifted his attention to Todd. She was his student, damn it. And perhaps someday again his friend. But thinking of her as a very attractive woman? An absolute no-no.

"We'll be seeing patients who had surgery the past couple of days," he continued, keeping his eyes off Katy. "But first we'll see Mrs. Patterson, on whom tests were run yesterday. I know you've made your work rounds, so a lot of what I'm going to say will be a repeat of what you already know."

Alec led the way toward Helen Patterson's room with the group of students following behind. Katy was closest to him, and her light, fresh scent seemed to waft to him, around him, pleasing his nostrils so much he picked up the pace to put another foot or so between them.

What kind of doctor was distracted by someone's sex appeal while in the middle of work? Not the kind of doctor he demanded he be, that was for sure. Not the kind of doctor he'd been at one time, long ago when he'd been younger and stupid.

"Dr. Pappas, will you tell me about this patient from your work rounds this morning?"

"This is Mrs. Helen Patterson, and she has been in a rehabilitation nursing facility for one week, post-op after surgery for a broken hip," Katy said. "She was admitted here yesterday for abdominal pain and referred to the surgery service. She had low blood pressure and her lactate was elevated."

Katy licked her lips nervously, and Alec yanked his gaze away from them. He tried to simply listen and not notice the serious blue of her eyes as she spoke. "We ordered a CT scan of her belly, and there was no evidence of perforation in the bowel or appendicitis. We observed her overnight, gave her IV fluids and pain meds and she has spontaneously improved. We've determined that she has a mild case of ischemic colitis. She had a normal breakfast, and her physical exam is normal, so she can be released today."

Her expression was both pleased and slightly anxious, and Alec hoped he wouldn't have to remind her about the low potassium he'd read about in Mrs. Patterson's chart, and that the repeat potassium was still slightly low. "And?"

"And her potassium was low this morning, but I gave orders that brought it up."

"Except that those orders were all wrong, Dr. Pappas,"

Elizabeth said. She had on her usual superior smirk that Alec had tried, with limited success, to get her to tone down when talking to less-experienced students. "You gave her forty mils to drink, which is way too much to give orally. How did you expect someone to drink that amount? I can only imagine how nasty it tasted to poor Mrs. Patterson. No surprise that she vomited it up and had to be given some intravenously to replace it."

Katy's smile froze, and all color seeped from her face, then surged back to fill her light olive skin with a deep rose flush. "What...? I... Oh. Oh, no! I didn't order forty mil. I ordered four ml!"

"Really?" Elizabeth raised her eyebrows. "Nurses sometimes mishear an order, but it's still your responsibility—"

To Alec's shock, Katy turned and tore into the patient's room, and he quickly followed. What in the world was she doing?

She slid to the side of the patient's bed and reached for the woman's hand. Katy's expression was the absolute picture of remorse. "Helen, I didn't know it was my fault you got sick to your stomach this morning. I feel terrible! I guess the nurse misheard me and gave you way too much to drink. That's why you vomited. I'm so, so sorry."

Alec was torn between being impressed that she instantly took responsibility for what technically wasn't her mistake, and concern that the patient might get angry and let loose on her. He stood next to Katy, placed his hand on her back to let her know he was there to support her. "It's unfortunate that orders get confused sometimes, Mrs. Patterson. You're feeling okay now, though, aren't you?"

"Yes, it was just an upset stomach. Don't be angry

with dear, lovely Dr. Pappas, now. She's such a good doctor. Everyone makes mistakes once in a while."

Dear, lovely Dr. Pappas? Alec smiled in relief. Obviously, the woman liked Katy and wasn't going to create a stink about the error. He glanced at the residents standing at the end of the bed and almost laughed at the variety of expressions on their faces. Michael was wide-eyed, Todd scowling, and Elizabeth fuming. Having been raked over the proverbial coals often during their training, the two more experienced doctors had obviously been hoping for the same for Katy.

"I'm glad you're feeling better." He looked at Katy and, luckily, she understood that he wanted her to stop holding the woman's hand and stand next to him in a more professional manner.

"Helen, as you can see, I have some interns and residents here with me this morning. Is it all right if they stay while we talk?"

"Of course, that's fine."

"Thank you." He proceeded to ask her questions and explain tests that were run, while palpating her abdomen and listening to her heart and lungs. In the midst of it she held up her hand and interrupted.

"Wait a minute." Helen frowned at him. "First, why don't you warm up that stethoscope before you press it on my skin, like Dr. Pappas always does? That thing is cold!" She shifted her attention to Katy. "And why is he asking me the same things you asked me already, dear? Don't you two talk to each other?"

Katy laughed a little, and glanced at him with a smile in her eyes that felt like old times, making him smile, too. "It's just how it's done when we're being taught by the attending physician, Helen. I know it's kind of annoying but Dr. Armstrong is an amazing surgeon. I promise you're in good hands."

How absurd that her words, which were just to reassure the patient, made him almost feel like puffing up his chest just like the teen Alec who'd always appreciated her faith in him. Helen nodded and waved her hand. "Fine. Carry on."

"I appreciate the endorsement, Dr. Pappas." Alec could hear warmth creeping into his voice as he spoke and concentrated on cooling it. On sounding professional and impartial.

Katherine Pappas was his best friend's little sister and his own student. He had to make sure no one thought they saw any kind of favoritism in the way he interacted with her.

The term "bone-tired" took on a whole new meaning after all-night call with minimal sleep followed by a long day of rounding and scut work. Katy thought she'd worked long and hard in med school, but that had been a veritable party compared to this.

As she stepped through the front door into Nick's living room, he emerged from the kitchen. "Katy-Did, you're finally home! You look beat."

"Now, there's a surprise. I'm sure I look every bit as hot, sweaty, and wrinkled as I feel."

"Living hot, sweaty, and wrinkled is an intern's existence pretty much. Sometimes it's a general surgeon's existence, too." Nick grinned. "I knew you'd be exhausted, so I'm fixing dinner. You don't have to do a thing."

"Aw, you're the sweetest big brother anyone could ever have." She gave him a quick hug, hoping she didn't smell too bad. "What are we eating?"

"Steaks from the grill, baked potatoes, veggies. To celebrate your first day, and because you probably need iron and protein after practically twenty-four hours of work. How did it go, rounding with Alec?"

"He's a good teacher, of course. I'm sure I'll learn a lot from him." She dropped into a chair in Nick's living room because she thought her legs just might give out if she was on her feet another minute. "But you know how I feel about him personally."

"Katy." Her brother's smile faded. "Alec is a good guy, and I regret that I ever told you what happened. Yes, he went through a hellion stage when there was too much partying and too many of the wrong kinds of women in his life, but that was a long time ago. You need to cut him some slack."

"Why? He's not the person I thought he was. I'm allowed to be bothered by that, aren't I?"

"You thought he was cool and smart and cared about other people. You liked him because he treated you great. And that's exactly who he is, along with older and wiser than he was back then. Hell, I'm still working on the older and wiser part."

"Don't worry, I'm not going to be unpleasant or anything. I just don't want to be friends with him again, that's all."

"Well, that's too bad. Just remember he's still my friend. And a partner in my practice." He frowned at her for a moment then sighed. "You never really knew that Alec's dad was always putting him down, and I think that's part of why he acted out some back then. But for a long time now he's worked hard to gain respect. It's important to him. While he never did get it from his dad, he has it in spades from everyone here."

"I'm sure he's a good doctor, so of course people respect him."

"It's more than that, but I'm not going to waste my breath trying to convince you." He turned toward the kitchen. "I'm going to get the steaks on the grill and play with the dogs out in the yard. I'll let you know when it's ready."

He disappeared, and she stayed slumped in the chair, closing her eyes. Which made ignoring the mess of stuff she'd left lying around the room, still packed and unorganized, much easier. She knew she should work on it right now since Nick was being so sweet about letting her live with him for a while, but she also knew he was happy to let her rest a moment.

Much as he'd teased her over the years, Nick had been good to her, too. All six of the Pappas kids were, in fact, close, which Katy was more than thankful for. As an only child, she knew Alec had never had a sibling that he fought with sometimes but who also always had his back, and she knew that had been a big part of why he'd been at their house so much. Her mother had welcomed him, and her dad had adored and mentored him.

Which was why learning of his unethical and distasteful behavior had cut Katy to her very core. Not only that, Alec's parents had shoved what he'd done under a rug then wrapped it up with a nice tidy bow while someone else had paid the price.

Ah, who was she kidding? It hadn't been just his mistake and the aftermath that remained stuck as a sharp barb in her soul. It was that he'd done it all practically right after she'd boldly kissed him and he'd pushed her away. Told her it wouldn't be "appropriate." Which obviously had just been another way of saying, *I think of you as a little sister, not a woman*, since "appropriate" clearly hadn't entered his mind before the scandal.

Her chest burned in embarrassment and disgust but at the same time she couldn't deny that the man was an impressive doctor and teacher. And, yes, even more ridiculously good looking than he'd been years ago. Today, in Mrs. Patterson's room, as they'd smiled together at the woman's comments, she had to admit it had felt nice. A little like old times, and thoughts of his past had momentarily faded from her brain until she'd sternly reminded herself.

She was smart enough to take advantage of his intelligence and experience and learn what she could from him, just as she had long ago. But as far as a friendship happening between them again? Never.

The doorbell rang and, still collapsed in the chair, she nearly groaned. The last thing she wanted to do was talk to anyone. Maybe if she ignored it, whoever it was would go away.

The bell rang again and with a resigned sigh she shoved herself from the chair and forced herself to open the door.

To her shock, Alec stood there, looking annoyingly handsome in jeans and a yellow polo shirt that showed off his broad shoulders. Sunglasses covered his eyes. The evening sun gleamed in his dark hair and his admittedly attractive lips were curved in a smile that no doubt had women flocking around him like seagulls. And yet again she looked like she'd been through the heavy-duty wash cycle and hung out to dry.

What was Alec doing here?

"Hello, Dr. Armstrong. What can I do for you?"

His dark eyebrows rose as he slipped off his sunglasses. "Oh, so formal. What happened to the old 'Hi Alec, come on in' you used to greet me with?"

How was she supposed to answer that? She wanted to say that had been back when she'd been young and naive and worn rose-colored glasses, but there was no point in going there. "I wasn't sure if I should call you Alec, as you're an attending and I'm a student."

"It's fine for you to call me Alec when we're not in the hospital. Unless you particularly like guys in scrubs and want to call me 'Doctor.'" The teasing grin he gave her was downright dazzling, and she turned away from its power, opening the door fully as she doubted he'd stopped by just to say hello then leave.

"Funny. Though perhaps you're saying that because I know that you particularly like women in scrubs. Or, even more, in nothing at all."

Crap, had she actually just said that? Her cheeks burned and she couldn't figure out what part of the room to focus on, because she sure as heck wasn't going to look at him now. She quickly walked over to the pile of stuff she'd pulled out of a box and left on the sofa yesterday.

"Katy Pappas, I'm shocked that you—"

"Sorry the place is a bit of a mess," she interrupted, the deeply amused rumble of his voice making her blush all over again. She did not want to hear whatever he'd been about to say in response to her extremely ill-advised comment. She grabbed up her things and shoved them back in the box. "I haven't had time to put away all my stuff yet."

"Don't worry, I saw the housekeeping police are busy a few blocks away. I think you're safe until tomorrow."

His voice still held laughter and she focused on the box. Not. Going. To look at him. "As you can see, I haven't had a chance to change my clothes. Excuse me while—"

Excited woofs drowned out her words as Nick's two yellow Labrador retrievers bounded through the house to greet Alec, slamming against Katy and nearly knocking her off her feet. "Whoa!" she yelped, her tired legs not quite balancing the way they should. Before she tumbled to the floor Alec lunged to grab her and hold her upright, flattening her tight against him.

Her hands slapped up against his muscular shoulders as the feel of his firm chest against her breasts, his strong arms around her sent her breathing haywire. Their eyes met, and the grin faded from his, replaced by what looked like a slightly confused frown.

The seconds ticked by and both stood motionless, oddly frozen, until Katy grabbed what wits she had left. She pushed against his shoulders and stepped back as his arms dropped to his sides, but their gazes remained locked. The tingling of her nerves and the imprint of his body that she could still feel against her own must be some sort of "muscle memory" thing, from the years she'd written in her journal about how much she wanted to be held close by Alec.

"I see you still have a little clumsiness problem."

Her gaze moved from the oddly disturbing eye contact to his lips, which disturbed her in a different way. She looked down at the dogs for a distraction. "I don't think being knocked into by these crazy pups of his makes me clumsy," she said, hoping she didn't sound as breathless as she felt. The dogs wagged their tails and rubbed against her for attention, leaving dog hair all over her black skirt. As if she wasn't already enough of a mess. "Nick can't have much company—they've acted like this every time someone comes to the door. If they hadn't been outside, we would have been mauled the second you came in."

"They're still young and rambunctious." He looked oddly serious, considering his teasing of just a moment ago. "And in case you don't remember, your dogs pretty much all acted this way at your family's house. I remember your mutt, Buddy, chewing up one of my shoes that I'd left at the door."

She looked up at him as she scratched the dogs' heads. "You had to put up with a lot at our house, didn't you? Utter chaos, with six crazy kids and badly behaved dogs."

"I think the term would be bedlam." The smile was back on his face, and why she was pleased to see it again she wasn't sure. "But I enjoyed every minute of the time I spent with Nick. And you. And the rest of your family, of course."

"You two sitting out there, socializing, with your feet up?" Nick's voice called from the kitchen. "Katy has the night off, but you don't, Alec. I need a hand here."

"Coming in a sec. Just realized I left the wine I brought in the car." His index finger reached out to give her nose a gentle flick, a soft stroke from between her brows to its tip as he'd done more times than she could possibly count, but the expression in his eyes seemed different than in the past. Hotter, more intimate, somehow, and her heart stupidly sped up in response.

Thankfully, he turned and went back out the door, and Katy sucked in a breath. She would not allow her old, youthful crush to muscle its way in and crowd out her older, smarter self. No way, no how.

She moved toward the kitchen, resolutely passing by the hallway to her bedroom with barely a longing glance.

She hadn't planned to do anything more than wash her hands for dinner and refused to give in to her sudden urge to clean up a little and change her clothes. Maybe it would even be a good thing, she thought as she shook her head at herself, if Alec noticed she didn't exactly smell perfume fresh.

"Why didn't you tell me you'd invited Alec for dinner?" she asked Nick in a whisper, even though she hadn't heard the man come back into the house.

"Because he's my best friend, and I didn't realize until tonight that you still felt such animosity toward him." Her brother glanced at her before he turned his attention back to the dinner. "Which I frankly hope you'll get over."

"No animosity. As I told you, I just don't want to be friends with him anymore." And her darned shortness of breath and flippity heart and awareness of his hunkiness quotient was far different from feelings of friendship anyway, dang it. Which made it even more important that they not be together anywhere but at work until her smart brain prevailed over her not-so-smart one. "But obviously, since he's my instructor for the month, I'm perfectly fine with spending work time with him. I just would've appreciated a heads-up."

"Okay. Hey, Katy-Did." Nick turned to her, the evil big-brother smile on his face she was more than used to. "Alec's coming over for dinner."

She rolled her eyes. "Thanks for telling me. If I'd known it wasn't just the two of us, I wouldn't have dressed up in my nicest clothes."

As Nick chuckled in response, Alec's voice filled the kitchen, followed by his tall, broad form. "You look good in whatever you're wearing, Katy."

She looked up at his eyes that were all golden and

warm again, accompanied by a beautiful smile that seemed absurdly sincere, since she knew she couldn't look much more of a wreck if she tried. Why did the darned man have to have the kind of charm that made it all too easy to overlook his not-charming characteristics?

"Thank you." She busied herself with getting the food together, despite both men's protests that she was supposed to be off duty. In short order, they were sitting at the small table, holding crystal glasses and lit, to her touched surprise, with candles.

"To Dr. Katherine Pappas," Nick said, holding up his glass of red wine. "Congratulations on finishing med school with honors and for living through your first day as an intern."

"Cheers to that," Alec said, his focus so entirely on her it was unnerving. "We always knew you were special, and you've proved it over and over again."

Special? And here she'd thought it had been her domain to think of Alec that way when they'd been young. "Thank you. And here's hoping I don't do anything stupid to embarrass you in rounds over the next month."

"You could never do anything to embarrass me, Katy, and that's a fact. I'm more than sure you're going to make me look good."

As if he needed her to make him look good.

They all sipped their drinks, and Katy wasn't sure if it was the wine slipping down her throat that made her chest feel so warm or something else. Something like Alec talking about the faith he had in her, as he had so many times in the past.

Despite it being just the three of them, their meal together brought a welcome feeling of normalcy. Almost like the years hadn't passed and Alec was just hanging out with the Pappas clan for dinner. Except those times would never come again. Her and Nick's father was gone, and Alec was not the knight in shining armor she'd painted him to be.

"I was called in to help with a rough surgery today," Nick said. "Bob Rollins had a teen girl with a torsion in her ovary, and when he opened her up she was a total mess. Had to bring in another gynecologist and me to dive in there with him to identify and try to save her entire reproductive system. So remember, Katy, don't be surprised if some surgeries turn out to be completely different than you expect." He gave her a pointed look. "Just like people."

It didn't take a genius to know what he was saying. "I'll remember."

Nick turned to Alec. "What time is your flight next weekend?"

"For the wedding? Nine a.m., I think."

"You were able to take time off even though you're doing teaching rounds?" Katy hoped she didn't sound as dismayed as she felt, but she wasn't excited about trying to keep her distance from him at another family event.

"You bet." A grin slowly creased his cheeks. "Maybe you can help me with my marginal Greek dancing skills."

She stared into his amused eyes then shook her head. Holding his hand in more ways than one? There had been a time when she'd have loved to. "You fake it well, Alec. You don't need anyone's help with that."

CHAPTER THREE

ALEC WONDERED WHY Katy's expression had become strained, just as he still wondered why she seemed so cool toward him. Surely she wasn't still upset about their little kiss from five years ago?

Then there'd be a brief moment when she was more like the old Katy he used to know. He couldn't deny that he wanted to see more of that Katy, who used to think he was great. Why did he miss her former adulation when he was no longer the troubled kid he used to be?

"Are your parents coming to the wedding?" Nick asked.

"I doubt it. They're both still in Russia while Dad teaches how to do his valve-replacement technique there." And he'd be just as glad to not have his father there, grilling him on his life and telling him his surgical work wasn't as important as a cardiologist's.

"I figured you'd have to work," Katy said, "so I hadn't even thought about you coming."

And didn't that make his ego feel great? Though the way she'd been toward him the past times he'd seen her at family get-togethers had shown she no longer thought of him much, period. "Are you really going to make me fake again that I can Greek-dance?" Alec asked, which earned him a small smile from her.

"Nick's the master dancer. He can teach you."

"Never did me much good in the past." It was pretty obvious Katy didn't want to teach him, which gave him a twinge of disappointment. He remembered well the times he'd watched her lead the dancing, mesmerized by her movements and her joyful smile. "What time are you two flying out?"

"Nick has us leaving at some crazy time, like six a.m.," Katy said with a scowl. "As though I'm not already getting zero sleep."

"Think of your lack of sleep as a rite of passage. Kind of like hazing in a fraternity," Nick said with a grin.

"Mr. Empathy, as usual," she said, punching her brother none too gently on the arm. Nick raised both fists, jabbing them in the air back at her.

"Okay, you two." Alec shook his head but at the same time he had to chuckle. Some things never changed. And when it came to the Pappas family, not changing was the best thing in the world, as far as Alec was concerned. "Truthfully, though, the more hours you're in the hospital, Katy, the more you're exposed to all different kinds of cases that are invaluable for learning. The time schedules aren't just for torture."

"I know, I know. I'll try to remember that in the midst of my zombie state tomorrow. I doubt we interns will even be able to stay awake for the after-work welcome dinner with the teaching staff," she said. Her tone might be grumbling, but those blue eyes of hers were lit with the enthusiasm and wonder he'd seen in them, and had always enjoyed, forever. She turned her beautifully lethal gaze on Nick. "Does it sound silly to say I'm really excited to be one of…of you now? A real doctor, like Dad?"

George Pappas. Alec's chest grew a little heavy, thinking of the man who'd been more of a father to him than his own. Knowing how hard it had been on every one of the man's family when he'd died. And on himself too, despite not being a real member of the Pappas tribe.

"Your dad would be proud of you." He reached for her soft hand and squeezed it. "He was proud of each one of you, but I think he had a special place in his heart for his youngest."

Tears filled her eyes, and he kicked himself. The last thing he wanted to do was make her sad. Then she smiled through the tears, and the jab of guilt eased.

"Thank you. I know I don't have much experience yet—that I have a crazy amount to learn. But I think you're right. I think he would be proud that I'm at least trying."

Trying? The Katy Pappas he knew never tried. She worked until she accomplished whatever damned goal she'd set for herself, from the most simple to the most difficult.

"There's no question about that, Katy," Nick said, his voice a little rough. "Here's another toast to you for always making him proud."

"To you, Katy." Alec raised his glass to hers. Maybe it was because she couldn't see too well through the tears in her eyes, but for whatever reason, as she tried to clink her glass to his, she completely missed. And managed to toss most of her glass of wine straight onto his lap.

"Oh! I'm so sorry, Alec!" Katy leaped from her seat, grabbing her napkin to dab vigorously at the wine staining the bottom of his shirt, moving down to dab even harder at the biggest pool of liquid in a place he didn't want her dabbing.

Or maybe he did, because seeing her hands on his groin, feeling them pressing against him, shortened his breath, stepped up the beat of his heart and invited an instant physical response he couldn't control.

"Let me handle it, Katy," he said, firmly grabbing her wrist before she could feel exactly what was happening to him and embarrass them both.

"But the stain is setting, and— Oh!" Suddenly her motions stilled and her widening eyes met his. Obviously, his body's response to her hands all over him was plenty clear.

"Yeah. 'Oh.'" What else could he say? Except maybe, *Touch me some more, please.*

"Katy, having you around sure livens things up." Laughing, Nick headed to the kitchen. "I'll get a wet towel."

"I'm…sorry. Really sorry. So, so sorry." Her face was nearly as red as the wine, and she stood staring at him as though she was frozen.

"It's okay. Really." He should be sorry, too. Sorry that she felt embarrassed, sorry that his clothes might be ruined, and sorry that his body had responded the way it had. In spite of all that, though, he found he didn't feel sorry at all. In fact, his primary feeling at the moment was wishing the two of them were alone so he could strip off his wet clothes and see if that led anywhere good.

As soon as the thought came, the heat that had surged throughout his body was quickly replaced by ice, and he wanted to pummel some sense into himself. Not only was Katy Nick's little sister, she was his student, damn it. He absolutely could not think of her in that way, ever, despite the fact that, right now, he clearly was. But that was not acceptable. Not under any circumstances, but especially while he was her superior at the hospital.

He'd already tried to blow up his own career with that kind of mistake, and had succeeded all too well in blowing up someone else's. The last thing he wanted was to lose the respect he'd tried so hard to regain since his stupidity of the past.

And risking Katy's career and reputation with the same kind of stupidity? Never.

Had she really rubbed her hands all around and pressed down on Alec's privates?

Katy walked down the hospital corridor, face burning as she thought about the reality that, yes, she sure had. Even worse, she now knew something she hadn't before. Which was that he apparently became aroused easily and was more than well endowed.

Long ago, she'd fantasized about—well—all of that. But she knew last night's impressive reaction had had nothing to do with her. Lots of men might respond that way to any woman fondling them, inadvertently or not. And since Alec had gone through girlfriends in high school like a patient with a bad cold went through tissues, she shouldn't be surprised he was one of them.

What was a surprise had been her own reaction. That in addition to feeling beyond embarrassed, she'd also found herself fascinated by the swelling beneath those jeans of his. As though she was some innocent kid and not a grown woman. She was quite sure Alec's swelling—and what a ridiculous way for her, a doctor, to be thinking of his erection—was no more impressive than any other man's. Well, she wasn't sure, but she no longer had any desire to find out. Did. Not.

For the tenth time that morning she shoved down thoughts of any and all of Alec's body parts and headed to her next patient's room. "Good morning, Helen!" Katy stepped to Mrs. Patterson's bedside and patted her thin shoulder. "Ready to go home?"

"I wish I could. But I'm heading back to rehab at the nursing home until I'm stronger."

"I know. But you're going to be out of there before you know it." She took her stethoscope from her neck and pressed the bell to her palm to warm it before she placed it against the woman's chest. "Do you have someone to help take care of you when you're home?"

"My daughter's coming for a bit after I'm home. Today, though, my son is taking me back to rehab."

"That's good." The woman didn't look too excited about that, but who would be? "I know it's not much fun doing rehab, but knowing it's going to make you independent again makes it worth it."

"I don't mind it, really. The nurses and physical therapists are lovely. But all this has been very depressing." Helen sighed. "Until I broke my hip, I was pretty strong and walked my little dogs every day. Now I feel just awful with this stomach pain. It's enough to make me want to move on to heaven to be with my Albert."

The sadness and frustration on the poor woman's face squeezed Katy's heart. She wrapped her arm around Helen's shoulders to give her a hug. "I can imagine how hard it is to feel weak and not well when you're used to being up and about. But your tests don't show any problems, so I bet you're going to be feeling good again soon. Hang in there."

A tall, skinny man with long hair knocked on the doorjamb, which surprised Katy. It couldn't be any later than seven a.m. "Can I come in?"

"Hello, Jeffrey." Helen shifted her gaze from the man to Katy. "Dr. Pappas, this is my son. Jeffrey, this is Dr. Pappas. She's been taking good care of me."

"Thanks for that," Jeffrey said, then came to stand between Katy and his mother, rather rudely. "Mom, I need a little cash to fix my car. Can you front me a loan? I brought your checkbook."

"I just gave you money for your car last week." Helen frowned, but took the checkbook he handed her.

"I know, but there's something else wrong now, so I've been driving yours. I'll pay you back soon."

"This has to be the last time. My medical bills are adding up." Helen scribbled out a check. "Please remember I need you to pick me up whenever I'm released today."

"Okay. Call me." He dropped a quick kiss on her forehead and headed out the door. Katy couldn't believe he hadn't even asked his sweet mother how she was feeling.

She squeezed Mrs. Patterson's hand one more time. "If I don't see you again before you're released, I hope you're back to walking your pups very soon."

Katy left the room and looked at her patient notes. Next was a seven-year-old boy named David, who'd had a complication when his appendix had ruptured. Alec had done the surgery nearly a week before Katy had arrived, but the poor child still had a drain in his belly.

About to knock quietly on David's door in case he was still asleep, she was surprised to hear the deep rumble of a man's voice. Then was even more surprised to see Alec in scrubs, sitting on the side of the boy's bed. What was he doing, seeing a patient so early?

She shoved aside the discomfort that again heated her cheeks. She had to see the man every day, for heaven's sake, and he'd probably forgotten all about the little fondling incident. "Good morning, Dr. Armstrong. You're an early bird today."

"I wanted to stop in and see our star patient before I start morning surgery." He stood and smiled down at David. "The drain's looking good, buddy. We just might be able to take it out in a day or two."

"I can't wait!" David grinned, showing a missing tooth. "But I'm feeling lots better, Dr. Armstrong. Thanks for the car stuff you brought me. Will you come back and see me later?"

"I'll try, David." He tousled the boy's hair and turned to leave, and his sweet expression and the warmth in his eyes made Katy's breath catch in her throat.

Had she ever seen him around children before? Except back when she'd been a child? She couldn't remember, but it seemed he was pretty good with them. His surgery schedule was so heavy she couldn't imagine he'd be able to come back to see the child later, not to mention that the welcome dinner was tonight, but it was nice of him to tell the boy he'd try.

"I've checked David out, so you don't need to, Dr. Pappas." They moved to the shadow of the doorway where he paused. "What patient are you seeing next?"

They stood so close together she could smell his aftershave, see a tiny spot next to his lips that he'd missed when shaving, feel the heat of his body near hers. Unwittingly, her thoughts turned to touching him the night before, and she started to feel overly warm. From embarrassment, of course.

"Mr. Lyons in 2215."

"Better watch out you don't spill anything on him. Mr. Lyons can be quite a character."

Lord, she'd hoped he wouldn't mention it again. Even in the low light of the room she could see the amused glint in his eyes. His lips tipped up into a slow smile, and she found herself staring at his mouth. Swallowing, she took a step away from him so she could breathe. "Can we please just forget about that? You know I sometimes have a clumsiness problem."

"I'll try to forget about it. But you know what, Dr. Pappas? I'm pretty sure that's not going to happen."

He left the room and she sucked in a breath. Their exchange had smacked dangerously of flirting, and she shouldn't let that happen. Also shouldn't enjoy it, but she'd be lying to herself if she claimed she hadn't.

About to head to her next patient's room, Katy realized she'd been so distracted she hadn't thought to ask Alec to sign Mr. Lyons' release papers. What was wrong with her? Work had to be her number-one focus, dang it.

She hurried down the hall to catch Alec, wishing their last conversation hadn't been about her grabbing his privates. His tall figure stood by an elevator, and she stepped up her pace. "Dr. Armstrong!"

He turned to her, and his gaze swept her slowly from head to toe. Feeling a little breathless from hurrying, she stopped next to him. "I forgot to ask you to sign Mr. Lyons' release papers."

She looked up at him, his eyes meeting hers for a long moment before he reached for the papers. "And I forgot to ask you if you're excited about helping with some surgeries in a few days. I've put you first on the list."

"Is that an honor, or is it because you want me in and out of there before I kill someone?"

"We try not to let interns kill anybody. It's against hospital policy."

So were some other things he hadn't worried about in the past. But, of course, he was joking. "I confess I'm not excited. But I'm sure it will be an interesting experience."

"It will be. Especially for you, Miss Science. Weren't you always the one conducting various weird experiments on the kitchen counter until your mom yelled at you?"

"Is this your way of calling me a geek? I—" Her phone beeped a text message and she looked at it then frowned. This couldn't be right.

"What is it?"

"The nurse says Mrs. Levitz is having a panic attack. Shortness of breath, chest pain, and a fast heartbeat."

"She's the one who had her gall bladder removed by Nick yesterday, right?" Alec asked, his teasing expression instantly replaced by calm professionalism. "Her chart said she's prone to panic attacks. Prescribe lorazepam and see how she does."

Katy frowned up at Alec. "I don't know. I left her only a short time ago and she was fine. Looking forward to being discharged. I just don't see her having a panic attack right now."

"Since she has a history of them, most likely that's what it is. You'll see this more often than you would guess." His eyes were thoughtful, seeming to study her. "But sometimes it's important to listen to your instincts. Go see her. Let Nick know your conclusion and what your thoughts are on what needs to be done."

"Okay. I will. Thanks." She turned and her chest felt suddenly buoyant. How could it not when Alec had basically just told her he had faith in her to figure it out?

She had a ridiculous impulse to look over her shoulder to see if he still stood there and was surprised that he was. Not just standing there but holding the elevator door open with his eyes still on her.

Something about his expression made her heart thump a little, and she realized she was failing miserably in keeping her former crush from rearing its ugly head. Also failing in re-erecting the cool wall she'd been so good at keeping between them before she'd started working there.

"Hello, Mrs. Levitz," she said as she walked into the patient's room. "I hear you're feeling upset."

"I don't know what's wrong." The poor woman was breathing hard and wringing her hands. The brown eyes staring up at Katy were filled with fear. "My chest hurts. I don't feel good. I'm scared."

"Okay, let's take a look," Katy said in a soothing voice as she took her pulse. No doubt about it, Mrs. Levitz was behaving completely differently than she had been only an hour earlier. But why? A panic attack seemed unlikely, despite her chart saying she was prone to them, since she certainly hadn't been worried about going home. Quite the opposite. But something was going on, there was no doubt about that.

"Did something upset or worry you, Mrs. Levitz?"

"No. No. I just started feeling bad all of a sudden."

"Her chart says she often has panic attacks," the nurse said in a low voice as she reset the monitor that had been screeching at the patient's elevated pulse.

"I know," Katy murmured. "But that just doesn't seem right to me, after speaking with her earlier." Think, Katy. What could be going on here that's not obvious? Chest pain, shortness of breath, and elevated heart rate were, indeed, consistent with a panic attack. But as she peered at the monitor next to the bed she noted that Mrs. Levitz's oxygen level was low, too. And a panic attack wouldn't cause that.

With tension rising in her own chest, she pulled out her little medical book and studied it. Thought back to the cases she'd had in med school. Then she nearly shouted *Eureka* as the answer struck her.

Pulmonary embolism. Unusual, but not impossible after gall-bladder surgery, and it would account for every symptom the woman was experiencing. It was a post-op complication she knew every surgeon dreaded. It also had to be diagnosed and addressed immediately.

"I want a CT scan run on Mrs. Levitz," she said to the nurse, adrenaline surging through her. *"Stat."*

CHAPTER FOUR

KATY STOOD IN the park by Mission Bay and breathed in the tangy sea air. This was exactly why she'd wanted to train in San Diego. The beautiful sandy beaches with tall, swaying palms, the emerald-green grass, the deep blue of the water were all utterly breathtaking. Why choose to work in a cold, gray, rainy place when you could be here?

All kinds of people mingled and chatted at this welcome party for students and staff, but she felt like she'd been talking nonstop all day and enjoyed having a little moment of quiet.

A server stopped next to her with a tray of champagne, and she swiped the last of the sand from her hands and took a glass. Hopefully no one had noticed her sneak down to the beach to dig in the sand and see what creatures lived in there. She'd found little gray crabs of all sizes, and the moment she did she found herself ridiculously looking at the crowd to see if Alec had arrived so she could show him.

Hadn't she decided to stay cool and as distant as possible? To keep their relationship strictly professional as student and teacher?

But the crab discovery had instantly taken her back to all their adventuring days together. To how he'd never made fun of her experiments and discoveries, and in fact had seemed to enjoy them as much as she had. She'd been shocked at the disappointment she'd felt when he was nowhere in sight.

How strange that she still had this ingrained habit of looking to him now that he was back in her life, so to speak. She knew it for what it was, though, which gave her complete power to control it.

She moved closer to the crowd, figuring she should socialize a bit and maybe learn something in the process.

"I had so much pizza last night I'm not going to do justice to the food here," a nurse said to the group of women she was standing with.

"I know." A different woman chuckled. "Dr. Armstrong bought enough to feed an army, which was really sweet of him. Just because we all worked so late on the emergency perforated ulcer didn't mean he had to spring for dinner for everyone."

"He always does that when we work late. I just love him. If I wasn't married, I'd have his babies."

The group of women laughed and Katy moved on, not wanting to be an eavesdropper. She'd heard women swooning over the hunky surgeon before—but the fact that he bought pizza after a long day? She'd probably want to have his babies too.

No. Wrong thought. All wrong.

As though drawn by some magnetic force, her eyes lifted to the opposite edge of the party, and there stood Alec. Looking even better in casual dress clothes than he did in scrubs—which seemed nearly impossible, since he looked incredible in them—his hair fluttered across his forehead as he spoke with the woman standing next to him.

The woman stepped closer until they were nearly

touching. There was nothing professional or distant about their body language as she rested her hand on his biceps, and the woman had a clear, come-hither look on her attractive face. The face of fifth-year resident Elizabeth Stark.

Katy's gut squeezed and her hand tightened on the stem of her glass. Here it was, right in her face. A cold reminder of who exactly Alec Armstrong was in addition to the good-with-children, pizza-bringing surgeon the nurses adored. Why she'd kept her distance from him until working together had made that impossible.

The image bothered her far more than it should have, considering she'd known all about his player reputation of the past, which clearly was also part of his present. Just as she was thrashing herself for feeling illogically disturbed, Alec stepped back from Elizabeth. His lips flat-lined from the cordial smile there a moment ago, and a frown creased his brow.

Then he walked away, leaving Elizabeth staring after him.

Had they had some kind of tiff? Or was it because Alec wasn't like that any more, as Nick had insisted? The thought lightened the weight in her chest. Maybe she'd held onto her disappointment in him for too long. Maybe it was time to let that go, to see the more mature Alec. The man who still had so many of the appealing qualities of his youth.

Surely she was more mature, too. Mature enough to put behind her old crush and hurt at his rejection and accept him as a friend again.

Alec tried not to stare at Katy, making anyone who might notice wonder why, but he couldn't seem to stop his gaze from traveling back to her. The fragrant breeze coming from the bay fluttered the floral dress she wore, which was significantly shorter than her conservative hospital clothes. He knew he damn well shouldn't but he couldn't resist letting his gaze slowly drop from her appealing face down the length of her body. To her breasts, which were completely covered by a neckline that went all the way up to her collarbone but were still all too well outlined by the filmy fabric.

He'd thought, more than once, that no woman looked better in scrubs than Katy. But watching her now, with the wind outlining her body and the evening sun giving her hair a golden glow, he realized she looked even more spectacular outside the hospital.

Smart, sweet, and gorgeous were one damned lethal combination.

When he'd first found out Katy would be coming to Oceancrest as an intern, he'd been pleased, thinking it would be a good chance to renew the friendship she hadn't seemed to want to continue. Never would he have dreamed he'd have so much trouble keeping himself from looking at her every curve, trouble keeping firmly in mind that she was a student and Nick's little sister.

Hell, who was he kidding? After the way he'd responded to her kiss long ago, he should have known. Shouldn't have been surprised at the stirring of attraction he'd felt the second he'd seen her that first day in the coding patient's room. More than a stirring when she'd wiped the wine from his body. Now every time he saw Katy he saw a special woman there was no denying he wanted more than friendship with.

This inconvenient attraction—hell, unacceptable attraction—was a problem he wasn't sure how to deal with.

"Alec." Nick came to stand next to him and he was glad for a reason to stop watching Katy. "You missed the speeches. Which I'm sure you're real sad about."

"Yeah. Not. After hearing the CEO give the same speech at every welcome gathering, I may be forced to write a new one for him myself."

Nick turned his head to the crowd of people mingling in the park then turned back to Alec. "What—or should I say, who—are you looking at?"

"Uh, nobody in particular. Just seeing who's here." Was it that obvious his gaze kept returning to Katy? Of all the many people he didn't want to notice that, number one was Nick.

"I saw one person here who's already singled you out. Elizabeth Stark," Nick said. "Tell me you aren't going to fall for her coming on to you."

"Why would you even ask me that? Since when are you my father?" Alec frowned at Nick as they walked up the slope of grass. Hadn't he tried his damnedest to make sure he never got involved with any woman at the hospital? To make sure he and his reputation were stainless now? "You know, it was five years ago. At a different hospital. In a different capacity. I think the chief medical officer is the only person here who even knows about it."

"I know that mess is in the past. You're the one who still avoids any woman within a ten-mile radius of the hospital."

"Then why are you on my case about Elizabeth? Who, for the record, I have zero interest in."

"Because Elizabeth is a student, who's made it clear she has more than zero interest in you." Nick stared at him like he'd grown two heads. "Which you sure as hell know is different than just someone working in the hospital."

No one knew that better than Alec. His gaze caught on Katy again, and his stomach twisted. Good to be reminded that he couldn't think of her the way he kept thinking of her. That he couldn't look at her smooth skin and imagine touching it, couldn't think about tangling his fingers in her soft hair, couldn't want to cover her sweetly smiling lips with his own.

Alec gritted his teeth and forced his attention back to Nick as they headed to the food table. "Don't worry. I'll never cross that line again."

Nick nodded, the conversation obviously over, thankfully. "How about that sister of mine?"

Alec's heart nearly stopped. Surely Nick hadn't noticed... Ah, hell. "What about her?"

"She's been saving lives all by herself."

"Saving lives?" The tightness in Alec's chest slid away. "What did she do?"

"You didn't hear?" Nick grinned at him. "One of my patients. Post-op gall bladder, with anxiety disorder. Everybody assumed she just needed a dose of lorazepam to calm her down, but Katy figured out what was really wrong."

Alec remembered Katy talking with him about the patient earlier. "So, what was wrong?"

"I guess Katy just had a gut feeling about it not being a panic attack, despite the woman's history. Ordered a CT scan and found pulmonary emboli. Got her into the ICU, got a heparin drip going and—bam! Alive and well." Nick looked as pleased as if he'd been the one who'd figured out the problem, though, of course, the woman was his patient, too. "Gotta say, I'm pretty proud of her. I don't think too many first-year interns would have thought of that, especially knowing about the patient's anxiety disorder."

"You've got that right." Alec felt a peculiar pride welling up within his chest, which seemed ridiculous. It wasn't as though his teaching had helped her figure it out. And she was Nick's sister, not his. "I've already seen that Katy has good instincts when it comes to patients. Great bedside manner and rapport, too. The only thing she lacks sometimes is self-confidence, so this is bound to give her that." And wasn't that the truth? He couldn't think of anything lacking in the woman, including the sex appeal that just oozed from her without her even being aware of it.

His gaze slipped back to where she'd been and saw she was headed their way. A good chance to congratulate her on her great job with Mrs. Levitz, then mingle with others to keep his distance.

"Hey, Nick! Alec. How can you two stand not to be out here every day? This place is beautiful!" Strands of her silky hair feathered across her face in the breeze, and her slim fingers shoved them aside as she smiled at him.

"It is beautiful. And I'm out here every day I can be. My condo is just across the bay."

"Is it really? I'll bet your view is amazing."

"It is. I could take you sailing or kayaking some time, if you want." Sailing with her sounded great to Alec. Also sounded like a hell of a bad idea, and he quickly changed the subject. "I hear congratulations are in order."

"Congratulations? For what?"

"I know you probably have many things to be congratulated on today." He had to smile at her questioning look. Did she really not know what a great job she'd done? "But I'm referring to figuring out that Mrs. Levitz wasn't having an anxiety attack. Most docs—and especially interns—might not have gotten the diagnosis until it was too late."

"I'm sure that's not true." Pink filled her cheeks, and he realized he loved to see her blush, for some reason. How many women blushed like that these days? "You would have figured it out."

"Probably. Hopefully. But too often we look at the first thing that comes to mind and assume it's the correct thing. With her history of panic attacks, no one could have blamed you for treating her for that and not even considering another possibility. Hell, didn't I tell you to give her lorazepam to see if that did the trick?"

"Yes. But you hadn't seen her as recently as I had."

"I'll bet that in med school you heard about looking for the zebra when everyone else is looking for the horse. That's what you did. You found the zebra no one was looking for, and I'm proud of you. You should be proud of yourself."

"Thank you. I guess I am."

They smiled at one another as the breeze whipped a thick strand of hair onto her face, and he nearly reached to slip it from her eyes and tuck it behind her ear. Nearly leaned forward to kiss her on the cheek. Just her cheek, in celebration, as he would have long ago when they'd been young.

Who was he kidding? He wanted to start on her cheek and work his way over to that smiling mouth.

"I'm proud of you too, Katy," Nick said.

Damn. He'd practically forgotten Nick was there. Alec shifted his attention from the temptation of her lips and noticed she had sand all over her dress.

"You been rolling on the beach?"

"Rolling on the beach?" Her gaze followed his. "Oops. I thought I'd wiped it off. I was digging in the sand to see what was down in there."

He had to chuckle. Typical Katy. "And what did you find?"

"I'm not sure. Can I show you? You might know what they are."

There it was again. That absurd puffing-up-his-chest feeling, as though it meant something that she thought he'd know the answer to a simple question about crustaceans. "You're not pulling a joke on me are you? Have you dug a hole and covered it with palm fronds so I'll fall in?"

"As if I'd spend party time digging a hole big enough to trap you in." She laughed. "You're suspicious because those are the kinds of pranks you and Nick liked to pull."

"Thanks for the reminder. I'll have to think up a good way to prank you for old times' sake," Nick said with a grin. "I'm going to catch up with a few other folks here. You're checking on patients after this, aren't you, Katy? I'll see you when you get home."

"Okay," she said to Nick, but her eyes were on Alec. "Come on. They're down here."

They walked across a long stretch of grass and down a small hill to the water, leaving behind the party guest chatter. He was struck with an absurd desire to wrap his arm around her shoulders or to twine her fingers within his. Maybe it wasn't all that crazy, though—when they'd been young he'd often given her a brotherly hug.

Nothing brotherly about what he was feeling now, though, damn it. What he felt was hot and insistent and getting more and more difficult to tamp down.

"See all these little holes in the wet sand?" She pointed as the gentle waves receded, leaving bubbly holes behind. "I saw sandpipers and black-bellied plovers poking in their beaks. So I dug down and found some funny-looking gray crabs, some tiny and some as big as a spoon. Do you know what they are?"

"I'm afraid I don't. Folks here just call them sand crabs. And why am I not surprised you know the names of the birds, Miss Science?" Just like when she'd been little, she was curious about everything and because of that had an amazing, encyclopedic brain. He had to smile. That curiosity was going to make her a fine doctor one day.

"Are any bigger than the ones I described?"

"I confess I haven't paid that much attention." He crouched down and she crouched along with him, steadying herself by grasping the back of his arm, her knee bumping against his. They'd explored things this same way long ago, and it felt natural, right, to have her hold on to him that way. "Let's dig up some more to find out."

He scooped into the sand and she scooped and dug along with him, finally pulling out a handful of the grayish crabs in all sizes. "Looks like that's about the biggest one," he said, holding up a fat one. "They do look pretty tasty, don't they? If you're a bird, that is. Sandpipers and…what kind?"

"Black-bellied plovers. Willets, too." She looked up at him and laughed, her blue eyes sparkling. Her face was so close he could feel her breath brush his lips warmly. Teasing him without knowing. Tormenting him. When all he wanted was to press his own lips to her smiling ones.

"I wish I'd brought a bucket to put some in. I'd like to take a few home."

"For what? To keep as pets? Give to the dogs to play with?"

"No, to study, silly." Her teeth flashed white in the wide smile she gave him. "Don't you remember how we'd do that back at home all the time with beetles and locusts and things?"

"I remember." How could he be feeling this sensual pull towards her when they were talking about crabs and beetles and science? Because it was Katy, and that had always been a part of who she was. Because watching her lips move, watching her speak made him think of how he'd felt when she'd kissed him long ago. How it would feel to kiss her now, which was all he wanted to do.

He turned to place the crabs back into the hole they'd dug, to somehow take his mind away from this nearly overwhelming desire to lower her to the sand and kiss her and touch her, and to hell with the consequences.

Their hands touched, her fingers sliding against his as she tucked the crabs into the hole and covered them with sand. About to stand and end the torture of being so close to her, she clapped the wet sand from her hands and lost her balance. Rocked into him, shoulder to shoulder. Crouched on the balls of his feet, Alec wasn't prepared for the impact and promptly fell backward onto his rear, his elbow in the sand holding him half-upright, with Katy falling practically into his lap. One sandy hand slapped against his collarbone, the other grabbed his shoulder.

"Oh! Sorry!" Katy stared down at him, and he thought he saw more in her expression than just apology. He thought he saw a flicker of something in her darkened eyes. Something that was hot and intangible and irresistible and that hung, suspended, between them. Something he'd been feeling all damned day. All damned week.

Without thought, his heart beating fast, Alec wrapped one arm around her. An instinctive movement that brought her against him, her breasts against his chest. Her hair fell in a curtain around her face and tickled his cheeks. He watched her lips part in surprise, breathed in the scent of her that tormented him every time she was near. His sandy hand began to slowly slip up her back to cup her nape, to bring the mouth he'd wanted to kiss all day to his.

The sound of someone laughing poured over his mind-less, surging libido like a full bucket of iced water, and he jerked up, nearly tossing Katy into the sand. He stared in horror at her, all too aware of what had just about hap-pened. With a student. With everyone at the hospital just a stone's throw away.

How many times had he vowed to never again make a foolish mistake that could jeopardize his career? Or, damn it, hers, too, which was even more important. He fought for calm in the midst of his self-disgust. "Sorry. I…didn't do a good job of catching you, did I?"

"I'm the one who's sorry. It was my fault. I lost my balance." Her expression was serious, that little frown creasing her brow again, and Alec figured it was prob-ably in reaction to his own expression. He could only imagine what it was. He heaved in a breath, then stood and stretched his sandy hand to hers to help her up. De-spite his anger at himself, the feel of her hand within his as he tugged her to her feet still sent that not-allowed zing, which he kept feeling when he touched her, all the way up his arm, and never mind that grit rubbed between their palms, masking her skin's usual softness.

Standing close, she still stared up at him, her blue eyes now wide. Questioning. Did she know how she affected him? She had to, considering she'd been practically lying on him a moment ago.

"Dr. Armstrong I don't think I've had the pleasure of meeting your intern."

Alec swung toward the voice that spoke from directly behind him, and felt like a second, even icier bucket of water had been dumped on his brainless head when he saw who stood there. The only person in the hospital besides Nick who knew about the scandal he'd been involved in long ago. The person responsible for ensuring doctors in the hospital were held to a strict code of ethics.

"Hello, Margaret." He struggled to sound calm and normal. "This is Dr. Katherine Pappas. Katy, meet Oceancrest's Chief Medical Officer, Dr. Margaret Sanders."

CHAPTER FIVE

NEARLY FINISHED WITH checking on patients for the night, Katy stretched her tired muscles and flexed her fingers. Which reminded her of how Alec's grip on her hand earlier, when he'd helped her up from the sand, had become downright vise-like after he'd turned to speak with the CMO. Then how he'd dropped it like it had been a red-hot coal...

And of course she knew why. The woman had likely seen Katy practically sprawled on top of Alec after she'd lost her balance. Might even have seen the way Katy knew she'd been looking at him, which had been with serious thoughts of kissing the man until he couldn't breathe. Alec had probably seen it, too. And since he knew better than anybody the potential consequences of inappropriate conduct between a supervisor and student, he'd practically left divots in the grass after he'd introduced them and taken off.

She smacked the side of her head. Clearly, there was something wrong with her. What kind of woman would kiss a guy again after he'd pushed her away and said he wasn't interested the last time? Only a woman who enjoyed rejection, and apparently she was that woman. A woman who also enjoyed flirting with danger, since that kind of relationship with Alec could jeopardize her own fledgling career anyway.

She looked at her patient list and headed to David's room. Poor little guy had been in the hospital for quite awhile, and she hoped Alec would be able to remove the child's drain soon.

As she approached the room, she heard a man's voice speaking in an almost melodic voice and stopped short of the door. This time she knew who the voice belonged to. Alec.

He'd actually come back to the hospital after the welcome party? After getting here by at least seven a.m. this morning, since that was when she'd seen him in this very room? She may be a newbie, but she'd spent a lot of time in hospitals during medical school and couldn't remember seeing any surgeon do such a thing unless there was an emergency.

He'd told David he'd try to come back, and obviously he'd meant it. Amazed, she couldn't resist peeking inside, even though she knew it was tantamount to spying. Her heart melted into a gooey little puddle at the sight of Alec sitting on the side of the boy's bed, a picture book in his hand with race cars on the front, reading out loud. David stared raptly at the pages, though his eyelids were drooping a bit.

Oh. My. She was supposed to try fighting her attraction to this man? This man who'd always included her in his and Nick's adventures? This man who was now this caring doctor who took the time to keep his word to this child when he could be home with his feet up?

The answer was, yes, she had to, for all the reasons she'd been thinking about just five minutes earlier.

She moved into the room. "Sorry to interrupt. Just wanted to see if you need anything from me."

Alec looked up and his eyes met hers for a long moment. Something about the expression in his eyes sent her heart thumping harder and made her think of exactly what she needed and wanted from him, even though she shouldn't and couldn't, and how come she seemed unable to keep that firmly in her mind?

"Dr. Pappas. Thanks, but I think David's all set. And ready to sleep, from the looks of it." He stood and pulled the covers up to the child's chin. "Sleep tight, buddy. I'll see you in the morning."

"Night, Dr. Armstrong. Thanks for my book."

Katy followed Alec out the door, where they stood silently. Awkwardly.

"Look, I just have to say I'm sorry I fell on you on the beach." Getting it out there was the best way to clear the air. "I could tell you were embarrassed that Dr. Sanders saw me sort of on top of you."

"I wasn't embarrassed. Don't worry about it." His serious expression said something other than his words, but she wasn't sure exactly what. Concern for her? Guilt?

"Well, anyway. Sorry." She cleared her throat. "I can't believe you came back to see David, and even read him a book. That's a lot more patient care than most surgeons offer."

"I had to come back to see a patient in the ER, so I was here anyway. And most docs would read a book if a kid asked."

"Still, that was really sweet of you."

"Sweet? I'm a lot of things, but sweet isn't one of them."

Oh, yes it was. He was. When he wanted to be. "What

about the time I had chicken pox and you smuggled me bubble gum? You stuffed it inside a teddy bear and brought it to me…remember? Or the time I jumped on Nick's skateboard after he told me not to and then fell and skinned up my knees? While he yelled at me, you ran inside and got first-aid stuff."

His face relaxed into a grin. "That wasn't sweet. I just used you as a guinea pig. Was practicing for someday when I became a doctor."

"I hope you've gotten better at it," she teased, glad to replace the awkwardness with their familiar banter. "You put so much ointment on my legs the bandages wouldn't stick. So you wrapped me with gauze and tape until I looked like a mummy."

He laughed. His cheeks, dark with five-o'clock shadow, creased and his eyes twinkled, and despite her prior stern talks to herself, her heart swelled a little in response.

"But you were a very cute mummy." Still smiling, he ran his finger slowly down her nose and her breath grew short at the touch. "I remember—"

Alec's phone rang, and she moved away discreetly to give him some privacy while he answered it. Wondering, since it was so late, if it was a woman he dated. Feeling ridiculously, stupidly jealous at the thought, she wanted to thrash herself all over again.

"We have a blunt trauma cardiac arrest in the ER," he said, moving toward her as he shoved his phone in his pocket. "Stab wound to the chest. I need to do an emergency thoracotomy." He grasped her arm, his hand slipping down to hers as he strode so fast down the hall she had to run beside him. "This is something you'll probably never have a chance to see again."

"Do I have to?" Okay, she knew she sounded like a little kid who didn't want to clean her room. But she wasn't going to be a surgeon, and knew the procedure was only done on someone in an extremely life-threatening situation. Wouldn't she just get in the way?

"Yes, you have to." His intense expression gave way to a quick grin. "I'm your teacher this month and I say so. Believe me, you'll be glad you came along."

He pushed open the stairwell door and released her hand to jog down the steps. "Don't trip," he said over his shoulder. "The stairs are faster than the elevator, and I need to get in there. You can join me when you're scrubbed."

"What, you think I can't keep up with you? You and Nick never succeeded in ditching me in the past."

She could hear his chuckle as he widened the distance between them. "Keep up with me? Sweetheart, you've always been ten steps ahead. See you down there."

Sweetheart? Her breath caught, and it wasn't from hurrying down the stairs. Never, in all the years she'd known him, had he called her that. She shouldn't read anything into it, but the word warmed her heart anyway.

He disappeared through the door to the ER, and she hurried to get ready, nervous but excited, too. An emergency thoracotomy was a rare and difficult procedure, and she knew it was lucky that she'd actually get to see it.

Nothing could have prepared her for the chaos in the OR. It seemed like a dozen people were moving everywhere. Equipment beeped. Tense but controlled voices talked over one another. The patient lay on the gurney as someone steadily performed cardiac compressions on his chest. Alec stood beside a young doctor, who was slicing through the patient's skin from his sternum down between his ribs.

"All the way down to the shoulder, Jason. All the way," Alec said, his voice authoritative but calm. He turned to someone next to him. "We need a bigger knife."

She stood there, taking in the astonishing scene, feeling the sense of urgency in the air, hanging back to stay out of everyone's way. In moments, someone handed another knife to Alec and he stepped close to the patient. "Good job, Jason. I'll take over now. Somebody get the blunt-tipped scissors."

Alec sliced deeper between the ribs, then reached for the scissors and began to cut rapidly, roughly, through the man's flesh and cartilage in a way only a supremely confident and experienced doctor could. Multiple hands reached to hold open the ribs as Alec hacked open the man's body. "Where's the rib spreader? I need it right now."

He lifted his gaze to take the spreader being handed to him, and for a brief moment his intense eyes met hers across the room. He maneuvered the spreader between the ribs and cranked it to widen the opening. And all of it had been done in about one minute.

Part of Katy wished she could see better exactly what was happening, and part of her wasn't sure she wanted to.

"Dr. Pappas, I need you to assist me," Alec said, without looking up.

She gulped and headed to the other side of the patient, listening to the urgent voices of the nurses and residents as they worked, seeing the ragged flesh around the now wide opening in the man's chest, the blood being suctioned out, the hands still performing steady cardiac compression as Alec finished positioning the spreader.

She felt a little hot and swayed ever so slightly on her feet. Do not faint and take people's attention from this man who might be dying, you fool, she scolded herself as she took a deep breath. She forced herself to move close to Alec. "What do you need me to do, Dr. Armstrong?"

"Hold the clamp in place. I want you to see how I snip then manually spread the pericardium to expose the heart."

Lord, why did he want her to see that? But she knew the answer. Because Alec had shown her so many crazy things over the years, and knew she'd benefit as a doctor to see first-hand how this was done.

Heart pounding, she slid her gloved fingers around the edges of the bloodied spreader and tried to hold it steady as Alec reached into the man's chest cavity.

He made a tiny incision in the pericardium then tugged the membrane apart with his fingers to expose the heart. He then grasped that vital organ in his hand and began to gently massage it. In moments the man's heart was moving, beating, pumping on its own right in front of her eyes, and it was the most amazing thing she'd ever seen.

"Oh, my God!" she exclaimed, looking up at Alec, whose eyebrows were lowered over his supremely focused eyes as he worked. "It worked! He's got cardiac activity!"

Alec nodded. "Somebody get me sutures to repair this small cut in the heart. Mammary artery is bleeding. I need a clamp for that. May have to cross-plant the aorta, too."

The flurry of activity continued as Alec, unbelievably calm, gave orders, repaired the cut in the man's heart, and worked to address the other issues for another hour and a half or so. Katy kept looking at Alec, wondering if he was tiring. Heck, her arms were numb and she was just standing there! But his posture and focused expression never changed.

Finally, it was over. The patient's vital signs were within acceptable range. He was moved to the ICU as everyone beamed, slapped each other on the back and chattered in relief, congratulating each other and Alec.

He stripped off his gloves and yanked down his mask, a broad smile on his face. "Great teamwork, everyone. You all made Oceancrest proud tonight."

"Awesome job, Dr. Armstrong," one of the nurses said. "I'll be honest, I didn't think he was going to make it until you got here."

"I wasn't sure either. But an amazing staff and a little luck made it all work out."

As everyone made their way out of the OR, Alec turned to Katy, his finger moving her hair from her eyes to tuck it behind her ear. "So was I right? Are you glad you were in here to see this?"

She looked at his smile and the crinkles at the corners of his tired eyes. Moved her gaze around the now empty room. Empty except for the blood spattered all over the floor and the instruments and tubing and sponges strewn everywhere, looking like a war zone of sorts. Which it had been. An epic battle to save that man's life.

It was an experience she'd never forget. And the most unforgettable part had been seeing Alec in action under extreme stress.

"Yes. I'm glad I was here."

"You did great. Held the clamp steady and didn't faint on me. I'm proud of you."

"I confess I did feel a little faint for a minute."

"But you controlled it. That's what's important. Besides, Miss Science wouldn't want to miss one of the coolest surgeries there is."

His eyes, full of admiration, met hers, and she could picture the little pit-pat her heart was doing in her own chest since she'd just seen, incredibly, that man's heart pumping inside his.

Alec may have made a big mistake in the past, but she could no longer deny that today he was pretty much the total package. Uber-talented. Generous and appreciative of his staff. Beyond caring for his patients.

"Thank you for including me." As he always had. "It was an incredible experience."

"We make a good team." He moved closer, cupped her face in his palms, his eyes focused as intently on her now as they'd been on his work.

To her shock, his mouth lowered to hers in a light touch, at first soft and warm, then firmer, hotter, and she found herself wrapping her arms around his neck, sinking into the incredible, delicious sensation of kissing him. Of him kissing her.

Her heart beat hard and her breath grew short, and just as she was about to open her mouth in invitation to a deeper exploration, he pulled away. His eyes now the darkest she'd ever seen them, his chest rose and fell in a deep breath.

"Congratulations on getting through it like the superstar you are," he said, his voice rough. "Tomorrow's rounds won't be as exciting as tonight's surgery but I promise to make it as good as it can be."

Staring after him as he walked out the door, she lifted

her fingers slowly to her lips, wondering why he'd kissed her. And thinking about what she'd really like for him to make as good as it could be.

CHAPTER SIX

CONSIDERING HER LACK of sleep all week, it was hard to believe anything could have kept Katy awake. But she'd found herself wound up after the exhilaration of watching Alec perform that amazing surgery. Not to mention the feel of his lips had still been imprinted on hers, questions swirling through her mind. She hadn't gotten to sleep until the wee hours of the night, and by the following afternoon even constant hits of coffee couldn't keep her from dragging.

She tried to come up with how many hours she'd slept the past couple of days, but finally decided it didn't matter. All she knew was that she was so tired her vision was starting to blur.

About to check on another patient on the floor, her call system buzzed.

"Dr. Pappas."

"Becky from ER here. We have a fifteen-year-old girl with abdominal pain and want Surgery to check her out, rule out any surgical necessity, and sign off on her."

As she headed to the ER, she realized her hands weren't sweaty and she knew exactly what to do when she got there. Interview the patient, give her a physical exam, order blood work then check the results. She'd come pretty far the past week, and the thought managed to perk her up a bit.

A resident was stepping out of the patient's room when Katy got there. "Anything I should know before I talk with her?"

He shrugged and shook his head. "Tenderness in the belly, but it seems unremarkable. I ordered blood work, CBC and urinalysis. Should be able to look at results soon."

"Okay. Good." A young teen lay on the gurney and a well-groomed woman sat in a chair next to her. "Hi, I'm Dr. Pappas. You must be Emma." She smiled at the girl then turned to the woman. "Are you a relative?"

"I'm Emma's mother. Barbara Brooks."

"It's nice to meet you both." Thank heavens the girl didn't look like she was in acute pain or at death's door. "I hear you're having some tummy pain. Want to tell me about it?"

"It just…hurts kind of right here." Emma pointed to her belly button.

"Okay, let me see." She snapped on gloves and gave her a general physical exam, noting no pain in the right or left quadrants. Probably not gall bladder or appendicitis. "Have you had any vomiting? Does it hurt when you go to the bathroom?"

"No. I did throw up a few times, but just in the morning."

"All right." She glanced at the mother and then back at Emma. "Do you have a boyfriend? Are you sexually active?"

"No! I don't have a boyfriend."

Barbara nodded in agreement. "No boyfriend so far, I'm happy to say. She's too young for that."

"Okay." She studied the girl's face and couldn't tell if she was fibbing or not. "Mrs. Brooks, would you mind if I speak to Emma alone?"

The woman bristled visibly. "I most certainly do mind. She needs me here to support her, and I want to hear everything that's discussed."

Katy inclined her head, wondering how she'd get a chance to talk to Emma privately. For now, she'd check the girl's blood work and see if the ER resident had ordered a pregnancy test. "I'm going to check what your blood work shows, but try not to worry." She patted the girl's arm and smiled at her, hoping to soothe the worried look from her brown eyes. "I bet this is just some tummy bug that's got hold of you. Back in a minute."

Katy dodged the nurses and techs, as well as the EMTs that were wheeling in new patients they'd brought in by ambulance, as she made her way to the computers.

"Dr. Pappas?" The ER resident stopped her in the hallway. "I need you to see another patient, Samuel Green in Room 26, and evaluate for surgery. Possible bowel obstruction. Evaluate and report back to me."

"I'll see him as soon as I check the test results for the patient with abdominal pain and I get my report to you about that." Whew! The ER was a crazy place, and she felt glad again that she'd decided to go into family practice medicine, where she could take time to get to know her patients.

Emma's blood work and urinalysis were normal, with no sign of infection, so Katy felt satisfied to report that she didn't have any condition requiring surgery. No pregnancy test on file, though.

She found the busy ER resident and reported her findings. "She's clear to have the medical intern take a look at her now, except for one thing."

He didn't look up from the computer files. "What?"

"There wasn't a pregnancy test ordered. Do you want me to order it?"

He shook his head and headed down the hall, speaking over his shoulder. "I'll have the medical intern do it."

She nodded and moved to see the next patient, studying the papers in her hand, when her head ran smack into Alec Armstrong's hard sternum as he strode down the emergency department corridor.

"Oh!" She stared up at Alec as his hands grasped her arms to steady her. He shook his head, and her gaze got stuck on the curve of his lips, which sent her breathing a little haywire as she thought of the way he'd kissed her last night. "I'm so sorry. I should have been watching where I was going."

"Walking in a busy hospital while staring downward is asking for trouble," he said, a touch of amusement in his voice. His hands still held her arms, warm and steady, even though she was no longer in danger of toppling over, which seemed to be a common problem when she was around him. As was her heart rate zooming and her mouth going a little dry.

"I know. I guess I can't chew gum and talk at the same time."

"There's no gum chewing allowed in the hospital." He grinned and released one of her arms, holding out his palm. "Spit it out before I have to give you detention."

"What, now you're Mrs. Smith from Highland High School?"

"She probably never gave perfect Miss Katy Pappas detention, but she slapped Nick and me with plenty."

He leaned closer, his eyes mischievous, his voice low. "Maybe I should keep you after class to sharpen my pencils."

"Sharpen your pencils? That would be a cakewalk compared to being in charge of washing every test tube and Petri dish, like you and Nick always had me do. Which never occurred to me was completely unfair."

He laughed. "You were so much better at it than we were, you probably would have done them over again anyway." A nurse headed their way, and Alec dropped his hand from her arm. "I was called down here to talk about the teen patient you saw. Did you—?"

"Dr. Armstrong." A nurse stepped up to them, standing close. She glanced over her shoulder then looked back at Alec again. "I know Dr. Platt called you down because your intern didn't order a pregnancy test for the patient." She leaned closer to Alec, waving a piece of paper and giving him a conspiratorial smile. "Just wanted you to know I got it ordered. And also wanted you to know that Dr. Platt didn't spend more than one minute with the girl and left the history and physical completely to surgery. So if he gives you grief about it, you have some ammo to throw back."

"Thanks, Ruth." Alec smiled and, to Katy's astonishment, gave the woman a little wink. "What would I do if you didn't have my back down here?"

Ruth beamed. "What would we do if we didn't have you to deal with some of the other docs around here?" She handed him the paper and winked back. "Good luck."

He looked at the paper and his lips twisted before he turned to Katy. "Okay, teaching moment here. Whenever—"

"Well, it looks like our little helpers don't know what

the hell they're doing, doesn't it, Dr. Armstrong?" A short man whose name tag said Dr. Edward Platt strode up to them, with the ER resident Katy had talked to walking behind him. The younger man's expression bore a strong resemblance to a dog who had his tail firmly tucked between his legs. "Both my resident and your intern apparently don't know that any adolescent female who walks through these doors is assumed to be pregnant until we know otherwise."

"I was just about to discuss the case with Dr. Pappas," Alec said in a surprisingly cool voice. Cooler than Katy could remember ever hearing him speak.

"So let's discuss it together," Dr. Platt said with a smirk that hovered between nasty and self-satisfied. "Why didn't you order a pregnancy test, Dr. Pappas? Do you have any idea the liability to this hospital, and to me personally, if we ran radiological tests on a pregnant woman because we were too lazy and careless to check?"

"I..." Katy swallowed, hands sweating, heart pounding, completely taken aback at the hostility on the man's face. She glanced at the resident. Should she say he'd told her he'd take care of ordering the test? "I asked the patient if she was sexually active, and she said no. However, I did—"

"Well, it's another miracle of immaculate conception." He threw up his hands and the condescending expression on his face made Katy literally quake in her shoes. "Was her mother in the room? Did you shoo her out before you asked? Anybody with half a brain knows a teenager isn't going to tell the truth about something like that when Mommy or Daddy are around."

"Actually, Dr. Platt, I am aware that—"

Alec took a step forward so that he was in front of

Katy, and she had an urge to slip all the way behind him to hide. She made herself stay put, but was grateful for the slight protection and distance from the man throwing figurative darts at her. "It's certainly true that not ordering the test is a serious mistake. A mistake both these doctors will make only once in their careers, and that day seems to be today. Luckily, we have great staff who ordered the test before anyone else even saw the girl."

"What if we aren't so lucky next time? I don't want a lawsuit on my hands or my ass raked over the coals because of these two being inept."

"Dr. Pappas is far from inept. She is excellent with patients and did a stellar job assisting me just last night in an emergency surgery." Alec's cool tone had grown harder, flintier, as had his eyes. Those tiger eyes, defending Katy as he'd done so many times in her life. "Maybe this wouldn't have happened if you'd done any kind of history and physical on the girl yourself. If you'd spent any time with the patient before either of them did."

"That's why we have the residents and interns." Dr. Platt's face flushed as his eyes narrowed at Alec. "That's their job."

"Well, that's where you and I differ. I think it's my job." He met the man's gaze, his expression steely. "The residents are my backup, not the other way around. Now, if you'll excuse me, I'd like to speak with my intern about this alone."

Alec turned and walked away. Katy followed, immensely glad to get away from the angry Dr. Platt. Alec may be upset with her, too, but she knew he wouldn't flay her skin from her body and leave her bleeding, figuratively speaking.

Silently, she followed him down the corridor and

through to another longer, empty corridor. She started to wonder if maybe they were going somewhere private enough that he could flay her after all. Or spank her, she thought, nearly laughing nervously as she thought of his earlier teasing. Except there wasn't anything funny about her messing up with the test.

He finally stopped short of the swinging double doors that led to Radiology and turned to her, his expression thoughtful. But not annoyed or disappointed, thank heavens.

"All right, Katy-Did. Fess up. What happened with the test?"

She inhaled a breath, glad it was Alec she was ratting the ER resident out to. But it didn't make her blameless. "I asked the resident if he wanted me to do it, but he said he'd handle it. I'm sorry, I realize I should have done it anyway. That was a mistake."

Her extreme lack of sleep must be making her embarrassingly overemotional, because just seconds ago she'd wanted to laugh and now, out of the blue, a lump formed in her throat, and to her horror tears stung her eyes.

Since when was she a wimpy, teary girl of an intern just because she'd made an error and someone had yelled at her? She wanted to be strong and tough and capable and the awful awareness that she was none of those things at that moment sent the tears spilling over. Quickly, she turned away, swiping her fingers against her cheeks. No way could she let herself be all weepy and weak like this.

She squared her shoulders and took a deep breath. "I'm…I'm sorry."

He grasped her arms and turned her toward him. His gaze had softened and his hands moved up to cup her face. His thumbs feathered across her cheeks, wiping away her tears with a gentle touch. "Hey, what's all this?"

"I just...feel stupid. I hate making mistakes." As she struggled to control her frustration with herself, she found herself staring at the fine lines at the corners of his eyes, at the thickness of his lashes, just before he gathered her into his arms and folded her against his chest.

His embrace was beyond comforting. His chest, wide and warm and firm, was the absolutely perfect place to lay her tired head. The sound and feel of his steady heartbeat against her cheek, the arms holding her close, and the heady scent of him in her nose had her wrapping her own arms around his back without even considering that she shouldn't.

"Hate to break it to you, but you're human, Katherine Pappas. And humans make mistakes. As for being stupid? Now, that's about the only thing I've ever heard you say that is stupid." His voice rumbled through her, warm and amused, as his wide palm held her cheek to his heart and his lips grazed the top of her forehead. "Being an intern is tough. There's a lot to learn and you thought someone else was going to do it. Now you know it's better to just take care of those details yourself. Remember this is a teaching hospital, and my job is to teach you. Every day that you're working, I'm here to help. I'm here in whatever way you need me to be."

Any way she needed him to be? She lifted her head and looked into his eyes, no longer the flinty tiger eye they'd been in the ER but now golden amber, looking at her with an expression she couldn't quite interpret. An expression that felt more than just comforting. And as she stared into them, she imagined that a hot flicker touched his gaze. His chest rose and fell against hers as his arms tightened around her.

"Thank you," she whispered, her breath short, oh, so aware of how closely they held one another. How good it felt. "I'm sorry to be a crybaby. I'm just really tired, that's all."

"You, a crybaby?" He pressed his smiling lips to one damp cheek, lingered, then kissed the other. "You were the toughest little girl in the world, and now you're one tough intern. Who dove into a thoracotomy without blinking an eye?"

With his breath feathering across her face, her lips, an overwhelming urge to lift up onto her toes and press her mouth to his was nearly impossible to ignore. Thinking about that, and how amazing it had felt last night, sent her back to all the years she'd dreamed of kissing him when she had been a teenager and he a young man.

And to the moment five years ago when she'd kissed him and he'd quickly given her the brush-off, saying anything but friendship between them would be all wrong.

It would be even less right today.

The memory of that humiliating moment had her lowering her arms and she began to step back at the same moment his face lowered an inch and his lips touched hers.

Her eyes slid closed as she savored the sweet sensation. Had he kissed her last night in congratulation? Was he kissing her now in comfort? As his mouth moved slowly, gently, on hers, she didn't care why. She just wanted to feel.

The radiology doors swung open and Alec's head snapped up before his arms dropped and he quickly stepped back. As someone wheeled a gurney into the hallway, a gust of air through the doorway cooled all the warmth she'd felt just a moment ago.

"I'll stop back into the ER after you work up your next patient," he said in a stiff, professional tone. "Sounds to me like he will be a surgical candidate, but we'll confirm that after you run some tests." Abruptly, he turned and strode back down the long hall.

Katy watched him. Couldn't help but notice how his wide shoulders filled out his green scrubs, his tight butt in those loose pants still somehow so unbelievably sexy she couldn't stop looking at it. Then wanted to smack herself.

Her focus had to be on becoming the best doctor she could be. The kind of doctor her father had been—confident, kind, respected and admired. She couldn't allow anything, even delicious Alec Armstrong, to interfere with that goal.

"That would be great, Barney. Thanks. I owe you." Alec turned off his cell, sucked in a breath of relief, and strode down the hospital corridor to check a patient's chart as tension eased from his chest.

Unbelievable that, after all he'd been through five years ago, he'd nearly been caught holding his student intern close against him, murmuring words in her ear and kissing her. Right there in the hallway outside Radiology.

How could he have let himself kiss her in the OR last night? Was he out of his mind? Apparently the answer was a resounding yes.

Something about Katy simply reached inside him. Something that made him want to be there for her, comfort her when she was distressed and not believing in herself. Something that made him forget their student–

teacher relationship, forget that she was his best friend and partner's little sister, forget she was completely off-limits for any kind of relationship other than those that came with a little distance.

He'd fought those feelings for the past week, and definitely wasn't doing a good job of it. He'd been so pumped after the successful thoracotomy, so impressed with the way Katy had hung in there, he'd found himself kissing her before he'd known he was going to. And when her beautiful eyes had filled with tears, he'd had only one thought in his head, which had been to hold her close. Once she'd been in his arms, kissing her again had seemed like the most natural thing in the world.

The final realization that he was in serious trouble had come when, as he'd been comforting Katy, he'd spied a roomful of empty gurneys and could think of only one thing. Which had been sweeping up his intern to lie down on one of those beds with him on top of her, making love together until she'd forgotten everything but the feel of him buried inside her.

Damn it. What the hell was wrong with him? Before tongues began to wag, before anything bad could happen to her reputation and career, he realized he had to take himself off the teaching service for the rest of the month. Not an easy thing to accomplish, since every one of the general surgeons had crazy schedules.

Barney Boswell, though, had been willing to switch. Take over for him now, and having Alec do teaching rounds in August. Barney had actually been happy to, since he had a second kid heading to college and wanted to be involved in helping her move in, which would require taking a few extra days off.

So now all Alec had to do was come up with some

excuse for why he'd switched with Barney, something convincing and not suspicious. Get through tomorrow, when he and Katy were scheduled to go to the free clinic together. Then after that somehow steer as clear as humanly possible from Katy Pappas.

"How's Katy doing, Alec?"

He looked up to see Nick had just walked out of a patient's room. Apparently not talking about Katy was going to be nearly as challenging as not thinking about her. But he couldn't mind giving her the praise she deserved.

"She's incredible. Did she tell you about the emergency thoracotomy? For a woman who's going into family practice, she was tough as nails through the whole thing."

"I can't believe you got her to go in with you. Good for her. I hear she's good with patients, too."

"She is. Unlike you, who has such a lousy bedside manner you probably should have been an anesthesiologist instead of a surgeon. Though at least your patients are asleep half the time you're around them."

Nick chuckled, probably because this was something he'd been razzed about more than once, not only from Alec but other hospital workers. His ex, too, and Alec wondered if his lack of empathy about her problems had contributed to their marital difficulties.

"Yeah, yeah. Having a touchy-feely bedside manner isn't as important to my patients as my excellent surgical skills. Which even you, Dr. Golden Hands, must acknowledge I have." He grinned. "I really just wanted to ask if there was anything I could do to help her."

"Starting tomorrow, you'll have to ask Barney, because he's taking over teaching rounds this month."

"You're kidding. Why?"

"He wanted off next month's rounds so he could move his daughter into her college dorm. So we switched." Which was true, except it had been Alec who'd initiated it.

Nick frowned. "Barney's a good guy, but you're a better teacher. I'd hoped—"

"Hello, Doctors. Doing anything fun after work?" Alec's fifth-year resident, Elizabeth, stepped over to put away a chart, smiling at Alec the way she often did, and it was a smile that made him feel distinctly uncomfortable. It was the smile of a woman trying to use her sex appeal to ingratiate herself with her superior.

While it didn't happen often, it did happen occasionally. Alec knew it was tough going for a woman wanting to be a surgeon, and it wasn't unusual for them to feel like they had to work harder to get respect. To be either hard-nosed and aggressive or use their feminine wiles to get ahead. He wished Elizabeth wasn't one of them, and he also wished he could just come out and tell her the way she was coming across. But that would open a can of worms he absolutely did not want to open.

"We have a couple of tough cases this afternoon, Elizabeth," Alec said, keeping the conversation on work. "Are you ready?"

"I'm always ready." The smile she gave made the double entendre more than obvious.

"Dr. Stark," Nick said, his tone and eyes cold, "Dr. Armstrong and I were having a private conversation, if you don't mind."

"Oh. Sorry." She looked both disconcerted and annoyed. "I'll see you in surgery later, Alec, er, Dr. Armstrong."

When she was out of hearing range Nick looked around before speaking. "That woman is getting more obvious every day with her come-ons to you. You need to talk to her about it. The last thing you need is rumors about you and a student to start up. It could dredge up your past and jeopardize your job."

Wasn't that the truth? The thought sent a cold chill running down his spine. He'd worked too hard to earn the respect of his peers. To put behind the lack of respect he'd unfortunately managed to earn five years ago.

The rumors he was worried most about had to do with his attraction to Nick's sister. And the thought of damaging her reputation was a hell of a lot worse than any thoughts of damaging his own. "Don't worry. I steer as clear of Elizabeth as possible. On the occasions I'm at the Flat-Foot Tavern and she shows up for a drink, I leave as soon as I can."

He knew it would take a Herculean effort to stay strictly professional with Katy tomorrow at the clinic, but he had to do it. And if Katy showed up at the bar for after hours "liver rounds," he'd have to somehow make sure he treated her just like any other member of the gang.

CHAPTER SEVEN

KATY TRIED TO keep her eyes on the road and thoughts on what she might learn at the free clinic, but found her gaze drifting more than once to Alec. To his attractive profile and the broadness of his shoulders in a dress shirt and tie instead of his usual scrubs. He swung his car into the lot of a strip mall and parked the car. Katy turned to him in surprise.

"This is where the free clinic is?"

"Yep. It's central to a lot of low-income neighborhoods, and easy to access by bus, too," Alec said. "You already know we have a sizable indigent population here also, and this location serves them well."

He led the way into the clinic, which had a modest but tidy waiting room, and through to a common room, with doors to exam rooms. "This is where the nurses take patients' vital signs, weigh them, and get general histories," Alec said, as he put down his bag then picked up some charts. "There are four exam rooms off it."

"What do you usually do here?" she asked, as she looked around the small space.

"Various stuff. Hernia repair, skin biopsies, chronic wound care, things like that."

"How often do you come? Do all the doctors at Ocean-crest work here sometimes?"

"No. It's on a volunteer basis. Nick and I come about once a month. We both think it's important to give to the community, and plenty of other docs do too, but not all of them."

Having already met a lot of doctors at the hospital, she could guess which ones might not. Then again, that would make her judgmental, and she knew from experience you couldn't always judge a book by its cover.

Alec being the most difficult book of all to read.

One minute he was the teasing Alec she used to know, then the new Alec who looked at her the way she used to dream he would. A new Alec who had kissed her twice now, and while she couldn't deny she had enjoyed it she wasn't sure exactly how it made her feel. Well, other than turned on, that was.

He'd turned her down flat five years ago when she'd kissed him. So could his kissing her now be all about the conquest and nothing more? Or was she reading something into it that wasn't there at all? That it really had been just his way of congratulating or comforting her? No matter what it was, Katy scolded herself, she had to stop wondering. While years ago a relationship between them wouldn't have been off-limits, as he'd stated at the time, now it most definitely was.

"Since you're going into family practice, why don't you see Miss Kraft first? She's twenty-four years old with possible cellulitis of the arm. She's already had her vitals taken and is waiting in room two," Alec said, as he looked at the chart, all business. Which was good. "I'm going to do a follow-up with a patient who is post-gall-bladder removal. Shouldn't take me long, then I'll join you."

"All right." She took the chart and knocked on the door of the exam room before going in.

A young, attractive woman sat there in a sleeveless dress, and even from across the room the redness of her arm was obvious. Katy introduced herself then sat next to her. "Can I take a look at your arm? Tell me what happened."

"It's been real red and hurting for a few weeks now. I went to the ER at Oceancrest and they prescribed me antibiotics, but they haven't helped."

Katy gave her a physical exam, and the woman's arm was hot to the touch. The redness ran from her forearm all the way up to her biceps. "Did you fall down? Did you have some kind of skin injury?"

"No. I don't think so. I don't know how it got like this."

Katy looked at her arm a few more minutes, asked a couple more questions, then decided to look at the records from the hospital. Excusing herself, she went into the hallway to the computer and saw that it was her nemesis, Dr. Platt, who'd seen the woman. The antibiotic he'd prescribed was clearly not the right one, and Katy couldn't help but feel a little smug.

Alec came out of the exam room he'd been in and stood next to her, looking at the computer screen along with her. "What do you think, Dr. Pappas?"

"Patient has cellulitis, and our Dr. Platt prescribed cephalexin. It seems clear it's MRSA and that she needs tetracycline."

"Slow down there, Katy-Did." His eyes crinkled at

the corners. "How do you think she got the MRSA? Did she fall? Have a pimple that got infected?"

"She says she didn't fall, and doesn't know why she has it."

"Okay, then, Miss Science. What did I say on your very first day? Why do you think she has it? It has to have come from something."

Katy stared up into his smiling eyes and heard loud and clear what he was saying. What he was teaching her. That she'd taken the cellulitis diagnosis at face value, had been pleased with herself, thinking she was smarter than Platt, and hadn't looked any further for a real diagnosis.

"I hate it when you're right," she said, and warmed at the grin he gave her in response. "I wasn't careful enough getting the patient's history. I don't yet have a real diagnosis, do I?"

"Bingo." His hand reached to cup her cheek, his thumb briefly stroking before he dropped it. "You're close to your gold star for the day, Dr. Pappas. Let's go talk to her together."

Alec sat on the stool next to the patient. Katy found herself studying the way he smiled at the woman, reassuring and warm. He asked a few questions and examined her infected arm then the other, though she resisted briefly. Looking more closely now, she could see a few tiny track marks on the skin of both arms, and shook her head at herself. How could she have missed them? Because she hadn't looked carefully enough, but she would never make that same mistake again.

"I hope you know that all we want is to help you, Miss Kraft. And we can't do that unless we're honest with one another. Can we be honest here?" The sincerity in his eyes as he spoke squeezed Katy's chest. Never could she remember hearing a surgeon speak with such understanding to a patient with addiction. With such compassion.

The patient stared at him a moment before her face crumpled and she began to cry. Katy reached for her hand, her own throat closing. "I don't know how it started," the woman said, sobbing. "I just thought it would be a one-time thing. My old boyfriend asked me to give it a try. But then I started shooting up more. And now I don't know how to stop."

"All right. I want you to know you're not alone in this." He reached to squeeze her shoulder. "Dr. Pappas and I are going to get your arm fixed up. I can feel a clot in your vein that's causing the infection and needs to be taken out. After that, there are people here who can help you with your addiction. Okay?"

"Okay." The patient sniffed and wiped her eyes with the tissue Katy handed her. "Thank you. Thank you for helping me."

Katy watched Alec give the woman a local anesthetic then make an incision in her arm to access the vein and remove the infected clot. Her attention kept going from his talented hands to his face as he worked. His dark lashes fanning his cheekbones, his lips pressing together, his eyebrows twitching as he cut and stitched.

Her heart stuttered as she watched him. What a beautiful man. How could she ever have thought he was beautiful on only the outside and not the inside too?

After tying off the vein, he showed her how to drain off the surrounding pus, then wrapped the wound and prescribed tetracycline. Once they were finished, he spoke to the nurse and social worker who took over.

"You were wonderful with her, Alec." Katy looked

up at him and wanted to cup his cheek with her hand, as he'd done to her. Wanted to wrap her arms around him to show him how much she admired what he'd done. Who he was.

"So were you. I'm glad you were here today. This is the kind of patient you might get in your practice. To look at her, you wouldn't guess she's a heroin addict. But there are more functional addicts out there than you would ever guess."

"I'm glad, too. Especially since you schooled me."

He laughed. "Schooled you? That sounds kind of negative."

"Not negative at all. You taught me again to not assume the correct diagnosis is the first thing that comes to mind. To look beyond that for a cause. I knew it, but promptly forgot it when it seemed obvious. You reminded me about looking for the zebra instead of the horse."

He touched his finger to her brow and tapped a few times before tracing it slowly down her nose. "If you can remember that, and I know you will, Dr. Pappas, you're going to be the best doctor at Oceancrest."

She lifted her hand to grasp his. Stared into his warm, smiling eyes, lowered her gaze to the curve of his lips, and knew she was right back to where she'd been all those years ago when she'd written about him in her journal. To when she'd kissed him at her brother's wedding.

But this time it was different. She was different. She was older and wiser and she no longer saw him through the filter of rose-colored glasses. Now she saw him for who he was. A man who was flawed like anyone else, who was capable of making mistakes. A man who was smart and funny and beyond talented, and who cared deeply enough about others to volunteer at a free clinic and take care of anyone who needed his understanding expertise.

A man she so wanted to know more deeply and intimately. Could there be any possibility of that happening, without risking her career in the process?

CHAPTER EIGHT

ALEC STOOD AT the edge of the crowded ballroom, watching the bride and groom dance their first dance together as husband and wife, their big extended family smiling and clapping.

Funny how being around the entire Pappas clan just felt right. The years he'd spent at their house, having lively conversations and disagreements over dinners, intervening in various sibling squabbles, going on day trips crammed into their van, had been some of his happiest childhood memories.

Even now, he felt the tiniest pang that he was, in truth, an outsider, looking in. Still wished, as his childhood self had, that his own family was as close and caring as the Pappas family. That he had a real brother or sister to argue with and be close to. A parent that respected him, believed in him.

The meal had been served, the cake cut, and traditional Greek pastries filled a long table. Earlier, as Elena Pappas had walked down the aisle of the Greek Orthodox church, on Nick's arm, he'd known everyone acutely felt the absence of the bride's father and were doubtless feeling it again at that moment. The wise and gentle man whose dry sense of humor had often found just the right

quip to bring strife in the house to a halt and bring on
laughter instead.

He thought of how cool Katy had been to him at the
past two family weddings. Even at her father's funeral.
It had bothered him. A lot. He'd wished he could go back
in time and react to Katy's kiss differently. How, exactly,
he wasn't sure, since it had shocked the hell out of him as
much as his own reaction had. But at least their friendship seemed back on track.

Friendship? Back on track? The smoldering attraction he felt for her now was nothing like friendship and
a whole lot like admiration and desire.

She'd constantly impressed him all week. Then working with her at the clinic, she'd made a typical young doctor mistake. But instead of bashing herself about it, or
making excuses, she'd quickly realized her error, back-
tracked, and listened, which too many students didn't
do. When she'd looked up at him, telling him how great
he was, he'd realized no one had ever made him feel the
way she did. Appreciated and admired, and he'd wanted
her to know he felt the same way about her. Had nearly
gathered her up in his arms for another kiss, but had
forced himself to keep his hands off.

His eyes had been on Katy through the whole wedding. The woman was attractive as hell in anything she
wore, including scrubs. But today she looked like an
angel from heaven, though as soon as the thought came,
he rolled his eyes at himself. How corny could he be? Yet
that was exactly what she made him think of.

The bridesmaids wore dresses that were a dark purple and strapless, showing off the smoothness of Katy's
shoulders and the golden skin above her breasts where a
strand of pearls lay. Her thick hair was piled on her head,

with wispy tendrils around her face and down her neck, and the sapphire of her eyes was as intensely blue as the stained-glass windows of the church had been.

As she'd followed the newlywed couple back down the aisle, her gaze had caught his, and her smile had somehow ratcheted even higher, seeming to reach right into his chest to squeeze his heart. To reach out and grab him by the throat. And he was damned if, as he'd watched her disappear through the doors, he hadn't thought of someday when she had her own wedding, and of how incredibly beautiful she would look. He felt a deep stab of envy for whoever the lucky guy would be. Knew that might be the first Pappas wedding he wouldn't attend.

He brought his thoughts back to the present and noticed that Katy had moved onto the dance floor with a groomsman. All he wanted to do was watch her, look at her. Ask her to dance with him next. Which was not a good idea, even outside the hospital. He had to find ways to keep his distance, not look for excuses to hold her close.

He forced himself to look away from Katy and glance around the ballroom to see who he might know. A number of attractive women stood in groups, laughing and smiling and openly flirting with the men standing with them. At any other wedding reception Alec might have been interested in meeting some of them. Maybe even enjoy a brief fling for a night or the weekend. But as he turned back to watch Katy dancing, as the music drew to a close and another man approached her, he knew he wouldn't find one other woman he'd rather spend time with than her.

He turned away, no longer wanting to see her in someone else's arms.

A soft hand closed loosely around his wrist, and his heart gave a little stutter when he saw Katy's sweet face smiling up at him.

"I haven't had a chance to talk to you all day," she said. "Wasn't it a beautiful wedding?"

"Beautiful." And watching her had been the most beautiful part of it, her every emotion sending shadows and joy across her face as she'd stood at the front of the church.

"I love Elena's dress. Though I guess men don't care about things like that."

Not unless the dress was wrapped around a smart, gorgeous, adorable woman. Then unwrapped off her. "Your dress is nice too. In fact, you look...very nice." And wasn't that a clumsy comment? But he couldn't tell her what he was really thinking and feeling.

"Thank you." Her smile seemed genuinely pleased, as though it had been a great compliment instead of the lame one he knew it was. It was just like Katy. A woman who was always herself and didn't fish for compliments or play coy with anyone.

"I can't believe I'm the last single sibling in the family," she said, smiling, before sadness flickered in her eyes. "Well, if you don't count Nick, who isn't technically single yet. I'm still hoping something good will happen there."

"You never know." Though Alec had his doubts that anything positive would emerge from the current cinders of that marriage.

"I haven't had any dessert yet. Want to check out the table? I heard Aunt Sophie brought her—"

"Come on, Katy!" Her cousin grabbed Katy's hand and yanked her toward the mass quickly forming on the dance floor. The band had apparently taken a break, and Greek music began blasting from speakers flanking the floor. "It's your favorite!"

Katy sent Alec a laughing shrug and shouted, "Come with us!" before she joined the circle that snaked around the floor. He had to smile. He'd been dragged to participate a number of times in his life the same way Katy had been just now, and while he'd never learned the steps of various dances to be particularly proficient at them, he could usually muddle along and fake it.

Unlike Nick, who was the real deal when it came to Greek dancing. As the line of dancers gyrated, he led the group, hand in the air holding a kerchief, his graceful turns seemingly effortless. And he supposed it was effortless for Nick, since the man had learned them literally at his father's knee and practiced for years.

His attention slid from Nick to Katy again. She, too, knew Greek dancing like she could do it in her sleep. Watching her as she held hands with those on either side of her, as she stepped in and out in one of the intricate patterns, it struck him how amazingly graceful she was.

Klutzy Katy? Not this woman. Not the woman who, with a wide, encouraging smile, helped the guest to her left whose hand she held, a guest who was even less adept at Greek dancing than he was. This wedding was a break from the extreme fatigue of an intern, and she simply radiated energy.

Had he ever really watched her like this? Ever noticed her proud posture and delicate footsteps as she danced? Ever noticed how slim and shapely her ankles were as she gave little kicks and circled the room in the strappy high heels she wore?

Entranced, he watched her approach his side of the

floor. To his surprise, she dropped her cousin's hand and grabbed his as she swept by, and he had no choice but to join the controlled chaos on the dance floor.

"Opa!" She grinned, any resemblance to studious Katy completely gone, replaced by this vibrant and exciting woman. Her hand was warm, nearly hot, as it clutched his. "You remember this one—it's the syrtos, one of the easiest," she said encouragingly, slightly breathless. Damned if it wasn't obvious that the tables had turned, and she'd become the teacher to the student. And what had changed her mind about that, when she'd been so clearly unwilling before? "One, two, three, four, five, six, seven, back, then again."

"I've only done this a couple of times at your family's weddings, remember?"

"Surely a brilliant surgeon can do a little Greek dance," she said in a teasing voice. "Just follow my footsteps and you'll do fine."

He tried his best to follow her lead, shaking his head as he messed up, yet feeling exhilarated, too, her hand clutched in his, her blue eyes laughing. The music pounded across the floor for what seemed like forever, and he felt his tension fade away, replaced by the simple pleasure of dancing with her. Finally, the music stopped, and everyone moved from the floor, catching their breath as the band returned to play popular dance music.

"Whew! That was a workout. But you did great!" Katy turned to him, her face flushed and dewy from exertion. Without warning, she flung her arms around his neck and gave him a smacking kiss on the lips.

Shocked, he stared into her laughing blue eyes and couldn't resist wrapping his arms around her, just like he had long ago. Unlike in the past, though, their embrace created a cyclone of emotion in his chest that threatened to burst out. The same emotion he'd felt both times he'd kissed her at the hospital. Emotion that nearly had him kissing her again right there in front of everyone at the reception.

He folded her close against his chest, savoring the moment. Let his lips touch her temple, slip to her soft cheek and linger there, before he forced himself to loosen his arms. To step back and shove his hands in his pockets before he did something he'd regret. Like grab her hand and pull her to his room and beg her to make love with him the rest of the night.

Her eyes had closed and she slowly opened them, her gaze holding his, and he wasn't sure what he saw within that beautiful blue. He just knew he wanted to keep looking there.

"YiaYia brought her famous kourambiethes. How about we get a few?"

"Sounds good." He knew he should find an excuse not to. But all he wanted was to spend a few more minutes with her. And what was the harm after all? They weren't at the hospital, around eyes that might judge them for talking together.

He let his hand rest against her back, touching her soft skin where the dress dipped low. They walked to the dessert table where the powdered-sugar-covered cookies were nestled in fluted paper cups.

"I'm betting you'll eat two," Katy said, as she put several on a plate.

"And I'm betting the extra one is really for you. As I recall, you had the biggest sweet tooth of the family."

"I admit nothing. I'm a doctor, so of course I only eat healthy foods." She grinned at him and grasped his hand, and damned if it didn't feel absolutely right for their palms to be pressed together.

Katy led them to a darkened corner of the ballroom and slipped the plate of cookies onto a tall, empty table. Her slender fingers picked up one of the cookies and held it to his mouth. "Remember not to do what you did last time you ate these," she said. The teasing tone had returned to her voice, her eyes twinkling with mischief.

God, he loved this Katy—the fun and relaxed woman who, outside the hospital work setting, couldn't be more adorable.

"What did I do last time I had these? Something stupid?"

"Not stupid. A rookie mistake. Inhaling while eating one, then the powered sugar makes you choke like crazy."

"Ah, yes, it's coming back to me." He grinned, remembering her teenage fists pounding on his back when the sugar had stuck in his lungs. "You almost injured my kidneys, whomping on my back like you did. It wasn't like I needed the Heimlich maneuver. What exactly did you think it would accomplish to assault me like that?"

"I guess it was silly." He liked her smile, both guilty and amused. "All us kids did that to one another whenever it happened, though there's clearly no medical reason for it. Maybe it was just an excuse to pound on one another. Sorry."

"Never be sorry." He couldn't resist running his finger down her cute nose. "Pretend to be confident, no matter what, and people will believe you are."

"Is this the secret to your success?" she asked, taking a bite of the cookie.

"I'm not sure I should share my secrets with you." In fact, he knew he shouldn't. The secret about his past that weighed on his present. That made it imperative he not think about Katy the way he couldn't stop thinking about her.

But as he stood close to her like this, seeing her lips covered with powdered sugar, he wanted more than anything to cover her mouth with his once more. To taste the sweetness of her along with the sweetness of the cookie.

Her gaze dropped to his lips, as though she'd read his mind, and her fingertip lifted to stroke her bottom lip. To lick the crumb of almonds and sugar there. His breath grew short, his pulse kicked into a different rhythm at that seductively tempting mouth. At the way she looked at him. He was no inexperienced kid. And damn if her eyes didn't hold the same intense heat and want that tilted his world sideways.

As though drawn by some unseen force, his head lowered and his mouth touched hers. His tongue slipped lightly across her lower lip, tasting the sugary sweetness there. His hand on her back drew her close as they shared an excruciatingly slow, soft, mind-blowing kiss. Her fingers slipped up his chest to the sides of his neck, and he heard a low, throaty groan, not sure if it came from her or from him. The sound had him pulling her closer, sent him deepening the kiss, until the band striking up a loud tune cut through his sensual fog.

It was all he could do to loosen his hold, to pull his mouth from hers, to leave the seductively sweet taste of sugar and of Katy. Panting slightly, they stared into one another's eyes for a long moment until Katy breathed, "Wow."

"Yeah. Wow." And wow was an understatement. But what, exactly, was he supposed to do now? Unlike the last time they'd kissed at a wedding, he was the one who'd started it. Along with the two others he hadn't been able to resist at the hospital. But she'd been so upset five years ago when he'd told her anything between them would be all wrong, how was he supposed to deal with the reality that it truly was?

"Who knew a kourambiethes kiss could be so incredible?" Katy said, her eyes heated but smiling, too, and he huffed out a breath of relief.

"How many kourambiethes kisses have you had in your life?"

"Ah, that's for you to wonder. You're not the only one who isn't sure they should share their secrets."

He smiled and shook his head. How the hell was he supposed to resist her teasing smile and beautiful eyes and incredibly sexy lips?

He would because he had to. Any sexual relationship between them—and God knew he wanted that more than he wanted his next breath—was strictly against hospital policy. Hurting her reputation or her career was something he couldn't risk, no matter how much he wanted her.

He shoved his hands into his pockets and cleared his throat. "I'm going to find your Uncle Constantine. Haven't seen him for years, since he couldn't make it to Nick's wedding."

"Before you go, will you dance with me, Alec?" The band had struck up a slow, dreamy tune and Katy licked the last of the sugar from her lips. Her eyes, now, oh, so serious, held his. Eyes he kept getting lost in when he let himself forget.

"I've already Greek-danced until my feet hurt." Until her hand had felt like it belonged in his. Until her brilliant smile had filled his soul to overflowing.

Her hand slipped from his arm to his wrist and, without thinking, he slid his hand out of his pocket. Her fingers, slim and still warm, captured his. "Please? Just one dance? I promise not to bother you the rest of the night."

Bother him? If she meant bother as in torture him with dreams of her naked in his arms and in his bed, he was sure she'd be doing exactly that for the rest of the night.

He moved toward the swaying couples on the floor, still holding her hand in his, anticipating the pleasure and torture it would be to dance with her. To let the scent of her warm perfume surround him, let his hand drift from her waist to the soft, exposed skin of her back, let the loose tendrils of her silky hair tickle his face.

"Alec! We thought you'd probably be here."

Alec turned and froze. Shocked to see his elegant mother and sophisticated-looking father standing there, holding glasses of champagne in their hands. "Mom. Dad. I thought you were in Russia."

"Just got back this morning, which is why we didn't make the ceremony. Staying home a short time before we head back," his father said.

"We spotted you over in the corner with your...friend. Can you introduce us?" His mother's eyebrows were slightly raised as she looked at Katy, an intrigued expression on her face.

Alec realized with sudden, sickening clarity that he was holding Katy's hand, tucked closely against him. And he remembered extremely well the long, intense kiss they'd shared.

Dropping her hand like he'd been bitten by a snake, he turned to look at Katy. That small frown he'd become accustomed to seeing dove between her brows again as her eyes scanned his face, and he wondered what the hell his expression looked like. He swallowed hard before he addressed his parents. "You remember Katy. Katherine Pappas. Nick's sister."

"Nick's baby sister? Why, I wouldn't have recognized you!" His mother shook Katy's hand. "What are you doing these days?"

"I just graduated from medical school and am interning at Oceancrest Medical Center."

"Interning at Oceancrest?" Charles Armstrong narrowed his gaze at his son, and Alec's gut clenched. He knew exactly what was coming next. "Are you an idiot, Alec? Cuddling up and dancing with a student from your hospital? Don't you ever learn?"

Alec set his jaw. Years of experience had taught him not to respond to his father's insults, and he certainly wouldn't react the way he wanted to. Not in the middle of a damned wedding reception. "Contrary to what you've always believed, I'm not an idiot. And what I do is my own business."

"Then don't be expecting me to bail you out again. I mean it."

"I never asked you to do that. Would never ask. And for what it's worth, Katy is like a sister to me." Which was a damned lie. Except he knew he had to double his efforts to remind himself that was all there could be between them. "If you'll excuse me, Katy and I were about to go talk with her Uncle Connie."

He turned and didn't even look to see if Katy was coming along or not. Hopefully not, because the last thing either of them needed was more speculation about their relationship. Then he realized she hadn't followed him at all…that she'd found someone else to dance with.

CHAPTER NINE

HER SHIFT THANKFULLY over after twelve hours, Katy headed to the changing room, grateful to put on real clothes for what seemed like the first time all week. She felt physically and mentally exhausted. Emotionally, too. Today was the anniversary of her father's death. It was the one day of the year she allowed herself to mourn and be sad. The distance between her and Alec added to the heaviness in her chest.

The heaviness had been weighing there since the wedding. Just as the two of them had been about to dance, after they'd shared a kiss so sweet she'd nearly melted to the floor, he'd yanked his hand from hers like she was a leper. Told his parents he thought of her as a sister, and the words had felt like he'd jammed his fist in her solar plexus.

The man had kissed her three times, damn it. Wouldn't any woman think that meant he wasn't thinking of her as a "sister"? Player or no player, she had to believe Alec didn't kiss every woman he met before turning as cold as the proverbial cucumber and running away. Then again, history had shown she was very capable of deluding herself when it came to Alec Armstrong.

It had been a week since Dr. Boswell had taken over

Alec's teaching rounds. Except for her current weariness, Katy felt like she was really finding her sea legs and not drowning in the hospital undertow. Dr. Boswell had proved to be a good teacher on rounds. Not as good as Alec, of course. But also not as distractingly attractive either.

She figured that had to be a good thing. Her goal was to learn how to be an excellent doctor, and being sidetracked as she noticed other things instead was a hindrance to that.

Noticed, for example, Alec's amazing bedside manner that engendered trust from even the most difficult patient. Diverted from listening to what patients had to say as he touched them with his long, beautifully shaped surgeon's hands. Engrossed by the vision of how incredibly sexy he looked in his green scrubs, his muscular chest and athletic tush filling them out in a way that would make any woman practically swoon.

She yanked off her scrub top and pulled on her sundress, thinking of how wonderful Alec had looked in his suit and tie at the wedding, how adorable he'd been, trying to Greek-dance. He'd seemed so much like the Alec she'd been getting to know again, teasing and fun and natural, and the memory of their kiss at the hospital had made her insides all warm and gooey. She'd felt a little Cinderella-like in her beautiful dress, dancing and eating with an oh-so-handsome prince then kissing him until she'd been breathless.

Then he'd just walked away, their planned dance apparently forgotten. Angry for deluding herself, she'd found someone else to dance with.

But then she'd seen him standing there, watching her. And the look on his face, a peculiar combination of fierceness and defeat and something she couldn't quite figure out, had brought back a small, budding hope that maybe she hadn't been wrong about him wanting her the way she wanted him.

With that tiny hope had come a tentative conviction. If presented with another opportunity to kiss him, she wasn't going to regret and wonder. She planned to be bold. To find out what might or might not be there between them.

She huffed out a long sigh. The unfortunate part of that plan was that she rarely saw Alec now. And today, of all the three-hundred-sixty-five days in the year, she would have loved to have his understanding support beside her. His presence would be a comfort, she knew, because it always had been.

Tears clogged her throat and she quickly swallowed to banish them. This year, the painful loss seemed even worse than it did most years. Her dad's absence at the wedding had left a sad emptiness in everyone's heart on an otherwise very happy day.

Nick understood a little. After all, it wasn't the best day of the year for him either. For some reason, though, they both seemed to want to handle it in their own ways. Separately, not together.

The door swung open and Elizabeth walked in and quickly stripped, throwing on her clothes like she was in a hurry. The fifth-year resident had seemed to thaw a little toward Katy, becoming nearly friendly since Dr. Boswell had taken over the teaching rounds. Katy didn't know what had motivated the change but was glad of it.

"You coming over to the Flat-Foot Tavern for liver rounds?" Elizabeth asked as she pulled a beaded shirt over her head.

"Liver rounds?"

"Yeah. Those of us off duty and not on call drink until our livers complain." Elizabeth grinned. "There'll be cute guys there from other services you might not have met yet. It's a fun break after a long week, and a good way to get to know people out of the hospital."

"I don't think I'm really in the mood to socialize."

"Suit yourself." Elizabeth shrugged. "But I'm heading over if you end up changing your mind."

Katy thought about her plan for the night. Which was to go to Nick's house and look through old family photo albums. Laugh and cry, then put them away for another year. Is that what her dad would want her to do?

No. He'd be so proud of her for getting through these first weeks of her internship, and even having a few successes. He'd want her to celebrate that. Make new friends. Maybe Alec would even be there, and her spirits would be lifted just by being with him, the way they'd always been.

"You know what? Mind's changed. I'm in."

Alec finished up the last of the paperwork on his desk, glad that this hell of a long day was finally over. He closed his eyes and let his head drop back against his chair, disgusted with himself that he'd had the gall to think he'd had a bad day. This latest news about a patient he'd liked and cared about, a patient whose family he'd become close with, was a painful blow. And he knew that, as painful as the sad prognosis for this man was for Alec, it was nothing compared to how it affected the man's wife and children.

His own unpleasant day had started with a phone call from his father in the morning, before his parents had left to go back to Russia for another week or two. The man had felt a need to ream Alec out yet again for his lack of good judgment and general failings as a doctor and human being.

Then Margaret Sanders had stopped by his office to talk about which fifth-year residents he would recommend being offered a permanent position. Talking with Margaret had made him think about nearly kissing Katy on the beach, which the CMO would have seen all too clearly if he had. Then thought about the times he had kissed her, and how much he wanted to do it again. Starting with her mouth and working his way down every inch of her beautiful body.

Damn it, he knew he couldn't act on this intense, nagging desire for her, but didn't need a constant reminder of that reality.

Or maybe the truth was he did need it. Should, in fact, welcome it. He couldn't ever make the same mistake again, no matter how much he wanted to. He could not risk Katy's reputation. Her future. And since he couldn't, avoiding her as much as possible was the least torturous solution to the attraction that felt inescapable.

He'd felt terrible after he'd walked away from her at the wedding. Then a different emotion—jealousy—had stabbed even deeper when she'd just moved on to dance with someone else. Though he sure couldn't blame her for that, since he couldn't be with her the way he wanted to be.

The deep breath he pulled into his lungs didn't calm the disquiet he felt. What he needed was a long run to clear his mind before the sun set. He knew running wasn't going to push the tragic news about his patient from his mind. Definitely wouldn't erase thoughts of

Katy. Not thinking about her had proved impossible, but it had gotten slightly easier since he no longer saw her every day on teaching rounds.

Damn it, though, he missed her. Missed seeing her warm bedside manner. Missed seeing that little crease in her forehead as she pondered a problem. Missed seeing the desire in her eyes that mirrored his own, making not kissing her impossible.

He nearly groaned when his phone rang in his pocket, wondering how he'd get through another surgery in his current state of mind, until he remembered he wasn't on call tonight. He looked at it, relieved to see it was Nick. "What's up?"

"I need you to do a favor for me. Are you able to go to the Flat-Foot Tavern tonight?"

He stared at his phone. Nick's favor was to go to a bar? "Why?"

"Katy's there with the crew. I'd hoped to join her and keep her out of trouble, but I just got called in for an emergency surgery and can't."

"Why do you need to keep her out of trouble?" Of all the people he knew, Alec couldn't imagine Katy whooping it up and getting drunk and out of control.

"Today's the anniversary of Dad's passing. It sure as hell doesn't feel like he's been gone four years, does it?" Nick sighed in his ear. "You know how tough that was on all of us, but especially Katy. She was his baby, you know?"

"I know." His chest compressed in sympathy for the whole family, but he had a bad feeling he knew where this conversation was going. "What exactly are you asking me to do?"

"Katy usually stays home on this day and, basically,

mourns. I expected to find her here, going through old family memorabilia, so I was surprised when she wasn't. Then she called and told me she was going to the bar. She's not a big drinker, and it doesn't take much for her to get looped. I'm afraid tonight might be the night she has a bit too much. To forget. And I can't be there to make sure she gets home okay."

Hell. "All right. I'll go."

"Thanks, Alec. I appreciate it."

A peculiar sensation rolled around in his chest. A strange combination of trepidation and anticipation at spending time with Katy, of being there for her. Thinking how much it would mean to him to be with her tonight as much as she might need him around.

He glanced at his watch. Just after nine. Surely it was too early for her to already be tipsy. Except liver rounds usually started around seven, so who knew?

He stacked the papers he'd signed, put them in his outbox and stood, ready to head out the door. Until he realized he needed a quick shower and to change into street clothes. And never mind that half the people at the Flat-Foot would be there straight after work, wearing scrubs.

Twenty minutes later he headed outside and across the street to the tavern as the sun dipped beneath the horizon. Even with the low light inside the bar, his gaze was instantly drawn to her. Katy.

He hadn't seen her for days, and he let himself stand there a moment to absorb the sight of her. Her hair gleaming, her smile surprisingly wide for a woman who was supposed to be feeling sad today. Laughing and bright-eyed and clinking a glass with some intern he hadn't met yet.

He remembered her trying to clink her glass with

his, dumping her wine in his lap, and touching him until he'd nearly exploded. Good thing he'd arrived to make sure she didn't have the same effect on the young guy, and never mind that it shouldn't be any of his business.

He weaved through the crowded tables, the thump of the bass music seeming to pound a primal rhythm into his body. He pulled up a chair next to Todd Eiterman, the second-year surgical resident. Close to Katy, but not so close as to raise eyebrows. Though eyebrows were raised anyway, since he didn't make a habit of doing liver rounds with the residents.

"Any lives saved today?" he asked, to make small talk, looking around the table of hardworking young doctors relaxing after a long week. Hoping no one saw him looking particularly closely at Katy, trying to see if she'd been drinking much. Trying not to think about how good it would feel to drape his arm across her shoulders. To feel her soft skin beneath his hand that was exposed by the spaghetti-strapped sundress she wore.

"Every day, Dr. Armstrong. Every day." Elizabeth smiled coyly and lifted her glass of wine.

Alec didn't have a glass to lift, so he simply gave her a return half-smile. "Good. Cheers."

"Here, Alec. I mean Dr. Armstrong. Toast with this— I'm going to get another one." Katy held her glass out to him. Her mostly empty glass, and what had been inside it, he wasn't sure. Margarita? Daiquiri?

He didn't want her drink, but he also didn't want her to be drinking it either. It was more than obvious from the over-brightness of her eyes and the slight slur to her words that she'd already had plenty. He felt an urge to sweep her up and out of there before she embarrassed herself, but forced himself to be patient. To wait for the right moment when it wouldn't seem like a big deal.

He held up the glass. "Cheers, everyone. You're all doing a great job."

The cheer was loudly chorused, and he took a sip to be polite. Margarita, and a strong one, at that. How many had she had?

He looked at Katy again, but her face was turned to Elizabeth next to her. Within the loud beat of the music in the bar, he couldn't hear her words, so he just let himself study her profile. Her cute little nose and generous lips. Her slender hands fingering the necklace slipping down between the hint of her breasts that peeked from the top of her dress. He found his breath growing short, wished he could replace her hand with his own to stroke that delicate skin. Then figuratively smacked himself for the thought.

Damn. He took a swig of her drink, grimaced a little since he didn't particularly like margaritas, and pretty much emptied the already nearly empty glass. He answered questions and engaged in chitchat while half his mind wondered how he was going to discreetly get her out of there without anyone noticing.

Katy stood, clearly wobbly on her feet, and picked up her purse as she turned, likely to go to the restroom. This was his chance to talk with her alone and get her home. The waitress stopped at the table, and Katy sent Alec a wide smile. "Alec, let me buy you a drink. I'm having another one."

Like hell she was. Time to scrap the idea of being discreet. "I can't stay. And unfortunately you can't either because your brother asked me to drive you home."

"I don't need a driver. I have my car here."

"Except you're not driving it."

"Says who? Besides, I'm not ready to leave."

Alec nearly laughed at the look she gave him, which could only be described as a death glare, coupled with a deep frown. Apparently the normally sweet and apologetic Katy had another side that was unleashed after a few drinks. Or, he considered, she might still be ticked about the way he'd left her at the dance floor.

"I'll make sure she gets home, Dr. Armstrong," Todd said.

He looked at the young man, who seemed sober enough. But he'd promised Nick he'd see her safely home. At that moment Katy turned and stalked—if you could call her wobbly gait stalking—to the restroom, and Alec exhaled in relief. This was his chance.

"Thanks, Todd. That would be great. I'll see you all later." He headed toward the door then pivoted back toward the restroom. Out of the corner of his eye he saw one person was still watching him. Elizabeth.

Damn it. Caught.

No matter. He was going to get Katy out of there without a scene, text Todd that he'd driven her after all and fulfill his duty.

Duty? Who was he kidding? This had nothing to do with duty and everything to do with the surge of protective instinct he was feeling. That, for whatever reason, he'd always felt toward Katy.

After what seemed like an eternity the door to the women's restroom finally swung open. She tripped over her heel and stumbled into him, grasping his arms as he steadied her against his chest.

"Oh! Sorry." Her big blue eyes blinked up at him, and that scowl settled on her face again. "Oh. It's you. Why do you and Nick seem to think I need taking care of? I don't need a babysitter. I'm a big girl now. I can take care of myself."

"I know you can. But you've had too much to drink to drive, and I think you know that."

She stared up at him, now with just that tiny frown between her brows that was such a cute part of who she was. Did she know her fingers moved on the skin of his arms, caressingly, tantalizingly, as they stood so close to one another in the dark, narrow hallway? His hands tightened on her shoulders, and he forced himself to loosen them.

"Okay." Her breasts rose and fell in a deep sigh. "I know I shouldn't drive. But I…I don't want to go home. Not just yet."

"Fine. We'll go somewhere else." How could he insist he take her home when her eyes looked so clouded and sad, when her lips trembled ever so slightly? He needed to take her mind off the pain of losing her dad. Off the stress of work. Off anything but simple pleasures.

He shoved down thoughts of the kind of pleasure he'd really like to offer her, and decided on where he could take her. Somewhere sure to bring the smile to her face that he needed to see again. "Let's go to my place and take a walk along the bay to clear our heads."

"That sounds good." Already the clouds in her eyes were fleeing, and Alec's heart felt a little lighter as he led her out the side door of the tavern.

Moonlight lit the lapping water of the bay as he swung his car into the driveway of his condo. Katy had been uncharacteristically quiet the entire ride. He turned the ignition off and looked at her, so close in the seat next to him. The sadness that was back in her eyes knocked the air from his chest.

"Come on. Something's happening soon I want you to see. Something that will make you smile."

"I don't feel much like smiling today."

"I know. To be honest, I don't either. But maybe we can find a reason to smile together." He walked to her side of the car and opened the door, reaching for her soft hand. "It's a little chilly, so wear your sweater." She'd need the light warmth, and it would be good to see less of her smooth skin that tempted him to touch it.

He led her down to the bike path that circled the bay, holding her hand because she was still a little unsteady on her feet. And because it just felt right to twine his fingers with hers. It would've seemed oddly distant to just walk side by side with her, when both of them could use the warmth and comfort of that small connection. After all, it wasn't as though some spy from the hospital was watching.

The simple act of strolling with her, the crisp night air in his lungs, the moon hanging in the starry sky, all seemed to clear his mind of everything that had weighed him down that day. He looked at Katy and hoped she felt a little of that, too. "I'm sorry about your dad. I know him being gone is hard on all of you."

"Things like a family wedding are a sad reminder, you know?" She looked up at him, and even through the darkness he could see the shadows in her eyes, a misting of tears that clutched at his heart. "He would've loved to live long enough to see a first grandchild and be a wonderful *papou*. He would've loved to see Elena married. He would've been so happy to see me graduate from med school. It...it really breaks my heart he never got to do any of those things."

He stopped walking to cup her cheek with his free hand. Wipe away the single tear that had escaped her brimming eyes and squeezed his heart. "I know. Life isn't fair, is it?"

She shook her head. "No. It definitely isn't. He gave me this necklace to remind me to always go after what I wanted. I wear it every day and can feel him with me."

Her eyes held wistful sadness as she fingered the necklace. Alec wanted to offer her comfort, to hold her, kiss her, until there was only happiness in their sapphire depths. But he couldn't. He could only offer words. "Your dad was proud of all of his kids, but I think you were special to him. You shared his love of puzzles and mysteries. I remember how much he got a kick out of the backward solutions you came up with when everyone else only thought forward."

"He did, didn't he?" The smile that touched her lips was small, but it was a start. "So tell me why you don't feel much like smiling today either."

Should he tell her? He rarely shared when he was upset about a patient. But she'd shared with him, so it was only fair that he open a little of himself up to her, too.

"A few years ago, I had a patient with colon cancer. I got to know him well, and his family, too. He's just a great person, as is his wife. They have three of the cutest kids." He sucked in a breath, thinking how they'd all been sure the worst health problems were over for the man. "I performed a hemicolectomy on him, then he had a course of chemotherapy, and he's been doing well until this week when he started having stomach pain. Today we found out the cancer has spread to his liver." He could still see the man's wife's tears, the way they'd clutched each other when he'd had to tell them the bad news. And damn if that wasn't the absolute hardest part of his job.

"I'm sorry." It was her turn to squeeze his hand, and he was surprised that telling her, and having her listen, felt good. "I haven't had to go through that yet, but I know I will have to help patients deal with bad news when I'm in a family practice. I hope I do okay."

"You don't have to hope. You have a wonderful way with patients. I've seen it firsthand and have had quite a few people tell me, too."

"Really?" This time a real smile touched her face, which made him smile, too. "That's good to hear. Thank you."

The first boom sounded in the air, and Katy stopped walking. "What was that?"

"What I brought you out here to see. What I said would make you smile."

More loud booms, and then red, green and white sparkles lit the night sky.

"Fireworks?"

"From the adventure park. You can see them across the bay."

"Oh! They're beautiful!"

He watched her face and was filled with a feeling of triumph when he saw her eyes light almost as brightly as the fireworks. As her smile grew wider she gasped with delight. And damned if the soft sound, the expression of pleasure on her face, didn't make him wonder how she would look, how she would sound, as he buried his nose in her soft neck and buried himself in her beautiful body.

He shouldn't think those kinds of forbidden thoughts,

but he just couldn't escape the fierce desire for her that had become a constant, intense ache.

He turned, not wanting to look at her. Not wanting to see her shining eyes and lush lips and her curves hidden beneath her dress that kept giving him these insane thoughts. Thoughts that gnawed at him. Thoughts of taking her to his condo and stripping off her clothes and making love with her all night.

No. He had to suppress it. And since he didn't seem to be able to accomplish that out here with the bright, silvery moonlight touching her hair and skin and smile, he had to end the evening and take her home. He took a few steps away, back toward the car.

"Nick will be wondering where you are." His voice came out gruff, hoarse, but it was the best he could do. "And I have an early morning tomorrow." It wasn't true. In fact, he had the day off. But a little lie was nothing if it helped him get her home before he did something he'd regret. That they'd both regret.

"Alec."

He looked back at her and, to his shock, she was right there. Inches away. His breath backed up in his lungs at the expression on her face.

It wasn't sad any more, or worried or studious or any of the things he was used to seeing on her lovely face. It was determined. And sensual. A combination that both excited and alarmed him.

"Yes?" he asked, wary, his heart beating harder, the excitement and alarm growing as she closed the small gap between them.

In answer, she rose up on her toes, wrapped her arms around his neck and pressed her mouth to his.

CHAPTER TEN

ALEC STOOD THERE motionless, as though he were a statue, as she kissed him. He didn't pull away, but didn't participate either. She'd known he'd be surprised, but she'd had to taste him. Had to kiss him one more time.

His lips were so warm, so soft. She ran her tongue across the seam of them, and was rewarded as he opened them slightly, as his tongue touched hers, and she drank in the taste of him.

His hands closed around her shoulders, tightened, and with a strange, strangled sound in his throat he seemed to give in. Tilted his head and opened his mouth over hers. Brought her body tightly against his. It felt so right, so wonderful, to be pressed so closely to his heart she could feel the pounding of it against her breasts.

His stiff form loosened, molded to hers, hip to hip and thigh to thigh. His hands left her shoulders to wrap around her back, his fingers digging slightly into her flesh as his mouth devoured hers. As though he was starving for her in exactly the same way she'd been starving for him.

Yes. Yes. Yes. The mantra broke through the fogginess of her brain. Each kiss before this had gotten longer, sweeter. Now they were sharing the kind of passion she'd dreamed of. She arched up, kissing him more boldly now, letting her fingers thread into his soft hair, the thick waves curving around her fingers, holding onto her. Her holding on to him.

Abruptly, his arms dropped from her back, his hands grasped her shoulders again, and he set her away from him. His chest heaved in deep breaths. Her stomach tightened as it became clear, even through the darkness, that his expression wasn't smiling and sensual. It was very serious.

"Katy. I'm sorry. I shouldn't have kissed you in the hospital and again at the wedding. I shouldn't have kissed you now."

"It's not for you to be sorry." She tilted her chin at him, refusing to let him take the blame. Trying to push down the regret she, too, felt. Not regret for the kiss. Regret that he wouldn't allow himself to be with her the way she so wanted him to be. "I kissed you, not the other way around."

"This time, maybe. But that still makes it three to one." His serious expression gave way to a glimmer of a smile.

"Actually, it's three to two, counting the time I kissed you five years ago."

"Okay, Miss Math. Though I didn't think you liked to remember that kiss too much."

"I don't. Do you have any idea how embarrassed I felt when you turned me down flat and ran away like a dog being chased by a cat?"

"I'm sorry. I was most definitely a dog that night." He lifted his hand to her hair, blowing in the breeze, and tucked it behind her ear. His fingers slowly continued down to stroke her cheekbone. "But I think you know

now it wasn't because I wasn't attracted to you. Which, to my astonishment, I was that day."

"And now?"

"Now I'm beyond attracted to you." Even in the darkness she could see his eyes grow serious again as he cupped her face in his hand. "But I can't do anything about it."

"Why?"

"You know why. You're a student and I'm an attending physician. Your teacher. It's not ethical."

"You're not my teacher any more. Dr. Boswell is."

"It doesn't matter. People love to talk—you know that. I couldn't bear to have you gossiped about, maybe even have your career jeopardized. Nick and I even worried about people calling favoritism just because you're his sister. Believe me, I know how it can be. We can't do this, no matter how much I want to."

"How much do you want to?" she asked. Wondering if it could possibly be as much as she did.

"You want a demonstration?" His eyes glinted. "Something you can quantify, Miss Science? Then here it is." He pulled her tightly against him, angled his mouth to hers, and kissed her hard. Fiercely and possessively and without reserve. A kiss that most definitely beat out all their prior kisses tenfold. A kiss that sent her heart racing and hot tingles surging through every nerve and was everything she'd dreamed for years and years that kissing him would be.

Katy clutched his shirt with her hands. A moan formed in her throat as his hot mouth explored hers so deeply and thoroughly that her knees wobbled beneath her. Then nearly stumbled as he released her and backed away. A chill replaced the warmth that had spread across her body on every inch they'd touched each other.

"Does that give you something to measure?" The dark eyes that stared at her glittered with a passion that shortened her breath even more. "I want you, Katy. I think about you all day long. Wondering if I'm going to run into you in some patient's room or the hallway or the lunchroom. I look for you, even though I tell myself not to. Even though I've tried hard not to. I want you, but we can't do this. I won't be responsible for damaging your career."

"No one has to know. No one will know."

"A dangerous assumption to make."

He grasped her hand and began to walk back toward his car, so quickly that she stumbled in her heels and he slowed down. "I'm taking you home now."

He'd told her he wanted her. Thought of her all day long. Just as she did him. But the huge problem keeping them apart couldn't be ignored, and she knew it. She didn't want her career damaged any more than he did. How could she be the doctor her father had been if she let her personal life cloud her judgment? A secret affair with a man who was technically her boss was not something her father would have wanted for her—even if that man was Alec. And she understood why he didn't want to go through that again either.

As they'd both said earlier, life wasn't fair. And that reality felt like a brick on her heart.

"Can I see your apartment before you take me home? Maybe have a quick cup of coffee?" She wasn't quite ready to say goodbye. Knew a cup of coffee wouldn't really make a difference but grasped at any reason to spend just a few more minutes with him.

He looked down at her, his expression now unreadable. "You want coffee?"

"Yes. Please."

He looked at her a long moment, so long she nearly fidgeted beneath his gaze, before he finally led her into his condo. Floor-to-ceiling windows looked over the star-lit bay from his living room, which was furnished with modern pieces in clean, sleek lines. They moved into a spacious kitchen with gleaming appliances and a huge island with bar stools on one side. "Have a seat at the counter. You'll see there's a plate of kourambiethes your *yiayia* insisted I bring home with me."

Mmm…kourambiethes. Instantly, she remembered the powdered sugar on his lips as it had been at the wedding, and knew she'd never again eat one again without thinking of him.

He had one of those single-cup coffee-brewing machines, and placed a steaming cup in front of her before brewing one for himself. She looked at his strong back, his shoulders broad in the blue polo shirt he wore tucked into the waistband of jeans. Watched his long, surgeon's fingers nimbly work the machine.

Why couldn't she feel those talented fingers, just once, touching her everywhere? Feel his skin and muscles under her own hands? Knowing he wanted her the way she wanted him but that they couldn't let it happen made her chest ache even more than when he'd rejected her five years ago.

Welcoming the distraction of hot coffee with a sweet cookie, she picked up one of the kourambiethes and handed it to Alec, then took one for herself. She took a bite then realized he was looking at her mouth. Watching her eat, his eyelids low, his eyes dark. She ran her tongue slowly across her sugary lip, deliberately tempting him. What could be wrong with one last, sweet kiss?

Still staring at her, he took a bite of cookie, and his chest lifted as he drew a breath.

Suddenly he began to choke. Lord, it was the powdered sugar! She jumped off the stool and ran to the other side of the counter, pounding on his back with her fists as his body was wracked by a violent cough.

"Ow, damn it, stop!" His eyes watered as he choked and coughed and finally got his breathing under control. He turned and grabbed her wrists. "Geez, Katy! Didn't we already talk about the medical necessity for this? Or are you just mad and trying to kill me?"

"Trying to kill you, I guess. Haven't you heard about hell and the fury of a woman scorned? But if you kiss me, I'll spare you."

One more kiss. Was that so much to want? She pressed her hands, her wrists still imprisoned in his hands, against his chest. His heart beat hard against her palms. Harder than it should have been just from his choking episode. As hard as hers currently pounded in her own chest.

"Katy." His eyes were dark and hot. His voice low and rough. "It's nearly impossible for me to resist kissing you as it is. Now you have to add a threat of bodily harm?"

"Just trying to even up the score. Which is currently four to two." She leaned up to press her mouth to his, softly, slowly, not wanting to be accused of assaulting him again. Just wanting to taste him. Wanting him to feel what was between them.

His warm lips moved with hers for a long moment until he broke the kiss. "Does everything have to be a competition with you? How about letting me win this? Leave it at three to four?"

"I don't think so. I'm liking this kissing contest a lot." She kissed him again, and he tasted beyond wonderful, a spicy hint of coffee mixed with sugar and him.

He pulled his mouth from hers, his hands tighter on her wrists now. Tension emanated from him, and heat, too. His eyes glittered, most definitely a wild, tiger-eye color as he stared at her, and she could see very clearly that his need was every bit as powerful as her own. "So now we're even. Are you happy?"

"Yes. I'm happy. But I could be happier." She pulled her wrist loose from his hold and grasped his hand. Brought his palm to her breast and held it there. His fingers tightened, his thumb sweeping across her nipple, and it felt so wonderful she gasped.

"Damn it, you don't play fair," he said in a low growl, still stroking her breast.

"All's fair in love and war." She used her free hand to tug part of his shirt from his pants, slipping her fingers beneath until she could feel him tremble.

"Is this love or war?" His hot breath slipped across her cheeks as his lips caressed her face.

"Maybe a little of both."

"Yeah." The word came out on a groan as he released her other wrist, wrapped his arm around her back and kissed her. No longer teasing and soft. This was a real kiss, deep and hot and nearly desperate, and she sank into it as one hand caressed her breast, the other sliding down to squeeze her bottom.

"Katy." The word came against her lips as he kissed her, delved deeply again, their tongues dancing together as he claimed her mouth for his own. The countertop pressed into her lower back as he molded his body to hers. She wound her arms around his neck and held on, feeling the tension in the muscles of his shoulders, in the tautness of his body. Her knees felt so weak she thought she just might slither to the floor.

"Katy," he said again, his voice ragged, his eyes dark. He gave her a small smile as he imperceptibly shook his head. "I'm going to hell for this, you know." Then he kissed her again.

A feeling of relief swept through her as she realized they'd both finally, finally surrendered to the force that was clearly bigger than both of them. His kiss was filled with passion and sweetness but no regret. Only want.

She brought her hands to his waist, tugging his shirt loose to feel his skin, his body. His muscles shivered beneath her palms as she stroked under his shirt.

He responded by pulling the straps of her dress off her shoulders, tugging more until it hung at her waist and her lacy bra was all that covered her breasts. With his agile fingers, he quickly flicked the clasp and slid it, too, from her arms.

"I've fantasized for more hours than you can imagine how your breasts look." His voice was hoarse as he looked at her. "Do you know how beautiful you are?"

"What I know is that I don't know exactly how beautiful you are," she said. She wanted to see him, look at him the way he was looking at her. She pulled his shirt up and off. Her breath caught at the width of his shoulders, at the muscled strength of his chest, at the fine layer of dark hair covering it. She smoothed her hands up and over all of it, loving the feel of him against her palms. Wanting the feel of all of him against all of her.

He grabbed a cookie from the plate on the counter,

his eyes gleaming. "Promise not to bruise me again if I choke?"

"I— Oh…!"

All thought of how she was going to respond left her brain when he rubbed the cookie slowly across and around one nipple, then the other, his mouth following to lick and suck the sugar left behind. The feel of his lips and tongue were so magical and wildly erotic she could barely breathe. She tangled her fingers in his thick hair, held him to her, and moaned.

With his mouth still on her breasts, he pulled her dress the rest of the way down her body until she stood there wearing only her panties. He sank to his knees, his mouth continuing down, circling her navel. Moving lower until his lips and tongue pressed against the damp front of her underwear. She moaned again, melting for him.

Perhaps he sensed that her legs were about to crumple beneath the erotic invasion of his mouth, because he suddenly stood. His long, warm fingers grasped her bottom and lifted her to his waist before he began moving from the kitchen. She wrapped her legs around his hips and clung to his neck, kissing him, still able to taste a little of the sugar on his tongue.

"You taste unbearably sweet," he whispered between kisses. "Even without the sugar." He carried her into a bedroom, and her heart pounded so loudly in her ears it was like a drumbeat. Finally. Finally. But he passed the big bed and moved to a sliding glass door.

"Where are we going?" Surely he wasn't going to go all noble now after he'd made her crazy with wanting him. "I'm thinking a bed is a good idea. Like now."

"Who knew you could be so impatient?" He grinned as he shoved open the door and stepped into the breezy night, onto a covered, private balcony accessed only from the bedroom. "Ever since you came to San Diego I've thought of you out here with me. Thought of how you would look, naked on the cushions of this chaise lounge with the breeze in your hair and the moonlight in your eyes."

He gently lowered her to the chaise and the bay breeze did tease across her nakedness, sensuous and wonderful, and she wanted him to feel the same thing. Needed him naked—now.

"You, too." She sat up and grasped the belt of his jeans, undid the buckle. "I want to see your body in the moonlight."

"Your wish is my command." His eyes crinkled at the corners, but in their depths was the same deep longing and desire that had filled her from the moment he'd kissed her on the bay. From the moment she'd first seen him again.

He stripped off his jeans, socks and underwear in a hurry, then settled his torso between her legs. Licked along the inside of her thigh as he pulled the last bit of her clothing down and off. Kissed his way up her body as his hands gently stroked her legs, opening them, as he settled himself in between to nuzzle her neck and nip her earlobe.

"Too bad the fireworks are over," he said against the hollow of her throat. "We could have heard and seen them from here."

"I'm willing to bet we're going to make some fireworks of our own." There was no doubt about that as her body was already consumed by an intensely sparkling heat she'd never known existed.

He chuckled against her neck. "I won't take that bet, because my goal is to make you explode."

He kissed her again as his fingers found her core, touched her, caressed her, as her own fingers explored his smooth contours. His face, his shoulders, his tight buttocks, his back. Clasped him in her hand until both of them were gasping into one another's mouths, their bodies moving, skin against skin.

She'd dreamed of this for so long. Wanted this so long. Part of her wanted to savor every second, to draw out their lovemaking all night. But the part of her that wanted him beyond anything she'd ever experienced couldn't wait. She wrapped her legs around his hips, drew him in to join with her. They moved together, creating an instant rhythm of perfection between them, giving and taking until the moment couldn't be held off any longer. Her climax making her cry out, he covered her mouth with his, absorbing the sound as they both fell.

Alec lay propped on his elbow in his bed and watched Katy sleep, listening to her breathe as she lay on her back next to him. He gazed at her sweet face in repose, her eyelashes resting on her cheeks. At her motionless body, positioned as a sleeping fairy-tale princess would be, her hands one on top of the other resting on her belly, her beautiful hair in a thick halo of waves around her head. Deep in the kind of sleep only someone who'd been without it too long could have.

The breeze from his ceiling fan lifted strands of her hair, and he gently stroked them from her eyes and tucked them behind her ears. His chest filled and his gut tightened with too many swirling emotions.

Pleasure. Regret. Worry. Joy.

He shouldn't have let it happen. Hadn't been able to keep it from happening.

He let his finger trace her eyebrow, slip down her nose, touch her beautiful lips. Her face twitched in response, and he had to smile. She was a woman of contrasts, like no one he'd met before. So smart, someone who thought deeply and carefully, who took her job seriously, and yet who could be almost childlike at times in a charming and adorable way.

Katy. He'd never have dreamed when she'd tagged along after Nick and him all those years ago that he'd be lying in bed with her, sated, happy, content. He should get up. Leave her to get her much-needed rest as he went for a run, fixed some breakfast for both of them. Then take her home and hope to hell her brother had no clue why she'd really spent the night at his home.

All this was dangerous. So potentially damaging to both their careers. But as he looked at her, he knew he couldn't walk away and end it now. He wanted to spend the day with her. Wanted to spend more time learning how her interesting mind worked. Wanted to explore the world through her eyes, which had always seen things a little differently than most.

He wasn't her teacher any more. And, yes, he knew it was a damned lame excuse for not breaking it off right now, before it had barely started. He wished he was strong enough, but he wasn't.

He could only hope and pray they wouldn't both regret heading down the path in front of them. The all-too-thrilling path that was also scary as hell.

CHAPTER ELEVEN

"HI, DR. BOSWELL. Dr. Armstrong." Could anyone tell her heart thumped absurdly fast as she tried to stand nonchalantly in the doctors' lounge by their lunch table? How hard it was to suppress a secret smile as she looked at Alec's handsome face? How hard it was to not reach out and smooth his slightly messy hair from his forehead?

"Hello, Dr. Pappas." The smile Alec gave back to her probably seemed normal enough to anyone watching. But Katy could see the glint deep in their amber depths that showed he was feeling exactly as she was. Still remembering their incredible and beautiful time together three nights ago. "Are you giving Dr. Boswell any trouble?"

"I'm trying not to. I don't think I've made any mistakes for at least a few hours."

"I think it's actually been an entire day." Dr. Boswell chuckled. "In truth, Alec, our student is doing a stellar job. She's the kind of intern who makes teaching rounds a pleasure."

"She is indeed." That glint in his eyes grew a little hotter as their eyes met, which made Katy feel short of breath. He must have realized how he was looking at her as he seemed to quickly school his face into bland professionalism and turned back to Dr. Boswell. "I hope the interns I get next month work as hard as she and Michael Coffman have been."

Elizabeth Stark stopped next to her as she stood at the men's table, holding an empty lunch tray, her gaze a little cold as it slid over Katy, which surprised her. A slight chill of anxiety slid down her spine. Elizabeth had been so much friendlier the past week. Had the woman somehow picked up on the vibe between Alec and her?

Elizabeth shifted her attention to the two surgeons. "Dr. Boswell, are you still planning for me to do the appendectomy this afternoon?"

The man nodded. "Should be a cakewalk for you by now, Dr. Stark. I'm impressed with the skills you've shown me so far. You're just about ready to go off on your own."

"Thank you." She inclined her head in acknowledgement of the compliment as her face relaxed a bit into a pleased smile. Katy knew Elizabeth put tremendous pressure on herself to achieve in the surgical arena, which was still primarily a man's world. Another reason Katy was more than happy that she'd chosen family practice for her future.

Elizabeth turned to Katy. "When you're done with lunch, come find me. I have a few patients I need you to see."

"Okay. I won't be long." She wanted one more quick look at Alec. Wanted to be the recipient of another smile that lit his eyes. But knew she couldn't linger and possibly raise any red flags, so she looked at Dr. Boswell instead. "I'll be here if you need me. Otherwise I'll see you for rounds in the morning."

Katy moved to a table at the back of the room and faced the wall so she wouldn't be tempted to stare at

Alec. After their amazing night and day together, she'd found it a little hard to concentrate when she'd first come back to work. Thankfully, she'd gotten back into the groove soon enough and was so busy working umpteen hours she didn't have time to think about anything but her patients.

Still, when she did have a free moment her mind instantly drifted to her wonderful day off. A day off that had seemed like far more than twenty-four hours. Probably, she thought, hoping the dreamy smile on her face wasn't obvious to the entire lunchroom, because she'd spent the day with Alec. A day filled with delicious lovemaking, laughter, and fun.

Kayaking on the bay, then lovemaking at Alec's place. Lunch by the ocean on Mission Beach, a little swimming, then back to his condo to make love. Sailing on Alec's small sailboat then making love again.

Could any day possibly have been any more perfect?

With a smile on her face she just plain couldn't suppress, she finished up her lunch. Alec had already left, and when she felt a twinge of disappointment sternly reminded herself that was a good thing. She contacted Elizabeth on the hospital call system to find out where she needed to be next.

"Twentieth floor. I have to be somewhere else in a few minutes, so I need you to get here quickly," Elizabeth responded. Was it Katy's imagination that her voice was a tad curt?

She hurried to the floor and found Elizabeth going over some charts. "What do you need from me?"

"That patient you tried to assassinate with potassium a couple weeks ago?" Elizabeth barely glanced up from the charts. "Like a boomerang, she's back again."

"Mrs. Patterson?" Katy frowned. "Why?"

"She actually was here a few days back when you were off work. Typical granny problems, but the nursing home sent her in anyway. She still had lactic acidosis, and the diagnosis was again ischemic colitis."

"So why is she back today?"

Elizabeth rolled her eyes. "Same old. Lactic acidosis again. In my opinion, she just has the dwindles and is depressed and nervous. Then the nursing home gets nervous, too, and sends her back. I remembered she liked you, so why don't you do her workup, see if you can reassure her before we send her back to the home?"

"Okay. I'll be glad to. Thanks." Katy took the chart and headed toward Mrs. Patterson's room. When she got there she stopped abruptly in the doorway, staring for a moment, shocked at what she saw.

"Helen?" She hurried to the woman's bedside. The woman looked astonishingly ill. Nothing at all like the energetic, chatty woman she'd been just weeks ago. How could she have lost so much weight in such a short period of time? She'd been the tiniest thing, anyway, when she'd been here before. Now she was practically skin and bones. She reached for the woman's hand. "Tell me what's going on."

"Who are you?" Her eyes had a hollow look to them as she peered at Katy, with none of the friendliness and vitality that had sparkled in them before.

Her words jerked Katy's heart. Was the woman delirious? "It's me, Katy Pappas. The intern. I took care of you the first time you came in. Just a couple weeks ago."

Helen stared at her, then gave a tiny nod. "Oh, yes. I remember."

Katy warmed her stethoscope, then listened to the

woman's lungs and heart and took her pulse. "Tell me why you're here. How you're feeling."

"My stomach hurts so much. I can't eat. I don't sleep well." Her thin hand rested on Katy's. "I think it's my time. I think I'm dying."

"Not if I can help it." Katy pressed her lips together. This didn't sound like a normal post-op problem. Or simply ischemic colitis. Before her hip surgery Helen had been a very active, healthy woman. What could possibly be going on? "I'm going to check some things and see what we can figure out. Hang in there." She squeezed the poor woman's shoulder and headed to the computers to look at Helen's lab results. And hoped and prayed there would be one little thing that would shed light on this peculiar mystery.

Katy closeted herself in one of the hospital computer labs where she'd have some quiet to study and think. She pulled up all Helen Patterson's records. Her hip surgery. Tests done at that time and during her next admissions. She turned to the mnemonic used for studying the anion gap of metabolic acidosis—MUDPILES.

Ruling out several of the various causes for acidosis in the MUDPILES mnemonic was fairly easy, but still didn't give her an answer. Then she called on the training her dad had given her. The puzzle master. The ultimate mystery-solver.

Define the goal. The topic. What did she already know on the subject? Set aside the first, most obvious solutions and keep an open mind. Place the facts in a pattern she could understand and evaluate.

She stared at all the information on the computer, gnawing her lip. Think, Katy, think.

It almost seemed as though the type on the screen

grew crisper, brighter, practically leaping out at her. The answer was right there. But what a crazy answer it was! Would anybody believe it? Who should she try to convince first?

Nobody. The first thing she had to do was prove her hunch, her conviction, through a blood test.

Sucking in a fortifying breath, she ordered the test and asked for the results to be determined STAT. Then managed to distract herself by seeing other patients, but checked every few minutes to see if the tests were done, practically jumping for joy when the results came in. Then stared in both triumph and disbelief.

Katy's heard thumped and her adrenaline flowed. She remembered Alec reminding her to look for the zebra while everyone else was looking for the horse. And, man, this zebra was a big one.

She turned from the computer, hands a little sweaty. She'd start with Alec. He'd advise her what to do and what steps had to be taken.

After what was only ten or so minutes but seemed like hours, Katy was able to find out where he was. And what could possibly make the elevators so painfully slow? Rushing through the corridors, she finally found Alec about to enter a patient's room and ran up to him.

"Dr. Armstrong! I need to speak with you right away."

A frown formed between his brows as he looked at her then quickly glanced up and down the hall. He took a step back and spoke in a low voice. "Dr. Pappas. As you know, Dr. Boswell is covering teaching rounds now. You need to address any questions to him."

"No. I know." She gulped. Obviously, he thought she was here for personal reasons and was worried about hospital gossip. Didn't he know she fully understood they had to keep their distance here? "I have a very peculiar situation with a patient and I need to talk with you about it. Have you advise me, because we may have to get the police involved."

His expression turned to one of surprise. "All right. What's going on?"

"You remember Helen Patterson? The patient who accidentally got too much oral potassium on my first night on call?"

"Yes. I remember."

"She's been back two more times for ischemic colitis, which seemed a little strange to me. Then when I went to see her I couldn't believe how different she was, really sick-looking and a little confused."

He stared at her intently. "Go on."

"I set aside the most obvious answers then did some critical thinking. I saw there was one thing that hadn't been checked because normally there wouldn't be a reason to. So I ordered the test. It's confirmed. Her ethylene glycol levels are through the roof."

"What? How is that possible? She's been living in a nursing home."

"Here's the crazy part. Are you ready?" She prayed he'd believe her hypothesis. "I believe her son is poisoning her with antifreeze. He needs money—I know he's been borrowing plenty from her, and she told him she wouldn't give him any more. I know it seems…unbelievable, but my gut tells me it's true and the lab results support it."

He studied her, his eyes thoughtful, then gave a nod. "I would have to agree that there doesn't seem to be any other way that her ethylene glycol levels would be high. I'll speak with Barney and the CMO. The hospital has specific protocol for situations like this, and the police will be contacted to investigate. Meanwhile, we'll get started treating her."

A huge breath of relief left her lungs. "Thank you for believing me. For not dismissing the idea because I'm a lowly intern."

A slow smile spread across his face, touched his eyes which grew warm and admiring. He reached out to cup her face in his hands. "Lowly intern? You, Dr. Pappas, are a superstar. Have I told you lately how much you amaze me?"

Without thinking, she pressed her own palm against the back of his hand. "Me, amazing? Not as amazing as you, Dr. Armstrong, surgeon extraordinaire."

A chuckle rumbled in his chest, and their gazes stayed locked on one another's. Memories of their night and day together hummed in the air between them, and both moved forward, their lips meeting for the briefest connection until a voice jolted them apart.

"What…the hell?" Nick was in the hallway, practically right next to where they stood, and Alec's hands fell to his sides as he took a step back. Nick stared then moved in, just inches away. His voice was quiet but filled with a confusion and anger Katy had rarely heard from him. "Are you kidding me?"

Alec's lips were pressed into a thin line, but he regarded Nick steadily. "Katy has come up with an impressive diagnosis for a patient, but wasn't sure anyone would believe her. She came to talk with me about it first."

Nick looked behind them before speaking again in a near whisper. "I may be as dense as my soon-to-be ex-wife claims, but I'm not totally stupid. The excuse you gave for Katy staying with you…" He shook his head, his eyes narrowed. His chest lifted in a deep breath as he glanced down the hallway again. "We'll talk about this later. My office. Tonight."

Katy's stomach churned. How had they let their guard down and allowed themselves even one second of anything smacking of a personal relationship between them while they were here? And a kiss more than smacked of that. It screamed it. Alec's expression had hardened to stone, and her heart sank at the worry and remorse in his eyes.

"Nick, I don't get what you're upset about." Could she play the innocent, clueless Katy and convince him he hadn't seen what he thought he had?

"You—"

"Alec, I need to speak with you."

They all turned to see Barney Boswell walking toward them. His expression was as grim as Nick's, and Katy's heart about stopped. Dear God, had he seen, too? And if so, what would happen?

"Yes?" Alec's voice was even, but his stony expression hadn't changed.

"I've received…bad news." The man rubbed his hand across his face. "My mother has passed away, and I need to help my brother with all the arrangements. I'm leaving in the morning, so you'll have to take over teaching rounds again."

CHAPTER TWELVE

ALEC PACED IN his office, wondering how the hell to handle this latest problem. His gut churned at what a mess it all was—what a mess he'd allowed it to become.

After his magical night and day with Katy he'd wanted more of them. Hadn't wanted it to end. Had convinced himself they could be discreet and completely professional in the hospital. With him no longer doing the teaching rounds, he'd been sure it wouldn't be too difficult to keep their distance by day and be together when their schedules allowed it at night.

That plan had now gone up in flames. How could he possibly justify what had been wrong to begin with if he had to take over the teaching rounds again?

He'd also clearly been kidding himself about their ability to be discreet. After only moments in the hallway with Katy, looking into the intense blue of her eyes as she'd spoken, listening to her impressive detective work on Helen Patterson's illness, he'd forgotten every damned thing except how amazing she was.

He dropped down into his desk chair, wanting to think about all this for a minute before he went to Nick's office, and closed his eyes. They'd been beyond lucky that the only person who'd seen him holding her face in his hands and kissing her had been Nick. And while that brought another dimension into the equation, at least Nick wasn't going to run to the CMO and report a suspicion that a teacher and senior staff member was hitting on a student. Or, at least, he didn't think so, unless Nick thought he'd be protecting his sister if he did.

"So what do you have to say for yourself?"

Alec opened his eyes and saw Nick standing in the doorway, arms folded across his chest, looking almost as angry as he had when he'd first seen them in the hall.

"Do you realize how much you sound like my father right now?"

"Apparently someone damn well has to." Nick came in and perched on the edge of the chair opposite Alec. "I still can't believe what I saw today. How the hell long has this been going on?"

Should he tell him? Or flat-out lie and try to make him believe it had been a friendly, congratulatory kiss?

Alec didn't like either option, but knew he couldn't lie to Nick. "What's going on is that, from the minute I saw Katy again, I haven't been able to stop thinking about her. About her beauty and brains and how damned all-around incredible she is. And, yeah, I knew it was all wrong but couldn't stop it. No matter how hard I tried." He leaned his elbows on his desk and braced himself for the censure he deserved. "When I found out she felt the same way, I couldn't fight it anymore."

"Hell, Alec." Nick stood and paced across the room. "First of all I'm having a hard time wrapping my brain around you and my little sister being...you know...whatever it is you are."

"I know." He couldn't believe it either. But he didn't

have to believe it for his attraction, his obsession with her to have consumed him anyway.

"To think, I was worried people would whisper favoritism because she's my sister. Which thankfully hasn't happened." Nick shook his head. "And I don't even have to say the rest of it, do I? I absolutely can't believe you've done this after all you went through before. You just can't go there. Period. It's bad for you, and it's bad for her. It's just plain bad."

"I know. You think I don't know that?" Alec clenched his fists, wanting to pound on something. "I—"

"It's only bad if you choose to decide it is," a quiet voice said from the doorway.

Both men looked at Katy. Alec's stupid, confused heart felt like it somehow squeezed and swelled at the same time. She stood there in green scrubs that were wrinkled and had some sort of orange stain beneath her breast. Her blue eyes had shadows smudging them and the hair he so loved to touch was pulled back into a messy ponytail that had numerous loose strands sticking out of it…and still she was the most beautiful thing he'd ever seen.

Nick walked over to her. "You two can't do this. A student having a relationship with an attending just isn't done."

"Really? Just isn't done? I've met several couples in this hospital who had exactly that kind of professional relationship before they had a personal one." Her eyes turned to blue steel as she stood toe to toe with Nick, and in spite of the whole damned situation Alec had to smile. This amazing woman standing in front of him was as tough as nails.

"Doesn't make it right. Doesn't make it ethical, and it

doesn't mean the hospital won't boot both of you out of
here on your asses. You know what happened five years
ago when Alec made exactly this same kind of stupid
mistake. It blows my mind that he's doing it again. To
you, of all people! I won't let you make the same kind
of mistake and have your reputation ruined, or worse."

Katy knew what had happened back then? Alec's chest
tightened, because he knew everything Nick said was
true. Risking her reputation was all kinds of wrong. Except their relationship felt so damned right.

Katy wrapped her arms around her brother's waist and
leaned up to kiss him on the cheek. "I keep reminding
you I'm a big girl. Alec and I will figure this out, and I
promise you—no tears, no matter what."

Nick's face softened slightly as he looked down at his
sister. "I love you, Katy, but the last thing you need is to
get fired because of misconduct." He turned and pointed
his finger at Alec, his eyes fierce. "This is my little sister you're messing with here, and you'd better end this
now before she gets hurt."

He stormed out and Alec and Katy were left to just
look at one another. Since simply looking at her made
him feel alive in a way he hadn't felt in a long time—hell,
had never felt—he didn't know what to do.

She took a few steps closer, surprisingly hesitant steps,
considering her firm response to her brother a few minutes earlier.

"So, now what?" she asked quietly, her eyes searching
his. "We've both known all along this might happen."

He stood and walked to her, wrapping her in his arms.
She laid her head against his chest and he pressed his
cheek to her silky hair.

If only there was a solution that would still allow him

to hold the softness of her body to his, still tangle his fingers in her hair, still kiss her lush lips whether they were covered with sweet sugar or just savor the sweetness of them alone. A solution where he could enjoy her inquisitive and quirky mind and find ways to make her smile and laugh, which he'd just recently discovered was the best part of any day.

"I didn't know you knew about what happened five years ago," he said.

"I don't know much. Just that you were involved with a teacher of yours when you were a resident, and she ended up getting fired."

Realization dawned. "Is that why you'd been so chilly to me for so long after the wedding when you kissed me? I thought you were just mad about that."

"Hey, wouldn't you be upset, too? I kissed you and you turned me down flat, saying anything between us wouldn't be appropriate. Then ran right out and had a fling with your teacher just months later. I wanted to hit you." She smiled. "But I know now that's not at all who you are."

"It's who I was then."

"We all learn and grow, don't we?" She stroked his cheek with her hand. "So tell me the whole story."

"I was young and careless. Probably tried to live up to my dad's poor opinion of me." He sighed. "She was only a few years older than I was. But still my teacher and superior. She came on to me and I thought, Why the hell not? Then found out why not."

"What happened?"

"The university and hospital ethics board had a fit. Wanted to boot me out of the residency program." He didn't want to confess the worst part of it, but knew he had to. "My father was furious with me besmirching the Armstrong name that just happens to grace the cardiology wing of that hospital after his revolutionary valve-transplant discovery. He swept my dirty deeds under the rug, while making sure she got fired."

"Did you love her?"

The blue eyes looking up at him had gotten so serious he actually smiled, despite everything. "Hell, no. I barely knew her. From then on I never dated anyone in the hospitals I worked in."

"Then why get involved with me?"

"You're not really asking me that, are you?" He loved the way her brows were drawn together, at the way she seemed to be studying him, trying to figure out what he was thinking. And good luck to her with that, because his mind sure ping-ponged back and forth from moment to moment on how to deal with his feelings and hers and the damned professional risks.

"Yes, I am asking. And you'd better give me an honest answer."

"Because I couldn't resist, Katy-Did. Because I'm crazy about you. So crazy it seemed worth the risk to your reputation and mine too. Even though Nick is right. Risking yours makes me a selfish bastard."

"I knew about your past and the potential consequences but decided I wanted to be with you anyway. And it's still a risk I'm willing to take, if you are."

Her arms tightened around him and squeezed his heart. What should he do here? Could he really walk away from her on the slim chance someone found out and reported it? Could he make himself say goodbye?

His stomach churned, and that sensation made him realize that it wasn't just the thought of damaging her career that had made it feel that way all afternoon. It had been the thought of ending things before they'd even begun to explore what was happening between them.

"I'd never forgive myself if people started talking and it affected your job here."

"I'd never forgive you if you don't let us find out exactly what this is between us."

"I don't think I could stand never being forgiven by you. Having you turn all cold to me the past five years was hard enough." He realized the office door was open a crack, and released her to shove it closed. "I don't know what's right. But I do know that I can't just walk away from you. From this. Without finding out exactly what this is. Even though I know I damn well should." He wrapped his hands around her shoulders and drew her close again, breathing in the scent of her that tormented and teased him whenever she was near.

"Smart man." She smiled, flattening her palms against his chest, warming him. "I was hoping you wouldn't make me turn loose my woman-scorned fury on you."

He chuckled then kissed her cute nose, touched his lips to each soft cheek, to one beautiful eye then the other, before drawing back. "Tomorrow I have to take over teaching rounds again. My having a jones for an intern while being her teacher, supervisor and, in just over a week, giving her an evaluation grade, is completely unethical."

"This is not a news flash, Alec. We—"

"Shh. Let me finish before you unleash the scorned woman on me." He pressed his fingers to her lips, trailed them across her jaw to cup her cheek. "This is a complicated problem I feel requires some special problem-solving skills that a certain beautiful intern I know has in spades."

The irritation in her eyes faded to a smile. "Go on."

"So, I'm borrowing the technique you told me you used to figure out Mrs. Patterson's illness. I defined the goal. And that goal is to put back the sparkle and excitement that's been missing in my life by spending time with you. To kiss every inch of your body until you're in delirious ecstasy, then start all over again. Teach you how to sail, because you nearly got knocked into the water by the boom when we went last time."

"You know I have a clumsiness problem." Her warm hands slid up his chest to rest on each side of his neck. "I like your goals. Except there are three of them, and to truly solve a problem you have to concentrate on one."

"All right. The goal is to add excitement to my life by taking you out on my sailboat and kissing every inch of your body while we're on the water."

She laughed, her eyes now twinkling, and he nearly lost his train of thought while thinking about kissing her delectable body. "Next," he continued, before they never finished the conversation and he ended up making love to her on the floor, "I determined the facts, which is that no one can know about my kissing you all over or anything else that may come to mind."

"I can see you're very good at problem-solving. Did you learn this from my dad, too?" She reached up to nip his lips, nibble, lick, tease. He nearly dove into her mouth to give her a deep kiss and to hell with any and all conversation, but this had to come first.

"No. I learned from you." He kissed her softly, her sweet lips clinging to his. Her fingers slipped from his neck, slid into his hair as she pressed closely against him and he couldn't wait to finish the talking so they could move on to something infinitely more pleasurable.

"Final step is critical thinking." He lifted his hands to her cheeks and looked into the smiling eyes he could lose himself in. "I want you. You want me." Which made him the damned luckiest man on the planet. "We should try being together, not apart. But we have to get through the ten days you're my student being as cold as ice to one another in the hospital."

"That won't be easy for me, since what I'm feeling right now is very, very hot." She pressed her mouth to his chin, his jaw, his throat. "But I'll rise to the challenge."

She always rose to any challenge in front of her. Her mouth on his skin was making his body rise to a challenge, too, and he pulled an inch away before he lost control. "There are still some risks involved. But when you move off of the surgery rotation, it will be fairly easy to be discreet. And if people found out, at that point it would probably result in just a slap on the wrist, nothing more. What do you think?"

"I think your conclusion is most excellent. Just like you."

"Am I allowed to add another goal now?"

"Since you've concluded the last one, you may work on a new one."

He reached behind her and locked the door. "My goal is to enjoy our last few hours together before rounds tomorrow." He tugged her scrub top loose from her drawstring pants and wrapped his hands around her ribs, let them travel upward to cup her breasts, lightly thumbing her nipples.

A pleased gasp left her lips as she arched into him, but touching her wasn't enough. He wanted to see her, too. Moving his hands upward, he grasped her arms to push the cotton fabric up and off her.

"Are you sure no one will walk in?" She covered her breasts with her hands and glanced behind her.

"The door is locked. And this is the private office of a big, bad surgeon. No one will bother me."

"Big, bad surgeon?" She dropped her hands to cover his as they cupped her ribs again. "And here I didn't think you were egotistical."

"Don't be fooled. All surgeons are egotistical." He kissed the top of her breast then slid his mouth across the swell of it to kiss the other. "I love your pretty, lacy bra. And what's inside it. Every time I see you in your scrubs in the hospital, I can't believe how sexy you look in them. Even more now that I know what's under them."

"Scrubs are not sexy. Not on me, anyway. But on you? Most definitely." Her breathy laugh turned to a low moan as his mouth moved to her nipple beneath the lace. "However, having them off of you is sexier still."

She tugged his shirt over his head, which unfortunately required him to lift his mouth from her. Which he figured was a good opportunity to see more of her skin. All of it. He unclasped her bra and slid it down her arms to the floor. Then tucked his thumbs into her waistband and tugged until she kicked them off her ankles, along with her shoes and socks, yanking off his own clothes in short order.

He paused a moment to just look at her stunning nakedness. At the golden glow of the smooth skin that covered her delectable curves, the sensual smile on her lips, the blue eyes that looked at him with the same desire he felt that nearly overwhelmed him.

Breathless, he tugged her ponytail loose from the band holding it, let her silky hair slide over his hands. Holding her waist in his hands again, he moved backwards, bringing her with him, until he sat in his swivel chair. Let his hands slide to cup the smooth curves of her rear and brought her onto his lap.

"I've never made love in an office before." She straddled him, wrapping her arms around his neck, her hard nipples teasing and tickling his chest. "Is this how it's done?"

"I don't know. I've never made love in an office either. Though I've fantasized about you enough as I sat right here in this chair. And I'm more than excited to have that fantasy become real." He slipped his fingers between her legs, caressing her slick core until she gasped and sighed and pressed against him. She closed her eyes, and the little sounds that came from her beautiful lips made his pulse pound and his breath short. Watching her face as he touched her was beyond erotic, and he nearly plunged inside her that second.

But he didn't. He wanted the moment to last. Wanted to go slow, wanted to hear her sighs, wanted to look into her eyes and the bliss in their blue depths. The scent of her hair and her skin and her arousal nearly drove him mad, and he covered her mouth with his, needing that connection. Needing to taste her sweetness. Needing more of her. The kiss became deep, frenzied, until she lifted herself onto him and they moved together in a primal rhythm. Moved together with a growing need that nearly swamped him.

"Katy." He grasped her hips, trying to slow the moment down, to savor every single second of their joining, but as she tossed her head back, her glorious hair spilling across her shoulders she cried out his name, and he had no choice but to give in to the release, her name on his lips as they fused with hers.

CHAPTER THIRTEEN

THANK HEAVENS TEACHING rounds for the day were almost over, with Mrs. Patterson as their last patient. It was nearly impossible to listen to Alec speak without watching his mouth and remembering all the places on her body it had roamed. To look at his hands as he held a patient's wrist, or touched them in a physical exam without thinking of the places he'd touched her own body and how incredible he'd made her feel. To look at his eyes and remember how they had gazed at her nakedness with a hunger that had set her on fire.

Through sheer force of will she'd managed to make work her number-one focus.

"You look so much better, Helen!" Katy took in the woman's rosy color and bright eyes, and thought she might even have put on a pound or two.

"I certainly feel like a new woman." Helen reached out her hand and Katy clasped it in hers. "Dr. Armstrong here tells me it's all because you figured out what was... going on."

"She did indeed." His expression held warm admiration as he glanced at Katy. "Dr. Pappas is smart and thorough, and we're lucky to have her as an intern here, Mrs. Patterson."

"I know you are." She squeezed Katy's hand. "I want to thank you for saving my life. It's not often someone gets a chance to say that. I know I wasn't far from being on the other side of the grass."

"You don't have to thank me. I'm just glad we were able to figure out what was making you ill." She couldn't imagine how beyond awful it must have made Helen feel to find out Jeffrey was poisoning her, and she didn't want to distress her by bringing it up.

"It's all hard to believe." Her eyes were sad. "A part of me feels bad for my son. That he would be so desperately in debt that he couldn't think of any other way."

Katy didn't reply. It was hard to feel sorry for someone who would do something so terrible to anyone, let alone his own mother.

"He wasn't trying to kill me, you know." The woman looked at them almost pleadingly, apparently hoping they'd believe her words. "He just thought I'd get sick enough that he'd have my power of attorney. Just long enough to get out of debt, then I'd be okay again. The judge will take into account his gambling problems, I think. I hope he can get over his addiction."

"Addictions are powerful things, Mrs. Patterson, but he's getting the help he needs," Alec said. "Meanwhile, I'd like you to focus on getting back to your old self and walking your dogs again."

Helen smiled. "I can't wait to have them jumping up in my lap. My daughter is bringing them down tomorrow, and I'll be so happy to be home and continuing my physical therapy there." She squeezed Katy's hand tight. "Thank you again, my dear. Oceancrest is very lucky to have you."

"Thank you, Helen. I'll be thinking of you with your pups."

They left the room and Alec paused in the hall to smile at her. "It's got to make you feel great to see Mrs. Patterson so fit and ready to go home. Congratulations."

"Thank you."

"I hope you both remember this." Alec turned to Todd Eiterman and Michael Coffman. "Sometimes you have to look for the zebra when the first answer doesn't seem to make sense. I'll see you for rounds tomorrow."

He strode down the hall without a backward glance, with Todd following, and she quickly turned her attention to her schedule as she pulled it from her pocket.

"Must be nice to be teacher's pet," Michael said. His tone of voice was light but his expression wasn't.

"I'm not teacher's pet." Her stomach constricted a little, even though she knew he couldn't mean it in a personal way. "I just got lucky with the diagnosis, and I'm sure you will too some time."

"Yeah. I can only hope," he said. "Got more scut work to do. See you later."

She breathed a deep sigh of relief. Had she and Alec actually managed to always keep poker faces around one another the past week? Had not a single person noticed how their eyes sometimes met and clung, before they both quickly looked away? She hoped and prayed no one had. Thank heavens they wouldn't have to be under such a strain much longer.

Only four more days. Four more days of the stress of hiding how she felt about him while they rounded together. Though they'd still have to be discreet at the hospital when they did run into one another.

A smile spread across her face, and she hoped no one

noticed that either. Because she knew it was a silly, lust-struck kind of smile that came every time she thought of their forced separation being over with. A smile from wondering what kind of quiet, behind-the-scenes relationship might blossom between them.

She shook her head to dispel all thoughts of Alec so she could concentrate on the work in front of her. Her next assignment was to give conscious sedation to a patient who required a special IV line that would be inserted into his neck vein. Just a few weeks ago she might have been a nervous wreck about doing it, and she felt a little proud at how far she'd come in such a short time.

Katy looked at the chart in her hand. Room 4280. Patient Richard Wynne. Elizabeth would be there to supervise as Katy performed the procedure.

She knocked on the doorjamb of the surgical intensive care room, then stepped inside with a smile. "Mr. Wynne? I'm Dr. Pappas. I'm here to insert the central IV line you need."

The man grimaced. "Sounds like it might hurt like hell."

"Don't worry." She came close and gave him what she hoped was a reassuring smile. "We'll be giving you an intravenous drug to make you drowsy. Technically, you'll be awake but you won't remember anything."

"I'll be awake but won't remember it afterward?"

"Strange, huh? But that's the way it works." She'd learned that patients didn't really have to know the details of how retrograde amnesia drugs worked, only that they did. She'd also learned not to tell patients she was a newbie at these procedures, unless they asked. Usually, they freaked out, and who could blame them? "I'll be assisted by Dr. Stark."

He nodded, seemingly satisfied. Katy cleaned up and put on a gown, mask, and gloves. The nurse brought all the necessary equipment, and Katy prepped the man's skin by sponging on a sterile soap solution. She and the nurse got the man draped to create a sterile field, his neck exposed by a hole in the fabric, and again Katy felt pretty darned proud how competent she'd become at all of it.

All systems go, she thought with satisfaction. She and the nurse sat there waiting quietly, Katy looking at her watch every few minutes. Where was Elizabeth? She should have been here twenty minutes ago. Katy tried calling her but got no answer.

"Is there some problem?" Mr. Wynne asked with a frown.

"I'm sorry, I'm not sure what the delay is." The man looked quite annoyed, which Katy could well understand. All draped and having to stay motionless, ready to get it over with, then lying there endlessly waiting. "Dr. Stark should be here any moment. I'll see if I can find her."

Katy looked up and down the hall, but there was no sign of Elizabeth. What should she do here?

"Something wrong, Dr. Pappas?"

Alec's deep voice seemed to rumble right into her chest, and her heart leaped as she looked up at him. His expression was carefully neutral as his eyes met hers, and she quickly schooled her own to look the same.

"As you likely recall, this patient is having extensive bowel surgery tomorrow, and we couldn't get a line placed in his arm. So I'm here to insert a central venous catheter in his neck, and Dr. Stark is supposed to supervise me. But she's not here and I can't find her."

Alec frowned and glanced into the room. "Obviously

you have the patient ready. I assume you haven't given him sedation yet?"

"Not yet. I was waiting for Elizabeth."

"We need to just get this done. I'll supervise you."

Katy's heart did a little pit-pat in her chest as they walked together into the small room. She was all too aware of him as he stood just an inch away. Aware of the warmth of his body in the chilly room. Aware of his distinctive scent. Aware of his eyes lingering on her before turning to the patient.

She sucked in a breath and focused her attention on the procedure she had to perform, her hands sweating a little inside her gloves. Why did she suddenly feel so nervous about him watching her do this? She knew the answer. She was afraid she just might not do as good a job as he would expect her to, and she so wanted him to be impressed. Maybe that was vain and shallow, when she should be most concerned about the patient, but couldn't help the feeling.

She reminded herself she was a professional and needed to think and act like one. Not a nervous nellie newbie who had to cut into someone's skin in just a few minutes.

Alec moved a short distance away to scrub, gown, and mask himself before he came to stand beside her again. "Go ahead, Dr. Pappas. I'm here to assist you with anything you need," Alec said. Katy glanced up at him and while his face was mostly obscured by the mask, she could see the small smile in his eyes, see him give her a little encouraging nod, which instantly helped her relax.

"Okay." She stopped short of saying, *Here goes nothing*, figuring the patient wouldn't exactly be reassured by that. She drew the sedation into the syringe and injected it smoothly into Mr. Wynne's arm. Within seconds his eyelids drooped and it was obvious he was already under its effect. No matter how many times she saw it used, the speed with which the drug worked always amazed her.

The nurse handed her the small knife and Katy looked up at Alec, who gifted her with another smile from his eyes and another nod. Steeling herself, she turned to make the tiny incision in the man's neck. When she was finished, she carefully slid the central line, half the width of a pencil, through the skin and down into the patient's jugular vein.

When it was finally done, Katy realized she'd been holding her breath, and let it out in a whoosh. "All done, I think. Did I do okay?"

"Better than okay. You did great."

Alec's eyes now weren't just smiling, they were crinkled at the corners like she loved to see, and she grinned back. "Are you sure you don't want to be a surgeon?" he asked. "It just might be your calling after all."

"No thanks. But I do admit I've loved being on this service and learning all this cool stuff. Thanks for being a wonderful teacher."

"Thanks for being a wonderful student." He placed his palm between her shoulder blades and gave her a quick pat before he turned to take off his mask and gown.

"Excuse me, Dr. Armstrong."

Both Alec and Katy turned to see Elizabeth standing there. A very angry Elizabeth, whose fists were clenched and lips were pressed together into a thin line. Katy's heart flipped in alarm at her expression. Then reminded herself nothing inappropriate had happened. Alec had just given her the same kind of congratulatory shoulder pat she'd seen him give to all the interns and residents.

"Yes, Dr. Stark?" Alec's expression was cool, neutral, but Katy didn't think she was imagining the wariness in his eyes.

"With all due respect, sir, it was my job to supervise Dr. Pappas for this procedure. Why are you doing it?"

"Because you weren't here, and the patient had been ready for some time." Alec's voice was firm and authoritative. "When Dr. Pappas told me she'd been unable to locate you, I decided to supervise. There's no reason to keep a patient waiting unnecessarily when another physician gets delayed, is there?"

"My delay was unavoidable. Dr. Pappas should have waited for me instead of soliciting you to do my job."

"It was actually I who volunteered to supervise when I realized you'd been delayed." Alec regarded Elizabeth steadily, seemingly not affected by her surprising anger. "At no time did I think you not being here reflects on the quality of your work or your reliability, Dr. Stark, if that's what's worrying you. If you'd like to talk about this further, please come to my office later. Meanwhile, you may finish up with Dr. Pappas."

Without a backward glance Alec moved past Elizabeth and left the room.

With Alec gone, Elizabeth glanced at the nurse then turned to Katy. "May I speak with you privately?"

Katy trailed after her into the hallway, dismayed when Elizabeth turned and pointed her finger at her. "You. What a gunner you are." The resident's voice was shaking. "Always trying to make yourself look good and to hell with anybody else looking bad because of it."

"I don't know what you mean." Katy's stomach knotted. "I've just tried to learn and do my work on this rotation."

"That is such a load of bull. Every time I turn around you're talking to Dr. Armstrong about this or that, asking questions, trying to sound so smart. Trying to make everyone else look stupid. I wouldn't be surprised if you tried to get into Alec's pants just to win points from an attending. Don't think I haven't noticed the way you flirt with him. The way he looks at you."

Katy gasped and felt all the blood drain from her face. Had Elizabeth really noticed the vibe between them? Surely this must just be her lashing out at her because the woman put so much pressure on herself to succeed in a man's world.

"Elizabeth, I hope you don't really believe that of me. That I was trying to build myself up by putting other people down. And I'm certain Dr. Armstrong views me only as an intern who needs all the help I can get. I've seen how hard you work and what a good surgeon you are. I know it's tough to be a female surgeon, and I honestly wish the best for you."

To Katy's shock, Elizabeth's eyes filled with tears before she turned away. "Head on to your next assignment, please, and I'll finish with Mr. Wynne."

Should she try to talk out this shocking hostility from Elizabeth a little more? As she watched the woman remove Mr. Wynne's drape, she decided she'd leave it for now. Perhaps it was a conversation better suited to the tavern.

She headed to the next floor to see a patient, a cold chill running down her spine as she recalled Elizabeth's ugly words about trying to get into Alec's pants to win points and noticing the way he looked at her. Would Elizabeth ever suggest to someone else that Katy might have done that?

The chill spread to every inch of her body when she thought of the ugly turn gossip like that could take if her relationship with Alec became public.

"Thanks, everybody, for staying late and for doing such a great job. As always, you make Oceancrest one of the best hospitals around," Alec said to the medical staff as he finished his last surgery of one damned long day.

"Dr. Armstrong, can I speak with you real quickly? Privately?" a nurse asked.

"Of course." Alec stripped off his gloves and walked out of the OR to the empty hallway, with the nurse following. "What's on your mind?"

"I really respect you, so I wanted you to know there's some talk going around."

His heart practically stopped before it sped up into a fast rhythm. "Talk?"

She leaned closer. "One of the residents was talking about Dr. Pappas being your favorite, and implying some things I'm sure you don't want implied."

"What kind of things?"

"Like she gets more attention from you because she's Nick Pappas's sister. Even worse, that she's been coming on to you to get a good evaluation."

Holy hell. His breath backed up into his lungs. "Is this…rumor all over the hospital, or confined to just a few people on the surgical service?"

"I don't really know. I've only heard it around surgery, but that's where I hang out most of the time. Anyway, I thought you'd want to know."

"Thank you. I do want to know. And for what it's worth, Dr. Pappas is a very upstanding intern, and my evaluation of her will be strictly professional."

She nodded. "Of course I know that, Dr. Armstrong. You're one of the most professional doctors at this hospital."

His chest compressed even tighter at her words. He moved on to the locker room and stripped out of his scrubs, feeling a little numb. His mind spun back to his interactions with Katy, and other than that brief kiss in the hallway that Nick had seen couldn't think of anything that would start the rumor mill going.

Except that he knew, damn it, the way he looked at her sometimes. Had caught himself giving her goo-goo eyes on a few occasions, but hadn't thought anyone had seen.

He could only hope and pray that the gossip was minor. Wasn't juicy enough to spread through the hospital or garner much interest. How could it be? From what the nurse had said, it was a minor comment that probably stemmed from jealousy at what a great job Katy was doing and nothing more.

Trying to relax his tense muscles and tamp down the nag of anxiety, Alec got dressed, glad the long day was over. Glad that what had seemed like the longest week ever was almost over. Just a few more days with the stress and pressure of being sure he didn't look at Katy or talk to her or smile at her in any way that might be misconstrued by observers.

Misconstrued? That was the crux of it, because there would be no misinterpretation to think his looks and smiles came from his all-too-vivid memories of making love with her, and thoughts of how he wanted more of it. More of her.

A nasty niggle of worry over this whole situation stayed stuck in his gut. A different, crappy feeling would definitely lodge there instead, though, if they decided the risk to both their careers was too big.

He picked up his shirt, realizing her addictive scent lingered on it. Realized it was the shirt he'd been wearing when they'd last made love. He lifted it to his nose and inhaled, and just that tiny memory of her stepped up his pulse and shortened his breath.

What a damned complicated situation. But surely they could keep their cool around one another for just a few more days until she was off the surgical rotation. After that the chances were good they'd barely see one another in the hospital and any germs of gossip would quickly die.

He'd call her to tell her what the nurse had said then double his efforts to keep his feelings hidden while they were at work.

CHAPTER FOURTEEN

"How much do you think they're paying this guy?" Nick whispered, leaning toward Alec. "I could put together a better lecture than this."

"Maybe. But then you'd alienate everyone in the room, because you wouldn't be able to resist throwing in a few opinions about how certain specialists are usually prima donnas."

"True." Nick chuckled, turning his attention back to the lectern.

The county-wide hospital meeting had been going on for hours, and Alec was glad this was the last speaker before lunch was served. Though, among the duds, there were always interesting presentations on new research and updates specific to general surgery and other surgical specialties. At their table sat doctors from three other medical centers, and it was always good to catch up with them, too.

Alec tried his best to not look across the room where Katy sat with other residents and interns, and was pleased he managed to accomplish that. Most of the time, anyway, until he occasionally caught his gaze sliding her way.

Apparently, he wasn't the only one ready for lunch as

chatter broke out instantly when the presentation ended and food was served. He found himself wondering if Katy had ordered the fish or the chicken then shook his head at himself. Why the hell would that even cross his mind? The answer clearly was that she was on his mind, period, even when the subject was inane.

"Her name is Pappas," he heard a voice say at the next table, and he and Nick both paused their eating and turned their heads at the same time as the name caught their ears. A man was pointing across the room toward Katy's table. "I can't remember her first name."

"Kathy, maybe?" another voice said, then chuckled as he looked across the room in Katy's direction. "Yeah, I heard the same thing about her. But there are always a few of them, you know. She's pretty enough to tempt any attending into thinking with the wrong head."

He stared at Nick who stared back at him, and his heart thumped hard as an ice-cold chill swept through him. What the hell were they saying about Katy?

"Doesn't the CMO know what's going on?"

"I hear she's got all the docs wrapped around her little finger. Or maybe it's because she's got her legs wrapped around them," someone said, eliciting chuckles.

"She's the kind of doctor that gives the rest of us a bad name," a woman said. "Most of us don't have to sleep around to get a good evaluation. Though I admit there was one resident I knew who slept with every attending she worked with."

A man chuckled. "And what I want to know is why I wasn't ever lucky enough to have a female student like that."

As the entire table laughed, Alec had trouble swallowing the bite of food he'd stuck in his mouth when they'd first heard the chatter. After he got it down, it sat in his stomach like lead and he had trouble catching his breath.

He turned to look at Nick, who stared right back at him. Nick's eyes were hard, his lips pressed tightly together, but he didn't say a word.

He didn't have to. Alec knew what Nick was thinking, and knew he was right. He also knew what had to happen next. And it had to happen in a way Katy couldn't argue with.

It was late in the afternoon when Katy made her way toward where she, Alec and Nick had arranged to meet up after the day conference. While the presentations had been interesting, she was more than glad it was over. After checking a few patients, she'd get to go home, put her feet up and have a leisurely evening with Nick and hopefully Alec, too.

Since her brother had been so disapproving of anything smacking of a relationship between her and Alec, the two of them had agreed to stay just friendly around each other while Nick was around. To let some time go by until she'd been off his teaching service for quite a while. Maybe by then Nick would see their relationship was important to both of them and that, hopefully, at that point it wouldn't jeopardize either of their careers.

She made her way through the crowd of people then headed out to the parking lot, spotting Nick next to the car, along with some woman. Alec was there, too, and seeing his smile made her heart swell. Quickly, she tamped it down, knowing her feelings would be written all over her face if she didn't.

Then realized Alec had his arm wrapped around the woman's shoulders. A very pretty woman, and his hold seemed more intimate than friendly. Her steps slowed as she stared then stopped completely as his arm slipped to the woman's waist, tightened around her to draw her close. His handsome head dipped down and he kissed the woman on the cheek.

Then moved on to her mouth, lingering. Their lips separated an inch and held that position, almost nose to nose, before he pressed his lips to the woman's again for a long, long moment as she raised her palm to his face.

Katy felt like she couldn't breathe. What in the world...? Surely this wasn't what it looked like. It couldn't be.

She forced herself to start moving again, reassuring herself this had to be just a friend of his or something. But her gut knew that no two people who were just friends kissed the way she'd just seen them kiss.

As she approached them she was sure Alec would drop his arm from the woman's waist, but he didn't. Numbness began to seep through her body when she stopped to stand next to Nick.

"Hey, Katy," Alec said, smiling at her. Smiling as though there was nothing strange about his holding another woman close when he'd made love to Katy just days ago. "Did you learn a lot from the presentations?"

"Yes. They were interesting." She managed to say the words through a throat so tight it hurt. "Aren't you going to introduce me to your...friend?"

"Oh, sorry. This is Andrea Walton. She and I, and Nick too, were residents together." To Katy's disbelief, he actually gave the woman another lingering kiss on her forehead. "I didn't know she was working at Holland Memorial now, and was pretty excited to see her here today. Andrea, this is Nick's little sister, Katy."

Nick's little sister. Pretty excited to see Andrea. Katy felt woozy, but told herself she was making a mountain out of a molehill. Maybe Alec held and kissed all old friends who were female.

"It's nice to meet you, Katy. I hear you're an intern. Alec tells me you're a good student," Andrea said.

"Nice to meet you, too."

"Hey, listen," Alec said, "Andrea and I are going to head out and get some dinner before I take her sailing. Just like old times." Alec smiled at Andrea and damned if he didn't give her another kiss on the mouth right in front of Katy.

Suddenly, her numbness and shock began to give way to anger. Alec was going to give her an explanation for all this, and what it did or didn't mean, and he was going to do it right now.

"Can I speak with you privately for a second, Alec?"

"Sure." He finally dropped his arm from curving around Andrea and followed Katy a few yards away.

She turned to him, and didn't know what to think of the expression of apology and guilt on his face. "What's going on here? Who is Andrea?"

"I told you, she and I were residents together. She was also my girlfriend for awhile, as you probably figured out."

"Yeah, since I have that analytical brain and all." Her voice shook and she swallowed to control it. "Not that it would have been hard for anyone to figure out since you were kissing her right here in public."

"I was pretty crazy about her, but she got a job all the way across the country." He gave her a crooked, apologetic smile. "Listen, I know you're not going to like this. But, well, seeing her made me realize I never really got over her. And I want to see if we can have what we had before."

Katy swayed a little on her feet, unable to breathe. Was this really happening? "You want to date her."

"I do." He leaned closer, speaking low. "I'm sorry, but it was never a good idea for us to be involved to begin with, you know that. It's not good for your career, and I frankly don't want to risk my reputation again. I'm sure you understand. Andrea is my peer, which makes her perfect for me."

Perfect for him. "Alec, surely you don't mean this." The words were out of her mouth before she realized she was dangerously close to begging him to stay with her. And she'd never do that with any man.

"It's best for both of us, Katy. You know, you look a little tired." Alec patted her on the head and smiled like he was her uncle or something. "Why don't you go to bed early and get some sleep?"

While he took Andrea to dinner and out on his boat and made love with the woman, just like he'd done with her.

She didn't know how to respond to his words without screaming at him and beating him with her fists like she wanted to. Tears threatened to choke her, and she dragged in a shaky, shocked breath before turning away.

He stopped her with a hand on her shoulder then ran his finger from her forehead to her nose. "I hope we can still be friends."

Friends? Was he kidding? When he'd given her the brush-off long ago she'd been hurt. What she was feeling now after being foolish enough to sleep with a man with his kind of history was so far beyond hurt it was off the charts. "Thanks for the offer, but I don't want to be friends with you."

Somehow she managed to turn and get into the car before the tears began to fall.

CHAPTER FIFTEEN

KATY HAD BEEN too stunned to speak as she and Nick had driven back to the hospital to check on patients before they went home. Too busy swallowing back the tears and trying to wrap her brain around what had just happened.

As she talked with her patients and did her work, she felt like an automaton. Going through the motions in a state of utter numbness. Even when they grabbed a carry-out dinner to take home she didn't speak about it to Nick. Didn't know what to say.

By the next morning, though, her disbelief had morphed into an anger so intense, so deep she had to let some of it spill out. Had to get some answers. When she and Nick walked into the hospital together, she turned to him and spoke.

"Can you explain to me what happened yesterday?"

"I assume you're talking about Alec?" Nick's expression was grim. "No. But I can't say I'm sorry, Katy. I am sorry that you feel hurt. But Alec was never right for you anyway."

And wasn't that an understatement? Still, she needed some explanation for how one minute Alec had been making love with her and the next he was kissing another woman. Except, oh, wait. That's the kind of man he was.

"Did he date that woman a long time when you all were residents? Was he…crazy in love with her or something?" Just the question made her chest hurt.

"They were close, I guess." His tone was strangely stiff and he wrapped his arm around her shoulders in a quick hug. "Listen, I know you feel bad right now. But it's for the best."

"Obviously." Her voice shook. "But you're the one who told me he wasn't the kind of guy I thought he was. A player. Why would you say that when you've known him forever? When you know exactly what he's really like?"

"He's my friend, regardless." Nick sighed. "I've got surgery scheduled and need to get to work. We can talk about this later but, honestly, I don't know what else there is to say."

She watched him head down the hallway, and fought back tears yet again. Then she squared her shoulders. She would not allow jerk-of-the-decade Alec to ruin even one day of her life. Somehow, some way, she'd have to get through rounding with him a couple more days. How, exactly, she didn't know. But she would not let him think for even one minute she was heartbroken.

Though at the moment that organ felt crushed into a million little pieces inside her chest.

She forced herself to march down the hall to meet the crew for morning rounds. When she saw Alec standing there talking to Elizabeth and Todd, her confidence wavered and a horrible feeling swept through her body. A peculiar tornado of fury and grief and humiliation, and the sensation was so overwhelming it was all she could do to keep going.

His eyes met hers for only the briefest moment before

he turned away. Her throat closed at how gorgeous he looked on the outside. How could he have turned out to be so shallow on the inside? She wanted to scream at him but shoved her anger and pain down as best she could.

Becoming a good doctor was tremendously important to her. She couldn't believe she'd allowed herself to fall for him, especially after trying so hard to remain true to her goal of becoming a respected, admired doctor. The kind of doctor her father would have been proud of. From this moment on she'd give every ounce of her heart to her work.

"Congratulations on a great job today and all month long," Alec said to the young doctors standing with him, beyond thankful the last day of surgical teaching rounds was over with.

He'd known it would be difficult to work with Katy for a few more days after the scene he'd orchestrated with Andrea. But he hadn't begun to realize the depth of that difficulty.

It had been torture. Torture to look into her beautiful eyes and see only ice blue staring back at him. Torture to hear the disgust for him in her voice when she spoke. Torture to be close to her, to have her scent wrap around him, to want to touch the silkiness of her hair and skin and know he'd never again have that pleasure.

He thought it had been disturbing when she'd been chilly to him the past few years? That had been nothing compared to the deep freeze he knew she'd feel toward him forever, and had to wonder if what he'd done had been a terrible mistake.

"I'll be finishing your evaluations and turning them in to Dr. Sanders, who will give them to you this eve-

ning. Best of luck to all of you." One by one, he shook
their hands. When he got to Katy's it felt as cold as the
eyes that stared at him but still he didn't want to let it go.

He didn't have to. Katy yanked it from his after only
the briefest shake and turned away. He watched her walk
down the hall with the others. Watched the slight sway
of her hips, watched her lustrous hair swish across her
shoulders.

Watched her walk out of his life.

With a painful hollow in his chest he went to his office to somehow work on the evaluations. But the papers
kept blurring into images of Katy.

He knew he'd hurt her badly. Hearing those people
saying such ugly things about her had sent him into protective overdrive, but he realized now that maybe he
hadn't thought it through well enough.

Andrea had been his friend for years. She'd been
around during the nasty scandal in his past, and had
been nice enough to go along with his ploy to end it with
Katy because she knew what it had been like for him.
Katy had stubbornly insisted she wasn't worried about
the risks to her reputation, and wouldn't have accepted
it then either, he knew.

But had handling it that way been the right decision?
Alec leaned back in his office chair and closed his eyes.
At this point he supposed it didn't matter. It was over
and done with.

Over and done with. Just like his relationship with
Katy.

"Katy," he said out loud, just wanting to hear her
name. She was smart and beautiful and wonderful and
would be an incredible family practice doc someday,
and he could not be the cause of others besmirching her

name. No matter how much it hurt, and it hurt beyond anything he'd ever experienced, he'd stay away from her. For her sake, and for the sake of her future.

Hurting *her* that way, though, stabbed like a knife so deeply in his own heart he could barely stand the pain. He hoped she'd get over it soon and move on to someone else who wasn't her superior in the hospital. That thought twisted the knife even deeper, but he'd somehow endure it for her.

A knock on his door had him opening his eyes. "Come in."

Nick appeared and sat in the chair opposite, slumping back into it much like Alec was slumped in his. He had a thick sheaf of papers in his hands. "Guess what arrived today."

"What?"

"My divorce papers from my beloved wife's attorney." His voice was both bitter and pained. "I guess this is really happening."

"You thought it might not?"

"I hadn't admitted it even to myself. But getting these made me realize I thought it wouldn't. I thought maybe she'd change her mind."

"I'm sorry, Nick." What else was there to say?

"Me, too." His lips twisted as he looked at Alec. "We're two pretty pathetic jerks, aren't we?"

"Yeah." He was pathetic and most definitely a jerk.

"I'm going to say something, and you're going to be shocked as hell by it."

Alec raised his eyebrows. "Is this going to be some deep confession about your marriage or your private life? I'm not sure I want to know."

"No. But it's my nearly over marriage that's made

me decide to say it." With his elbows on his knees, Nick leaned forward. "I was upset as hell about you and Katy, and even more upset when I heard those people talking about her. But seeing how sad and hurt she is now is upsetting me in a different way."

"Breakups hurt, Nick, as you well know. But we all eventually get over it and move on. Katy will, and you will, too." Though he wasn't too sure about himself.

"I do know. But I also know that sometimes when you really love someone you have to be willing to make a sacrifice. I wasn't willing to sacrifice what I thought was most important, which was my job at Oceancrest, and never mind that I worked so much it was one of the things that killed my marriage." He looked Alec in the eye. "Do you love my sister?"

Alec hadn't thought about putting his feelings into words. But as he sat there, nearly overwhelmed by the awful emptiness in his chest, he knew he did. "Yes. But it doesn't matter."

"It's the only thing that matters. That's what these papers made me realize today." He held them up. "It's probably too late to get Meredith back. But I am going to do something that, if I ever have a chance to fix things, will go a long way to help make that happen."

"I hope it's not that you're going to bomb the company that talked her into moving to New York."

"No." Nick gave him a glimmer of a smile. "I'm going to leave Oceancrest and start a private surgical practice so I can be in control of how many hours I work. And I'd like you to consider joining me."

A private surgical practice? Alec knew that usually meant more flexibility with the work schedule, and sometimes even more money, but he hadn't considered doing anything like that so early in his career. He'd been convinced he needed to establish the respect of everyone in the medical community first. Earn his father's respect first. "That alone would take a huge amount of time and effort to get going."

"I know. But then I'd be in charge of my own destiny. For a lot of reasons I've realized I want that." He stood up. "Think about it. And while you're doing that, think about one more thing. Which is that you love Katy and I know she loves you. I hate to see you both miserable the way I am about Meredith. If you join me, you'll be out of Oceancrest. Ethical problem solved."

Alec sat up straighter. Could that work? And would Katy ever forgive him for lying to her?

It was time to do some thinking. And the best place to do that was in the middle of Mission Bay.

CHAPTER SIXTEEN

KATY HAD NEVER been a person who wanted to drown her sorrows in alcohol, but she was about to make to-night the exception.

The residents and interns were extra-happy at the tavern happy hour, celebrating the end of the month's rounds before they moved on to the next rotation. Most were beaming at the good evaluations they'd received, though a few looked a little glum over their drinks. Katy felt more than glum, and never mind that Alec had given her the highest evaluation possible.

She should be proud and happy. Instead, she just felt relieved that she wouldn't have to work with Alec again. Wouldn't have to look at his amber eyes and handsome face and sexy body and picture him with Andrea, which made her feel so angry she wanted to hit something, and so hurt it gouged all the way to her soul.

She had to get over it. She'd known he was a player. A man who did as he pleased and twisted the rules to suit himself. Then she'd promptly forgotten all that when he'd kissed her. She'd let him wiggle inside her heart just like the worm he was until he'd dumped her like a hot potato when he'd tired of her.

She took a swig of her margarita to swallow down the bitterness filling her chest.

"What are you looking so mad about?" Elizabeth asked as she sat down beside her. "I am absolutely sure Dr. Armstrong gave you a great evaluation."

"Why are you so sure?" Probably because she thought what she'd said before. That Katy had dived into Alec's pants for good marks, and, boy, did she regret diving into them for a whole different reason.

"Honestly?" Elizabeth regarded her steadily. "Because you are one of the best interns I've ever worked with."

Katy stared at her in surprise. "Thank you. That's... nice of you to say."

"It's just the truth," Elizabeth said. "And I have another truth. A true confession about something I'm not proud of. Something you need to know."

Katy looked at her, wondering what she could be talking about.

"I was jealous of the way Alec looked at you, then it became pretty obvious there was something between you two. I think he's hot, but he never looked twice at me. I'm ashamed to admit this now but I said something to a couple other residents. Next thing I knew, a bunch of people were talking about you sleeping with him."

Katy gasped. "Are you kidding?"

"I wish I was." Elizabeth's lips twisted. "It's my fault, but I swear I never meant it to go any further than my few friends. I'm really sorry. Honest."

She looked at Elizabeth and realized she was telling the truth. That she did feel bad about it, and Katy had made enough mistakes in her own life that she wasn't going to judge Elizabeth too harshly for it. After all, it didn't really matter any more anyway. Alec had moved on.

"Thank you for telling me. Hopefully any more talk will die off since I won't be around him now."

"Won't you be? Anyone paying attention could tell he's crazy about you."

"No, he's not. He's got a girlfriend."

Elizabeth stared at her. "You're not his girlfriend?"

"Nope."

"You're just saying that because you're not supposed to be involved with an attending. Believe me, I was more than willing to be involved with him, and to heck with the rules." Elizabeth smiled. "I swear I'll never gossip about you again. But I have to tell you. I saw him kissing you in the hall."

Ah, damn. But again, it didn't really matter. But since Elizabeth knew, for some pathetic reason Katy wanted to unload on her. Maybe she'd feel better talking to another woman about it all.

"Okay. I thought we were involved. But when we were at the hospital meeting at the hotel he told me he didn't want to see me any more because he'd run into an old flame named Andrea Walton he hadn't known was in town." Just saying the woman's name made her stomach cramp. "She must work at a different hospital. And he kissed her right in front of me. The jerk."

To her surprise, Elizabeth burst out laughing. "Andrea Walton worked here for a while, so I can tell you she's not new to town. She's also married to a hunky cardiologist who happens to be a partner in her practice, and they have two cute little kids. I guarantee you they are not seeing one another. At least, not in a romantic sense."

Katy stared at her. Was there any way what she said could be true? And if so, why would Alec lie about it?

"I want to make it up to you for being catty and starting tongues wagging, so here's my advice," Elizabeth said, leaning in. "Ask Alec why he would lie to you, because he obviously did. I wouldn't be surprised if he heard the gossip about you and couldn't stand being the reason for it. If I were you, and I frankly wish I was, I'd be his girlfriend no matter what the hospital policy was on that. Go for it, girl."

Alec *had* been worried about her reputation and about any gossip. Was it at all possible that was why he'd broken up with her?

Maybe it wasn't. Maybe he really had moved on. But it was worth risking one more bash to her heart to find out for sure.

"Thanks, Elizabeth." Katy shoved her drink aside, grabbed her purse and headed out the door. Twenty minutes later she was pulling her car into the parking lot outside Alec's condo, her heart thumping nervously. What if Elizabeth was completely wrong? What if she banged on Alec's door and a half-naked Andrea opened it?

She gulped, but got out of the car anyway. She knew he'd still been at work just an hour ago, and did the math. Even if he'd left the second she'd been given her evaluation, which was unlikely, he would have gotten home only a short time ago.

In any case, she reminded herself sternly, whatever happened this evening would be good. If she found a naked Andrea there, she'd have that answer. If it was just Alec, she'd pay more careful attention to his expression and the tone of his voice if he rejected her again. After all, she'd known him most of her life and could read him pretty well. Or thought she could. Which brought her full circle to thinking she didn't really know him at all.

She shook her head at herself then squared her shoulders, about to head to his front door. Out of the corner of her eye she saw a distinctive sail coming from the center of the bay toward shore. The sail of Alec's boat, which was white with a cobalt-blue triangle in the top corner.

Lord, please do not have Andrea sailing with him and kissing him, she prayed. Going through that again would be beyond torture.

She pulled off her shoes and walked along the sand toward the dock, reaching it just as he smoothly slid the boat in. Her heart pounding so loud in her ears it nearly drowned out the sound of the surf, Katy stepped onto the planks of the dock. Alec stood on the boat, his tanned arms reaching to tie a line to the dock post.

Her heart stuttered at how gorgeous he looked with his muscular legs wide apart on the rocking boat, his hair tossing in the wind, his chiseled features covered only slightly by his sunglasses. At least they could have this conversation alone, she thought as a breath of relief left her chest.

He looked up at her, and his hands and arms stilled in the middle of tying the line. She wished she could see the expression in his eyes behind the lenses of the sunglasses but had no idea what he was thinking. Hopefully it wasn't horror that she'd shown up on his doorstep.

"I'd like to talk to you, Alec," she said, summoning every ounce of bravery she could muster.

Without saying a word, he finished tethering the line and reached his hand out to her. She grasped it in hers and stepped onto the boat's deck.

Now that she was there, she felt utterly paralyzed. What, exactly, should she say? Have you had sex with Andrea yet? Were you being truthful, or were you lying? I love you, please don't leave me.

And wouldn't the last be beyond pathetic? But standing so close to him now, holding his hand and staring up at him, the words nearly fell from her mouth anyway, and she swallowed.

"I'm glad I found you here. I need to know if you really are involved with Andrea. I need to know if you really don't care for me. That you don't want to be with me. I want the truth."

Her chest felt both heavier and lighter now that she'd asked. Relieved that she'd managed to get the words out but scared to death to hear his response.

"The truth?" Alec took off his sunglasses, and the deep seriousness of his eyes closed her throat. "The truth is I'm an idiot."

"Right now, I can't disagree."

"I don't blame you." He nodded. "What would you say if I told you I lied to you? That I never had anything with Andrea, not in the past and sure as hell not today."

The giant weight on her chest lifted a little, but at the same time her lungs burned with anger. "I'd say you are a giant jerk to hurt me so badly. To make me suffer the way I've been suffering. Then I'd ask you why you lied."

"Ah, Katy." He dropped her hand, shoving his own through his hair. "I'm so sorry I lied. I'm sorry I made you suffer. If it means anything, I can tell you I'm pretty sure I've suffered even more than you."

The anger burned even hotter in her chest, realizing that he'd set up the whole scene with Andrea intentionally to hurt her and drive her away. Yet with the anger came hope that what he said next could bring them close again, instead of driving an even deeper and permanent wedge between them. "Why would you lie and tell me such a horrible thing if it wasn't true?"

"Because people had started to talk and say nasty things about you. I couldn't bear it. And my being the cause of it was even more unbearable." He lifted her chin with his hand to look into her eyes. "I knew if I told you we couldn't be together for that reason, you'd say it didn't matter. But it did matter, Katy. It mattered to me that people were telling ugly lies that could damage what should be a stellar reputation for a stellar intern. It mattered to me that it was my fault."

"And so you, almighty surgeon Alec Armstrong, thought you should play God and decide what's best for me? Lie to me and break my heart, all in the name of what's 'good' for me? I'm more than capable of deciding what's good for me. I can make my own decisions regarding my life and my future."

"I know. I'm sorry. I know I was wrong to lie to you in such a terrible way. It seemed like the best thing at the time, but since then I've thought about what that must have felt like. How much it would have destroyed me to have you do something like that to me. All I can do is tell you I'm sorry and beg you to forgive me. Will you?"

"I don't know. Give me a reason to forgive you."

"You want a reason?" He cupped her cheek in his hand then lowered his lips to hers in a soft, tender kiss. "I don't have a good enough reason for what I did. The only reason I can offer in asking for your forgiveness is that I'm crazy in love with you. So crazy it makes me do crazy things. I love you. And now I know I need you in my life no matter what it costs."

Her heart nearly burst with joy at his words. "I might forgive you if you promise to never worry about either of our reputations again."

"I do promise. I've come to realize that having a spotless reputation doesn't mean much unless you have the respect of the person you love." He gave her another soft kiss. "But I've decided to take a path that won't let tongues wag anyway. A path I considered in the past but rejected because I thought I needed everyone in the hospital to think I was great beforehand."

"What path are you talking about?"

"Nick and I are going to start a private surgical practice. It will take a lot of work, but the benefits will be worth it."

She frowned. Surely he wasn't doing something so extreme just so they wouldn't have to work together? "Why?"

"He wants more control over his schedule and his life, and I want the same thing. I'm not doing it just for us, Katy, I promise, though I would if I had to. But it does take that worry out of the equation."

"And no more playing God?"

He signed an X on his chest. "Cross my heart."

"Then I forgive you. And I love you too. So much."

He pulled her close and pressed his forehead to hers. "Thank you," he whispered. "For loving me back and forgiving my stupidity. What can I do to make it up to you?"

"I think we should get started on those goals we talked about." Just the thought made her breathless. "The one involving excitement and sailing and you kissing me all over."

"Goals are good things to have." A gleam filled his eyes and a slow smile curved his lips. "Must be fate that we're already on the boat, as I'm more than ready to get started on our first goal. Then work on a list of others that will take a long time to achieve."

"Any thoughts on new ones?"

"Yes. I know exactly what the first goal should be. Well, the first one after the other first one."

She had to laugh. "All right, what is it?"

"A big Greek wedding starring Dr. Katherine Pappas." He drew back an inch, and his gaze grew both serious and tender. "Will you marry me, Katy? I think maybe I loved you all those years ago when you were conducting weird science experiments, and insisting on helping Nick and me build a tree house, and even when you out-fished us with some special bait you'd come up with. But I'm absolutely sure I'm totally in love with you now, and I want to spend every day of the rest of my life with you."

Her heart swelled to bursting at his words, but before she could speak his lips touched hers with the sweetest of kisses.

The eyes gazing into hers weren't amber or tiger eye but gleamed like polished gold, precious and dazzling. "Will you marry me? Please, say yes."

"Yes." The easy answer barely squeezed past the lump in her throat. "Yes, I will, Alec Armstrong."

"Thank you." His arms wrapped around her and he caught her close against him. "How fast can a Greek wedding be pulled together?"

"Not very fast, but we'll see what we can do to expedite the process." She hugged him and whispered in his ear. "You do realize you'll have to practice Greek dancing."

"I might have to fake it. But one thing I'll never have to fake is how in love I am with you."

* * * * *

MILLS & BOON
MEDICAL
Pulse-Racing Passion

Set your pulse racing with dedicated,
delectable doctors in the high-pressure
world of medicine, where emotions run
high and passion, comfort and love are the
best medicine.

LET'S TALK
Romance

For exclusive extracts, competitions and special offers, find us online:

 facebook.com/millsandboon

🐦 @MillsandBoon

📷 @MillsandBoonUK

Get in touch on 01413 063232

For all the latest titles coming soon, visit
millsandboon.co.uk/nextmonth

MILLS & BOON

THE HEART OF ROMANCE

A ROMANCE FOR EVERY READER

ODERN

Prepare to be swept off your feet by sophisticated, sexy and seductive heroes, in some of the world's most glamourous and romantic locations, where power and passion collide.

STORICAL

Escape with historical heroes from time gone by. Whether your passion is for wicked Regency Rakes, muscled Vikings or rugged Highlanders, awaken the romance of the past.

EDICAL

Set your pulse racing with dedicated, delectable doctors in the high-pressure world of medicine, where emotions run high and passion, comfort and love are the best medicine.

ue Love

Celebrate true love with tender stories of heartfelt romance, from the rush of falling in love to the joy a new baby can bring, and a focus on the emotional heart of a relationship.

Desire

Indulge in secrets and scandal, intense drama and plenty of sizzling hot action with powerful and passionate heroes who have it all: wealth, status, good looks…everything but the right woman.

EROES

Experience all the excitement of a gripping thriller, with an intense romance at its heart. Resourceful, true-to-life women and strong, fearless men face danger and desire - a killer combination!

To see which titles are coming soon, please visit

millsandboon.co.uk/nextmonth